THE LAST HOPE

MARCUS LEE

THE LAST HOPE
THE CHOSEN BOOK II

Copyright © 2023 by Marcus Lee

All rights reserved. The rights of Marcus Lee to be identified as the author of this Work has been asserted by him in accordance with sections 77 and 78 of the Copyright, Design and Patents Act 1988.

This is a work of fiction. Names, characters, places, and incidents either are the product of the author's imagination or are used fictitiously. Any resemblance to actual persons, living or dead, events, or locales is entirely coincidental.

No part of this publication may be reproduced, stored in retrieval systems, copied in any form or by any means, electronic, mechanical, photocopying, recording or otherwise transmitted without written permission from the publisher except for the use of quotations in a book review.

Paperback ISBN: 9798371329653
Hardback ISBN: 9798378021895

For more information visit: www.marcusleebooks.com

First paperback edition Feb 2023
First eBook edition Feb 2023

BY THE SAME AUTHOR

***

THE CHOSEN TRILOGY

Book 1 - THE MOUNTAIN OF SOULS

Book 2 - THE LAST HOPE

Book 3 - THE RIVER OF TEARS

***

THE GIFTED AND THE CURSED TRILOGY

Book 1 - KINGS AND DAEMONS

Book 2 - TRISTAN'S FOLLY

Book 3 - THE END OF DREAMS

***

Follow the author at:

www.marcusleebooks.com
Twitter: @marcusleebooks
Facebook: marcusleebooks
Bookbub: @marcusleebooks
Instagram: marcusleebooks

Frozen Sea

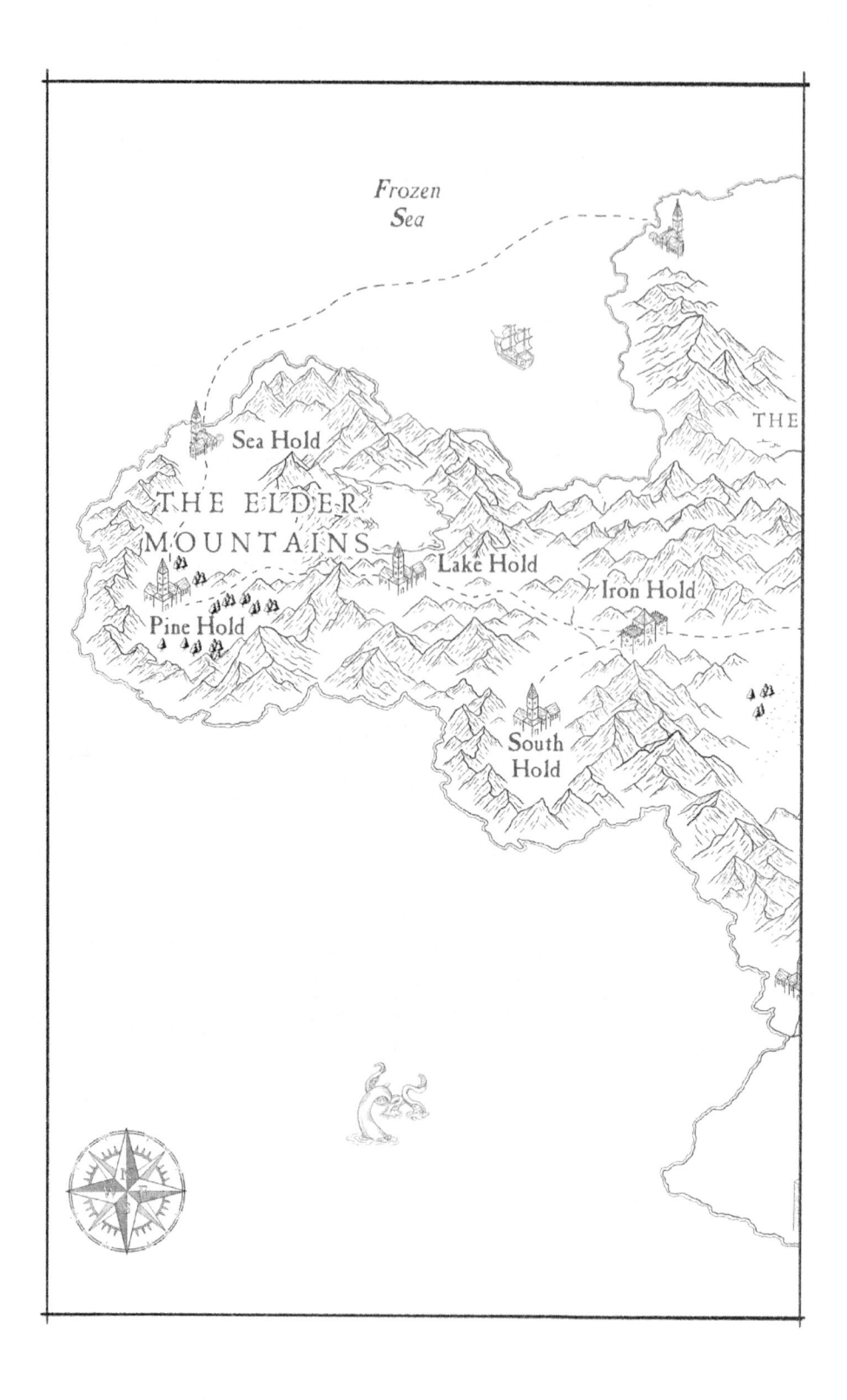

Sea Hold

THE ELDER
MOUNTAINS

Pine Hold

Lake Hold

Iron Hold

South
Hold

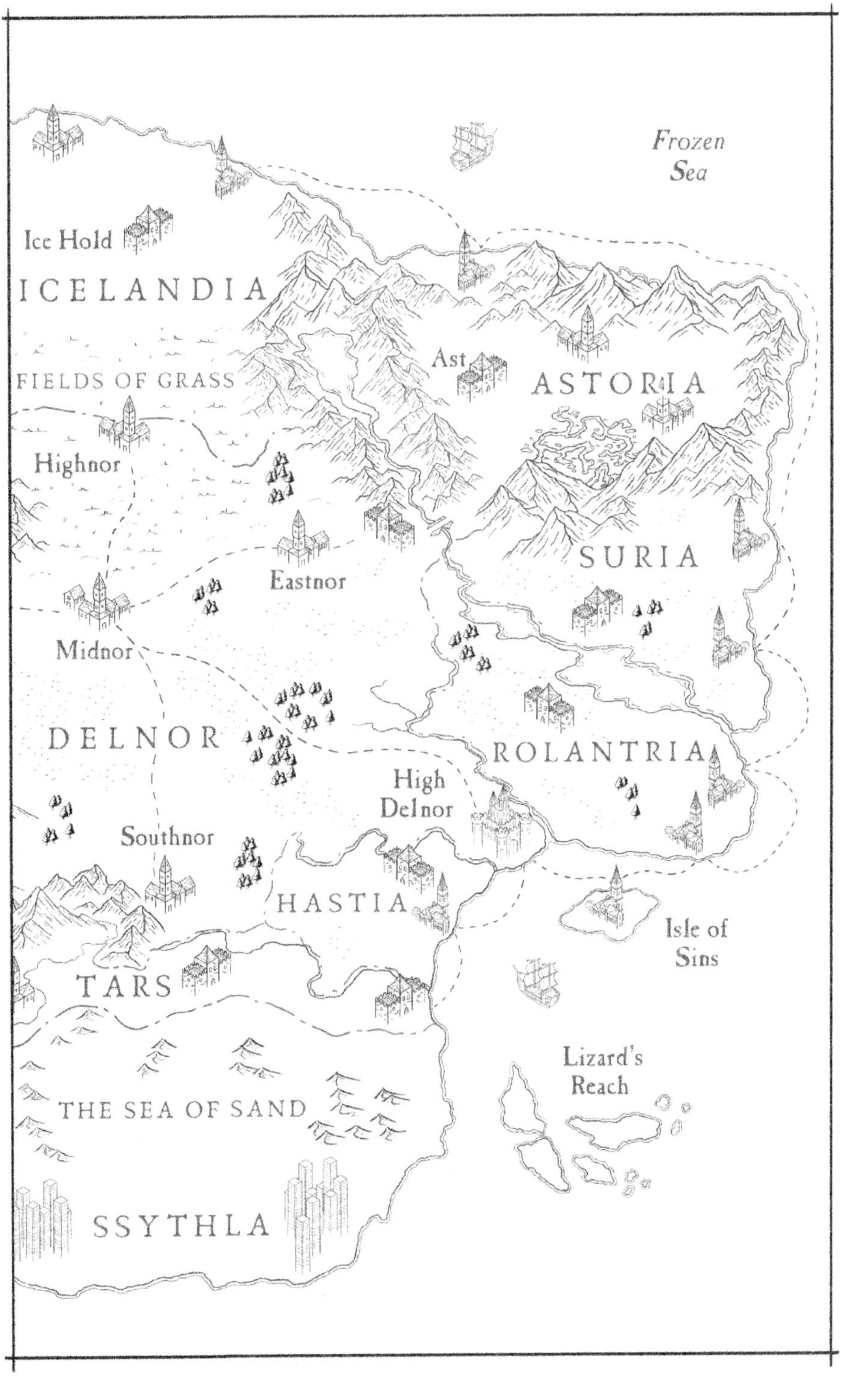

Frozen Sea
Ice Hold
ICELANDIA
Ast
ASTORIA
FIELDS OF GRASS
Highnor
Eastnor
SURIA
Midnor
DELNOR
ROLANTRIA
High Delnor
Southnor
HASTIA
Isle of Sins
TARS
Lizard's Reach
THE SEA OF SAND
SSYTHLA

CHAPTER I

I'm dying.

Even without my soul I should be able to live for weeks, perhaps even a month, at a push, yet I'm dying already. The cold of the grave seeps through my bones, and it's like nothing I've ever experienced. If only I could reach my magic and have the heat of fire burn away the ice freezing the blood in my veins.

My head is heavy, and my limbs are unresponsive like stone blocks. There's a sensation of falling even though I'm lying on a cold floor.

Or am I?

Perhaps instead of falling, I'm moving. Voices are loud yet distant, familiar yet unknown, but they fade into insignificance as I shiver and convulse. Surely it's impossible to be this cold and live. This is how my victims must have felt when I left them to die, stripped of their souls.

I don't want to die. There's too much work left undone, and then there's Lotane. Yet the skeletal hand of death grips me firmly, relentless in its pull.

'Malina.'

The voice is powerful, familiar, and commanding. It reaches out, finding me when I was about to let go, to give up the fight. Somehow it briefly dispels the agony, but moments later, I'm slipping away again.

'Malina. Look at me!'

Falling into oblivion offers the path of least resistance, but there's a compulsion to obey that I can't resist. Light filters past my eyelids as I force them open to find Nogoth leaning over me. It's impossible not to drown in those violet depths.

'Now is not the time for you to die, King Slayer.'

Nogoth's strong hands lift my head easily despite it weighing more than a mountain, and a chalice is pressed to my lips.

'You must drink, Malina. Drink deeply, or you'll be lost to me forever.'

He is my king; I want to please him and am bound to obey.

My eyes convey my agreement, for I can barely move anything else.

Then my pain fades into nothingness as liquid fire burns down my throat to work through my body. The piercing screams I hear can only be my own. To distract myself from the agony, I look through my spirit eye as a glowing light starts pushing back the blackness that's taken hold of me. It's incredible to watch, for it cleanses the foulness in my veins, stimulates my magic, and brings it dancing back to life.

What kind of enchanted elixir I've drunk doesn't matter; for now, every nerve ending tingles and the pain gradually recedes.

Nogoth's fingers gently brush a strand of hair from my face.

'Sleep.'

His voice has a magic of its own, resonating with endless wisdom.

This time when I close my eyes, death is no longer beckoning.

***

I awaken in a bed, cold and weak, the vibrant glow that had brought me back from death absent.

As I sit up and lean tiredly against plush cushions, the four polished wooden posts of the bed stand over me like sentinels. Between them, gossamer thin curtains sweep, tied back with cord. The sheets beneath me are the smoothest I've ever felt, and I marvel at their texture, never having experienced their like.

I'm no longer wearing a Tarsian robe and have been dressed in a short-sleeved shirt and loose trousers. I'm used to being changed during a long training sleep, so it doesn't bother me.

Looking beyond the bed, on one side, there are exquisitely carved statuettes of strange creatures on lacquered cabinets and on the other, a window through which rays of faded sunshine splash the room.

My head spins. It sickens me to be this frail. It won't be more than a day or two before my body succumbs to the pull of death again. A bell is on a bedside cabinet, and even picking it up saps my strength as I ring it to draw attention.

A panelled door opens, and a robed figure observes me from under a dark cowl. I can't see their face, for absent my soul, everything is in shadow.

'Our king will be with you shortly.'

The voice has that strange sibilance of a ssythlan, and sure enough, as it turns away, the flowing movement confirms my suspicion.

Groaning, I swing my legs out of bed, testing their strength before I commit to standing. They can hold me, but not for long.

Unsteadily, I make my way to the window, my toes sinking into a plush carpet floor, opulence supporting me with every step. Leaning against the stone frame, I stare out over an unfamiliar grey landscape.

'It's good to see you back on your feet, Malina.'

I turn at Nogoth's voice and drop to my knees from respect and dizziness. He doesn't glow with light as he did when I first gazed upon him through the mirror, nor does he need to. His majesty is almost overwhelming. He's not wearing plush robes or fanciful attire. Instead, his clothing, while of perfect cut, is practical. A loose shirt with rolled sleeves, trousers tucked into boots and a belt. Perhaps the cloak is the exception, for it's secured with a delicate chain.

'No, no. That will not do,' he exclaims. 'Come, child. Let us put such formalities aside. You're a guest in my home, and I can't have you on the floor every time I pass by!'

The next moment he's kneeling before me, offering me his hand. None of my training has prepared me for this. I can go into combat with my heartbeat barely above normal, but it almost bursts out of my chest as I place my hand in his.

'Now, look at me.'

I raise my eyes, looking into his ageless face, to find myself the subject of his scrutiny.

'It seems you've found a way to surprise me again, Malina. You might be interested in knowing that you're not the first Chosen to have made their way here by accident or design. Yet you're the first to have survived the journey. Welcome to the world of Serenity.

'Now your ordeal has affected you badly, and without your soul you'll perish, so let's do something about that, shall we?'

'Serenity? I'm on another world?' My legs tremble, and I feel faint.

Nogoth, sensing this, leads me to a chair and sits me down.

Moving away, he takes the bell I'd rung earlier and shakes it three times before turning back with a smile. A moment later, the robed ssythlan opens the door and offers Nogoth a chalice on a tray.

'There are many amazing things in this world, Malina. This one not only saved your life but will keep you alive until you're reunited with your soul.'

Taking the chalice from Nogoth's outstretched hand, I look inside and gasp. In this world of greys, here is a liquid that glints and shines with an iridescent light. It's almost too beautiful to drink.

Lifting it to my lips, I hesitate for a moment, but with Nogoth nodding reassuringly, I take a sip. The liquid tingles across my tongue, then as I swallow, fire shoots through my veins ... but this time without pain. It's like a flood, sweeping aside my weakness, replacing it with vigour beyond the norm. I feel stronger than ever before: invincible even. Then, to my amazement, streaks of colour flash across my sight, a shining display that momentarily blinds me. Then as my vision returns, the world around me is no longer grey.

Never before have I seen with such clarity. Even the incredible experience of returning home through the Soul Gate and reuniting with my soul doesn't come close.

My nerves tingle, my breathing shallows, and as I look upon Nogoth, I feel a desire awaken inside me. His lips and eyes are mesmerising, and a hunger that has nothing to do with food stirs deep in my core.

Shocked by these sudden thoughts, I shake my head, desperately reaching for something to distract me. Lotane. I need to be near him again, to rid myself of these unwanted desires.

'My mission,' I gasp gratefully, suddenly conscious of having left Lotane and my fellow Chosen waiting for me. 'I have to get back!'

'Malina. You needn't worry. I've sent word of your arrival here. The mission you refer to is now complete, and others besides. You've been asleep here for three days, but over a month has passed in your world. Be assured, everyone that matters knows you're alright and will accompany me on my return to your world.'

'Why can't I return now?'

Nogoth laughs, and it's like seductive music to my ears.

'I forgot how full of questions you can be. You could try, and indeed it will be your choice. Sadly, I doubt you'll survive the journey. When my acolytes found you, you were on the edge of death. Your world doesn't enjoy our magical healing abilities, so even if you made it through alive, you'd perish shortly after. Why take the risk when you can travel with me in little more than a month.

'I asked you to be my advisor. Are you so swift to want to abandon your duty? Do you not want to be near me?'

Does he know how his choice of words stirs my blood? Yet despite this strange attraction, I'm also ashamed and realise how ungrateful I must sound.

'Forgive me, my king. Of course, I want nothing more than to be at your side.'

Uttering these words makes me flush, and I stumble on.

'My troubled thoughts had me thinking of seeking your wisdom when I entered the Soul Gate on my last mission, and,' I spread my arms, 'here I am.'

'Here you are indeed, and we can't have you calling me by such a grandiose title if you're to be spending time with me. I am called Nogoth by those who know me well. It's a title as much as a name, so I'd be pleased if you'd call me that.'

I bow my head in acknowledgement.

'Now, I've matters to attend to. Clothing not unlike what you're used to wearing is in the wardrobes, so choose something you're comfortable with. I'll send someone to answer your questions and keep you company until my return later tonight.

'Would you care to join me for dinner?'

His stare is intense and holds me in a vice-like grip, turning my insides to water. Even though it's posed as a request, I feel obliged to say yes. My desire to do as he wishes isn't just because of the privilege or the blood magic that binds us; it's his sheer animal magnetism.

'I'd be honoured.'

The smile he bestows upon me is genuine, as though relieved at my acquiescence. Is he so unaware of the effect he's having on me?

Grow up, Malina. You're like a star-struck girl!

I should be thinking of Lotane. Lotane, who presumed me dead for a while, and who cried at night when I didn't return. He of the strong arms, a cheeky smile, endless teasing, and jokes.

My head clears, and relief washes over me.

'Until this evening then.'

With an elegant bow and a flourish of his hand, Nogoth smiles a final time as, opening a door, he sweeps from the room.

***

The emptiness inside me at Nogoth's departure is hard to fathom. My surroundings are as beautiful as before but seem diminished now he's absent. My elevated heart rate begins to slow.

Shaking my head, embarrassed and amused by my initial reaction, I wander over to a wardrobe.

Upon looking inside, I find several robes of varying colours hanging from hooks. My eye is drawn to a dark green one, a similar hue to my skin for the most part, and after first swapping my nightwear for a pair of heavier trousers and a shirt from some shelves, I pull the robe over my head.

Thankfully, my old boots are within, which makes me wonder where my Tarsian robe and, more importantly, my Soul Blade is. I move throughout the room, pulling open drawers and wardrobe doors, but to no avail. I discover only other clothing.

Frustrated, I bang the last drawer shut, at which point the door to my room opens. Instead of the ssythlan, a fair-skinned woman stands there with a fixed, polite smile. She enters, and despite the robes concealing her frame, there's no denying the assurance and balance with which she moves.

This woman is more than just a helper, I'm sure. But there's one way to find out.

Smiling, I open my arms in greeting, knocking, as if by accident, a figurine from the top of a cabinet.

She flows with perfect coordination, stepping smoothly, catching it just before the floor, then flicks it hard and fast at my face.

My hand snaps up to intercept, and I replace it gently from whence it came.

THE LAST HOPE

This time, her smile is somewhat warmer, a hint of respect apparent.

'Unless you have more tests for me?' She pauses momentarily, then carries on. 'My name is Aigul. I'm ... one of the king's bodyguards.'

Her hesitancy isn't lost on me, but now isn't the time to question.

'Nogoth has asked me to make you welcome, show you around, and answer most of your questions.'

'Most?'

'Yes, Malina. Most. Let's start with a tour of your new home, shall we?'

So saying, she bows with a gently mocking smile, sweeping her arm toward the doorway.

'After you.'

As I step through, I find myself at the end of a corridor near the head of a wide circular staircase. The landing on which I stand is decorated in a martial fashion. Suits of armour are positioned every dozen steps, and I wander over, intrigued. With some, the only difference between what I'm used to are the embellishments. However, others are enormous. Twice the size with thick spikes jutting from shoulder guards or thigh protectors.

'Are these for real?' I ask, running my hand over different pieces of armour. 'This doesn't feel like metal. What is it?'

Aigul brushes a strand of hair from her face. She's quite the beauty and reminds me of Lystra.

'It is real, and you're rather astute at recognising that it isn't metal. It's made from a type of ceramic unlike any you've encountered. It's almost as hard as steel, a little lighter, and doesn't shatter easily as you'd expect.

The corridor is lined with polished wooden display cases full of small hand weapons.

Every conceivable weapon is displayed against a lush red cloth, from dirks to hatchets, daggers to spiked knuckle guards. I'm so intrigued by the different designs and colourings that I'm unaware my steps haven taken me to the end of the corridor, where I stop in surprise. Alongside some leaf-bladed throwing knives, standing out because of their blunt crystal appearance, are several Soul Blades.

I cast an enquiring glance at Aigul.

'Yes, one of those is yours, but for now, it remains where it is. Now, please, follow me.'

Together we return to descend the staircase. Wherever I look, there's both the familiar and the abnormal. As we reach the ground floor, two ssythlan warriors stand guard, motionless like statues and all along the walls, large, brightly coloured paintings hang.

'How are there ssythlans here?' I ask.

'You're a long way from home, so why not ask how humans are here instead?' Aigul retorts.

Her indirect response is frustrating, but I'm too busy taking in my surroundings to press further. Ahead are a pair of gigantic doors. They'd have suited a castle entrance and are out of place in what appears to be a comfortable mansion. The two ssythlan guards pull on ropes, and the doors edge open with a creak.

'They arrived here in a similar fashion to you, through a gate,' Aigul volunteers. 'The ssythlans' homeland is beyond the Sea of Sand, yet they worship Nogoth and desire to be close to serve him better.'

Aigul's answer just leaves me wanting to ask more questions, but the ssythlans aren't where my main interest lies. It's time to be direct with my questioning.

'So, what's Nogoth like as a leader? He's coming to my world to bring about a golden era of change.'

It's a bold question, but one that needs to be asked. After all, I'm here to set my mind at rest, ease my doubts and satiate my desire for knowledge.

'What can I say that you haven't already fathomed in your time with him either through the portal or your recovery here.'

Aigul shrugs, trying to brush the question aside. Yet I continue looking at her until, with a sigh, she relents.

'He's knowledgeable beyond anyone I've ever known, a true king to his people who worship him as divine, and in some ways, he is. Now, Nogoth asked me to show you around, and what you'll witness will answer your questions far better than my words ever could.'

The doors are open enough for us to step through, and as we do, it finally hits me that I'm in another world. I'd believed the Mountain of Souls and its island was paradise, but I was wrong.

'Is this where the gods live?' I ask, barely aware I'm posing the question.

THE LAST HOPE

Aigul's laugh has a hint of something strange about it.

'The gods, no. Although I admit it matters not how often I gaze upon this land, its beauty strikes to my core every day.'

Whilst inside the mansion, there were things I found unusual; here, I'm captivated by the unknown. I'm not sure what I'd expected, but walls to keep Nogoth safe and apart from his subjects were the minimum. Yet, there's little to be seen of anything that hasn't been created by the hand of nature. It rules here, and this world is a better place for it.

Lush grasses sway in the breeze; the greens I'm used to are joined by purples, oranges and yellows. Trees with full canopies are laden with a myriad of ripening fruit under a sun that warms my skin with a tenderness that reminds me briefly of my mother's touch. Brightly coloured insects and birds fly everywhere, often drawn from one flower to the next by the pollen's heady perfume.

It's like a painter has created a scene with the most vibrant colours on the palette, yet with a harmony that defies belief. In plain contrast, healthy-looking men and women dressed in bright white, harvest the bounty that this world of plenty bestows on them. Despite the warmth of the day, white scarves adorn their necks.

Amongst them are others in green robes much like my own, overseers of some kind. As they move, they dance, their arms and bodies twisting in a sinuous, almost sensual way. They hold richly embellished skins from which they dispense sparkling golden drops to the soil. The workers touch fingers to their lips and smile warmly if the overseers come close.

One of the overseers, a woman from the way her robes fit, catches sight of us. She approaches, whirling around, eyes fixed on me. It's mesmerising to watch; an unchoreographed display that perfectly fits the natural surroundings.

Suddenly she halts, facing me but a few steps away. With light green skin, she melds into these lush surroundings perfectly. Her features are fine, delicate even, with arched eyebrows, high cheekbones, and a thin nose. To my surprise, she has yellow eyes, although a darker shade than mine. She tilts her head one way, then another, her hair moving almost with a life of its own. Then, with a half-smile and bow, she spins off again.

'Who or what was that?' I ask, intrigued.

'She's one of the Saer Tel. An ancient race that has served Nogoth since he came to power. Their devotion and loyalty see them sit at his right hand. He holds none in higher regard. Amongst other things, they're responsible for the beauty that surrounds us. They're creatures of nature, of the forest, and were on the verge of extinction with just a few hundred alive before Nogoth saved them, later gifting them eternal life for their service.'

'Eternal life!' I gasp, briefly unbelieving. But why should I be, for the king himself enjoys such longevity. How truly noble to share this gift of the gods with those who deserve it.

Aigul smiles, shining with pride as she extols Nogoth's virtue.

'Likewise, the other denizens of this world have been saved by our king. Once, they were hunted and persecuted, numbering in the hundreds, now, it's the hundreds of thousands, and they all worship Nogoth as their saviour.'

To think that Nogoth saved the peoples of this world, giving them life when all they'd known was death, is nothing short of miraculous. I wonder who he saved them from, what mighty battles were fought and what obstacles he'd had to overcome.

Something Nogoth had said when I'd summoned him comes to mind.

To appreciate the greatest view, you must not only climb the highest mountain but have first plumbed the darkest depths.

Now I truly appreciate the truth of those words. I breathe deeply, savouring the moment.

Aigul clears her throat, catching my attention.

'I'm sure that Nogoth will be better positioned to tell you further about the history of this world. Now, even though you won't get lost in the valley, let's familiarise you further.'

In the distance, toward the valley rim, are fields of what are probably crops. More interestingly, here and there, dotted throughout the landscape, are large, grass-covered mounds.

'What's that?' I ask, pointing toward a large mound covered in pink flowers.

'The workers here need somewhere to live. Not everyone gets to stay in Nogoth's residence.'

Aigul surprises me by taking my hand and leads me across the mansion lawns. Even this building is somewhat disguised by nature. Flowering creepers climb every wall whilst the roof is covered in grass.

Even the giant gates we'd stepped through appear half alive, with small flowers growing upon their surface.

Throughout the day, Aigul shows me around much of the valley. Every step is a pleasure, a chance to see something new, from sparkling brooks full of colourful fish to animals with shining gold fur resembling cattle.

We move slowly, frequently pausing so I can relish the scent of every bloom that catches my eye, run my fingers through grasses as soft as feathers, and enjoy the birdsong.

'You remind me of myself when I first arrived,' Aigul laughs. 'Even now, after all these years, it's the beauty of this place that keeps my nightmares at bay.'

'The only nightmare would be if this all turned out to be a dream!' I laugh. Then the meaning of her words register. 'You weren't born here then?'

Aigul scuffs her feet as if unsure of revealing more but then takes a deep breath and stops to face me.

'I was born in Astor a long time ago. My story is likely much like yours, Malina. In times past, I survived the training and purges to become a Chosen. They were glorious times, and sometimes I miss them. But what I've gained from living at Nogoth's side far exceeded my wildest dreams.'

I'm perplexed.

'But, Nogoth told me I was the only one to survive journeying here through a Soul Gate.'

'He spoke truly, Malina. Well, mostly. I returned with him following a previous conquest when the World Gate was open. It's far larger than the Soul Gate that you're thinking of; a direct passage between worlds. It doesn't require a soul to travel, for it derives its power from the moons.'

'But his last conquest was a thousand years ago!' I exclaim in amazement.

Aigul smiles. 'Here, it's only been one hundred, and I've been here longer than that, but I'd like to think I still look good for my age!'

Her laugh is infectious, and I join in, enjoying the moment of camaraderie with a fellow Chosen from another time.

'Is there no death in this world? Are the workers here all from home?' I ask, my curiosity straining to be satisfied. I've a hundred questions to ask, all begging to be answered.

Aigul's face twitches, a frown disappearing before it's half-formed.

'No, there's still death here. As for the workers, they're indeed from home, albeit another age, and are lucky to enjoy life in this incredible place.'

Every one of the workers appears well-fed, content, and despite not getting close enough to converse, several bow respectfully in our direction.

'Come,' Aigul says, looking at the sun nudging the horizon. 'Enough talk of the past for now. It will soon be dark, and we must hasten back for dinner in the present.'

Walking faster, she pulls me gently along. Her hand is hard, calloused, and strong like mine. I'm no longer surprised, for she is a Chosen.

Aigul leads me along a wooded avenue of red canopied trees. Fallen leaves cover the ground, creating an illusion of a bloody river. It reminds me of the dreams that I used to have of Karson. No doubt he'd have something ominous to say rather than exclaiming at its beauty. However, despite the incredible sight, the thought makes me a little uneasy.

'Are you up to running?' Aigul challenges me, nodding to the mansion in the distance. Then, without waiting for my answer, she lets go of my hand and sets off at speed.

I laugh happily as I begin my pursuit.

Aigul had been right. What I'd seen had answered my earlier question about what Nogoth was like more than words could convey.

I've seen only contentment in those I've witnessed, albeit from afar. For The Once and Future King to be willing to leave this exotically beautiful place behind, to come to my world and lift it from the darkness, he must be the purest of souls.

***

Long shadows hold the valley in their embrace as we reach the mansion. Only the eastern rim is still ablaze with colour as the last of the sun's rays give me a final chance to relish the vista's beauty.

Aigul has just beaten me back, but I'm not bothered. She knows the countryside better, and I'm far from my best. I can detect my life force ebbing away, drop by drop. Sadly, the elixir wasn't a permanent solution to being parted from my soul.

Aigul can obviously tell.

'Tonight, when we dine, your needs will be taken care of,' she smiles, a hint of something in her eye that I can't fathom. 'Now, come, let's hurry.'

Following her lead, she takes me around the side of the mansion, skirting a small pool that sits near its foundations. Pausing, I kneel at the edge, drawn by its unnatural stillness, watching dozens of colourful insects fly about their business, none of which disturb the waters. Something catches my eye, a reflection of ... yes, a black moon. Turning, I look upwards, but to the naked eye, it's unseen.

'It's a strange and powerful phenomenon. One of so many in this place,' Aigul says, understanding the reason for my perplexed gaze. 'I'll often look down from my balcony to see Nogoth sitting here on a calm evening, gazing into that pool's depths. Magic holds the waters perfectly still, courtesy of the ssythlan mages who helped build this place.'

'It's beautiful,' I whisper.

'Come.'

Despite our near-silent footfalls, the mansion doors open at our approach, the ssythlan guards somehow perceiving of our presence. Their tongues flick in and out as we pass, and I realise they've tasted our scent from a distance.

'Aigul. Why isn't this place fortified? There are so few guards, and they're lightly armed. How can they protect Nogoth if this place is ever assaulted?'

The look I receive from Aigul makes me feel like I'm in the orphanage again, being spoken down to by a teacher.

'Malina. Nogoth is loved by everyone in this world. The guards here are the bare ceremonial minimum, an honour for any ssythlan who takes the role voluntarily.'

As Aigul directs me along the entrance hallway toward the stairs, I admire the artwork on the walls, highlighted by moon globes. Each one is of a landscape similar to what I'd seen outside, and they have something else in common: the black moon.

'I don't have a trained eye to determine whether these are good or not, but to me, they look amazing,' I say, my fingers softly bushing the canvas, feeling the texture of the paint.

'Nogoth would be pleased to hear that.'

I'm astounded at the revelation, although why a king shouldn't be an artist is beyond me.

With my interest piqued, I peer closer as we walk until a familiar landscape and sky are captured perfectly in deft brushstrokes before me. The picture also depicts the black, blue, and white moons in perfect alignment.

I point, my look conveying the question without verbalising it.

'Yes,' Aigul smiles. 'That's the view from Pine Hold in your world.'

Her mouth snaps shut immediately after she utters the words.

Pine Hold. An ancient town on the furthest western reach of the Delnorian Empire. From memory, it's an unremarkable place except for one thing, a crumbling fortress built into the side of a mountain from ancient times. The location isn't strategic, so it had baffled people for ages as to why it had been built.

I smile to myself, for I now know the answer.

I'd always assumed Nogoth would step through the portal into the Mountain of Souls. However, it seems in times past, he'd arrived at Pine Hold and built himself a fortress there. The seat of his power before he'd expanded east.

Aigul's eyes flicker to an ornate clock made from some translucent crystal.

'Let's make ready. We're expected in an hour.'

'But I'm ready now,' I respond, shrugging.

Aigul laughs, but not unkindly.

'Let me show you something that might change your mind.'

She leads the way upstairs, back to the room I'd woken in.

Once inside, Aigul walks to a flat panelled wall between two cabinets and presses with the palm of her hand. There's a soft click, and when she steps back, an artfully concealed door opens, beyond which is a cleansing room. A toilet, a washbasin with some water jugs beside it, and a beaten metal tub in the corner full of steaming water are inside.

'I'll be back in half an hour,' Aigul states. 'Choose fresh garments for dinner and leave the old ones in the basket by the door.'

Without another word, she turns and leaves.

A fragrant scent lingers in the air, enticing me toward the tub. When I look inside, dozens of petals are floating on the water. Chuckling, I slip out of my robe and clothes. I've been out all day and raced back to the mansion. Even if I can't smell my odour, I'm certainly not at my most presentable.

I'd only ever showered in cold water, and whilst Lotane sometimes used his fire magic to warm up the basin water back at the mountain, I'd never been in a hot bath before.

Lotane.

He hasn't crossed my mind the whole day, and as I slip into the tub, I wish he were here to share it with me. The hot water envelops my body, easing some tiredness away, but the warmth in my heart is from thinking of Lotane. How strange. Without my soul, there should only be the knowledge that love exists between us. Yet, there's no denying the feeling.

Lowering my head beneath the water, I hold my breath, listening to my heartbeat. It's an exquisite moment, secure in the water's embrace, the love in my heart loud in my ears.

Reluctantly I surface, push my hair back and wipe the water from my eyes.

I wish the bath could be a little hotter. In response to my thoughts, my magic wriggles to gain attention, and I silently assent to its help. Opening my hands beneath the water, two small orbs of fire coalesce, heating the water around them. Both water and fire work in harmony, attuned to my contentment, subsiding as the perfect temperature is reached.

It's been too long since I've spent time connecting with my magic, so I close my eyes, mentally embracing the swirl of colours and enjoying their subsequent happiness. Then, having spoiled them with my affection, I turn my spirit eye outwards to gaze upon my surroundings.

Amongst the swirling elemental colours, a thick red thread of blood magic runs from my heart through the bottom of the tub. It must lead directly to Nogoth, for it's so vibrant.

How does it really work, I wonder? In all this time, I'd never thought to examine it closer or put it directly to use … assuming that's even possible.

What do I already know?

It binds someone to another person or something physical like the Heart Stone.

But perhaps I should be asking how I was bound to the Heart Stone, Nogoth and the others.

Even as I ruminate, my blood magic answers, such is its sentience. From within me, a tendril of red whisps outward, questing, scenting, awaiting direction on what to attach itself to.

Laughing softly, I wonder if I bound it to the bathtub, I'd find it hard to leave. However, is just attaching it to something enough to create a bond, or does some kind of emotion or instruction need to be given?

What about the blood magic that binds me to Nogoth?

In response, the tendril moves to wrap itself lightly around the bright thread, and I hear whispers of long-spoken words.

Unending love. Instant obedience. Unshakeable loyalty. Goodness. Hope. Salvation.

What if my investigations are felt?

Enough for now.

The tendril responds to my thoughts and withdraws happily, leaving me pondering.

Yes. Without question, emotional instruction and feeling were conveyed during our binding whenever it happened.

Does it bother me?

No.

Nogoth deserves my love, obedience, and loyalty because he is good, and the promise of hope and salvation shines within him.

'Malina. I hope you're nearly ready!'

Aigul's scolding voice shakes me into action.

'I'll be right out,' I call, stepping from the bath and grabbing a towel.

It takes only a matter of moments to dry myself, and, fortunately, my hair is short. I grab a brush and then realise there's no mirror.

Strange.

Nonetheless, I pull it through the tangles, straightening it out, then rush to the bedroom, tossing my worn clothes into the basket across the room, smiling with satisfaction that I don't miss. Opening the cupboard, I grab a fresh pair of trousers and a shirt, pulling them on, followed by a red robe.

THE LAST HOPE

The colour appears to fade as I adjust it on my frame, and a wave of fatigue washes over me, leaving me shaking.

Pulling my boots on, I head unsteadily to the door, opening it to find Aigul waiting with a hint of an impatient frown.

She utters just two words, that send a shiver down my spine.

'Nogoth awaits.'

***

Swiftly through the mansion, she leads me, down the staircase, along the hall, through numerous chambers, some filled with books, others with charts and maps. I want to pause and see what treasures of knowledge are held here, but I'm impatient to see Nogoth.

Despite being distracted the entire day by a never-ending myriad of new flora and fauna, the thoughts that led me here resurface. This will be my opportunity to lend Nogoth my knowledge and see if there might be a diplomatic path to pursue on his return. The death of the High King comes to mind, accompanied by the familiar feeling of regret.

We approach polished wooden doors, and a ssythlan guard holds one open as we approach. Stepping through, we enter a small room with a fire blazing warmly in a hearth. Before it is a semi-circular couch with a small table between the two. Around the walls are detailed stone sculptures of women in various poses. As I inspect them closer, I recognise the Saer Tel I'd seen in the valley.

Candelabras add a further homely glow to the room, boasting plush carpet on the floor and bookcases along the walls.

I'd been expecting some grand dining chamber, with a long table, formal sitting and with numerous staff to attend to the king's every need. Yet here I am in a comfortable, informal setting that, despite the sculptures, reaffirms Nogoth as a King who is not interested in pomp, ceremony, or overt displays of wealth.

A side door opens, and in he walks, making me catch my breath.

Kralgen and Lotane are both physically bigger, yet Nogoth exudes a strength beyond any mere mortal. He's wearing hunting leathers; the trousers dyed a deep blue but with a loose-fitting white shirt that's open at the neck. Surprisingly he's barefoot, but as this is his home, I surmise that's how he feels most comfortable.

He fixes me with those violet eyes, and a warm smile parts his full lips.

'Malina. I'm glad you chose to join us.'

As his gaze turns toward Aigul, I suffer an instant loss, as if something has been torn from me. I grab a chair, feeling unsteady as my head spins. Whatever remedy Nogoth had given me in the morning has nearly worn off, and the colour of everything in view is fading.

'Aigul. Malina isn't looking her best. Would you kindly source some elixir for us?'

With a soft smile and a lowering of her eyes, Aigul leaves the way we entered, and the door closes softly behind her.

I'm alone with Nogoth, yet his relaxed manner puts me at ease.

'Sit and make yourself comfortable,' he says, indicating the couch in front of the fire. 'You've been through quite an ordeal. However, I hope today has renewed your spirit, even if not your soul.'

As I move to sit at one end, he chooses the middle and, draping his arm over the back, turns toward me. I'm self-conscious under his scrutiny, but also feel special to be the centre of his attention.

I feel warmer, and not just because of the fire's proximity, there's a heat radiating from Nogoth himself.

'So, Malina. What caused you to travel between worlds to see me? The last time we spoke, you had doubts. Do they persist, or did I come to mind for other reasons?'

His violet eyes are mesmerising, and I find myself leaning toward him.

Look away, Malina! I berate myself and break eye contact. I focus on the fire and order my thoughts. Then, with a deep breath, I recount my misgivings about the mistake I believe was made in killing the High King. I talk for what seems an eternity, then suddenly stop, embarrassed that I've spoken for so long without pause.

'That you have such regrets speaks for the goodness of your soul, and now I share your concern. Being so far removed from your world, I rely on my ssythlan clerics to find the best path they can. Sadly, they sometimes err in their decisions. I told you once that I wanted you beside me, advising me, and that I'd listen to your counsel.

'Be assured that on my imminent return, there will be no deaths beyond those that are unavoidable. I'll offer a peaceful resolution at every opportunity. Every life is more valuable to me than you can imagine. Look at me, Malina, and know I speak the truth.'

I know from his voice that he is, yet I'm strangely reluctant to meet his gaze. His magnetism is nigh on overwhelming, and I have other questions to ask.

'So, where's your army? Other than a few ssythlan guards, there's no military force here. How large is it, how long will it take to establish your rule, and will it be enough to hold order across so many nations?'

Realising just how many questions I'm throwing at Nogoth, I restrain myself from saying any more ... at least for now.

Nogoth chuckles.

'Where do I begin? Well, this valley is my escape from all kingly matters. So, you're right; there's no army here. Outside of this valley, my forces gather, and they are more than sufficient to subdue the kingdoms of which you speak by force. But as I mentioned a moment ago, I will always offer surrender first, so bloodshed can be avoided.

'My rule will be established wherever we travel. But, and this may surprise you, I don't intend to stay for longer than two years.'

'What? But why? After all these years of waiting, why wouldn't you stay longer?'

'If I'm to end inequality, what kind of hypocrite would I be to stay as the king of not just one nation, but them all?'

Nothing but the crackle of the flames in the fireplace follows this statement as I consider what he's told me. His words are true and inspiring too. To attain such power at likely a high cost and then willingly cast it aside once attained is the most selfless act I can imagine. Yet, he surely needs more time to make lasting changes.

'Will two years be enough to bring about what we're fighting for?'

Nogoth's smile is as bright as a spring sunrise.

'I can assure you, once I'm king, my influence will be felt for centuries, and while not forever, I will return again and again in the future.'

My smile matches his.

'The Once and Future King.'

To laugh with him is as close to pure happiness as I've ever been. However, I'm beginning to feel cold despite the fire's warmth, and I shiver.

Nogoth looks at me closely, then leans over to pick up a small bell and rings it three times.

Moments later, Aigul reappears with a chalice on a tray. Her pupils are wide, a sign of excitement perhaps, as she places it on the table in front of Nogoth, then sits on his other side.

The shimmering golden liquid inside triggers my stomach to growl as a mixed wave of hunger and thirst sweeps over me. It takes every ounce of my willpower not to grab the chalice and drain its contents.

Nogoth is peering intently at me, his violet eyes appearing to shimmer. An intense pulse radiates from his body, permeating my core, and a surge of desire takes me by surprise.

Lifting the chalice, Nogoth takes a sip, the golden elixir coating his lips. Turning to Aigul, he leans toward her, and I watch, astonished, as she kisses him full on the mouth, her eyes closing in ecstasy. He gently pulls away, then allows her to take a sip directly from the chalice.

My heart is hammering. My need to drink the elixir, to feel alive, is only equalled by my desire for this man beside me. Perhaps his interest is in Aigul alone. But then his eyes turn upon me, full of desire and violet power. Again, a pulse of energy moves through me, igniting my passion like never before. My breathing is shallow, my heart fluttering like a bird's wings.

No, Malina! I scold myself. *Lotane is waiting, don't break his trust!*

Nogoth slowly dips his thumb into the elixir, and I watch, swallowing in anticipation as he leans toward me. Gently, ever so gently, he wipes the shimmering liquid across my parted lips. I try to resist, every heartbeat a small victory, every heartbeat a terrible punishment. Yet the moment it runs into my mouth, I'm lost.

Grabbing his hand, I lick and suck the elixir from his thumb, my stomach growling as it demands more.

This time when Nogoth drinks from the chalice, his lips meet mine, parting to allow a flow of liquid into my mouth. Our tongues entwine, and his hands pull me close as my body thrums with pleasure.

Another pulse of energy, and I can't restrain a shudder as pleasure rips through me.

Nogoth looks intrigued as he briefly pulls away.

'Only one of the Fey can respond to the quickening. I suspected as much the moment I laid eyes on you,' he whispers, his voice husky. 'You have the blood of the Saer Tel in your veins, Malina. Your eyes, your skin, and the magics that you wield. No mere human could bond with and command the four elements.'

I can't believe my ears. It's impossible to concentrate as desire overwhelms my senses, but his words are impossible to ignore.

He believes I'm a Fey? The Fey are spoken of only in children's tales and poems. Yet, there's no denying my resemblance to the Saer Tel. The Fey are supposed to have been evil, yet how wrong those tales are.

Nogoth raises the chalice to my lips.

'Drink, but share this with Aigul,' he commands.

I sip, savouring its incredible effect on my body, but when I offer the cup to Aigul, Nogoth shakes his head.

'Not like that. Like this.'

Taking a mouthful, he kisses Aigul on the lips, letting the elixir flow into her willing mouth.

Following his lead, I lean across Nogoth, my hand resting on his thigh. Aigul's parted lips meet mine, and I wonder if I'll ever feel this way again. Nogoth's lips brush my neck while his hands rove over my body.

Aigul's lips are softer than I could believe, and she moans with desire.

Then as our robes come off, I lose myself to the heat of the moment and the power of Nogoth's quickening.

***

CHAPTER II

I awaken to the faint light of a moon globe.

My body tingles warmly as I lie alone in bed, reminiscing over the last three crazy weeks.

Of an evening, Nogoth has been a consummate lover and, allied to his gift of the quickening, has taken me to unbelievable highs, again and again. I recall Aigul telling how Nogoth had saved the denizens of this world when they numbered in their hundreds. Having experienced the quickening's power, It's easy to understand how its use would have created a mating frenzy that saw the Fey numbers explode.

Yet, despite my relative inexperience, I know I've intoxicated Nogoth with my willingness, wild abandon, and creativity. The mysterious power of the quickening had stirred my imagination, and using my magic, I'd raised a heat inside of me that had Nogoth screaming in pleasure, verging on pain. I smile at the memory of me outlasting him the previous night. He hadn't quite hidden his wonder and disbelief as he bade me leave him to rest.

During the daytime, Aigul keeps me company as we wander within the confines of the valley. We've grown close, and it's not surprising, considering there's never an evening when we don't share a bed. Like Nogoth, her sexual prowess is breathtaking, but in an entirely different way. Her soft sensuality has been an exquisite complement to Nogoth's raw physical passion.

Something from the night before niggles at my mind.

Yes.

After all these weeks, she'd suddenly become jealous of something that happened between Nogoth and me.

What was it?

My memory is blurred by hunger, and it's hard to concentrate. I recall the events of last night, visualising the naked bodies next to me, under me, above me, reliving and relishing in the remembered pleasure.

Then, just as I see that look of jealousy appearing on Aigul's face, my stomach lurches, and light-headedness sweeps the pleasurable thoughts aside.

I reach for the chalice beside my bed to find it empty.

Damn!

Despite having partaken in some elixir the night before, I crave, no … I *need* its taste and nourishment. I haven't eaten since I've been here, as the elixir is so potent that it negates the need for food.

Groaning, I reach over and ring the bell on my bedside table.

It's time to get up, so I swing my feet out of bed, aching from the last night's physical activity. Had I been at the Mountain of Souls, I'd have leapt out full of vigour unless Lotane had other ideas.

Lotane's warm eyes and loving arms come to mind. For three weeks, he hasn't crossed my mind, not once. Guilt washes over me as the magnitude of my betrayal hits home.

What have I done?

I'd have cut his heart out if he had been unfaithful to me.

As I consider the hurt my actions would cause him were he to find out, I sob softly, and an emptiness grows to accompany my craving for the elixir. I'm desperate for a sip to banish all my misgivings alongside restoring my body and spirit.

No one has responded to the bell, and while frustrated, I'm not some noble who expects to be waited upon.

Quickly pulling on clean clothes, boots, and a robe, I slip out of my bedroom and pad across the hallway to Aigul's room. Despite knocking several times, there's no response, so I open the door and peer inside.

Empty. The bed is made, and there's no unfinished elixir for me to slake my thirst. Aigul being absent is quite unusual. She's always here to accompany me while Nogoth leaves to meet his generals. The notion of actually eating food comes to mind, but I quickly discard it.

If I want some elixir, I need to find it myself. But where to find some?

I feel a tugging from my magic in response to this thought, and an idea coalesces.

Yes. The elixir has a wonderfully unique sweet aroma. Perhaps I can find it by following its scent.

Help me.

In response, a wriggling in my stomach is followed by a gentle breeze as my magic responds.

There it is!

The ssythlan guards are as still as the statues atop their plinths and take no notice as I follow my senses down the staircase and toward the aroma's source. Passing through several chambers, I let myself in through a kitchen entrance. Half a dozen men and women are cleaning, dressed in their usual white, with scarves around their necks. They nod and smile but say nothing, as is the norm.

I breathe deeply. The scent is definitely more potent here, and I look for a jug or bottle containing what I need. However, there's nothing. Instead, I'm drawn to another door at the rear of the kitchen. Feeling the inquisitive stares of the staff follow me, I open the door to find steps leading down into the pitch dark.

Simply imagining the gentle warmth of a flame in my hand is all it takes for a small but bright ball of fire to coalesce in my palm.

Everyone falls to their knees, touching two fingers to their lips in the salute I've seen them use when a Saer Tel passes close by.

I'm surprised by their reaction, and whilst my needs are too great to ponder on something so trivial, it would appear I've just learned something. The Saer Tel can use magic if that makes these people acknowledge me as one.

The stairwell walls are polished, reflecting the fire, undoubtedly the work of a mage, ssythlan, or Saer Tel, I don't know. I curse silently. All this time, I've been revelling in my surroundings and enjoying intimate pleasures, yet I haven't trained or studied anything to better serve Nogoth.

Lystra would be so disappointed.

I don't know whether the ssythlans originate here or who exactly the Saer Tel are. I haven't seen the army, met any generals, nor discussed what responsibilities I'll have when we return to my world. The only thing I've served are my personal desires, and whilst, without question, I haven't disappointed Nogoth in the bedroom, as a Chosen he must believe me sadly lacking.

THE LAST HOPE

Yet, in my defence, he's driven every conversation we've had, inquiring about everything from my childhood to the present day. He's been especially intrigued by the descriptions of my mother and brother. I'd even told him about the children's bedtime tales that depict the Fey as evil and the poem in the book Arcan had given me.

His laughter had been rich and deep. Even now, I can hear his words in response.

'Every good lie has an element of truth to it, and therein lies the art of deception. But look around us. Can you point to this evil that is alluded to?'

I need to make amends. Start my training again and ensure Nogoth knows I'm ready and worthy to serve by his side in the forthcoming campaign. But first, I must attend to my hunger.

The elixir's scent grows more potent with every step. The storerooms must be down here, far below the kitchen. No wonder Aigul had taken her time fetching the elixir that first night.

As I think of Aigul, I see her face again, momentarily twisted in jealousy.

Now, why was that?

All the memories of these last few weeks were full of shared desire, passion, and pleasure between the three of us.

I pause. Something is tugging at the fringes of my mind, something that happened last night for the first time in the height of our frenzied joining. What is it? I slide my free hand beneath my shirt. There, just behind the meat of my shoulder, the skin is broken. I recall Nogoth's teeth biting my neck gently. It was exquisite, sensual, and arousing, but as his teeth moved to my shoulder, somewhat painful.

Aigul had been Nogoth's uncontested lover for so long that, unsurprisingly, she must have felt a little aggrieved as he focussed on me.

Reaching the bottom of the stairwell, I'm snapped from my thoughts by a ssythlan guard in heavy clothing, standing next to a closed wooden door under a single moon globe. From around the frame shines a golden light that waxes and wanes with every heartbeat. I close my palm, extinguishing the magical flame.

I pause, unsure, yet the door is opened for me, and beyond is no storeroom but a large dome-shaped cavern. The stone floor is polished, white, and from its centre rises a circular stone dais on which a dull metal archway stands.

If there is a room that holds this kingdom's treasures, then this is it. There are no jewels or coins, but surrounding the arch is a golden aura that fills this room with light and warmth. At the base of the arch, golden elixir gathers in a trough. It appears almost alive, for small waves churn the liquid, sending shimmering light reflecting from the seamless white ceiling. My stomach rumbles, and I have the craziest desire to immerse myself in the elixir and sink beneath the surface.

Four robed ssythlans stand equally distanced around the dais, heads bowed as their hands slowly weave, twist, and mould the air. They must be mages, but whether they're guarding or controlling what happens here, I can't fathom.

To one side of the chamber, chalices and elixir skins stand atop a white crystal table. I can't control my thirst any longer, and stride across the room to help myself to a chalice.

The relief as I quaff the shining liquid is instant. I feel strong, assured, and full of life.

Replacing the empty vessel on the tabletop, I notice a gently sloped passage and decide to investigate. The ssythlan mages don't even register my presence as I cross the chamber to walk up the gentle gradient toward a tree-lined exit about a hundred steps away.

Sure enough, the passageway exits within a beautiful copse encompassed with the mansion grounds. I find myself near the reflecting pond, enjoying the crispness of the early morning air. Not far away, a Saer Tel dances, a golden mist falling around her from an elixir skin.

The life this magical liquid bestows upon me and the land is beyond incredible. To live forever in such a world of plenty, where the land's bounty is only outweighed by its beauty, must be such a gift.

I'm invigorated by the landscape and the elixir, bursting with unspent energy.

Exercise and training are part of my daily routine, and I feel remiss having neglected them for so long. I'll have to ask Aigul later about weapon training. Her callouses indicate she's no stranger to them, and she's Nogoth's bodyguard as well as his lover.

A pang of jealousy rips through me. I don't want to share him with anyone.

Malina. What about Lotane?

The voice of my conscience rings loud. I'd hoped the elixir would banish my misgivings, but only rigorous exercise can truly take my mind off things.

Looking up, I see the valley's edge on the horizon. The gradient to get there is steep, and the distance far enough to challenge me.

'Right, Malina. You're a Chosen. So, time to train like one,' I growl.

The pace I set will hurt like hell, but with Lotane's face vying for position in my mind against Nogoth's ... I deserve it.

***

Peering upward, I note the sun's position and smile smugly.

I've made it to the valley's rim, and it's only mid-morning. Yet the smile gives way to a perplexed frown as I look at the strange sight before me. The valley's rim has been smoothed by magic and rises vertically above me for at least a hundred hands before giving way to natural rock. As far as the eye can see, this incredible feat stretches, creating a perfect barrier. Nestor would love it.

But why do this?

It must be to ensure no livestock escapes, or perhaps if there are wild animals beyond the valley, they would die if they fell in.

I'm still full of energy. Thankfully, my body is finally back to its usual strength. A climb will do me good.

Stepping forward, I call upon my magic, and it eagerly responds like a playful kitten. My hands and feet sink into the rockface, and I begin my ascent. It's a heady feeling being this high up. I always loved climbing the volcanoes back home, and by comparison, this climb is easier. There's no loose scree, and as far as I'm aware, no red wolves either.

Yet, that thought gives me pause. However beautiful this land may be, it will surely have its predators, and I'm unarmed. I imagine Lystra's scolding voice lashing me like a whip.

Heaving myself up, I finally reach the natural rock and carefully look for any trails. Even this high, trees and large grasses sprout everywhere. They're not quite as lush as those in the valley, but they look healthy, considering they're rooted in a mountainside's sparse earth.

I pick up a fallen branch and strip off the twigs. Using a fist-sized rock, I smooth one end to give me a comfortable grip but leave the other knobbled and spiked. This, my magic, and remaining unseen will be my defence.

The spine of the valley edge isn't far above me, and I'm impatient to see what lies beyond. Will bejewelled cities rise from a golden plain, or will people live in harmony with the land instead, their homes amongst the trees or under mounds?

Pushing myself the last few steps, I stay low and close to a tree trunk so as not to silhouette myself against the skyline, more out of habit than any belief there are predators around. Before me, mountains reach skyward to the northwest, while far to the northeast, forests of verdant trees stretch as far as the horizon.

Yet it's what's between the two, rising above the sparsely wooded grasslands, that beggars belief. What can only be an enormous black Soul Gate stands atop a giant stone ramp. No. This must be a World Gate, I'm sure of it. On either side, two columned buildings, perhaps temples, add to the spectacular view. Surrounding them for leagues are lines of what appear to be thousands of large, evenly-spaced rocks.

Whilst verdant and colourful, something about the landscape sends a whisper of warning through my mind; however, there's no threat that I can see. Turning, I look behind to where Nogoth's valley shines like a jewel, radiating light and goodness.

Perhaps I should return.

No. My concerns are simply about leaving such a paradise. With my curiosity piqued. I decide to examine the World Gate and see what is inside the temples. To understand more of this land, its history, the people, and Nogoth's reign is an irresistible lure. Depending on what I find, I can return to the mansion by mid-afternoon if I'm quick.

'Help me,' I whisper, calling my magic for assistance. Then, as I sense its understanding, I head down the steep slope toward the plain below. I leap as if I have wings, my magic buoying me, allowing me to descend at an insane speed as I ignore any kind of danger, at times jumping down vertical drops.

Soon I'm at the edge of the grassy plains, and projecting my thanks, I set off running toward my goal. Yet almost immediately, a growing tickle of unease plucks at my senses as I move further from the valley's sanctuary.

Pausing briefly, I survey the landscape again, searching for predators, yet perceive nothing apart from birds and insects. My gaze travels to the large rocks and scattered trees. Perhaps danger lurks in their shadows. Ignoring my senses would be foolish, so I continue at a reduced pace.

Yet the grasses remain soft and healthy beneath my feet, the sky like an azure blanket. I wish I could share it with Lotane; he'd have loved it here.

Damn.

One moment my mind is full of Nogoth, my desire to know and serve him better, then it's replaced by Lotane and my guilt over betraying him. The elixir is a blessing and a curse. Returning emotions such as love and lust have led me to betray Lotane but also allow me to feel the guilt I'd otherwise not have been bothered by.

Coming to the first line of rocks, I'm distracted from my thoughts, for I now know what had set my senses tingling. These are not just rocks but intricate statues. Their detail and the sculptors' imagination are beyond belief. I'd read once of old Surian kings buried with small statues of warriors, servants, and concubines that would grow flesh and serve them for eternity in the afterlife. Perhaps the temples hold the bones of Nogoth's ancestors or kin, and this fearsome army guards their bodies, meaning I'm trespassing on holy ground.

And what an army.

The statues depict hideous winged creatures with fangs and talons.

I smile as a familiar scene comes to mind. The wall carvings back in the Mountain of Souls had shown Nogoth sheltering both ssythlans and humans while evil like this cowered at his feet.

When I'd hunted evil on the streets of High Delnor, I'd assumed the carvings represented what we saw in those we killed, what Nogoth was coming to deliver us from. Yet perhaps it wasn't just symbolic. Maybe Nogoth actually defeated evil beings in the past, for undoubtedly, every statue is shaped like the stuff of nightmares or a scary children's story.

It's inconceivable how long it must have taken to craft such a homage to Nogoth.

I jog toward the temples, passing through the shadows of these beastly creations. Occasionally the ground beneath the grass crunches and snaps as if I'm stepping on twigs.

Finally, I pass through the last row and turn around. Everywhere I look, these statues face inward. It's strange. They're not in any martial pose; instead, they sit or squat as if waiting patiently for all eternity. It's incredible; there are thousands.

Yet my attention is pulled inexorably toward the World Gate and the temples. Now I'm close; they tower above me, their majestic presence impossible to ignore.

The grey ramp leading toward the gigantic World Gate is over fifty paces wide, and I kneel briefly to examine the myriad of scratches and deep scars in the stonework. When all the statues here have been perfectly smoothed, it seems odd that such flaws are allowed to remain.

With a shrug, I walk up the gentle gradient, the World Gate drawing me like a moth to a flame. I don't know what the arch is made from as I make my way closer. It's as thick as my waist and appears to be a shiny blackened metal inlaid with golden runes of a type I've never seen. It looms above me, at least eight times my height and ten paces wide.

I gaze into the shifting grey light that fills the arch's void and occasionally discern a faint landscape. Does this gate lead to Pine Hold, or are there other gates dotted around this land? The random thought gives me pause. Why wouldn't there be? Perhaps there are dozens, even hundreds, linking worlds together. Another reason Nogoth can only afford to spend two years assisting my world if others are crying out for his help.

Descending the ramp, I turn left toward what I've decided is a temple.

It's as tall as the gate, but this time made of bright white stone. I squint against the glare as I clamber up the strangely riven steps to its columned entrance. There are no gates, just a large square opening leading into a dark interior that radiates a calm that only a religious building or a library can exude.

Small windows high on the walls shed just enough light for me to peer around. Soulless, my eyesight should be able to pierce this gloom, but the elixir has returned that to normal too. Then, as my eyes adjust, I begin to perceive artwork painted all around.

Even in the semi-darkness, a striking depiction of Nogoth in his recognisable pose on the east wall draws my eye. Arms outspread, his majesty has been perfectly captured. My heart thumps as I remember his touch and how we couldn't take our eyes or hands off each other.

Another large opening in the north wall beckons, the darkness hiding what lies beyond. But the dark holds no fear for me, and I'll soon uncover whatever wonderful secrets lie within.

THE LAST HOPE

Summoning a ball of fire in my hand, I head toward what turns out to be a tunnel entrance in the north wall when a chill runs down my spine.

I'm afraid to turn, to see, but fear cannot hinder or conquer me, only warn me of danger. Yet there's no danger, not physical anyway. In the pit of my stomach though, I know it's something far worse.

Turning back to the painting, I raise my hand higher, willing the fire to banish the shadows. In response, it flares, and every stroke of paint around me is brought into vivid relief.

First, I take in the image of Nogoth, and then I gaze around the room in shock as a hideous story is revealed, recorded in vibrant colours on the walls around me.

'Please, no.'

My voice echoes back at me, a useless denial.

Nestor comes to mind. Following his return by the ssythlans after trespassing into their holy place, he'd been upset and emotionally changed. Now, it makes sense why he often muttered about the carvings being wrong. Deep in his subconscious, a distant memory lingered, despite the ssythlans' attempts to bury it.

I step closer, looking at the centrepiece image. The ssythlans stand behind Nogoth's left and the hideous monsters his right, while at his feet, men, women, and children, their bodies torn, plead for their lives.

'Every good lie has an element of truth to it, and therein lies the art of deception,' Nogoth's words echo from my lips as I study the pictures.

The artist's skill vividly shows human armies slaughtered by hordes of beasts, kings and queens butchered, and their bodies devoured. Then, what appears to be the weeping survivors of towns and cities are shepherded back through a World Gate and delivered to … temples shaped like the one I'm standing in.

Nogoth had told me he'd bring as many back as possible and that every life mattered to him. So much misdirection and deceit.

'This can't be,' I whisper. Even now, I'm desperate for this story laid out before me to be untrue, the work of some twisted enemy of my king.

That must be it, surely!

There's an easy way to prove it.

Turning to the tunnel, I begin to descend into the fetid depths.

***

As I tread stealthily along the tunnel, I note similar scars as those I'd witnessed on the ramp and steps. A memory of following such marks while tracking the red wolf comes to mind. These were caused by claws or talons ... I have to be extra cautious.

Help me.

I project my wish, and the air stirs as the softest breeze attempts to bring me sounds from far further than my light can penetrate. There's only an occasional drip of water, and I begin to relax when a hideous stench causes my nose to wrinkle.

This isn't good.

I should turn back, return to the valley safely, and put all this behind me. My resolve falters as I consider the beauty and peacefulness of that incredible place. The people are happy there, and Nogoth is warm, considerate, and passionate. He'll be able to explain all this.

The lure to turn away is strong.

'No. I am a Chosen!' The words armour me with determination.

Even though I can't detect any concealed enemies nearby, I bid the fire dim. The darkness enfolds me, and while I'm usually comfortable within its embrace, a sense of trepidation causes me to shiver as I continue.

I've no idea how far I am below ground, but the tunnel descends quite rapidly. The sides and roof are uniform, the result of magical construction.

The tunnel turns, and before me, thick, vertical bars block my progress. They're smooth under my fingertips, flawless, and are the same ceramic substance from which the armours at Nogoth's mansion were crafted.

A broad, double gate is set amongst the bars, a heavy lock securing the entrance. I pause, wondering whether to try and shatter the lock with fire or use my earth magic to create a way around the bars. I have to be frugal in its use, for even keeping my light aflame is draining my strength, albeit slowly.

Yet before I decide, I brighten the flame, then snort in satisfaction.

A large key hangs from a hook embedded in the wall a dozen steps behind me.

Moments later, I'm through the gate. Pushing it to, I leave it unlocked. If I need a quick exit, I don't want to be fumbling with a key.

THE LAST HOPE

As I descend deeper, the stench of decay and misery becomes so thick that I can taste it with every breath.

Ahead of me, a moon globe casts its dim light across the tunnel. After no magical lighting for so long, I'm surprised, but it also means I don't need to drain myself further. Projecting my thanks, I close my hand, extinguishing the flame, and pause, listening intently. There are noises, but it's hard to determine what they are, so I press forward.

Another gate appears, and fortunately, the key I'm holding opens this too. Once again, I leave it unlocked behind me.

Then, turning a corner, I come to a standstill.

Before me, there's a cavern so large that it could swallow a whole city. Moon globes intermittently dot the ceiling and walls for as far as my eye can see, akin to stars dotted against the black canvas of a night sky.

The stench is overwhelming. I gag but force myself onward.

Continuing my descent, the smooth tunnel floor becomes uneven as I head toward what might have once been a group of primitive shelters made from rocks and petrified wood.

Large boulders, some whole, some fractured with a terrible force, are dotted everywhere amongst these broken dwellings. What creature could have done this? Then, from the corner of my eye, I catch sight of a distant rock falling from the cavern roof to splinter against the ground. The noise echoes around the chamber before being swallowed up in the distance.

I try to gauge the ceiling above me, but to no avail. The moon globes spread more shadows than light up there. This was not a beast's work, just the instability of the cavern. Death could come silently from above at any moment, and I wouldn't even see it coming.

Wandering a little deeper, I turn a corner to see movement to my right and instinctively grip my makeshift club tighter. A group of a dozen bedraggled men and women, barely more than corpses, are pulling brightly glowing lichen from the cave walls. Every handful goes straight into their mouths as they scavenge for sustenance in this tomb.

Here's the proof that the pictures in the temple above showed something of the truth.

Other groups are everywhere. Skeletal and pale, some wear rags, but mostly they're naked. Many appear deformed, with twisted limbs and eyes like saucers in elongated heads.

I'm tempted to back away, but I want to communicate and find out what's happened to them. Then, if they let me, I can assist their escape.

All these people hold clubs, and as I approach cautiously, I correct myself; they're actually human thigh bones. A frightened whisper ripples amongst them as they catch sight of my intrusion. They begin to back away, frightened eyes looking at me and beyond.

'I mean you no harm,' I call, laying my club down carefully behind me, spreading my arms wide. 'It is just me.'

The muttering intensifies. The occasional word in the common tongue makes no sense amongst a jumble of frightened mewling that emanates from almost a hundred gaping mouths.

For how many generations have these sorry souls been kept here? Could these be the remnants of...? I can barely force myself to consider it ... those who were brought here after Nogoth's last conquest?

A woman, her breasts empty and sagging, with filthy, matted hair covering her features, shuffles forward from the rest, hands pressed together as if in prayer. Every rib is visible, and oozing sores cover her entire body.

Closer she comes while the others crowd together, watching intently. They must be so scared but also so hopeful. I don't move other than to smile encouragingly, nor do I speak in case the noise frightens them.

Halting a mere step away, her fingers reach out like gnarled twigs to take my hand. Behind her hair, tear-streaked eyes peer at me in disbelief.

Slowly, she bows her head, shoulders shaking with emotion. I'm close to crying, too, for these people must have been subject to untold horrors beyond any even I've experienced.

Then a searing pain shoots through my hand as she bites down hard, her sharp teeth tearing my skin.

As I yank my hand away in disbelief, she looks up, blood around her filthy mouth and howls like a wolf before lunging at me, her jagged fingernails reaching for my face.

Years of training have my body reacting, even as my mind reels in disbelief. I duck under her arms before rising, my left hand flashing out, open-palmed. Her nose breaks, sending her stumbling back, crying in pain.

I begin to back away, for her primordial howl has the others coming forward, yellow saliva dripping, blackened teeth gnashing in anticipation. My heel catches on my club, and I fall hard.

Even as I roll painfully to my feet, I hear Lystra's voice admonishing me for moving backwards on unfamiliar terrain. Taking this as a sign of weakness, the pack howls in a frenzy and surges forward, clutching at me as I twist away.

Where's my club? I look around frantically to find it lying within reach, and I duck frantically under a thrown rock to scoop it up.

Another rock glances painfully from my shoulder as I turn, making me stumble again, and then I'm surrounded. The longer I wait, the slimmer my chances become.

Help me, I ask of my magic.

With a cry, I sweep my free hand upwards, and all the loose stone and scree is flung into the faces of those between me and the way I entered. As they clutch at their bleeding faces, screeching and howling in pain, I run between them, my club smashing several to the ground, escaping from the circle.

Turning to face my foe, I back away from the advancing swarm. As I retreat, I stare at this wave of broken humanity full of feral hunger. I've faced death too many times to count, standing my ground, revelling in the challenge, unafraid, for I am one of the Chosen.

Nonetheless, in the face of so many, I turn and run. They don't deserve death by my hand; they've suffered enough already, and it's unlikely I'll prevail against so many. Even if I did, what would I achieve?

They charge, yet despite this, I outpace them easily. Years of malnutrition and living in utter squalor underground have left them weak.

I don't slow, but nor do they give up.

Flame blossoms in my hand as I set a swift pace into the tunnel. I know now why there's no light for the majority of its length. It's to discourage these lost souls from trying to escape.

I reach the first gate and am about to lock it behind me when I stop.

It's doubtful they'll follow into the dark, but if they do, who am I to keep them from tasting freedom, even if the odds of them surviving in an unfamiliar environment are slim.

Leaving it wide open behind me, I continue upwards. Amazingly, I can hear with the aid of my magic that they're continuing their pursuit. Perhaps their vision has evolved after so long underground.

I leave the second gate ajar, retracing my earlier steps until I reach the temple. A final look at the paintings has me shake my head in sad disbelief, but I don't linger. Bright sunshine calls, and I dash into its warm embrace.

Hurrying down the steps, I turn back, unable to believe that such awe-inspiring buildings can house such horrors. I'll have to confront Nogoth on his return. There must be some reason behind this. I can't believe someone so full of majesty is evil. He saved my life, and the people in the valley are so happy and good.

Then relief washes over me like a wave. That's it. These barely human creatures are descended from the evil ones of my world.

But a frown replaces my smile before it's even fully formed. What about the monsters in the paintings, slaughtering armies and herding the survivors here? To ally with or command such creatures is impossible to explain ... unless they aren't real, and the pictures, and indeed these statues, represent Nogoth's victory over evil.

Yet, is incarcerating evil people for generations more humane than killing them, considering what they've become? And here I am judging Nogoth when life sentences and executions are commonplace in every kingdom of my world.

Gah. It's ridiculous jumping from one conclusion to another and back again.

I'll return to the valley, drink a chalice of the golden elixir, and remind myself of the purity I've witnessed. Nogoth will make sense of it all.

The sun is approaching its zenith. Despite my adventure underground, I've made good time and can spare a little more. Those shambling creatures won't pose any threat in the open.

Moving over to the closest statues, I examine one carved to represent a winged beast like those on the paintings inside the temple. Its head has sharply pointed ears, flaring nostrils, and broken fangs protruding from a slit of a mouth. The cheekbones are too high and grossly defined and create a long, drawn face that sits at odds with the heavily muscled shoulders. There's no sign of chisel or file on its rough, corded musculature, so maybe these were crafted by magic.

THE LAST HOPE

A snap beneath my feet has me kneeling down to investigate. I drop the club and push the grass aside to discover shards of old bones glistening whitely against the dark soil beneath. This must have been the site of an old battle. Was this where these monsters were defeated, and the statues serve as a reminder?

Stretching my legs, I cast a glance at the temple entrance.

Nothing.

I run my hands over the statue's armour, noting that what I thought was rock is, in fact, the same type of ceramic armour displayed in Nogoth's mansion, but covered in a heavy layer of dust. Gingerly I reach out, taking hold of a dagger hilt, and, with a gentle tug, the weapon slides free, the blade razor sharp.

A small shiver runs down my spine as I carefully replace the weapon.

Moving around, I run my hand over the wings, and beneath the dust layer, they're leathery and give off a hint of warmth.

Leave, Malina. Leave. Something isn't right.

'Do I pass the Saer Tel's inspection?' The voice grates like grinding bones in the common tongue.

I freeze, ice running through my veins. I recognise my fear, but conditioning keeps its effects at bay, but that doesn't mean the chill of the grave doesn't lay its hand upon me.

The statue's beastly head swivels, eyes shining red, yet it makes no aggressive move. This is no statue, and if this isn't one …

Suddenly, the eyes of a dozen more *statues* close by snap open, fixing me with their piercing gaze. Several shrug their muscled shoulders, stretching out tattered and spiked wings, dust falling around them, before settling back down again.

The beast that has spoken looks at me intently, and its nostrils flare. It sounds like an ox drawing breath.

'You smell strangely like a human for a Saer Tel, and it stirs my hunger. Yet, you have the scent of our king all over you. You are favoured, however strange your smell.'

I keep quiet, just nodding as I walk around, my thoughts in turmoil. This *thing* hasn't attacked me, and nor has its fellows. It's hard to believe, but it would seem every one of these statues is a sleeping creature, and Nogoth, despite my hopes, is their king.

Are they charged with guarding the gate and temples or held here by his will for all eternity, penance for their ill doings?

'Why have you woken me, strange one?' It grumbles, looking to the sky. 'The black moon isn't in alignment, so it isn't yet time for battle. Nor is it time to feed either. Yet I'm so hungry.' It drools, a swollen red tongue slipping from between its thin lips. 'Perhaps our king won't miss one Saer Tel.'

Claws extend from its fingertips.

I don't hesitate. Opening my palms, balls of white flame form. Would fire harm this creature?

It recoils away, an apologetic look replacing its ferocity.

'Forgive me, mistress,' it pleads.

Suddenly its head, and those of the others I'd awoken, snap around, looking behind me. I know what I'll see before I turn, and I'm not wrong, as, from the temple, dozens of people stumble down the steps, blinking in the sunlight.

'It *is* time to feed,' the creature hisses.

With a whoosh, its wings snap open, and it leaps mightily into the air as dozens of its brethren join it in flight.

The downdraft of their beating wings almost knocks me off my feet, but I stay standing, watching in morbid fascination as they fall like rain upon their horrified prey. There's nothing I can do to save these wretches, and guilt falls heavily on my shoulders.

However grisly the sight, I force myself to briefly watch the feeding frenzy as talons, claws, and fangs rend flesh before retrieving my club and walking away through the ranks of the un-awakened.

To understand how to defeat one's enemy, one must first study them.

***

CHAPTER III

A beautiful tinkling stream amongst the lush grass is a welcome find, and I wash my hand beneath the cool water.

Bites by animals can often turn bad, and whilst those creatures back at the temple had once been human, I'm in no doubt that my wound, however superfluous, might get infected. I agitate the broken skin beneath the surface, making it bleed, to help it cleanse. There's a light blue clay on the stream bed, and after ripping a strip of fabric from the hem of my robe, I make a poultice and wrap my hand with the strip. Everything here is so healthy, full of life, and I feel confident that the treatment I've applied will be sufficient as the bite isn't deep.

Now I bear both the bite marks of animal and human.

My uninjured hand goes to the painful skin on my shoulder.

What is Nogoth? He appears human, but no human lives for thousands of years. But, even if he isn't, does it really matter?

He is my king and lover. He is love, goodness, and honesty, the salvation of my broken world.

A buried memory surfaces from a nearly forgotten dream, and Karson's voice echoes in my mind.

Don't always believe what you see in the mirror.

At the time, I'd gazed upon my reflection and believed he was talking about me. But no, he referred to Nogoth.

I haven't seen an army of virtue, gilded in shining armour, surrounded by an aura of righteousness, just a horde of creatures from the bowels of hell and paintings showing an entirely different story from what I believed.

I mustn't be blinded by blood magic ... not after what I've seen.

So, what if he's the opposite of everything I've been taught and come to hold dear.

The King of the Fey. A creature of hate, evil, and lies, the damnation of my broken world.

How to be sure without Nogoth's honeyed words confusing me?

Some workers are busy far below where I'm sitting. Yes, these people will be able to tell me the truth or at least their version of it.

The sun's position above the valley rim indicates I'll have a couple of hours before dusk when my absence will be noted. I heft my club but decide approaching anyone with the blood-stained weapon won't be a good idea. So, dropping it in the long grass, I push myself upright, then stride down the hill, the workers in my sights. How can I broach this delicate subject without drawing attention?

Then a perfect opportunity presents itself.

A young man moves away from the group toward a copse of tightly bunched trees. He's probably going to relieve himself, and whilst he won't appreciate the intrusion, what better place to find privacy than in a wooded glade.

I approach from the north, weaving through the trees, placing my feet carefully in the lush grass where it's almost impossible to make noise. Frustratingly my progress is slow, with thick bushes hindering my progress, and just when I think I'll be too late, I spy him through the trees.

He stands in the centre of a grass circle, arms hanging by his side, eyes closed as if meditating. The glade is deeply shaded, yet, in his white robes, it's as if he's illuminated. I'm about to call softly so as not to scare him when a Saer Tel dances into the glade.

Damn.

A tree trunk provides me cover as she dances around, her movements hypnotic and frenzied, spinning, leaping, and tumbling until she stands behind the young man, pressed against him.

I can see him visibly trembling as the Saer Tel's hands rove over his body.

It appears I've come across two lovers, and now I'm a voyeur to their mating ritual. I'll surely give myself away if I move, and nothing will explain my hiding here.

The Saer Tel nuzzles the back of the young man's neck, her moist lips moving to his ear, her tongue flicking out to gently lick the lobe. The man's arousal is obvious through his loose-fitting garments, and she slides a hand down the front of his trousers to his obvious pleasure.

I'm frozen in place, embarrassed at my voyeurism but also tingling at the eroticism of the moment, especially when she kneels before him, pulls his trousers down, and takes him in her mouth. From his face, he doesn't last long before she brings him to release.

Licking her lips, the Saer Tel reties the trouser drawstring, then moves sinuously around behind him, her arms, hands and fingers caressing throughout.

Slowly, the man's hands come up to his neck, untying the white scarf they all wear.

As it drops away, wafting down like a falling leaf, the Saer Tel opens her mouth, and a shift occurs. Not the ones I witness when I hunt evil souls, but an actual change. Her incisors become needle-sharp, and then with relish, she bites into the man's shoulder. Not a sound leaves her victim's lips as I watch, mesmerised as he crumples to the ground, their bodies writhing erotically as she sucks noisily. His face is now a mixture of pleasure and pain, and he pales as the Saer Tel feeds.

No!

This can't be happening. I'd hoped this morning's events could somehow be explained, but now Nogoth's oldest and closest allies turn out to be monsters too. I feel as if the whole world is closing in. My vision narrows, and I find it hard to breathe.

What should I do?

'ENOUGH!' I shout, storming into the glade.

The Saer Tel releases her prey, lifting her head. Blood runs from her chin as she crouches before me, baring her teeth, hissing.

I curse silently for leaving my club behind. Fortunately, the Saer Tel appears confused by my intervention. Her head tilts sideways as she observes me, perhaps realising, as did the winged beast, that I enjoy Nogoth's favour.

'Enough,' I repeat. 'Leave him alone.' I point to the path. 'Go.'

The Saer Tel lowers her head as if in deference, and I sigh with relief.

Suddenly she springs toward me, her robe billowing around her.

Caught by surprise, I'm thrown off my feet, but even as I go down, I grab her throat as she snaps at me with those blood-stained fangs. Yet her hands go to the back of my neck, pulling hard.

Sharp nails puncture my skin, and this time I'm the one who hisses … but in pain. There's a burning sensation from the wounds, and I wonder if poison is working its way into my blood.

The strength of this creature is beyond what I imagined, and I don't know how long I can keep her teeth from ripping my face off or my neck open. It matters not how hard I squeeze; her throat is hard as a tree trunk.

I twist desperately, but she remains firmly astride me, and I'm tiring fast.

Elemental fire envelops my hand, but fades without any effect. I call up a howling wind, yet it dissipates just like the flame. It appears this creature is resistant to or somehow stymies my magic. She tosses and twists her head, causing her hair to dance in shimmering waves. By return, the ground moves beneath me, and my magic reacts instinctively, counteracting hers before it does any harm.

We both hiss in frustration now, but I can feel my arms weakening, her body weight and strength taking their toll. Those teeth will be as deadly as daggers when they find my flesh.

Push Malina.

With a strength born of desperation, I manage to lock my arms, then release her throat with my right hand. The heartbeat my left arm holds out for is enough. As it gives way, my thumb jams into the Saer Tel's eye, driving deep.

The scream that erupts from her throat almost bursts my ears, and she pulls away, grabbing at my wrist, while I continue to push home. She throws herself backwards, but I hold on, rolling with her, getting my knees firmly astride her chest.

Her agony reaches a new crescendo as my other thumb drives into her right eye socket, blinding her entirely. I draw back, my hands covered in jellied gore as hers clutch fruitlessly at her face.

Keeping my weight on her, I remember the two rocks within my robe that I'd picked up off the mountain. I draw one out and smash it down again and again until there's nothing left to smash.

I'm exhausted, barely able to rise. Before my unbelieving eyes, the corpse and even the bits of the Saer Tel scattered around first turn grey, then purest white. I bend down, touching her, incredulous as her body turns to dust. A sweet aroma fills my nostrils, not the stench of decay I'd expected, and a breeze blows through the glade scattering her remains.

Remembering the man I'd saved, I turn around.

He pushes himself to his knees, tears coursing down his cheeks. With shaking hands, he picks up his scarf and ties it around his neck.

'Why didn't you help me? I saved your life!' I croak, limping toward him.

My vision blurs. Yes, I've been poisoned, or maybe I'm just completely drained.

He looks broken and upset but also fearful. He turns around before me and unties his scarf, letting it fall away again. He believes I've also come to feast!

With morbid fascination, I note dozens of scarred puncture wounds across his shoulders and lower neck. I often wondered why they wore scarves, and now I know.

'You've nothing to fear from me. I'm not Saer Tel,' I say, moving around to kneel before him.

Yet even as the words come reassuringly from my lips, I know it's not entirely the truth. I'd always known I was different, and despite Nogoth misleading me so much, his revelation of my heritage wasn't a lie. Somewhere in my ancestral past, the blood of the Saer Tel had found its way into my bloodline.

However, one thing's for certain, I'm not some bloodsucking harridan.

The man's eyes stare into mine, yet he utters no word. Perhaps he's traumatised by what he's just witnessed. Reaching up to the neck of my robe, I pull it to one side, leaning forward to show where Nogoth had bitten me. I almost fall, the effects of the poison, no doubt.

'I'm like you, and I need your help,' I whisper. 'Bring help, please. I need somewhere to hide before I'm found.'

Not even a flicker of acknowledgement registers at my words, but his mouth falls open in surprise as he peers closer at the bite marks.

Now I know why he didn't cry out in pain, call for help, or even say anything to me.

His tongue has been cut out at the root.

Suddenly the grass is cool against my cheek. I don't remember lying down, but it's so soft, and if I just close my eyes, I can sleep ... forever.

***

'She's coming around.'

The voice is female, soft, and familiar.

'Wake her!'

This one, I know for sure.

Freezing water hits me, and I cough and splutter, coming fully awake.

I'm not sure what I'd expected as I passed out, but my hopes of being helped by the man I'd saved were ill-founded because Aigul and Nogoth are the only ones present.

Till now, Nogoth had been a figure of majesty, wisdom and power, someone to worship, love and obey. The king before me bears no resemblance.

He stalks back and forth, violet eyes glowing with such force that the small cell around us is brightened by their radiance.

Here is barely controlled rage, hands balled into fists, corded muscles standing proud on his arms.

Here is a creature of immense power, and my life hangs by a thread.

Yet, at the same time, my heart is breaking. I've displeased my king and brought him to the edge of violence with my actions.

'I'm sorry, my king. I'm sorry.'

The words tumble forth, as do my tears. I've never felt more despondent in my life. Rune-covered manacles bind my hands as I raise them in supplication. A chain is also locked around my waist, securing me to a thick ceramic ring embedded in the cell floor.

However, righteous anger also begins to boil below my sadness, fighting for dominance against my conditioning and the blood magic. Anger at the lies, the deceit. The fear I've been serving the king of all monsters.

'You've surprised me again, Malina. But for all the wrong reasons. I should kill you for what you did. Not one of my Saer Tel has fallen in nearly a thousand years. They're gifted to live forever. Tell me why I should spare you when a whole race cries out in grief?'

THE LAST HOPE

Aigul looks smug behind him, dangling an empty elixir chalice by its stem. She's glad I've invoked Nogoth's ire. Gone is the warmth, the friendship, the fellowship of another Chosen. Instead, the jealous lover is revealed, relishing in her rival's demise.

I cannot answer with anything but the truth, even if I tried.

'We've been trained to take the souls of the evil we encountered. What I witnessed the Saer Tel do to that man was evil.'

'EVIL. You dare to judge one of my children as evil?'

I'm shocked. Are they his children in the literal sense? It doesn't really matter.

'She fed off his blood, his life. What else is she if not evil?'

Nogoth is still agitated, but I can sense the danger has passed when he sighs, fists relaxing.

'So, you believe she deserved to die because she drank a man's blood. This symbiotic way of life has gone on for centuries in this world. The Saer Tel take care of their flock here and in the forests. She wouldn't have killed him; the bond they share is too intimate.'

Now his anger has dissipated, that velvety smooth voice returns, caressing my ears.

'Malina, you mustn't judge a person or a creature by their looks. Didn't you suffer unjustly for just that reason throughout your whole life? You have their blood in your veins, and you're no different to them. In your land, do you not kill to eat, to survive? Here it's just a little different.'

How can he twist things to make so much sense, diminish what I saw, and make me feel wrong?

I can hear mantras in the back of my mind. Obey; love; serve.

Yet righteous indignation pushes me to argue further.

'I am different. I'd never feed off the blood of another human to extend my life!'

'But you'd drink their souls instead for the same reason, and that makes you better?'

Dread rips through me as I look at the chalice in Aigul's hand.

'Yes.' Nogoth confirms my worst fears. 'The Elixir of Life is farmed from the souls you and the other Chosen harvest. It saved your life when you came through the Soul Gate and keeps you alive, absent your soul even now. Under its magical influence, you can stay forever young like Aigul should you stay and continue to serve me. It has other uses, such as making this valley a place of beauty. From death comes rebirth, Malina. Those dark souls in their final moments are used for good.'

It all makes some kind of twisted sense now.

Despite being stripped of my soul, I can see in vivid colours and experience love or hurt.

I've been drinking souls!

How many it takes to fill a chalice or how it can even happen is beyond me. There is evil upon evil here; however Nogoth tries to explain it. The thought is tearing me up inside. All these years of training, the purges, the deaths, the hope for a better world. All are built on lies and evil.

If only it wasn't true.

I consider his army to the north, the horrific creatures that will invade my world, killing and eating their way across the lands. I could challenge Nogoth, tell him I know of their existence and that I've seen the paintings. However, I'll give him one last chance to give me something ... anything to believe in.

'What of your army, my king. Tell me. Are they close by? What are they like, and will they help restore balance to my world?'

He could tell me that they're the stuff of nightmares and will only harvest the evil, leaving the pure and the good behind. If he does, I'll embrace him once more. Not blindly, but with eyes wide open. I'll work to effect change, to guide him along a better path as he asked me to do so long ago.

'Malina, you should see them.' Nogoth's eyes glow a warm violet, yet his gaze is unfocused, far away. 'They're camped less than half a day to the north and are glorious. I assure you that they'll treat all they encounter equally, and balance will be restored.'

Lies, the art of misdirection. Again, there are no actual untruths, which is why he's so believable.

Thankfully, at last, there's clarity in my mind.

'Please forgive me, my king. Allow me to fulfil my duty as a Chosen.'

Nogoth's eyes bore into mine as I unflinchingly meet his stare.

There are no lies in my statement. I've learned this lesson well. Say what needs to be heard with the true meaning hidden in plain sight.

Nogoth's smile extends to his eyes, and relief courses through my veins. I let it show, for it isn't faked. I'm not ready to die yet, and this further completes the deception.

'You are forgiven, at least by me, Malina. You are unique, and I have plans for you if only you remain loyal.

'Aigul, fetch the guards,' Nogoth commands over his shoulder.

Disappointment at my redemption flickers briefly across her face, but there's no denying any order of Nogoth, least of all while blood magic binds Aigul to him.

Sighing, Nogoth returns his attention to me.

'The Saer Tel you wrongfully killed was an elder of this valley, and her kin are mourning. For your safety and to show contrition, you'll confine yourself to the mansion until such time as they extend their forgiveness. You can return to your chamber or mine if the desire takes you.

Two ssythlan guards glide up to the bars. How they achieve this flow while walking is always beyond me.

Nogoth's ssythlan is perfect as he addresses them. His hissing pronunciation is as precise as if he has a forked tongue. He speaks calmly and openly, without concern, not appreciating that I understand their language.

'The Lady Malina now enjoys my favour again. I've ordered her to stay within the mansion until I deem otherwise. Her training and our bond will ensure her compliance. Now, she is special to me, so you will treat her as such ...'

Nogoth pauses, and despite discovering him to be the opposite of everything I believed, his words make my heart pound. He genuinely cares for me, and even if everything else is a lie, that remains true.

Nogoth rubs his chin, then smiles at me reassuringly before continuing.

'Despite this, if she attempts to leave and ignores your warnings to remain, you may restrain or kill her if necessary, without fear of reprisal. Our conquest begins in just over a week, and no one can be allowed to jeopardise that.'

From the very lips of the king I love, to whom I've given my body and, for a brief time, my heart, a sentence of death is passed without sign of remorse.

I should be upset, perhaps feel betrayed, yet instead I smile. The warmth I feel for him is genuine, and despite everything, my feelings of love haven't diminished.

I'd told him that I would fulfil my duty as a Chosen, and I intend to do so.

For I am Malina the Chosen. I am the Wolf Slayer, but more than that, I am the King Slayer, and I intend to live up to that name.

***

I nurse a headache to end all headaches as I look around my room.

Fortunately, with the smallest sip of elixir, it's banished in a heartbeat.

Perhaps I should be sickened by drinking the souls of the deceased, but to complete a mission, I have been conditioned to do anything.

My mission is to kill Nogoth.

Again, the searing pain, and once more I sip, claiming a few moments of relief to reflect on how.

I can't go on like this.

I've spent an entire day considering what I've been manipulated into doing, ensuring my anger fortified my resolve ... to do what has to be done. I can admire the devious web of deceit mixed with truth and magic that had us enthusiastically doing this dark lord's bidding. With the High King of Delnor dead, and the leaders of other nations assassinated after a long period of war, my world is broken, any armed resistance weakened, ripe for the picking.

However, any thoughts of doing Nogoth harm directly while the blood magic binds me is impossible.

To think clearly and act upon any plan I might stumble upon, I first need to rid myself of the invisible chains that bind me. Then and only then might I have a chance to consider whether Nogoth can even be killed and how to do it.

Before the searing pain can take hold, I take a sip, keeping my eyes averted from the golden liquid. I'm afraid that I might see the twisted faces of the damned swirling in the liquid like when I first looked at the mists within the Soul Gate.

Laying back on my bed, I relax into a meditative state. Through my spirit eye, the colourful harmony of magic residing within me scintillates, and when it becomes aware of me observing, it sparkles even more.

THE LAST HOPE

Turning my focus outward, I gaze upon the thick red thread that binds me to Nogoth. There are others, faint, barely discernible, that must link me back home.

Home, on another world. The Mountain of Souls, where I'm bound to Lystra, the ssythlan clerics and mages ... but also ...

My heart aches with such intensity that I gasp.

Lotane.

I yearn to be with him, protected by his strength, having forgotten what I've learned, unaware, oblivious, enjoying a life of blind, blissful obedience.

No.

My happiness isn't worth the end of the world when Nogoth's hordes invade, and it's unlikely we'd survive it anyway. I wonder if it's possible to kill Nogoth, return to my first love, and find a life together. Yes. I must find a way to get back to him.

Surely I can travel through the world gate when the moons align. But will that return my soul to me? I'm doubtful. If only I could collect a soul with my Soul Blade to pay for my return passage through a mirror. But there are no mirrors in this mansion.

A chill runs down my spine as my mind leaps from one branch of thought to another.

What's to stop Nogoth's army from invading through the World Gate once it's open, even with their king dead. Even worse, without Nogoth to command their return, they might stay.

I'd need to return immediately, expose these lies, and see what can be done to prepare the world for the fey invasion.

Focus, Malina. I've allowed my thoughts to wander beyond more immediate concerns.

'Help me break this bond,' I project.

In response, a red tendril of blood magic emerges from my body, seeking, questing. Upon seeing the object of my attention, it coils itself around the thread binding me to Nogoth.

Obey, Serve, Love. These mantras and more whisper in my mind, weakening my resolve, yet I thrust them aside with sorrowful thoughts of the High King and this army of darkness waiting to invade.

Slowly the tendril constricts like a snake around its prey. Yet, however tight it squeezes, the thread doesn't break.

Damn. Why can't something just be easy for once?

And if that's not difficult enough, I also need to break the other threads connecting me to the ssythlans, Lystra and the other instructors.

In response to my thought, the tendril now extends to wrap itself around the others.

Unsurprisingly, the combined threads easily resist the tendril's efforts to break them. On its own, my blood magic simply isn't strong enough to break any of these threads.

Would my elemental magics be any help?

Even though it's barely more than a passing thought, orange, blue, green and white tendrils suddenly join the red one. Combined, they're thicker than the blood magic threads binding me to Nogoth, Lystra and the ssythlans. Thrumming with power, it coils around again and again.

What if Nogoth feels the thread break?

The thought chills me. I need to plan further before it ...

Damn.

The threads tear, and an instant later, there's a feeling of separation followed by an emptiness through which an ethereal wind blows, whistling softly in my mind. For the first time in longer than I can remember, my thoughts are crystal clear, unclouded by magic.

'MALINA!' Nogoth's voice echoes through the mansion.

That answers my question.

He's definitely felt the thread break.

'BRING ME THAT DAMNED CHOSEN!'

***

There's no time to come up with a detailed plan. However, sometimes the simple ones are the best. I'm going to kill the evil, lying bastard and any bloody lizard who tries to stop me!

Even before Nogoth's voice dies away, I jump from bed and run to my bedroom door. I know there's a guard outside, likely waiting for reinforcements, but maybe not.

To stay here is to be trapped like a rat. I could use my magic and drop through the floor to the level below, but what I need is nearby, outside my room.

I open the door, stepping to one side as I do so. A ssythlan lunges, arms extended, hands grasping to restrain me. I can't really afford to sap my strength by using magic, but I can't afford to lose this or any other fight either.

Grabbing its wrist with my left hand, my other grabs its throat, and suddenly the guard is a hissing, shrieking pillar of flame stumbling backwards into the hallway, skin popping and sloughing away from the bones.

With my first obstacle overcome, I sprint to the weapon cabinet that holds the Soul Blades and exotic daggers as booted feet pound on the stairs behind me. Smashing the glass with my elbow, I frantically tuck some into my robe. I've no idea if traditional weapons can harm Nogoth, but I intend to find out. If not, a Soul Blade just might work. Let Nogoth feel its bite and know what it's like to live without a soul!

I grab six smaller knives and, turning, throw them two at a time at a ssythlan guard running past the bubbling corpse of his dead brethren. My throws are accurate. I've been training for years for moments such as this.

The ssythlan twists like a snake, evading the first three, but the others find their mark.

Nogoth's complacency in keeping such a small force here, lightly armed and unarmoured, is a serious mistake. He rightly believed those of this world would never attack him, but I'm not from here, and I'll rip his dark head off.

The ssythlan sinks to its knees, plucking the blades free, dropping them from nerveless fingers to the floor. It would have done better to leave them in, the foolish creature. As it pushes itself to its feet to continue the fight, the black ichor pouring from the opened wounds has it falling over almost immediately.

Two more reach the top of the stairs but don't advance. They're waiting for reinforcements.

Turning to one of the armour stands, I pull a double-bladed staff from an empty mailed glove. It will be somewhat poetic to kill them with one of their favoured weapons. I twirl it in a figure of eight, testing the balance.

Exquisite.

'WHAT'S GOING ON?'

Nogoth's roar coincides with three additional ssythlan guards joining their brethren.

Kralgen, who we'd often teased as slow, had a theory about these deadly creatures, and it's time to put it to the test.

The ssythlans, seeing I'm heavily armed, have pulled weapons from the suits of armour lining the hallway. Two have small war hatchets, great for close combat or throwing, and a superb complement to the daggers they started with.

Two have swords, and one has nothing, yet his hands are moving, shaping, forming.

A ssythlan mage!

It's unlikely he can directly harm me, yet he's not about to conjure flowers either, and my success rests entirely on my magic remaining unopposed.

I sprint forward.

I'm ten paces distant when I spin in the air and, using the force of my momentum, launch the double-bladed staff spinning end over end toward the foremost ssythlan.

It's an incredibly rash move, and the guard sees it coming. Blocking such a heavy thrown weapon would be foolhardy in the extreme and unnecessary, so it slips to one side in a contemptuous fluid movement.

Thank the gods!

Unobstructed, the blade punches into the mage's chest several paces behind, who, distracted by his summoning, and thinking himself protected, is caught unawares. He's flung from his feet, dead before he hits the floor.

Swiftly, I grab a short spear from a stand, the only weapon within reach. The four remaining guards flow forward, confident in their lightning reflexes, knowing I've no avenue of escape.

If Kralgen wasn't right, then I'm dead or captured … which will surely lead to a prolonged death. Yet if I didn't believe in him and my observations, I wouldn't take such a risk.

Visualising what I need, I sweep my arm in a dramatic arc.

My breath plumes, clouding in the air, and a cold wind whistles down the corridor, sending the temperature plummeting along its length. The ssythlans' flowing movement disintegrates under this onslaught, and they only manage two more steps before coming to a complete standstill.

I could walk past, and they'd be unable to do anything until the corridor warms again.

Kralgen was right. Like the much smaller reptiles on the mountainsides, these creatures are cold-blooded. They wear heavy clothing when inside and live in the hottest region, south of the Sea of Sand, back home.

They simply cannot function in such cold.

I'm about to stride past when I recall one of Lystra's teachings.

Never leave a Chosen behind to die, and never leave an enemy behind to live.

The short spear's point is needle-sharp, which gives them all a quick death. Dropping it, I wrench the double-bladed staff free of the mage's chest, reach the top of the circular staircase and pause.

Rather than run down, I sit on the balustrade. Leaning back to take my feet off the floor, I begin a swift sliding descent, silent save for the whisper of my robe against stonework.

As I near the bottom, in the entrance hallway, Nogoth stands with Aigul beside him, while two further ssythlan guards are already running up to meet me.

Leaning backwards, I fall off the balustrade and land in a crouch on the polished hallway floor before straightening up. The ssythlans leap over after me, and I step away, giving them space, visualising how my magic can help.

As the ssythlans hit the floor, it ripples, and they sink to their waists before it solidifies around them. However skilled they might be, so restrained, they're easy prey. I knock their swords aside and dispatch them, the double-bladed staff cleaving through their skulls in a bloody spray.

A slow clap has me spinning back to Nogoth.

'Truly magnificent,' he says, voice smooth and level, unconcerned. 'You can control the elements by sheer thought alone, which is almost unheard of, and somehow, you broke the magic that bound us. If ever I had doubts about how special you are, Malina, you've just dispelled them.'

I let Nogoth talk. Using my magic has tired me, and every moment is precious as it allows me to recover a little strength for what's to come.

'This is a fight you can't win, Malina. However, what perplexes me is why you'd even try. You just reaffirmed your commitment to serve, yet here you stand, stained with blood, come to do me harm.'

'ENOUGH!'

My anger is incandescent.

'Enough of your honeyed words and deception. I KNOW everything. I've seen the story of your mighty victories painted in the temples by the World Gate and witnessed your monstrous army feed on the remnants of humanity that live below them.'

Nogoth's eyebrows raise in surprise, and I continue, fortifying myself with the spoken truth.

'Yes, you've said every human life matters to you, but that's because we're the livestock that sustains your fey. You promised equality, and you'll deliver, but only because those left behind will all have nothing!' Bitterness drips from my voice, and my outburst is greeted by a moment of silence.

Nogoth approaches me unarmed. He's dressed casually in leather trousers, a green shirt open at the neck and barefoot as ever. He holds no weapons, and I can't perceive any concealed on his person. He's so sure of himself that it gives me pause.

'You're right in everything you say. I admit to it all and more besides. However, I've never lied to you. So, believe me when I say that our future together could be both bright and eternal. It won't be long before you're more fey than human, so why not embrace your destiny. The world of humans will shun you again one day, Malina, but here you'll have a home. Why squander your life for a world that mistreated you and is broken so badly?'

How can his words resonate so perfectly with my very soul? Even without the blood magic binding us, his charm is nigh on irresistible.

'What do you mean I'll soon be more fey than human?'

'Live and find out, Malina. Simply lay down your weapon and embrace me as your king once again. You shall stand on one side of me as Aigul stands by the other. Just like you, she had to come to terms with the truth, but look at her now ... there is no one more loyal and deserving of my love.'

Nogoth's smile is warm, his voice full of wisdom.

'What do you say?'

Images of Lotane and the other Chosen flash through my thoughts. The gentle voice of the High King and his screams while he burned echo alongside them. Then, like an ethereal parade, the ghosts of generations of Chosen who died to feed Nogoth fly by, alongside parents who cry for their children without realising they're already dead. Lastly, I remember the remnants of humanity held captive in the caves, awaiting death at the jaws of their worst nightmares.

THE LAST HOPE

My legs quiver as Nogoth uses his power of the quickening, and I momentarily feel a rush of heat and desire reminding me of the pleasures that await if I only lay down my arms.

Yet, the only desire I now feel is to cut out his rotten heart.

'That worked once,' I laugh bitterly, channelling my thoughts. 'But let me assure you, I'm coming for you, just not in the way you hope.'

***

Stepping back whilst keeping my eye on Nogoth and Aigul, I drop the staff, taking up the two swords the dead ssythlans have dropped. These will be far better when facing two foes at once.

Aigul raises her sword, but surprisingly Nogoth gestures with a flick of his fingers, and she moves to the wall, her disappointment evident.

Despite this, neither she nor Nogoth looks concerned. Perhaps they think I'll allow him to get a weapon, maybe even armour, and we'll meet with honour in a duel to the death. He must be skilled beyond belief after so many lifetimes of practice.

To hell with honour or a duel.

Nogoth is but two long steps away, having just kept out of reach of my swords, but I close the distance in a flowing lunge, my right blade lancing out to take him in the chest while he remains unmoving, perhaps transfixed by my surprise attack.

Even as the point of my first weapon hits home, I'm spinning, and the second blade cleaves into the side of Nogoth's head.

Yet my right wrist spasms in pain, and my sword bounces off Nogoth's smiling face as if it's hit stone. It vibrates in my hands, giving off a high pitch tone as I sidestep swiftly back.

Nogoth's shirt is torn where his heart is, but there's no sign of blood anywhere. His face is grim as he raises his arm, almost as if to block the next blow, and I accept the invitation. With a grunt, I bring the blade of my left sword down to hack off his limb.

But it doesn't.

Once again, it's like hitting stone, and Nogoth's fingers grasp the blade twisting it savagely from my grip.

'I could kill you quicker than you can blink, but I'm going to take my time and teach you a lesson instead.' Nogoth laughs unkindly while examining the blade, running his thumb along its edge before tossing it toward Aigul.

His words send a chill through my veins but knowing he won't kill me immediately gives me options.

Taking the other sword in both hands, bastard style, I cut down, intending to cleave him from neck to groin. After my first few attempts, I should have known better. The blade shatters into a thousand pieces, leaving my face cut by an errant shard. At precisely the same time, Nogoth steps forward and punches me in the stomach with a blow so swift, I barely have time to flinch.

The air whooshes from my lungs as I'm flung back, skidding across the polished floor to crash against the staircase.

I gasp, sucking in what small amount of air I can while trying not to throw up or moan with pain. I'm lucky he didn't break any ribs.

'Is that all you've got?' I taunt.

It's a foolhardy tactic, but I need Nogoth to keep to his word and extend the fight. The longer it goes on, the better chance I'll have.

Reaching over, I grasp the double-bladed staff. Perhaps the magic that protects him will wear off if I sustain my attack.

I twirl the weapon, not allowing anything other than a fierce determination to show.

Advancing, I attack, and the blades bounce off his arms, legs, and head repeatedly until he manages to grasp the shaft. I can't compete against his strength, so I release the weapon, backing away, but not before receiving a mighty kick to the chest. I'm sent spinning, crashing to the ground.

He's so bloody fast and powerful.

I laugh mockingly on the outside, screaming with pain on the inside. Violet eyes glow like embers as he holds the staff and, with contemptuous ease, snaps it in half before tossing the pieces aside.

Advancing swiftly across the hallway, he grabs my robe in his fist and pulls me upright.

'No weapon can harm me, Malina. So why not use your magic?'

Indeed, why not. I have a little strength left.

Fire envelops my hand as I visualise Nogoth bursting into flame, but it dies away instantly as it did with the Saer Tel. I resist the urge to keep trying, saving my strength; what little remains.

THE LAST HOPE

'You'll never have a chance to discover what you might have been capable of!' Nogoth rages.

Holding me upright with one hand, he bunches the other into a fist which crackles, encased in what appears to be a small cloud of lightning. He punches me in the face, the searing pain blurring my vision as my body jolts and shudders under the lightning's effect.

My magic resists, diminishing what otherwise might have been a lethal blow, but I'm still twitching like a puppet with a broken nose and salty blood running into my mouth.

'You could have had everything!'

His words reach me through a sea of pain, yet I smile through it all.

'Eternal youth!'

Another blow lands.

'Magical power you can barely comprehend!'

My head spins.

'My child!'

What?!?

Nogoth's now holding me so close that I'm in striking distance.

Quickly reaching inside my robes, I grab the hilt of the Soul Blade and, pulling it free, drive it into his heart.

'Die!' I scream as I land the blow.

Nogoth slaps the weapon from my grip and then drops me in a heap. The blunt Soul Blade hasn't penetrated, let alone marked his already torn clothes.

'Haven't you realised that neither the fey nor I have a soul? We can only travel when the World Gate opens with the lunar cycle. But let me assure you, when it does, over two hundred thousand of my fey will follow me through. Giants, trolls, gargoyles and more. They're steadfast and loyal, like you used to be!'

Another kick, and I'm curled up in a ball, whimpering as blood pools on the floor from my broken nose, face and mouth, gathering in the cracks between the flagstones. Nogoth walks away, wiping the blood from his hands onto his shirt.

Grabbing onto the edge of the stone steps, I haul myself upright, collapse, and then make it to my feet again. I push my hand into my robes, clutching my stomach, moaning.

Nogoth nods to Aigul, and she steps forward.

I'm his gift to her. A beaten, broken love rival who can offer no resistance.

Swaying, I wait, looking around vacantly, my dazed eyes uncomprehending of death approaching.

Aigul raises her sword in both hands, ready to strike the executioner's blow. I lower my head in exhaustion, staring at her feet, perceiving her muscles tense, followed by a transfer of body weight.

I can't beat Nogoth. Not now, and perhaps not ever, but to have a chance of defeating a superior opponent, one should study them first, and I've learned a lot in this encounter. Now all I need to do is survive it and escape.

NOW!

I pivot, the hissing blade missing me by a hairsbreadth as I pull out my hand from within my robe. When Aigul's sword clangs against the ground, leaving her unbalanced, I slam the second Soul Blade into her neck.

I'd gambled everything on her having a soul as she'd travelled here through the World Gate, and I was right. Before she even registers the stunning blow, I vault over the balustrade onto the staircase and run up as fast as my shaking legs can carry me.

I don't know what's loudest; Aigul's scream as her soul is ripped from her, or Nogoth's shout of denial.

'No, Aigul. NO!' he roars as he streaks forward to catch her falling body.

I've delivered a killing blow, and she only has a minute to live.

My desperate last-second plan to survive depends on this moment.

As I sprint up the spiral staircase, I catch sight of Nogoth running with Aigul in his arms toward the kitchens and the cellars beyond where the elixir is gathered. He'll be too late to save Aigul, but I'd rested all my hopes on him trying.

Nothing is stronger than love.

I smash the first window I come across. Hopefully, any pursuers will believe I escaped into the valley. I need every hour I can get.

Continuing past the slain ssythlans, I enter Aigul's room and swiftly cross to a wardrobe. I tear off my bloodied robe and throw it to the back before snatching a simple black one which I pull over my head. Shutting the door, I hurry to her balcony. Climbing onto the stone railing, I hold the Soul Blade tightly.

THE LAST HOPE

Leaning forward, I dive off the ledge, head first, arms extended before me.

There are no mirrors in the mansion, whether to stop someone from escaping using a Soul Blade or for some other reason. Yet below me is the shallow reflecting pool, and there's my mirror image flying toward me.

This had better work.

***

CHAPTER IV

For the briefest moment, wetness engulfs me, and I tense, expecting to break every bone in my body as I crash into the bottom of the pool. Yet, the wailing of tormented souls reassures me that all is well.

This long return journey will be torturous, and I steel myself, trying to focus instead on what the hell I'm going to do back at the mountain.

How am I going to make anyone believe what I've discovered? Even if they do, they're still bound to the Heart Stone, to obey Nogoth, and the ssythlans. If they're ordered to kill me, they won't hesitate.

Maybe I should try and escape the moment I arrive. Yet that plan isn't as easy as it sounds. Even assuming I could make my way unseen to the docks, the small fishing boats there won't survive a crossing to the mainland, and I've no hope of sailing one of the huge ssythlan vessels alone.

The only other way is the Soul Gate. I'd had the idea that a Soul Blade already carrying a soul wouldn't require another to pay for passage. If I'm right …

But ssythlans apparently have no soul, meaning I'll have to kill another human.

I can't just randomly kill an innocent person to save myself. Can I? No, not unless they try to kill me first.

My thoughts come full circle.

I need the other Chosen. The six of us can escape using a large ssythlan ship. It won't be easy, but we can do it using our magic. But where would we go, and what would we do?

Even as that bigger question enters my mind, I fall onto the stone dais beneath the Soul Gate.

I'm home!

Once, returning here would have filled me with a sense of security. Now, I've rarely felt in more danger. Nonetheless, I breathe a sigh of relief.

If Nogoth had reached out to the ssythlans, there'd have been anything from the ssythlan mages to a dozen guards waiting to take my head. With me unarmed and my magical power almost depleted, I'd have had no chance.

Thankfully, just the usual one remains, standing straight and immobile, swaddled in thick robes, guarding the entrance into the ssythlan side of the mountain. It makes no step nor turns its head toward me. Only the trusted Chosen come and go through the gate, so my appearance isn't untoward, and we probably all look the same to them as they do to us.

However, it won't be long before the ssythlans are alerted to my betrayal. I need to make haste without drawing attention.

My head is spinning, and I get to my hands and knees, attempting to steady myself. I push against the blackness, relieved that the return journey hasn't affected my body so severely.

As my nausea recedes, I rise unsteadily and return the Soul Blade to the gate's frame. I don't want to raise any suspicions if those dark eyes are watching me.

As I step off the dais, it takes all my willpower to appear composed. I head toward the giant lens and, stooping down, peer through it at the night sky. There they are, the three moons, almost in alignment. Nogoth had said it would be one week till the invasion. But one week there, or one week here?

One week till the beginning of the end.

I have to find Lotane and the others and break the blood magic that binds them here as I did mine.

Yet how will they feel if I do?

My question makes me falter.

If I break the magic that binds them and show them the truth, I'll take away their home, their happiness, and maybe their lives.

Yet I've a feeling they'll die anyway. Either in service to Nogoth or at the hand of his servants once they eventually discover the truth. It's better I act now and at least give them that choice.

Making my way to the stairwell, I pause, looking at the carving of Nogoth, his arms spread, protecting both humans and ssythlans against the horde of evil that cowers at his feet.

My brow furrows as I consider a course of action.

Yes. The best way to get Lotane and the others to believe my story is for them to witness what Nestor must have seen and been made to forget.

As Lotane comes to mind, my heart swells with love. The desperate need to hold him in my arms lends me strength to increase my pace, and I surprise myself, flying down the circular steps of the stairwell two at a time, arriving at our level shortly after.

I straighten my robe, push my blood-matted hair back, and then choke back a laugh. I want to look beautiful for Lotane, yet I know I'll remain a broken, bloody mess from the beating I took, whatever I do.

A cold fist grips my heart.

What if they're not here. Everyone could be away from the mountain for days, even weeks, on a mission. I don't even know what day it is!

Quietly but with urgency, I hurry along the corridor, then pause by the first doorway to Kralgen and Alyssa's room. Steadying myself, I look around the frame into their chamber to see them both asleep under a softly glowing moon globe.

Now my heartbeat quickens as I tread stealthily past Nestor and Fianna's room. Likewise, they're peacefully asleep, and tears come unbidden to my eyes.

Here are my friends, who I've fought beside and bled for. I trust no one but them in this broken world, yet just as easily, they could shortly become my enemies.

As I arrive at my room, all I want is to run inside and throw myself on Lotane. I need his arms around me, his strength protecting me. I rest my forehead against the cool stone of the mountain, calming myself before looking inside.

He lies with his back toward me, all tousled hair, and broad shoulders. My room is the same as I'd left it. The wolves' heads and the Heart of Delnor still hanging from the walls.

THE LAST HOPE

Tears run freely as I enter tentatively, step by small step, afraid to wake him, drawing out this moment so I can remember this feeling for as long as I live.

I'll gently ease myself onto the other side of the bed, so the first thing he sees as he opens his eyes are my own, filled with love looking straight back.

Walking around to the foot of the bed, I falter. Pain like nothing I've ever felt, irrespective of whether it was caused by hand, tooth or claw, rips through me. I gasp like a fish out of water, struggling to hold back a tidal wave of emotion that threatens to wash me away.

Balls of fierce elemental fire spring from my palms, lighting the room with blinding incandescence. I don't have the strength to waste on this, yet my emotions lend me strength.

The flames don't affect me, but my robe begins to smoulder.

Lotane sits up, looking shocked and puzzled, before a bright, lopsided smile blossoms.

Lowering my arms, I bid the fire die. The Heart of Delnor hangs there, mocking my pain, and I snatch it before storming from the chamber, heading toward the communal balcony.

The words called after me sound distant, buzzing like a thousand swarming bees.

Pushing past the other Chosen who come rushing from their chambers in response to the noise, I hardly register their faces, for they're obscured by a burning image.

All I can see is Lotane, with those arms that had held and protected me now shielding the body of Lystra beside him.

***

'Malina.'

Is this the first or the fiftieth time my name has been called? I've no idea.

Everything is pushed to one side as I ask myself one thing.

Why?

How many times have I asked this? Likely a thousand in the last five minutes.

What's the point of returning if this is the price I pay for betraying my king and the man I loved? I want to hate Lotane and Lystra, but every time I try, I recall surrendering myself to Nogoth the day after I stepped through the gate. Undoubtedly, I was the first to stray, to break the unspoken vow, and now …

Who am I to judge?

And, does anything matter anymore when my heart is shattered?

I've nothing left … except perhaps one thing. Pain. I turn the Heart of Delnor over in my hand, gazing into its depths, seeking answers.

'We should send for a ssythlan cleric!'

Fianna's high trill penetrates my melancholy.

That mustn't happen. Even if I've broken free of the shackles that bind me, years of conditioning remain. So, I push the pain aside with an iron will, burying the hurt in my subconscious as if it were a flesh wound. I know it's only hidden, not defeated, but for now, it's enough.

'No!'

That one spoken word acts like a powerful spell. I am a Chosen, even if what that stands for has been twisted and corrupted. I'm still the remorseless weapon I've been forged into.

I was created under the lie of fighting evil and bringing in a new era. Now it's time to turn that lie around and make it the truth. For the first time since it was presented to me that fateful day, I hang the Heart of Delnor around my neck.

Everything comes back into focus.

Fianna, kneeling, tending to my cuts with a damp cloth, sponging the blood away. With an apologetic smile, she resets my nose with a sharp twist of her palms. She has always cared for me, and I smile my thanks as I gently take her hands in mine.

Kralgen, Alyssa, and Nestor talk animatedly toward the other side of the balcony while keeping their voices low. Occasionally their arms wave in my direction.

Lotane and Lystra stand close, a little behind Fianna. They both appear upset, but I don't know for what reason.

Enough of my strength has returned, and I cannot afford to linger. I need to act.

Rising to my feet, I squeeze Fianna's hand a final time before moving to stand before Lotane.

'Welcome home, Wolf Slayer.' Lystra greets me, stepping forward, unusually awkward. 'Report.'

Once, I'd have responded in a heartbeat, obedient to the bonds of blood magic. Now, despite her commanding voice, I ignore her.

'How long?' I ask, staring at Lotane.

I need to know. Then I can store this information alongside the pain so it doesn't gnaw at my focus when I can't afford to be distracted.

Lotane looks like he's going to cry.

My resolve begins to crack, but I force my emotions down. He's with Lystra now, and who am I to judge, having slept with Nogoth. To make matters worse, I broke the bonds of blood magic that ensured we loved one another.

I can feed off this pain but must never succumb to it.

Then suddenly, his arms are around me, and he's crushing me to his chest, his tears hot on my neck as he sobs uncontrollably.

'Everyone th-thought you were d-dead. You've been g-gone almost a whole y-year, Alina. I tried to never give up h-hope.'

A whole year? It's not what I meant when I asked the question, but I'm glad of the answer. I'd only been gone a month. But of course, time flies here compared to the fey world. Also, they'd believed me dead, which means Nogoth lied about telling the Chosen I lived.

No, Nogoth had said he'd sent word of my appearance but hadn't directly mentioned the Chosen. He'd told me the truth and let me hear what I wanted.

The emotional armour I'd encased myself in joins my heart and shatters as though it's never been. My arms wrap around Lotane, pulling tight as I breathe in his scent, and the harder we hold each other, the more my heart begins to mend. Even if it's just for this moment, I'll take this and never forget it.

'Hush,' I whisper, pulling his head down to my shoulder.

Feeling his love has dulled my initial shock, anger, and pain. Should I unburden myself of the guilt I carry by sharing my indiscretion? Will it help things? No. Not yet. Now is not the time.

'Everything is fine. We've found each other again, and that's all that matters. What's behind us can stay in the past.'

While I lose myself in Lotane's embrace, another pair of arms wrap around us.

Lystra appears regretful as she fixes me with a sincere look.

'Lotane refused to give up on you. He always swore he could tell you were still alive. But last night was the first time he doubted since you disappeared, and his grief was all-consuming. We didn't join, for no love or lust is binding us, just loneliness. I was just there to comfort him and fell asleep. You understandably misread what you saw, but I swear that's the truth. The others here can vouch for what I've told you.'

Last night ... was that when I severed the ties of blood magic? It must have been. He's been faithful to me all this time.

Then, it's not just Lystra's arms holding us; the other Chosen gather around too.

Now I'm surrounded by those I love, my doubts and fears are banished by the need to protect them.

'Are Darul, Ranya, and the other Chosen here?' I whisper.

They'll be invaluable if I can sway them to my cause.

'No. I haven't seen them in months. They must have died.' Lotane's simple words belie the magnitude of their loss.

I'd learned a lot from Nogoth. One of the most important lessons was that the best lies hold an element of truth. More importantly, is how subtle manipulation can be incredibly powerful. To save my friends, I'm willing to do anything. I'm going to beat Nogoth at his own game, at least to start. I'm going to tell them the lies dressed as the truth.

'I need you all to listen.' I fill my voice with strength and practicality, shrugging off the arms that I'd happily have stayed within for the rest of my days. Stepping away, with a final squeeze of Lotane's hand, I find myself the centre of attention.

'I just survived an attempt on the life of our king!'

***

A shocked silence greets my announcement, and only the gentle howl of the night breeze interrupts, setting a mystical tone. Then, bedlam breaks loose as everyone starts barking questions.

'What happened?'

'Was he hurt?'

'Did they catch who did it?'

Cursing inside, I realise I've already made a mistake. I should have attempted to sever everyone's magical bonds while they slept, but it's too late now.

'Quiet!' Lystra snaps.

Order is restored. Having been woken by the noise, a few birds squawk before settling down again.

'What do you mean?' Lystra demands. 'How by the gods have you been anywhere near the Once and Future King?'

Think fast, Malina!

I need to lie artfully because, at this stage, telling everything will condemn me and likely the other Chosen to death. However, It needs to be sprinkled with as much truth as can be.

'Before my disappearance, I'd conversed privately with The Once and Future King on several occasions. During our last conversation, he asked for my counsel, so when I entered the Soul Gate, I used it to travel to him. Since then, I've been by the king's side.'

'You mean to say any of us could have used the gate to go see the king?' Alyssa curses, her eyebrows coming together. 'If only I'd known!'

'I only hope that one day I'll be as honoured as you've been, Wolf Slayer!' Fianna smiles, slapping me hard on the back.

A moan escapes my lips. I'm so battered and bruised, and there's not a part of me that doesn't hurt.

'It looks like you had a good fight without us. So, what did we miss?' Kralgen booms, talking over Lystra, who's about to ask something else.

'The short version is all isn't as it should be. Just yesterday, an attempt to assassinate the king was foiled. I've come here directly from his side on a mission to discover whether the evil that infested the ssythlans there has spread, and I require your help.'

I speak with calm assurance. Using the word mission will also trigger the conditioning everyone has been subjected to.

Kralgen grimaces.

'I've never much liked 'em, but this is hard to believe. All their worshipping The Once and Future King, and now they're evil. I don't buy it,' he mutters.

Alyssa, ever supportive of Kralgen, grips his forearm, nodding in support.

My heart sinks. I can't afford for anyone to doubt me.

'You need to report your story directly to the ssythlan High Cleric,' Lystra orders, coming to a snap decision.

'No!'

Lystra's eyes open wide as I countermand her decision.

'Explain why!' she demands, her lips pressed thin, a dangerous frown marring her brow.

'Until the depth of the betrayal is understood, we cannot risk it!'

Lystra takes my arm and pulls me to the balcony railing.

'Give Malina and I a moment,' she orders over her shoulder. There's steel in her voice once again. It's all business, with no hint of softness evident anymore.

Turning to me, she speaks quietly but firmly.

'I was honoured many years ago by being entrusted with the king's name on condition of never sharing it. Having spent time by his side, you must know it. Now, name him to remove all doubt from my mind.'

'Nogoth.'

Lystra sighs, shaking her head from side to side in denial.

'You're speaking truly, I can tell. But I also know you're not sharing everything.'

Her eyes are hard, unflinching, and challenging.

'I swear to tell you all before the night is out,' I say, hand over my heart. 'But before then, we must learn the truth.'

Lystra nods in acceptance, then beckons the other Chosen to gather around.

'We follow Malina!'

This will be the biggest bluff of my life, and I smile, briefly recalling how I duped the Delnorian galley captain into thinking I was a princess of Delnor. If I can pull this off, there's a chance for …

A chance for what?

It just has to be escape. After that, we'll have to decide.

But for now, I need to lead with authority.

'We don't have much time,' I begin, my voice as strong as my eye contact. 'The worst scenario we might face is corruption on both sides of the Soul Gate. If so, and a message is passed across, they'll come for me, and perhaps you too. So we must move swiftly and covertly to ascertain the threat.'

Lystra grimaces, her mind grappling with such unpalatable thoughts.

'What if we find evidence of their betrayal?' she asks. 'We can't overcome the force the ssythlans have here and elsewhere on the island.'

THE LAST HOPE

There are no smiles anymore. Everyone is fully focused, taking in everything I say.

'I'll communicate with the king and seek his instruction. Let's hope we find nothing untoward!'

I have to keep the momentum. I lower my voice, not that we'll be overheard, but to emphasise the secrecy of what I'm saying.

'Now, listen carefully. Before my return, I discovered that the ssythlans had been worshipping a false god. Their sacred temples had been corrupted, the effigies changed. The Once and Future King will soon cross between worlds, and we must uncover the truth before he does. Nestor once saw something that was erased from his memory. It's my concern that this might have been what I also witnessed, and if so, we need to find out tonight.'

Nestor begins shaking badly as what I've said hits home.

'I c-can't go back. It w-was all w-wrong,' he stammers.

'Be strong, my love.' Fianna wraps her arms around Nestor. 'You're fearless, and nothing can hurt you,' she soothes.

Kralgen, who looked like he'd voice his reservations again, subsides. Nestor's comment seems to have silenced him for now.

'So, do we arm ourselves?' Lotane asks.

I shake my head.

'No. We go now. The ssythlans are least active at night, and we must take advantage of that. We aren't looking to fight, only observe.'

I point to the wall covered in Nestor's artwork.

'It's time to retrace Nestor's footsteps.'

Lystra moves forward, the runes on her arms writhing as she motions painfully with her hands, bringing them slowly apart.

The wall splits, and there, as before, is the tunnel Nestor had discovered.

I just hope it doesn't end up as our tomb.

***

We move silently. It's what we do, and we do it well.

My body complains with every step, yet I draw strength from the Chosen around me and from Lotane's broad shoulders as he leads us along the narrow passage. A small globe of fire sits on his right shoulder, shedding just enough light for us to move by.

I'm next, with Lystra alongside me.

Behind comes Fianna, her arms and hands moving as if strumming a harp, directing her magic to listen for anything untoward. I must trust her as I would myself, as I'm too exhausted to risk using mine further.

Nestor comes next, shaking as if freezing to death, with Alyssa's arm around his shoulders, offering support.

Kralgen is our rear guard. A solid, reassuring presence at our backs, although it's unlikely he'll be needed with the passage sealed behind us. I wish he didn't have his doubts, but hopefully, I'll dispel them soon.

The passage meanders as we descend deeper and deeper. Thin rays of light occasionally shine through angled viewing slits overlooking sleeping and training chambers

Then, a long flight of stairs appears, this time lit by moon globes, and we pick up our pace.

Down we go, into the bowels of the extinct volcano, the passageways crafted by nature and ssythlan magic. The staircase ends abruptly at a solid wall.

Lystra steps forward, pressing her hands against the rock. Moments later, a small hole appears. Fianna takes Lystra's place, listening with her magic, before nodding to Lystra, who opens a passage wide enough for us to pass through.

Once on the other side, she seals it behind us but leaves a slight indentation in the otherwise flawless wall, marking where we'd entered.

Alcoves have been fashioned into the passage walls, and fires burn within. Whether from oil, gasses, or magic, I don't know, but now isn't the time to investigate. Yet they cause the temperature down here to be significantly higher than what we're used to.

Without knowing which way to turn, we chose right. Every dozen steps or so, we pass small chambers with open doors. Looking inside, we discover nothing but dust and cobwebs, and we continue on.

I wonder whether we're going in the right direction, but as I catch sight of Nestor, I feel reassured we are. He's getting ever more agitated. Even Kralgen respects Nestor's ability to deal with pain, so for Nestor to be on the verge of crying shows that something is tearing away at his insides.

Fianna, who leads alongside Lotane, raises her fist sharply above her head, and immediately we duck inside a chamber. She holds up two fingers as we press ourselves against the walls.

Two ssythlans are heading our way.

There's no reason they'll suspect we're here, so all we need do is let them pass.

Looking across the chamber in the dim light, I'm surprised to see Kralgen enfolding Nestor in his enormous arms. It's a sound move, giving Nestor a sense of security, without which Nestor might give our position away.

My heart holds its steady tempo thanks to years of training, and no one around me looks worried. We're used to the shadows, remaining unseen, even as people look directly at where we're hiding.

The approaching ssythlans' footsteps, whilst softly placed due to their fluid grace, seem loud as they continue steadily along the corridor. The measured pace means they're probably guards. Another few heartbeats, and they'll pass. We'll shortly be on our way.

Except they stop outside of our hiding place.

We're not making any noise. So what's drawn their attention? We've left no trace of our passing.

I scream silently as the obvious comes to mind.

They've detected our scent.

And now they're contemplating what to do. They can probably determine how many of us are here, so they're calculating whether to confront us or wait for other guards. Perhaps one will head off to get help.

In any of those scenarios, this will end badly for us.

I look across at Lystra and draw my finger across my throat.

A subtle shake of her head.

Again I repeat the gesture, and this time the shake of her head is determined.

'We're coming out,' Lystra says firmly, challenging me with her stare. With raised hands, she steps through the doorway.

Morosely, the other Chosen begin to follow suit, but I hold out my hand, grabbing Lotane's arm.

'Do you love me?'

'Yes, of course,' he whispers, holding my hand. 'Don't worry. When they know the king sent you, this will all be resolved. Like Kralgen, I can't believe they're corrupted here.'

'Would you kill for me?'

'Don't even think about it!' Lotane hisses, shocked at my words.

'Our mission cannot be compromised. Do it out of love for me or loyalty to the king, but do it. We live to kill!'

Following the others out, we keep our heads bowed.

'Kneel,' hisses a guard, barely able to pronounce the word in the common tongue, jabbing his scaled finger downward to emphasise his command.

Lystra obeys, sinking to the ground. I doubt blood magic binds her to them, but disobeying a direct ssythlan command is as alien to her as it was to me up until just a day ago. The other Chosen begin to follow suit.

Pulling Lotane, I go to stand ahead of Lystra. The ssythlan guards hiss, then take a step back, scaled hands wrapping about the hilts of the swords they carry scabbarded at their waists.

'We won't resist,' I assure them and breathe a sigh of relief as they release their weapons. Nonetheless, they keep a safe distance. Their tongues flick constantly, and I wonder if this is a silent way for them to communicate.

I squeeze Lotane's hand, then close my eyes. He shifts nervously beside me as I call upon the remnants of my magic. If I were rested, I'd duplicate what I did to the ssythlans back at Nogoth's mansion and freeze the air. Instead, I need to do something far more specific.

Help me.

Opening my eyes, I fix them upon the scabbarded weapons. In response to my thoughts, I feel that familiar drain, the emptiness, and know my bidding has been done. I just hope it's enough.

Turning, I smile at Lotane.

'I love you.' I mouth silently, squeezing his hand.

We are seven paces distant from the ssythlans, far enough away for them to react, draw their weapons, and kill us.

I surge forward with Lotane beside me.

Before I take a step, the ssythlans' hands fly to their hilts. This is the moment of truth.

We close the distance as they tug fruitlessly, and then, we're upon them without our guts spilling to the floor.

My plan has worked. The weapons are frozen in place inside their scabbards.

I launch myself, then snap my right foot out, catching the ssythlan guard opposite me in the chest. Lotane, at the same time, grabs his opponent by the throat and crotch and slams the ssythlan horizontally into a door frame.

'Stop!' Lystra cries, horrified.

Lotane freezes, bound to obey, standing still over the comatose ssythlan. However, I still close the distance on the ssythlan I'd kicked, only to have its foot lash out, sweeping me to the floor.

As I crash onto my back, it leaps for me, pulling a dagger from within its robes.

Grabbing the creature's wrist, I lock my arms, preventing the blow from landing. However, its weight is on top with its second hand bearing down on the dagger's pommel. I won't be able to resist much longer.

None of the other Chosen will intervene while Lystra's command hangs in the air, and they wouldn't reach me in time anyway.

Thin ssythlan lips lift in a smile, knowing it has the better of me.

Suddenly, I change the direction of my resistance, pushing my hands back over my head. The ssythlan topples forward on top of me while I continue to hold its wrists.

Its chin smashes against my nose, and pain lances through my face. I can no longer resist its superior strength, but this is what I wanted. Twisting frantically, I sink my teeth into the side of its throat. It's a huge bite, and I clamp my teeth as if into a piece of meat at the dinner table.

With the last of my fading strength, I hold onto its wrists as it attempts to pull free, a strange whistling noise from its throat loud in my ear.

I bite harder, my teeth meet, and I'm tearing its throat out like a wolf. The black ichor that gushes over my face tells me all I need to know as it twists away, gurgling its last.

Rolling wearily to my feet, I stagger toward the Chosen, who are slowly coming to theirs. I don't fault them for not helping. Lystra's face is white, and her fists open and close.

I'm not ready to confront her, not yet.

Approaching Lotane, I kneel at his feet and grab the sword from the moaning ssythlan's waist. Despite it being cold, the blade now slides free. Without hesitation, I thrust it through the creature's neck.

With blood streaming down my battered and bruised face, I turn toward the others, raising the dripping blade to point at them.

Now, I'm ready.

'I come directly from the king's side. Nothing and no one will stand in the way of completing my mission. Do I make myself clear?'

Without waiting for an answer, I look at Kralgen.

'Take the other ssythlan's sword and dagger. You and Nestor deal with the bodies and blood. Don't leave a trace! You have one minute!'

Flipping the sword in my hand, I catch it just below the hilt and turn to Lystra.

'You're the next best with a weapon here. Take this!'

I pass it to her in a show of confidence.

Along the corridor, Kralgen carries both ssythlan corpses into the empty chamber as if they're mere ragdolls. The man's strength is unbelievable.

Nestor is more his usual self now he's doing something he loves. Kneeling on the floor, his features etched with pleasure and pain, he sweeps his arms as if swimming and the solid stone ripples then settles without a trace of blood apparent to the naked eye.

He disappears into the chamber after Kralgen to forever entomb the bodies in stone.

It isn't long before they reappear and give me a nod.

'Lystra. You're up front with me!' I snap. 'Kralgen, rear guard. Fianna, as before. Now, follow me.'

Walking between them, I don't allow myself to run, despite knowing we're living on borrowed time.

I don't look back. To do so would show I'm concerned they might not be following. To be a leader, I have to act like one.

Pushing the pace, I trust Fianna to warn us of threats. After another few minutes of swift progress, we come to an intersection. Fortunately, choosing which way to go is easy. The passage continues left and right, but a large cavern can be seen straight ahead beyond an archway.

Ducking through, we look about.

It's empty, although row upon row of stone benches fill it in neat lines. They all face toward a giant dais, above which the familiar visage of Nogoth is carved … and my heart sinks.

***

This is what I'd been hoping to find, yet at the same time, I feel no sense of victory, just sadness at what everyone is about to witness.

Slowly, the Chosen come to stand alongside me, following my gaze, open-mouthed and dumbfounded.

Except one.

'I knew I wasn't going mad,' Nestor moans, rubbing his temples and wincing in pain. Closing his eyes, he shakes his head as if that will clear it away.

This is a vulnerable moment for everyone, and I hope our luck holds out for a while longer. I've lost track of time, but it will be morning soon, and then who knows how many ssythlans we might come across.

'Heresy!' Lystra hisses, finally finding her voice. 'Tell me. What is the meaning of this!'

She grabs my robe with one fist while pointing the sword behind her at the hideous image.

In fact, this carving is more gruesome than most, for the stonework is coloured. Every panicked, bloodied, horror-stricken feature of the humans pleading at Nogoth's feet are brought into stark relief. It's such a work of art that the ssythlans and the drooling creatures at Nogoth's shoulders appear to loom over him, impatient to leap upon their cowering victims.

'It's a mistake. It has to be!' Fianna's voice, which is usually so clear, sounds choked.

Kralgen nods. 'Yes. It's a mistake. There has to be an explanation for this.'

I hear them repeat the same words of denial I'd used myself. Logic is fighting against conditioning, and conditioning is winning.

'This is my real mission,' I explain. 'To show you the truth. For you to begin to understand the evil we've been serving. There's no mistake, I can assure you. I've come straight from the king, and I've seen his armies, and witnessed them feast upon people. Everything we've fought for is a lie, artfully concealed with promises of equality and a new era, but still all lies. Evil is coming, and none is more so than The Once and Future King himself.'

Lystra brings her sword tip to my throat.

'How dare you! The only reason I'm not going to kill you now is so that you can face the justice of the king himself. YOU have something to do with this … this travesty. You will not resist, and if you do … you die!'

'Lystra!' Lotane steps forward, hands raised.

'You will not interfere, nor will any of you,' Lystra snarls. 'That's an order, and you will obey me.'

Lystra is on the verge of skewering me without a moment's thought if I make a move. She's far too experienced and will sense any subtle shift if I prepare to strike.

'It's wrong!'

I'm shocked. It's unheard of and impossible for a Chosen to disobey a direct order. Had Lystra commanded Lotane to kill me, he'd do so despite his remorse. Yet the words aren't his, and they're not even in response to Lystra's edict.

'It's been changed!' Nestor groans as he stumbles away from the group, clutching his head.

Fianna runs forward, putting her arm around his shoulders, but he shakes her off, moving across the chamber.

'I'm not mad!' he cries. 'It's been changed. There was something else!'

Now, he's on the opposite side of the chamber, hands and forehead pressed to the cold, unforgiving stone.

Lystra turns to Kralgen.

'We need to leave, now! Go get him and carry him if you have to!'

Yet before Kralgen takes a step, Nestor's hand sinks into the wall, and he pushes sideways. The stonework parts before him, revealing an opening from which spews clouds of freezing fog. He steps forward and disappears before us, with Fianna chasing after him.

'Move,' hisses Lystra, shoving me ahead of her toward where Nestor had disappeared. 'Everyone. We grab Nestor and Fianna, and then we get out of here.'

I was sure that seeing the carvings would be enough to sway everyone's thoughts, to help them challenge their beliefs and conditioning. But, it hadn't been enough. What can I do now?

The sharp point of Lystra's sword jabs between my shoulder blades, and I hurry across the chamber, the air temperature dropping with every step.

Together, we push through the freezing clouds to find Fianna and Nestor staring at the walls.

'You see. I wasn't mad. It was all so wrong.'

Nestor's voice is deep and strong again. The trembling has disappeared as though he's rid himself of an evil spirit.

THE LAST HOPE

The sword point drops away as we look around, yet I do nothing. There's no need for me to escape from Lystra, not now.

We're in a large chamber that serves as a larder of sorts. That magic was used to create the ice that keeps the meat frozen is likely. That evil is responsible for what's trapped in the ice is without question.

Hundreds of bodies are encased here, from youths to adults, probably those who've fallen during the purges but not necessarily all. Bloodstained saws, hatchets and cleavers rest in a corner next to an equally stained wooden bench. It appears this is where the meat is butchered, not just stored.

Raising my voice in this tomb feels like desecration, but everything hangs on this moment. There isn't much time, but my friends need to understand what brought us here and the peril we're in.

'Without you seeing something like this with your own eyes, I knew you wouldn't believe what I'm about to tell you, so I apologise for the necessary deceit that had you follow me here.

'When I was in the land of the Once and Future King, I discovered something like this, but worse. The few people there are enslaved, imprisoned and used as livestock to feed the hordes of creatures that worship the king.

'I told you I survived an attempt on the king's life, and that part is true, but it wasn't by the ssythlans. After I discovered his evil and understood his genocidal plans, I tried with all my might to kill him but failed.

'Nogoth, King of the Fey is his true title. He swore that he'd come with an army to bring down our corrupt kings and deliver equality. He will honour that promise, but not in the way we believed. The army he brings is one of darkness, and the equality they deliver will be everyone suffering the same horrific fate, be they peasant or noble. He will come for two years, and in that time, his armies will sweep across the world like a firestorm.

'I came back not just to escape but to warn you. If these are my last hours, I want to be with those I love and trust.'

As I say this, I take Lotane's hand.

'Without question, Nogoth will soon notify the ssythlans here of my escape if he hasn't already. They'll come for me, and if they know of your involvement, all of you too. There will be no mercy, and we'll end up the same as these poor souls if we stay here any longer.' I nod toward the frozen corpses for emphasis.

'I beg your forgiveness, Wolf Slayer.'

Lystra comes to stand in front of me. Then, to my surprise, she kneels, offering me her sword hilt.

'That I've been a party to all this for years, never questioning, never seeing the truth, is unforgivable. Take this sword and my life for what I've done to you and the hundreds before you!'

The other Chosen gather around, except for Kralgen, who stands transfixed, one hand on the ice, unable or unwilling to believe his eyes … I don't know.

'There's nothing to forgive. You had no choice, not then, and not now,' I say, addressing not just Lystra but the others too. 'You were bound to obey by blood magic, blinded by years of conditioning, and misled by lies and deceit. It was just luck that opened my eyes to the truth and good fortune that I had the means to break the chains of blood magic that bound me.'

'Can you break our chains too so we can follow our hearts and minds?' Nestor demands. 'I've doubted my sanity this last year, but now I've seen this truth again; I don't want to ever forget.'

'Set us all free, Malina, if you can,' Lotane says, tugging my hand so I turn to face him. 'You always wanted to leave this place. Help us do the same.'

'When I broke my bonds, I broke them all.' I warn. 'Nestor and Fianna, Kralgen and Alyssa, the blood magic binds you together too …'

'I'll love Kral no matter what,' Alyssa states firmly, interrupting me, understanding the implications.

The others voice their assent, except Kralgen, who stares into the ice. Do I have the power to break their chains? I'm exhausted and unsure.

Stepping over to Kralgen, I rest my hand on his shoulder.

'Kralgen. The others want me to break the blood magic that binds them to this place, to Nogoth and one another. Are you fine with that?'

Kralgen turns toward me, and I'm shocked to see his eyes puffy and red.

'He was always a nasty bastard,' he sighs, leaving me perplexed. 'I wasn't much better, but he was worse. Yet, he was my brother and deserved more than being turned into lizard food!'

Now I understand. For there, features forever frozen in endless sleep is the distorted face of Bardel staring back at me.

'You want to know if I'm fine with you breaking my chains?' Kralgen chokes out. 'Up until an hour ago, I didn't believe you, and I didn't want to. I loved this life and would have done anything to protect it. Now, I just want you to set me free, so I can kill every one of those scaly bastards.'

I sweep my gaze over the Chosen. They're awaiting my command.

Taking Kralgen's arm, I gently pull him away from the ice.

'Stay close together!'

I close my eyes, focus, open my spirit eye and turn my attention outward.

Even though the circumstances are dire, excitement races through my veins. If I can do this, then we stand a good chance. Seven Chosen will be a force to be reckoned with.

There are the threads, intertwining, a knot of unsolvable complexity. Even if I wanted to selectively break some and not others, there isn't the time. Fortunately, unlike when I'd severed my bond with Nogoth, distance apparently weakens the thread. The thickest are between Lystra and the others, but even those are negligible compared to what I'd broken previously.

Come, help me.

My blood magic responds immediately. A questing tendril emerges from my heart, awaiting my guidance.

Focussing on the threads, two words come to mind.

Free them.

Like a striking snake, the tendril lashes out in a frenzy, attaching itself to thread after binding thread before squeezing and tearing them apart. Words flash through my mind. Obedience, loyalty, love, and so many others before they fade as the bonds are broken.

It's over within a few heartbeats.

When I open my eyes, I find the other Chosen all staring at me. I stagger in exhaustion, and Lotane wraps an arm around me, concern etched on his face.

'It's done!' I gasp weakly.

'I don't feel any different. Are you sure?' Alyssa asks, her hand holding Kral's for reassurance.

The others shrug, looking unconvinced as well.

'I'm sure. It doesn't mean these years of conditioning won't still affect you, but the irresistible compulsion to obey and even return here has, I assure you, been broken.

'What now?' demands Lystra.

I'm conscious of the sudden weight of responsibility and uncertainty I'd never felt before. My friends' lives now rest in my hands. I'd feel supremely confident if I fought alongside them, but thinking strategically like this is new. If an hour or two has passed here, then barely a handful of minutes have passed since I fought Nogoth. He's probably still holding Aigul in his arms, feeling her last few breaths leave her body. If his rage and grief blind him, it might take him several hours to conclude I'm not in his valley or the lands beyond. That would mean a couple of days here before the ssythlans start hunting for me.

Yet Nogoth is no fool, and with me having stolen Aigul's soul, he'll realise it was to pay for passage. A new sense of urgency pulls at me as I recognise the truth. We have to leave now.

'We head straight to the docks, commandeer a ssythlan ship, and use our magic to get underway without a full crew. If we're lucky, we can press-gang some fisherfolk into joining us.'

Lotane's sharp bark of laughter matches the grim smiles of everyone around me.

'If that's your master plan, it's already sunk.' He chuckles with gallows humour. 'Those three ships set sail weeks ago with about six hundred ssythlans aboard. There's nothing but small fishing boats left, none of which are sturdy enough to cross the sea.'

'Then we just escape through the Soul Gate,' Kralgen offers, smiling broadly at finding the solution.

Alyssa takes Kral's hand gently in hers.

'The problem is, my love, that we'll die without our souls. Either that or we'd have to return in a few weeks. We'll be butchered.'

'Then our choices are simple,' Lystra says firmly. 'I've no wish to die without my soul in a world of grey, nor will I return to be butchered. I'd rather die here with honour, killing as many serpents as I can!'

'I'm with you, Lystra. Care to wager on who'll kill the most?' Kralgen quips.

'It goes without saying,' Alyssa pipes up, 'I'm with Kral and always will be.' She takes his hand, looking around for support.

THE LAST HOPE

Fianna raises her hands, palms outward, a grimace marring her beautiful face.

'But what about the other Chosen in training and the instructors? Do we kill them if we come across them? They'll believe we're traitors and will attack us without knowing what we do. I've no qualms about killing ssythlans, but cutting down the others doesn't sit well with me. They don't know better!'

Lotane adds his voice to Fianna's, and as they argue back and forth, my thoughts drown out their voices.

What a disaster my return has turned out to be! Having revealed everything to the Chosen and with no means of lasting escape, everyone is now in imminent mortal danger.

'Enough!' Nestor snaps.

Surprised, everyone halts mid-sentence. He rarely says a word and never talks loudly.

'None of you has it right. This isn't just about us escaping or killing a few ssythlans before we die. We're so used to our small world that we're forgetting the bigger one. Nogoth's arrival is only ten weeks away, and the world must be warned. If we die here, then not only have we helped bring about armageddon, but we're dying selfishly, leaving the world unaware and unprepared. The Delnorians might hate us, but as the strongest power, they must be convinced first to help rally a defence.'

Silence meets his announcement.

'Damnit!' Kralgen kicks the stone at his feet. 'I prefer it when you don't say anything.'

No one disagrees. Nestor has voiced what we instinctively know to be true.

Everyone is looking at me, not Lystra, and staring expectantly.

'We return the way we came, head to the Soul Gate and through to Delnor. We'll meet at the library and work out our next steps. Let's just make sure we aren't seen. Stealth remains our ...'

'It's too late for that.' Fianna interrupts, pointing.

We've dallied too long, or perhaps it was just bad timing. The clouds of freezing mist have parted, and there in the chamber, a dozen ssythlans stand staring at us.

***

CHAPTER V

Seven Chosen now have a new mission; to escape.

Years of conditioning kick in reflexively.

We're trapped in a dead-end, and whilst the ssythlans before us aren't guards, they're the enemy, and every moment we give them is a moment we'll regret.

I twist and grab a hatchet, tossing another to Lotane.

Alyssa has already claimed the one cleaver leaving only Fianna and Nestor unarmed.

'They're vulnerable to cold,' I say, grabbing Fianna's shoulder. 'It slows them down, but save your power for when we need it the most! Nestor, you watch her back!'

Then the time for talk is over.

We move forward, knowing that staying here will mean our inevitable death when reinforcements arrive. Lystra and Kralgen take the end of the line, with Lotane, Alyssa and myself in the middle. With their swords, Kralgen and Lystra have the longest reach and can try and counter any flanking manoeuvre. Nestor and Fianna stay behind us.

Yet we needn't have worried. These aren't warriors, but that doesn't stop ten of them from surging forward, while two at the back retreat into the passageways seeking help.

The hatchet is light in my hand as I face the hissing fury of a ssythlan leaping for me, another one right behind. But when I swing my hatchet, I purposely aim my blow to miss. I don't want my strike to be blocked by my faster opponent nor my strength to be pitted against his should he seize my wrist.

So instead, I swing sideways, severing the arm of the ssythlan attacking Lotane whilst ducking under my foe's clawed swipe. It's a tactic often employed by heavily shielded infantry who defend to the front whilst killing to the side. An inexperienced enemy often doesn't see the strike coming.

As the ssythlan who'd attacked me bears down, he stiffens, Alyssa's cleaver having hacked into the side of its neck. As she yanks it free, ichor spurts across us both.

I push the falling body away but there is no one left to fight. Kralgen and Lystra have already cut a terrible swathe through the unarmed ssythlan ranks, bodies are littered across the floor, black blood pooling around them.

Lystra meets my gaze. In times past, I'd have deferred to her instantly, but I can perceive expectation in her look.

'We return the way we came.' I reiterate my earlier order.

Everyone follows as I stride purposely to the chamber entrance.

'Fianna, you're our ears. Take the lead with Kralgen. Lystra, rearguard with Nestor.'

A leader should be at the front, yet I haven't recovered and am currently a weak link.

Fianna tilts her head to one side. 'Many are coming!' she points up the passage where we'd killed the first two ssythlans. 'Too many!'

'Lystra, you and Nestor seal the passage. It's unlikely they'll have a mage with them and will buy us some time.'

I indicate right.

'Everyone else, get going.'

Damn. We'll be lost down here in this unfamiliar warren. Moving without purpose can just as likely lead to a confrontation as the one we're avoiding, but according to Fianna, staying here will guarantee one we can't win. We have to get going even if we have no idea of direction.

Nestor nods, a rare smile creasing his features, and then he and Lystra concentrate, frowning as they scoop and mould the rock from the passage walls. It isn't long before they've blocked off the passageway, and we set off at a run after the others.

'Good idea, Wolf Slayer.' Lystra smiles.

Her face is as hard as the rock she'd moulded. All levity has disappeared. This is a life-or-death race we can't afford to lose.

It's not long before we find the others waiting at an intersection as the rough passageway breaks upward to the left and right.

'Left!'

There's no reason for my choice. I just hope the gods of chance smile on me.

Kralgen sets a quick pace, but not so fast that we make any undue noise.

Suddenly Fianna comes to a halt, holds up her fist, and twirls it around her head. Then she's running between us with Kralgen following, and we retrace our footsteps at speed.

There's no point asking why.

Back to the intersection, and there's no option but to take the other fork.

Lystra taps Nestor on the shoulder, and the two pause, frantically working their magic. Sweating with the pain, they're almost finished when a large group of ssythlan warriors run into view. Fortunately, the gap that's left isn't wide enough for them to fit through, and as we turn and run after the others, we hear them hissing and hacking away at the stone with their weapons in an attempt to break through.

'I can do that maybe one more time,' Lystra gasps as I run alongside her.

'Likewise,' Nestor adds, his face creased in pain as he struggles to breathe and run.

A warning shout from up ahead is accompanied by the clash of steel and war cries. The sounds of combat echoes along the passage as we sprint, trying to close the gap.

I burst into a wide chamber ahead of Lystra and Nestor and assess the situation instantly.

Kralgen to my left is fending off a ssythlan warrior bearing a fearsome double-bladed staff. The short, one-handed sword and dagger Kralgen wields can't be used to parry such a heavy weapon, despite his prodigious strength. He's backing away, moving around a wooden table, deflecting every strike from his lightning-fast opponent, staying on the defensive.

Lotane and Alyssa are baiting another armed ssythlan, who is keeping them both at bay. The ssythlan has a long sword against

THE LAST HOPE

Lotane's hatchet and a chair he's using as a shield. Alyssa only has a cleaver but grabs everything she can from shelves and tabletops to throw at the ssythlan. Neither side can commit. If the lizard goes for a killing stroke on one, he'll die from the other and thus bides his time, waiting for a mistake or his comrade to prevail.

Fianna is on her back, hands pressed to her side. Blood-soaked robes tell me she's taken a nasty wound.

Without pause, I hurl the hatchet, spinning end over end across the chamber at Kralgen's opponent. It's a snap throw, but I haven't missed in so long and know it will find its target.

The honed edge cleaves into the side of the ssythlan's head, leaving Kralgen free to help Lotane and Alyssa finish the remaining lizard.

I run and kneel at Fianna's side just as Nestor and Lystra catch up.

'They were so quiet that I didn't hear them,' Fianna hisses between gritted teeth.

Her face is pale, not a good sign.

'Hold her legs, Lystra. Nestor, take her hands, quickly now!'

As Nestor pulls Fianna's bloodied hands away, I yank the torn robe further apart, revealing a deep gaping wound from which blood flows heavily.

'Fianna!' Nestor cries piteously, seeing the extent of her injury.

I focus my thoughts, visualising what needs to be done. Thankfully a small amount of my power has returned. Pinching the sides of the wound together with one hand, I allow my magic to flow through the other. Elemental fire leaps from my forefinger, searing the wound closed. Fianna's scream echoes around the chamber and then dies as she faints from the pain.

When I stand, I find the other ssythlan has met a bloody end.

I'm at the edge of exhaustion, while Lystra and Nestor are visually fatigued from using their magic. Its use drains strength as quickly as physical exertion.

Kralgen, Lotane and Alyssa are upending the tables and stacking them against the door we'd come through. None of the doors have locks, but even if it buys us a minute or two, it's worth it.

Most everyone bears minor cuts from our encounters. Lotane now carries a double-bladed staff, and Kralgen hefts two swords. Alyssa grasps a hatchet and a cleaver while Lystra wields a sword and

Kralgen's discarded dagger. Lotane passes me my hatchet. We're better armed than before but now have to carry an unconscious Fianna.

'We need to get going,' Lystra prompts.

Nestor slides his arms under Fianna's limp body and stands up, glaring.

'Don't slow down for us!'

'Lotane, you and Kralgen on point,' I order. Sadness taints my voice as I watch Nestor cradling Fianna, her usually bright face a deathly pallor against his black clothing. Until a few hours ago, everyone here was happily asleep, and now ...

We head off through the other side of the chamber, grim as the death that hangs over us. At every intersection we come to, I listen carefully, and each time the downward passage has the sound of pursuit. Several times we come across groups of ssythlans, none of which are warriors. Yet that doesn't stop them from attacking, nor us from slaughtering them.

Everyone is breathing heavily. Nestor and Lystra take turns carrying Fianna, who has regained consciousness but is too weak to walk, let alone run or fight. The rest of us are bathed in our own blood and the ichor of the slain ssythlans.

'How many?' Kralgen cocks an eyebrow at Lotane.

'Ten. You?'

'Thirteen!' Kralgen growls.

'Lies. You can't even count that high!'

I watch the pretend joviality. It has a part to play, keeping their minds distracted when our circumstances are so dire. I know they're not indifferent to Fianna's plight or Nestor's.

'Take a short break,' I order as we reach the top of some stairs. 'I don't know how they communicated our discovery, nor how they're coordinating their search, but one thing's for certain, they know we're heading upwards.'

Lotane puts his arms around me, and I briefly surrender to his warmth before pushing him gently away. Now isn't the time. Or perhaps it should be. I'd never let him go if I knew I'd be dead five minutes from now.

'How are you doing?' Blood trickles from the corner of Fianna's mouth as I brush back her golden hair. It's strange that it shines so brightly when she's in such a terrible state.

THE LAST HOPE

'Nestor is holding me in his arms. I couldn't be better.'

She smiles wanly. Nestor smiles too, but tears run down his cheeks.

What I've done suddenly becomes too much, and I freeze, my mind overwhelmed by the host of bad decisions I've made.

'Lystra. Take the lead. Every choice I make is the wrong one.'

'No!'

In all the years I'd known Lystra, I'd seen her many faces. From the cold, remorseless killer of children to the warm face of a friend. Now her eyes shine with something I've seen only when she talked of Nogoth; that of belief ... but now it's directed at me.

'Don't forget who and what you are,' Lystra says firmly, gripping my wrist. 'You're the best of us and have been for longer than you know ... the King Slayer whether you enjoy the title or not.'

'But I couldn't kill Nogoth when I tried, and this time, even if we escape, we won't live long enough to try ... unless.'

Lotane leans in toward me.

'If there's something on your mind, and you're reluctant to say it. Whatever it is, voice it. Now is not the time for reticence.'

I'm reluctant to share. To raise false hopes at this time seems cruel, but Lotane is right.

'What if we don't have to give up our souls to use the gate. What if we collect another before we travel and pay with that one instead?'

Nestor nods.

'I have often wondered that too.'

The others look shocked, but a dawning light of understanding spreads across every face.

'Then what are we waiting for?' Kralgen laughs. 'A minute's gone. Come on, Nestor, see if you can keep up.'

Nestor grimaces, lifting Fianna again.

'I'm fine,' he says, shaking his head when Lystra steps forward, mutely offering her help.

We set off again with a renewed sense of hope and purpose. But the question plays on my mind with every step. Whose souls will pay for our journey?

***

My legs and lungs ache. In fact, my whole body does. We're near the mountain's summit; of that, there's no doubt.

Everyone is spattered in gore, the enemies and our own. The ssythlans behave like ants protecting their nest. From passages and chambers, they swarm with no regard for their own lives. Few are warriors, yet regardless, every single one fights with martial ferocity.

We've changed direction several times to avoid large enemy groups. Sometimes we've run through what could be classrooms, and others, sleeping areas or places of worship. Irrespective, I've lost count of the carvings of Nogoth we've passed, each depicting humanity cowering at his feet.

Nestor continues to carry Fianna, relying on us to protect him, and we continue to do so.

It's been a few minutes since our last encounter, and I'm a little more optimistic. We've kept ahead of our pursuers and can taste a hint of fresh air in our lungs. We must be nearing the outside. If we're lucky, we'll come upon the Soul Gate.

But whose souls will pay for the journey? What's that nautical saying? A captain always goes down with his ship.

As the leader, I'll sacrifice my soul for Lotane, so he can escape with his intact. It's the least I can do to pay for my sins.

As for the others, who knows? But I expect each of them is asking the same question of themselves. There's no need for me to point out the obvious ... unless perhaps to Kralgen, who looks too cheerful to have stumbled upon the truth.

The fresh air is joined by a breeze, and we pick up the pace.

'Wait.'

Everyone comes to a reluctant stop. Discipline is too ingrained to allow anyone to continue, even if salvation is only a matter of footsteps away.

I listen, sending out my magic, irrespective of my weakness, and there it is; the gentle hissing breath of countless ssythlans, just waiting. We'd just passed a junction, so I circle my hand above me, pointing back the way we'd come.

Turning left at the next junction, it's not long before we come to a large, luxuriously furnished chamber. The walls are lined with tapestries, whilst a large bed with purple sheets stands proud from one wall. Wardrobes and chests of polished wood covered in strange symbols stand upon a thick carpet. Even the ceiling is covered in hanging sheets. Large mirrors reflect the light coming in from a wide balcony. Whether this is the High Cleric's bed chamber or perhaps once belonged to the ssythlan prince doesn't matter.

'It's a dead end!' Kralgen points out the obvious.

'No, the other way was a dead end; there were too many ssythlans waiting in ambush. We'll go over the balcony and work our way around the mountainside!'

Kralgen and Lotane begin barricading the door behind us, heaving two wardrobes into place. If the ssythlans think we're taking refuge here, so much the better.

Lystra is already at the balcony, helping Nestor lift Fianna over the railing, and the rest of us quickly follow.

The mountainside is steep, but we've trained so often on similar slopes that it holds no fear. Nestor has Fianna slung over his shoulder and barely makes any headway along a narrow ledge. His foot slips, stone dropping away to tumble down the mountainside, and Lystra frantically grasps him, pulling him close against the rock face.

'Don't argue,' grumbles Kralgen and reaches over with his meaty fist. Grabbing the back of Fianna's robes and clothes underneath, he plucks her like a baby from Nestor's shoulder and places her on his own. 'She's safe with me. Now move faster. I'll give her back soon enough!'

Even so, we don't move as fast as I'd like.

Weapons hinder us, but we daren't drop them, and we aren't wearing sheaths or harnesses to secure them. Lystra leads, and it seems forever before we come to more forgiving terrain that allows easier passage.

Quietly we scrabble across, our fingers lacerated, adding to our myriad of wounds. The sky is blue above us, full of birds calling in frustration as we invade their territory, yet we ignore their cries.

Kralgen passes Fianna back to Nestor, and she smiles weakly in gratitude. Her chin is stained from coughing up blood, and Nestor tries to wipe it away. However, our clothing is filthy, soaked with blood and now rock dust. It's a losing battle, but he tries anyway, knowing she'll take comfort from his attention.

I look around, noting our position. We must be close as I recognise the view.

Holding my finger to my lips, I point, drawing everyone's attention, and they nod, understanding my signal. The mountain face curves here, and just on the other side, we'll find the Soul Gate. If our luck holds, we'll make it through before the ssythlans realise we're not where they thought we were.

I point to Kralgen, Lotane and Lystra in turn, holding up one, two, then three fingers, indicating who'll go first. Circling my hand, I encompass Alyssa and myself to follow, with Nestor and Fianna last.

Time is of the essence, but by an unspoken understanding, we all hug briefly.

Kralgen has never once stopped smiling. Sometimes I wish I were like him. He has an unbreakable belief that he will always be alright. He holds up his hand, counting down on his fingers, and Lotane looks at me and winks.

I know what Lotane is thinking. Kralgen is showing off that he can count backwards, and I can't help but swallow a laugh despite this dark moment. Then, we're all moving.

Seconds later, there's a clash of steel, and I move as fast as I dare, rounding the rocks to jump down onto the balcony. Kralgen, Lotane and Lystra have positioned themselves around the entrance to the ssythlan quarters and are picking off the lizards one at a time. Yet with every passing moment, more swarm out like bees from a hive.

Fortunately, no reinforcements are joining the ssythlans from the other entrance leading down into the human side of the mountain, but it might not be long.

'Alyssa, stay and help Nestor and Fianna,' I yell as I rush toward the others.

This isn't going well. If the balcony had remained uncontested, some of us might have been through the gate and gone by now. It's a bloody mess as I take my position to the side of the entrance, allowing Kralgen and Lotane to do most of the killing. Lystra is opposite me, and we manage to contain the ssythlans. The passageway is a narrow bottleneck, and as bodies pile at the exit, they hinder those coming from behind.

'Nestor and Fianna have made it!'

I can barely hear above the noise of combat and my own pounding heart, and have no idea who shouted the words.

'Another minute or two of this slaughter, and we'll be able to make a break for the Soul Gate if the dead block the passage enough,' Lystra shouts.

Damn!

THE LAST HOPE

Unbelievably the passage exit starts to expand. Slowly at first, but then noticeably, allowing three ssythlans to push through at a time. In a matter of heartbeats, our chances have gone from good to non-existent. If this goes on, we'll soon be overwhelmed.

'There's a damned lizard mage in the passageway,' Lystra yells, cleaving her sword through a ssythlan skull as she blocks a spear aimed at Lotane's thigh.

I wait for a warrior to pass by, step sideways, fling my hatchet in one swift movement, and then twist savagely away from a sword thrust. I'm too slow, and the blade glances from my ribs even as I recognise my weapon hasn't hit its target.

'This isn't looking good,' Lotane shouts as he's forced to take a step backwards, having killed my attacker.

I grit my teeth against the searing pain in my side, picking up the fallen ssythlan sword.

Then the unthinkable happens. Kralgen cries out, a dagger plunged deep into his calf by a fallen ssythlan. In a heartbeat, Alyssa takes his place, taking his weapons. But, with the best of us injured, this losing battle will be lost even quicker.

We're all tiring, and this fight is almost over. The widened passage has sealed our fate. Even if I order the others to flee, I doubt I could hold the ssythlan flood long enough.

'NESTOR, TO ME!' Lystra bellows above the clamour of steel on steel, jamming a dagger up under a ssythlan chin and into the brain. 'DO WHATEVER IT TAKES, BUT SEAL THE PASSAGE!'

It's an impossible task Lystra is demanding. The flow of ssythlans won't allow Nestor the time to complete the task.

'NOW' she yells, and then Lystra does the unthinkable.

With a war cry, she charges into the swarm. I'd seen her fight more times than I could remember, marvelling at her composure, perfect form, and the deadly grace she moved with. Now, almost all of that has gone, replaced by a berserk rage. She's discarded her swords and now wields two long daggers. In the confines of the passage, there isn't room to swing for the ssythlans side by side, but she doesn't need to. Her hands flash, almost as if unleashing a flurry of punches, and each time she delivers a deadly blow.

Nestor frantically pulls at the stone side of the passage, dragging it across like some kind of curtain, his face a nightmarish mask of blood and pain.

Lystra's charge is doomed. A sword thrust takes her in the side. She drops briefly to her knees before driving a dagger into the forearm of the ssythlan who'd delivered the blow, forcing him to let go of the weapon. Then she's surging upright again, lunging forward into the packed ranks, reaping a terrible toll. A spear gashes the side of her neck, and blood spurts.

It's not going to be enough, and I get ready to throw myself after Lystra when a freezing wind howls past down the passageway. With the remnants of her strength, Fianna has thrown everything into this final roll of the dice.

The ssythlans slow under the icy gust, albeit briefly, as Lystra sways unsteadily before them, a mist of blood in the air coming from her throat. Yet, with a sudden twist, she launches a dagger end over end. Hindered by her wounds, it's a superlative throw that takes the ssythlan mage in the chest. The wind drops away, leaving a moment of stillness and silence, but the ssythlans recover and charge forward. Lystra looks briefly over her shoulder, then disappears under their massed ranks.

I stumble backwards in shock even as Nestor brings the other side of the passage across, sealing the gap. We can hear the clash of metal on stone as the ssythlans hack away. It's unlikely they'll get through without the mage to unseal the passage, but the stairwell remains open.

Nestor staggers across the balcony and closes the stairwell exit enough to hinder any attack while we stand, weapons ready for a foe that never comes.

Now the immediate danger has passed, the reality of what is about to unfold hits home. We may have survived, but now it's time for some of us to die.

***

My head is spinning as Lotane takes my arm. If I look anything like him, I must resemble the dead walking. By unspoken agreement, we stumble to the Soul Gate.

Kralgen passes us Soul Blades, and we remain silent, lost briefly in thought, the moment of choosing upon us. I know what I must do but delay the inevitable, enjoying Lotane's presence a little longer. The others are doing the same.

Fianna is propped against the curved frame of the gate. Her eyes are half-closed, skin white where it isn't covered in blood and filth.

THE LAST HOPE

Unbelievably her hair shines like gold, unblemished even to the end. Nestor kneels beside her, holding her hand, pushing his ear close to her mouth as she murmurs softly.

Nestor nods, and his eyes are puffy as he looks to the sky, searching for something. Then, turning back to Fianna, he kisses her soft lips while pushing the Soul Blade into her heart.

Tears run without shame down his face as he moves over to me.

'Fianna insisted you have this gift. She always loved you in a way I could never comprehend.' His hand shakes as he offers me the blade.

'No! It has to be you. Her heart and soul belong to you!'

Despite his tears, Nestor smiles, and I break down, sobbing uncontrollably. Lotane stands to the side as Nestor pulls me close.

'Her heart and soul do belong to me, Malina. Just as mine will always belong to her. Gently he takes the dull blade from my hand, replacing it with the one holding Fianna's soul. 'And I want mine to be with hers, wherever it may be, however painful it may be.'

To my horror, he plunges my dull blade into his thigh and looks around.

'If only we'd seen this place at the beginning as I see it now, perhaps we'd have recognised the evil before it was too late. Sadly I can see it has touched us all.'

Pulling the blade free, he carefully presses the hilt into Lotane's hand.

'No soul should be without its mate. Keep the King Slayer safe.'

I watch Nestor turn away. He lifts Fianna into his arms, her lifeless head resting against his shoulder as he sits on the balcony wall. Time appears to slow at that moment, as with a final smile to us all, he topples back off the balcony and is gone.

My heart feels broken, and my body shakes as Lotane holds me close. He's standing strong for me, but I know he's torn inside.

Heart-rending sobs of utter despair that aren't my own draw my attention. Kralgen, the strongest of us all, holds Alyssa tightly to him. They're standing by the gate and have come to their own decision.

'You t-take my s-soul and l-live, do you hear me,' Kralgen stammers, as his words are broken apart by misery. 'One of us has to live. Promise m-me!'

'I promise,' Alyssa cries, her head buried in Kralgen's chest.

Kralgen pulls away, looking at the Soul Blade in his fist. It looks tiny in comparison. Something so small shouldn't have the power to kill such a giant.

'Don't you dare do it before you kiss me goodbye, you lummox!' Alyssa cries, tears running unchecked from her reddened eyes. She slaps him hard, taking the blade away. Reaching up, she wraps one arm around his neck, pulling him down for a kiss.

'Do you remember the rose garden in Delnor's northern district where I took you ... the one with the trellises and those gigantic flower pots?' Alyssa asks once their lips part, her arms wrapping around him. 'It had that amazing mosaic of two lovers on the ground.'

Kralgen nods.

'Tell me you love me,' she whispers.

'For all time,' Kralgen chokes out, crushing Alyssa to his chest.

Alyssa pushes the blade into her hand behind Kralgen's back.

Then, swiftly dropping it into his robe pocket, she breaks free of his embrace, kicks him hard on his injured leg, and, as it buckles, shoves him through the Soul Gate.

Without her soul, Alyssa calms again, her face losing its despair. For a moment, I'm jealous. To be rid of this pain might be worth ... if only I could.

'You need to go and quickly,' Alyssa says matter-of-factly. 'But I have something to ask of each of you beforehand.'

Turning to Lotane, she takes his hand, holding it firmly.

'Find Kralgen quickly and look after him for me. Can you believe it, but he looks up to you ... always wanted to be like you? You know where to find him. Please go now before he does something stupid.'

Lotane nods.

'I know the place. It's not far from where I've entered the city in the past.' He looks to me, seeking approval.

'Go. I'll follow right after. Once you find Kralgen, get out of the city quickly and camp a day's travel north alongside the River Del. Wait for me. If I'm not there in a week, then you must act alone. Tell our story to everyone who'll listen.'

Lotane kisses me briefly, cupping my face in his hands. They're caked in gore, bleeding, and disgusting, yet I don't want him to let go, ever. Then in the next moment, he's gone.

THE LAST HOPE

Only Alyssa and I remain. We're all alone. There's a moment of silence, but it's interrupted by crashing. The blocked stairwell entrance is being breached.

Alyssa bends to pick up a discarded sword and looks across the balcony.

'I'm not sure I can do what Nestor did,' she says. 'Nor do I want to give those ssythlans the satisfaction of killing me. Even worse, they might torture me into sharing your plans.' Reversing the sword, she offers me the hilt. 'Make it quick and clean.'

I haven't any words left as she turns her back to me, then kneels, looking into the distance. She closes her eyes and starts mumbling a prayer. The sound of falling rubble tells me all I need to know. Time has run out.

I tighten my grip on the sword hilt. My hand shakes, something it hasn't done in years. Then, in the next heartbeat, conditioning kicks in. It steadies, the blade whispers through the air, and I leap for the gate before Alyssa's body hits the ground.

I don't even notice the screams of torment, nor do I want to. What if I recognise the voices of Nestor, Fianna and Alyssa?

Moments later, I fall to the library rooftop in High Delnor. Rain falls in sheets, and I'm soaked within moments. Looking up, the sky is a soulless grey.

By the gods, no! Were the others' sacrifices in vain?

The first time I'd travelled through my weakness had been overwhelming, and now I feel exactly the same. I open my mouth, allowing the rain to trickle in, hoping to quench my raging thirst. The salty taste of blood is so strong that I turn my head to the side and spit.

A gooey red blob falls to the roof beside me, and I begin to cry again, this time in relief. I still have my sense of taste, and if my blood is red, the greyness is just a summer storm. My soul is intact.

'Thank you, Fianna!' I cry out into the gale, praying my words will reach them. 'Thank you, Nestor, Alyssa, Lystra!'

Have I ever hurt this much? I think not. It's all I can do to crawl to the shelter of the small temple. I look at the dull Soul Blade clenched in my hand as I reach cover. If only I could break it into a thousand pieces. Instead, I hide it behind one of the stone benches and hope I never see it again.

In a way, this torrential rain is a blessing. I go to stand under the edge of the sloping roof in a torrent of water that batters me like a fist.

Wincing, I pull my robe over my head. It's in tatters, but I can't discard it. My clothes underneath are in a little better shape. I kick off my boots and stand naked under the eyes of the gods.

I take my time, however difficult and painful, to wash away every bit of blood I can. My wounded ribs are bleeding, and with my other cuts, they're being cleansed by the rain.

Sitting on a bench, I clean my fingernails before picking up my clothes. I alternately squeeze them out and soak them at least a dozen times till the water finally runs clear. Next, I rip the legs off my trousers. One, I tear into strips, while the other serves as wadding as I bandage my wounds. I'm dizzy, exhausted, and on the verge of collapse, but I push myself.

Just as I finish, the rain stops, and the sky begins to brighten. I'm fortunate it's spring, or I might die of exposure. There's a hint of warmth through the clouds, and I crawl to the parapet. Pulling my shirt back on seems to take forever as it clings to my wet body. The trousers … no, shorts are easier. The robe I lay on the edge of the roof.

Leaning back against the parapet, I close my eyes just for a moment to catch my breath …

***

CHAPTER VI

I awaken to the fading warmth of a setting sun.

These last two days have almost broken me. I gingerly touch my nose and immediately regret doing so. Everything hurts to some degree or another, from my head to my feet. Added to that, I'm famished. On the positive side, even if my stomach is empty, I can feel my magical power is almost replenished.

If only I'd had the foresight to stock this roof with some siege rations when I'd frequented this place. Standing, I steady myself against the rooftop, then quickly step away as I spy the teeming crowds of people below. Standing silhouetted against the sky is a sure way to be noticed.

It's too soon to check my wounds; I'll only disturb them. They'll have to wait until I can get some cleaner bandages. Fortunately, my robe has mostly dried through, and I pull it on, careful not to tear it anymore. Without it, my eyes and complexion will have me arrested or killed by a vicious mob before I can explain anything.

At least Lotane and Kralgen don't have green skin. Yet two hulking brutes don't easily go unnoticed. Hopefully, they've managed to exit the city before its residents came out from wherever they'd sheltered from the storm.

But what do I explain, and why should anyone believe me; the assassin who killed the High King.

Hello Major Conrol, Commander Farsil, I'm sorry I killed your friend, the king, but I've some other bad news. My king, who, by the way, I also tried to kill, is coming here at the head of a fey army from another world. Yes, fey. The monsters from the fey tales we hear as children are all true ...

I doubt I'll get anyone to listen to my story before I'm gutted unless I have a captive audience. Hmmm, there's a thought. Yes, that might be the only way.

Ye gods. The task before me hardly bears thinking about and will almost certainly end in death. I'm glad I told Lotane to get out of the city, for at least only one of us will die delivering the message. Until, of course, he comes looking for me and tries to do the same when I don't return.

Damnit.

Pondering my next move, I go through a stretching routine. If I don't, my body will seize up from the punishment it's taken. Never has success been more crucial than now, yet never have I been in a worse state at the start of a mission. My newly formed scabs pull, but a little blood loss is nothing compared to being unable to fight.

Whatever I do will require money and I can always just rob someone.

'Perhaps we'd have recognised the evil before it was too late. Sadly I can see it has touched you all.'

Nestor's words. When he'd looked upon us at the end, bereft of his soul, he'd seen our inner darkness. From here on, I'll strive to be better.

The gold I'd secreted back at the Broken Arrow should still be hidden beneath the boards. As for the other equipment I'd left there, well, that was over a year ago. It will be long gone, I'm sure.

I find it hard to come to terms with how much time has passed here when to me, it was just last month that I stepped through the gate into Nogoth's realm. I don't even know who the High King in Delnor is now, although, from memory, a year of mourning was always tradition before a new monarch was anointed. So, perhaps one has yet to be chosen.

Shadows settle across the city like a blanket, street lights are lit on the main roads, and the citadel on the hill becomes awash with light.

'I'm sorry,' I whisper into the distance, the painful memory of my heinous deed within its walls still fresh.

Why is it getting so dark? I stifle a laugh. Being without a soul had made some things so much easier. If it weren't for the moonlight, I'd be almost entirely blind.

THE LAST HOPE

I wait a while, letting my eyes acclimatise. Should I travel the streets below instead? Unarmed and this late, the risk of a confrontation outweighs the risk of falling. Up here, I'll remain unseen and with my magical power returned, a fall won't be deadly.

Despite it being a while since I've travelled this city's rooftops, they feel as familiar as my old boots. Occasionally I'm buoyed by magic to ensure a leap is made safely. Perhaps it's frivolous, but the pleasure I perceive as I call upon its help warms me. Darul comes to mind as I move silently north toward the Broken Arrow. I wonder how he met his end? The ssythlans probably culled the older Chosen every so often, ensuring our ranks remained thin, so we could never become a threat. Maybe his corpse was frozen in the ice along with Bardel below the Mountain of Souls.

For the first time in years, a feeling of utter vulnerability pervades me, and I long for Lotane by my side, protecting me.

Why?

It doesn't take me long to arrive at the answer. Before, when I'd walked these paths, dying in service of my king wouldn't have worried me ... because other Chosen would follow in my footsteps to carry on.

Now, apart from Lotane and Kralgen, any Chosen who follow will be enemies, and if the three of us fail, it will be the end of everything. The burden is almost too heavy to bear.

The roof terrace of Ariane's establishment hasn't changed from when I'd last been here, and with a final leap, I land there, rolling to absorb the impact before rising to my feet. I regret the automatic move as my wounds complain.

Will I forever see Delnor in shades of black and grey as I walk in the shadows?

Stealthily moving down the steps, I let myself in through the unsecured terrace door, smiling in satisfaction to find my old keys in their hiding place where I'd left them. It's dark, the only light coming through the filthy glass door pane behind me. No lanterns are lit, a sure sign the rooms are vacant. Nonetheless, I listen carefully, but there's no tell-tale sound of breathing or snoring.

Reassured, I quietly let myself into my old room.

It feels strangely comfortable and familiar. Yet, there's no hint of me ever having stayed here, and as I run my finger across some thick dust on a shelf, it's apparent no one else has recently either.

Unsurprisingly the few things I'd left here are long gone.

Carefully shifting a chest of drawers, I spend a few minutes prying with my broken fingernails at a floorboard. Finally, it comes free, revealing the heavy pouch of gold. If only the world wasn't ending, this wealth could buy Lotane and me a happy future.

Moving back into the dark hallway, with my eyes accustomed to the gloom, I note the peeling wallpaper and lack of care in what had once been a pristine establishment.

Darul's old keys are where he usually hid them too, and I let myself into his room to find it in a similar state. Dust, stale air and dampness. I know Darul will have hidden some essentials in here.

Having pulled the curtains open to shed some meagre light on my search. I spend a few fruitless minutes carefully searching and moving empty furniture before discovering the wardrobe seems slightly heavier than it should be.

Opening the doors, I kneel down. There! A tiny tell-tale scratch on some lacquer shows that the bottom of this wardrobe can and has been lifted. It's fit too snugly for me to get my fingers around, so having pulled a picture nail from the wall, I spend a few minutes wriggling it headfirst down the back. Fortunately, despite my tenuous grip on the thin nail, the bottom lifts, and my efforts are well rewarded.

Within the false bottom, which is about two hands deep, is spare clothing, a dagger and shortsword, more money, some leather straps, and a thin, chainmail shirt. Everything is black, even the mail.

'Thank you, Darul,' I whisper. To say he was prepared for any eventuality was an understatement.

I take my time and cut the sleeves and legs of the shirt and trousers to the right length. I use the offcuts for clean dressings and take care of my wounds.

Donning the new clothes, I pull on my boots, then lift the chainmail over my head. It hangs long, halfway down my thighs, but that's fine. It's incredibly light, and whilst it won't stop a determined thrust, it will give me decent protection from cuts or deflected blows.

Next, I fashion a leather belt, and the scabbarded weapons soon hang at my waist alongside the bulging money pouches. A fresh robe slips easily over my head, and I don supple leather gloves to finish. They're a little big, but concealing my appearance is a priority.

With my old clothes stashed in the wardrobe, I quietly exit Darul's old room, retracing my steps along the corridor, then pause. I need to eat, and what better place.

I take my time descending two long flights of stairs, placing my feet carefully, trying to avoid creaking boards. I'm only partially successful, but no disgruntled patrons make an appearance. Then again, no lamps are lit anywhere, which is strange for such a successful establishment. However, light shines under a door at the end of the hallway, so at least one person is there.

Finally, I reach the ground floor. Light from the streetlamps permeates through dirty windows, showing me an unkempt shop floor. Cobwebs are everywhere, and the tables, despite being laid, are covered in dust. Dead flowers in small vases complete the sad picture.

I move behind the counter, following the aroma of fresh cooking to the kitchen. There's no light here at all, so I summon a small flame onto the palm of my hand, lighting my way. Despite the overall neglect, someone has cooked fresh food, and dozens of tea cakes are on a countertop. It appears this is the only room in the building that's in regular use and hasn't been left to rack and ruin. I wonder what's happened.

Despite moving quietly, my stomach rumbles louder than thunder, and I suppress a chuckle as I'm drawn to the food. I dip my head, smelling the recently cooked cakes. Their aroma is heavenly, and I remember the times I'd eaten them, tasting like wet clay. Yet there's another smell … smoke, and I spy a large candelabra on a table top. Using my magic, I light it, then realise the smoke I'd smelled must have been from it being recently extinguished.

A scuff of a heel has me spinning, twisting to one side as a large pan swooshes down where, until a heartbeat ago, my head had been. The wielder of the makeshift weapon, a woman, stumbles forward, unbalanced by her missed blow. A swift kick to the back of her legs sends her crashing face down on the floor. Jumping astride her back, I grab a handful of hair and yank back. Her neck is stretched taut, the veins throbbing with life blood … mesmerising. I'm about to drag the dagger across her throat when I stop.

What the hell am I doing?

'Please, please don't kill me,' the woman begs.

I recognise the voice of Ariane.

Damn, damn, damn.

The mission is everything, and if my presence is discovered, it's immediately jeopardised. Maybe I could just smash her over the head with the hilt. I raise it, about to deliver the incapacitating blow, when again I pause. Just because I've been taught to be ruthless doesn't make it right. Nestor's last words will haunt me forever ... I don't want to have a dark soul.

'If you raise your voice, if you scream, or draw any kind of attention, I'll have to kill you. Do you understand?' I whisper, my voice close to Ariane's ear.

A small nod answers my words.

'I haven't seen your face. Nor do I want to,' Ariane says, her voice trembling. 'Take whatever you want. I don't have much, but you'll enjoy the food, and my purse is in the right-hand drawer. Take that too. Just please, don't kill me.'

I feel sick. She's a good woman, and I almost killed her, and now she's trapped beneath me, frightened half to death. Yet I also know she's lying.

The ball of flame I'd carried, the lit candelabra, and with my hood down ... she must have seen me, and yet I can't blame her deceit.

'You can get up, but remember what I said about staying quiet. Your life truly depends on it.'

Standing, I put my hand under Ariane's arm, helping her to her feet. Even so, she keeps her face averted.

'Look at me!'

Ariane shakes her head, her hair falling about her face.

'Ariane, stop pretending. Look at me. If I was going to kill you, I'd have done it by now. Just don't give me a reason to change my mind!'

'Malina, the King Slayer!' You've killed me once already, so forgive me if I don't believe your promise!' She sniffs, wiping away tears and snot.

Will I forever be known as the King Slayer? I hate that damned title. I point to the table in the corner where she'd hidden from view when I entered. Indicating for her to sit down, I join her, having brought over the trays of cakes.

'It looks like someone gave you a little taste of what you deserved,' she says bitterly, eyeing my broken face, then looks down, perhaps afraid she'd said too much.

I'm intrigued by her earlier words.

'Tell me what you meant when you said I'd killed you once? I've never directly done you harm, nor would I ... unless I have to.'

The pain that shines from her eyes could never be faked.

'Look around you at what's become of my beautiful place.'

I pick up a cake, turning it over in my hands before popping it in my mouth. It dissolves on my tongue in an explosion of taste. Ariane is a cook of undeniable skill.

'Yes. What happened? It was thriving the last time I was here, and your food is unbelievable!'

A second cake immediately follows the first.

'You happened! After you ...' She pauses, reconsidering her words. 'After what you did and the wanted posters going up, I knew it was you. I notified the town guard, and they and others came here to take your things and look for information. They kicked out all my other patrons, and as soon as word got around that I'd given lodging to the King Slayer, my customers disappeared overnight.

'People I'd known years just spat at me in the street as if it was my fault. My staff left, not that anyone was coming to be served. Now the only things that come through the door are the debt letters. They'll take my beloved shop next month, and then, I'll have nothing left whatsoever. I make a few cakes every night to try and remember how good it used to be.'

Ariane chokes on the last few words, dropping her head into her hands, shaking with emotion.

I have killed her. She won't survive on the streets. Even if she sold her body, prostitutes have a short lifespan.

Duty and responsibility fight for control. There's so much I need to do and so little time. Lotane will be waiting, and who knows what state of mind Kralgen is in. They're also injured to a lesser or greater degree. Even a minor cut can cause infection, and Kralgen's wound was deep.

'I need a bag and the rest of the cakes,' I say, thinking of what I should bring to the rendezvous. 'Also bread, meat, cheese and water if you have any. Clean cloth as well, and any healing herbs.'

Ariane sighs, levers herself out of her chair, and opens cupboard doors. She pulls out everything I've asked for, leaving empty shelves, not that they'd held much in the first place.

With a thud, she drops the satchel on the table, draws breath to say something, but then bites her lip and sits down. She wrings her hands together, steadying herself.

'I'm ready,' she says. 'You can kill me now. Just please make it quick!'

These last few hours, I've been overwhelmed with sadness. Friends have died because of me, and just when I thought I couldn't feel any worse, I do. My word to Ariane means nothing. All she sees is a dark soul, a killer, a King Slayer. When I die, I don't want everyone to remember me this way.

Reaching into my robe with one hand, I note Ariane tense. She thinks I'm going for a dagger.

'Ariane. I'm guilty of many heinous things. I've killed more people than I can remember, although, in my defence, they were, for the most part, evil. Yet the killing of the High King was a dark deed and something I regret with all my heart and soul, whether you believe me or not. However, despite my blood-soaked past, there's perhaps one thing I can still take a little pride in … my word.

'So, I tell you this. If you promise to keep my visit to yourself, I'll take you at your word and leave you unharmed and unbound as I leave.'

A simple nod is the only answer I receive.

'I need to hear the words!'

'I promise. I promise.' Ariane whispers.

Standing, I reach inside my robe and, with a tug, pull out the heavy pouch of gold coins. She could buy the whole street with this amount of money. I empty them all in a jingling, shining avalanche onto the table in front of her.

Ariane's eyes are as wide as an empty plate as she stares at the fortune.

'This is for the cakes. They truly are the best I've ever tasted. Now I hope you can begin to rebuild the life I stole from you.' I pick up the satchel. 'Just remember your promise. If you break it, you'll lose more than just the gold!'

As I leave Ariane sitting there, I sigh. Why did my parting words have to be a threat?

Irrespective, despite that small misgiving, I feel a little more optimistic. My stomach is full; I'm clothed, equipped, and even have Darul's pouch of coin left. Now it's time to make my way north and find the others.

I only hope they're alright.

As I reach the roof terrace, the moons are shining favourably, illuminating my passage.

For a moment, their radiance lifts my heart ... a sign of good fortune. But then I remember that alongside them, hidden by their radiance, is the black moon. Invisible to the naked eye, it will soon align with the other two, heralding the end of days.

A shiver runs down my spine, spurring me to action.

Now is not the time to dally, so I set off, the weight of responsibility a heavy mantle that seems mine alone to bear.

***

The horizon to the east is glowing, and the clouds spreading across the sky like an ocean's waves are a thousand shades of red. It's the type of sunrise that usually fills me with tranquillity, but not this morning. I wonder if I'll ever be able to lie back and enjoy the passage of time again.

The sound of wooden bolts and latches being undone has me peer over the side of the low roof I've been resting on, and below me, the doors to the stable slowly creak open.

I wait for the stablemaster to turn back into the hay-scattered interior, then after a quick look around, vault off the roof and expend a little magic to soften my landing, and follow the man into the gloom.

The horses snicker as I pass their stalls, and ahead the stablemaster grabs a pitchfork and spins toward me, the wickedly sharp points raised.

'Creeping up on a man in such a fashion likely means yer up to no good,' he growls. 'Best ye go!'

I hadn't meant to creep up on him, but after years of training, my every step is unconsciously light and silently placed. Also, with my hood up and face in shadow, I probably look exactly like the assassin I've trained to be.

'My apologies, good stablemaster. I mean you no harm.'

I start in High Delnorian, putting him at ease with the musical tongue. He likely doesn't understand a word, but no mere cutthroat could speak even a few words so flawlessly.

'My apologies,' I say again in the common tongue. 'If my approach was silent, it was only so as not to disturb the animals, not for ill intent.'

The pitchfork is lowered, and the man scratches his head looking somewhat horrified at having threatened a noble. It's well within a noble's rights to take this further if I were who I pretended to be.

'Let me put you at your ease further. I require a fully equipped mount of good stamina for maybe two days.'

The stablemaster steps closer, trying to see my face, so I dip my head imperceptibly, ensuring it remains little more than a shadow.

'I'm sorry, M'lady. I sold my last available mounts yesterday, and those you see here were all bought at auction the day before that. I won't get any fresh mounts until the day after the morrow.'

The man shrugs apologetically, and from the look on his face, he is genuinely sorry. I sigh. Why can't things just go smoothly? It would be so easy to render him unconscious, steal a mount, and be on my way, but I've determined to be a better version of my former self.

I walk up and down the stalls under the watchful eye of the stablemaster, pondering what to do. Maybe there's another stable nearby, and he can tell me the way.

'How much did you sell that one for?' I point to a black gelding who snorts as I look at him.

'That's a fine beast, eh. You know your horses. That's the best one here, and already fully trained. He cost a full three gold pieces, would you believe. Between you and I, he's only worth two, but the lady who bought him seemed quite taken with his look. She's picking him up next week as a gift for her son.'

Pulling out Darul's pouch, I look inside and am pleased to find it is swollen with predominantly gold coins.

'I'll give you five gold coins just to hire him for just two days, maybe three,' I say, opening my gloved palm to show the thick pieces to the stablemaster.'

The man gulps, and I can sense his dilemma as he wrings his hands. I can't afford him to choose the wrong way, and it's not as though I'll have much use for the money I'm carrying anyway.

'Oh, and I'll make it six if you have him ready and provisioned to go in the next twenty minutes,' I add.

It's an extravagant offer, and the stablemaster moves like his life depends on it. I place the stack of coins on a small wooden stool and stand back, watching in admiration as the horse is brought to readiness. He finishes by hanging saddlebags, some grain pouches and water skins from the saddle.

'Add a few horse blankets if you wouldn't mind,' I ask as I step forward, putting the food satchel inside a saddlebag. I doubt he'll refuse, given the small fortune he's receiving.

With a nod, he opens a cupboard, pulls out three, and then ties them into a neat roll which he attaches to the back of the saddle.

'If you don't return him, I can live with that.'

The man's smile is bright against his bearded face as he pockets the gold. He could reimburse the buyer pretending the horse died, give her an extra gold piece as recompense keeping his reputation intact, and still be two gold richer.

'As a matter of interest, who bought your last horses?' I ask conversationally. 'Did they pay as much as me?'

The stablemaster laughs, and the black gelding snorts at the sudden noise.

'Hah. It was just one man buying my last two mounts. Big fella. I first thought he was a vagrant when he walked in. Not a man you'd want to cross and certainly not one I'd have tried to get more coin from than the horses were worth.'

That sounds promising. It could be Lotane had been here.

I swing up into the saddle with fluid ease, exerting a little pressure with my thighs, and grunt in satisfaction as the horse responds, wheeling first left, then right. I take the reins loosely, nod my thanks, and heel the horse into the street, turning north.

There are no pedestrians out, just tradesmen who scowl as I clatter along the streets. Only a noblewoman would have the arrogance to ride so noisily this early, but speed is of the essence.

It isn't long before I'm approaching the north gate, and momentarily my blood turns to ice. What if the city is still under attack? I'd suggested the others come here without even thinking about it till now.

Wake up, Malina.

I can't afford to overlook such things, not now.

Thankfully the gate is open, and only a bored guard stands in the roadway, motioning for me to stop.

It's light now, and if I stop and he recognises me, I won't have any choice but to kill him, or news of my return will spread like wildfire. I slow, fumbling under my robes and pull out a coin. It's silver, way too much … a copper would have been sufficient, but it catches the light nicely as I send it spinning through the air.

I stifle a laugh as the guard drops his spear to make a desperate but successful grab for the coin.

'That's for your good work, soldier,' I call as I canter past without stopping. Then the darkness of the wall tunnel engulfs me briefly before I'm free, the open trade road before me.

'Come on, boy; show me what you've got,' I shout, urging the horse into a gallop. I lean low over his neck, eyes half-closed against the wind as I let him have his head. After so much death and sadness, I welcome the feeling of exhilaration. The clatter of hooves on the paved surface helps to reinforce my sense of urgency.

Ten weeks till Nogoth arrives. That time will disappear like sand through an hourglass. Every day, hour and minute matters. However, an exhausted horse won't be of any use to me, so I rein him in, patting his neck gratefully as we slow to a gentle walk.

Low mounds dot the landscape. They remind me briefly of those back in Nogoth's valley that housed the human workers. Then I shake my head in recognition. These are burial mounds for those who probably died when the city was encircled. It reminds me that danger is ever-present and that despite the summer's day and an open road, I can't afford to be complacent.

I dismount briefly, and take a few moments to unbelt my hidden sword, then refashion the leather straps to sling it over my back.

It's not long before I spy the River Del that sustains the capital, and I nudge my horse off the paved road toward its winding course. I don't attempt to conceal myself and ensure my sword hilt is plainly visible.

Birds sing, flying through the air, oblivious to my pain. Insects whir and buzz, likewise going about their business. I envy them for their life of simplicity. Would they even notice or care if humankind was slaughtered and enslaved in the hundreds of thousands? Somehow I doubt it.

The question is, can anything be done to stop it?

Thanks to both the ssythlans and the Chosen, the Delnorian Empire is in tatters. The armies of every nation are already locked in battle, unaware their every move has been orchestrated, ensuring Nogoth's return meets a fractured opposition.

Even if the kingdoms somehow put aside their differences, would their combined forces be enough to stop the army that will shortly flood through the World Gate?

No. Not in an open battle. But there are other ways to fight an enemy if forewarned of the attack.

It's one thing for me to ensure Delnor becomes aware, assuming they believe me, but the rest of the world must know too.

I urge the gelding to a trot with my mind set on a new course of action.

***

A flash of light in the early dusk catches my eye. Turning to locate the source, I see the looming shapes of Kralgen and Lotane under a copse of trees further along the river bank.

The timing couldn't have been better as I was shortly to make camp and was beginning to worry that somehow I'd missed them. I hadn't even come across their trail.

I resist the urge to heel the horse faster, unwilling to risk its well-being if it stumbles on uneven ground. It's a torturous five minutes.

My horse snickers as I approach, and in response, two other horses reply, making me smile. It appears Lotane and Kralgen had indeed taken my gelding's stablemates as their mounts.

Kralgen limps forward, his demeanour dark, not a glimmer of his innocent happiness showing anywhere.

'I'll take care of your mount,' he says, ignoring my attempt to embrace him. 'The perimeter of our traps starts here,' he indicates.

'Thank you, Kral,' I reply, walking past as he takes the reins.

Lotane is standing there, the setting sun highlighting every feature. A latticework of cuts across his face and hands is complimented by bruised skin. His robe has been poorly repaired, and I don't think I've ever seen him in such an utter mess.

Yet he's a sight for my sore eyes.

The embrace we share isn't one of unfettered joy, nor do we lose ourselves in the moment and enjoy a deep kiss. The wounds we bear inside and out and our situation make that entirely inappropriate.

Nonetheless, I rest my head on Lotane's chest, enjoying the steady beat of his heart.

Kralgen has led my gelding past by the time we let go.

'We've got good visibility from here,' Lotane explains, pointing around. 'We've set traps at intervals fifteen paces out, not that we've encountered any threats. We've fresh water from the river, and there's good grazing for the horses. We have money, but except for the horses, we couldn't risk staying around to spend it. We're effectively weaponless as the trees hereabouts don't offer good enough wood to even make a staff. Kralgen's wound is deep but will heal given time. It needs attention, although he won't sit still long enough for me to tend it. I'm sure the wound he carries inside hurts him a hundredfold more. He's barely said a word to me; it's eating him up.'

I follow Lotane back to the camp. It's rudimentary, but in a lovely spot overlooking the River Del. As I gaze toward the far bank, the dying light showcases a fertile land full of long grasses dotted with lush woodland.

Suddenly an image of thousands of bodies imposes itself, all rent and broken, twisted in death, while above winged daemons fly. I shudder.

'The temperature does drop out here as the sun sets,' Lotane comments, mistaking my reaction for being cold. With a brief frown of concentration followed by a flicker of pain, he uses his magic to set a stack of kindling on fire in a shallow pit.

Two large logs on opposite sides of the fire have been pulled over, and we sit in companionable silence. The crackle of burning wood and the music of flowing water create a soothing harmony.

Not long after, Kralgen limps over, dropping the gelding's saddlebags at my feet along with the horse blankets before standing a few paces distant, staring into the distance.

'Please tell me you bought food,' Lotane asks hopefully. 'Kralgen's growling stomach kept me awake all last night.'

I know he's trying to get a reaction from Kralgen with the tease, but it's mistimed or perhaps unheard, for Kralgen doesn't respond.

Opening the saddlebags, I pull out the food satchel and water skins, lay a horse blanket on the ground and divide the food, putting the portions onto separate cloth wraps.

Lotane reaches out to take a cake, but I smack the back of his hand.

'Not yet!'

'Kralgen, come join us. We need to eat, and there's a lot to discuss.'

He stands still, a dark statue, looming and brooding.

'KRALGEN, come here, NOW!' I snap the order and am relieved that he responds to the command in my voice. He sits on the log opposite, his face lit by the flame, and I can see he's barely holding himself together.

'I, I n-need to ask you s-something, King Slayer,' he stammers, eyes bright with unshed tears.

I've been dreading this moment, for I knew it would come.

'How did my Alyssa die?'

There it is. How I answer might even determine whether another of us lives or dies. If Kralgen doesn't like what I hear and enters a blind rage, he's close enough to be upon me before I draw my weapon.

Be ready.

My magic responds, coiled, waiting to strike. A blast of wind to knock Kralgen backwards, allowing me to draw my sword and dagger. Then likely a hopeless exchange of words while I try to calm him before the bloodletting starts.

But, if I play this right, it won't be necessary. He'll want to hear that Alyssa died like a goddess of war. Charging the ssythlans as they broke through the stairwell wall, hacking and cutting a bloody swathe through their ranks as she died in a blaze of glory.

Indeed, it's the only way to avoid bloodshed. A lie to begin the mending of a heart broken by losing a soul mate. But it would be a lie to a friend and a fellow Chosen. Someone who should be able to trust me with their life.

'I killed her.'

The words tumble from my mouth almost of their own volition, followed by guilty sobs wracking my body.

'I killed her,' I whisper, almost scared to hear the words out loud.

Kralgen's enormous hands ball into fists, yet I don't call upon my power.

He stands, limping around the fire, his face lit by the flames, a frightening caricature of its normal self. Lotane rises guardedly to his feet next to me, but against Kralgen in a rage, he'll be swatted aside.

Kralgen stops before me, and I rise, meeting his gaze through blurry eyes.

What must be mere heartbeats seems to stretch for an eternity, and I wonder if I've even drawn breath in that time.

Then those hands that could crush my skull or snap my neck in the blink of an eye are rising toward me, and still, I cannot move.

'Thank you.'

I don't know what shocks me most, the words or the warm embrace that Kralgen enfolds me in. He keeps repeating the words over and again, softly, reassuringly, as much perhaps for him as for me. Kralgen's gigantic form shakes with emotion, an outpouring of grief that has Lotane in tears too, his arms around us both.

Kralgen's gratitude and this moment we're sharing, allowing our defences to drop, has a cathartic effect. When we finally step back, wiping our faces, at least some of the emotional trauma has been removed. I know conditioning has played its part, but on its own, it wouldn't have been enough.

'I feel lost,' Kralgen admits as he sits opposite. 'I've never been happier than these last years. I excelled at every task demanded of me and had Alyssa to share those moments with. Every day was golden.'

His voice breaks a little, but he struggles on.

'I'm a fighter, I always have been, but I've never felt more like lying down than right now.'

'Now is not the time for lying down, Kralgen,' I say, leaning forward earnestly. 'There's so much that needs to be done if we're to have revenge.' I use the word on purpose and see a twitch as the word hits home.

'Revenge.' Kralgen says the word as if he's tasting something for the first time. 'Tell us first, Malina, now we've the time. What happened? Everything moved so fast back at the Mountain. One moment Alyssa was asleep in my arms, and the next ...'

Kralgen chokes a little, blinking back tears again.

'Anyway, start at the beginning when you disappeared. Then I want to know about the army Nogoth's bringing. How many, and what kind of units. Finally, tell us what happens next. Once I know all that, then maybe I can think about revenge.'

Kralgen is right.

'Here.' I hand out the food. 'There might be sparse days ahead, so consider that as you eat.'

We're fortunate, for Ariane had packed away everything from meat to bread, and of course, there are her tea cakes. There's enough food here for several days.

Taking a deep breath, I gather my thoughts and realise there's so much of the story I mustn't share. One day I'll tell Lotane about what transpired between Nogoth and I, but hurting him now will serve no purpose. At least, that's how I justify it to myself.

THE LAST HOPE

'I've often had doubts,' I begin, 'but it all came to a head when I killed the High King. Before I took his life, I could see he was so pure of spirit, and I knew the deed was wrong. Afterwards, as Lotane knows, I was troubled by guilt. At that time, I believed that Nogoth, in his goodness, might choose a different path if only he knew. Inadvertently, when I went on our mission, thoughts of when we'd spoken through the mirror entered my mind. One minute I was at the top of the Mountain of Souls, about to follow you all, and the next, I was waking up in another world.'

'Another world.' Lotane shakes his head. 'If someone else said that to me, I'd just laugh in their face and believe them touched by the gods. Yet it's you, and if we can travel around this one using a Soul Gate, why not to another.'

Kralgen growls, eyebrows knitted together as he glares at Lotane.

'Sorry, please, go on.' Lotane apologises with a shrug before chewing on a chunk of bread.

'Well, at first, it was everything we could have dreamt of. Nogoth lived in a valley unlike anything you've ever witnessed. Nature ruled there, and the flora and animals were colourful, vibrant and exotic. It was a utopia. When I first saw that, I hoped with all my heart that this world could become the same under Nogoth's kingship.

'Bizarrely, it was my conditioning that shattered this vision. After a period of inactivity, the need to train had me explore outside the valley, where I discovered what's known as The World Gate, flanked by two enormous temples. They were surrounded by what I first thought were thousands of hideous statues.

'When I entered the temples and saw the true effigy of Nogoth, with paintings that told the tales of his conquests here, I was in denial. They showed cities sacked, and the surviving inhabitants herded back into captivity through the World Gate, to be used as livestock. I didn't want to believe what I saw, yet, under those very temples, I found the remnants of the survivors, and when I freed them, they were slaughtered. The statues were, in fact, part of Nogoth's monstrous army, sleeping, waiting for the World Gate to open, and they fell upon those survivors in a feeding frenzy.'

Kralgen leans forward, interest driving aside his sorrow a little. Anything to do with a fight, and he wants to know all the details.

'You escaped though. How?'

'They mistook me for one of their own.'

'What?'

The shock is evident in Lotane's voice, and Kralgen's eyes narrow.

'There's a magical race there called the Saer Tel. They're evil but appear as creatures of nature, full of grace and poise, with green skin and yellow eyes, just like mine. They're Nogoth's most favoured, so I was left alone.'

I artfully leave out that I had Nogoth's scent upon me. Will I ever share this secret with Lotane? Once, I'd intended to unburden myself, but now I'm not so sure.

'What magic do they wield?'

I'm relieved Kralgen is asking such direct pertinent questions, his mind responding to the years of conditioning, signs of the human weapon he needs to be resurfacing from below the grief.

'I never saw it, but the one I fought attempted to summon hers with a simple thought and felt no pain like me.'

Lotane looks a little puzzled and hurt by my revelation.

'You can summon your power so easily? For how long?'

'Since the beginning.' I shrug. 'I kept it to myself, for I was worried the revelation might put me in jeopardy and hiding it became a habit. It wasn't for lack of trust, my love. I promise.'

Lotane appears mollified.

'How many of them are in Nogoth's army?' Kralgen is ticking off his fingers.

In the past, Lotane would have taken this opportunity to tease Kralgen but holds back. I wonder if I'll ever enjoy their banter again.

'I don't know. I only saw a dozen or so.'

'How many ssythlans?'

'I killed all I came across in Nogoth's household. Beyond them, I don't believe there were any.'

'What was the size of the army by the World Gate you mentioned?' Kralgen is snapping the questions at me, a look of concentration furrowing his brow.

'There were perhaps ten thousand on the plain. But Nogoth mentioned he had an army of nigh on two hundred thousand ready to march through.'

'How many spearmen, swordsmen and cavalry. What about siege engines?'

THE LAST HOPE

'I have no idea, but when I said it was a monstrous army, I meant it in the literal sense, just like on the carvings we've seen. There are no people in Nogoth's army, although the Saer Tel and ssythlans could be mistaken for such at a distance. The creatures I came in close contact with had fangs and claws, and were also armed with swords and such. Body-wise, they were about as large as Nestor but were winged and flew like birds of prey. I think they were gargoyles. But Nogoth also mentioned giants and trolls.

'Giants and trolls like in children's fey-tales?' Kralgen asks, pulling on an earlobe.

'That's what he said. If so, I only saw a fraction of his army, and being winged creatures, they're his scouts, I presume.'

'What about Nogoth?' Kralgen presses onward. 'Tell us about him. How good was he?'

Unbidden, those violet eyes come to mind, the full sensual lips, the strength of his limbs and the vigour of his body. The way he made me …

'W-what do you mean?' I ask, flustered, flushing deeply.

'When you fought him, how good was he?' Kralgen demands as if talking to a simpleton.

I sigh with relief, but notice Lotane studying me, a strange look on his face, and I turn my attention back to Kralgen.

'He never fought with weapons, but with centuries of practice, he must be deadly. He let me land blow after blow, but whatever weapon I used, including my Soul Blade, they bounced off as if he were iron. He said no weapon could harm him, and it's hard to disbelieve. However, knowing how much he manipulates words, I can't say for sure if that's entirely true. My magic had no effect, and his own mastery far exceeded mine. During our fight, he hit me with a fist surrounded by lightning. I've never seen anything like it.'

'Maybe because we never considered it.' Kralgen offers. 'Lotane or I could have a flaming sword, but summoning that during combat would take too long and cost too much for little purpose. Yet, if like you, he can summon by thought alone, who's to say you can't also?'

'He told me I could have magical power I'd barely comprehend if I continued to serve him,' I muse.

Clenching my fist, I imagine it's covered in lighting. Sure enough, for perhaps two heartbeats, my hand glows with frightening power, but after, like an upturned water jug, I feel empty.

Lotane's arm goes around my shoulder as I sway, almost fainting from being so drained. Nothing I've ever conjured had brought me to the edge of collapse so quickly ... apart from when I first managed to summon the fire magic.

'Impressive.'

Kralgen isn't mocking. He's impressed by anything powerful.

'But about as useful as a blunt knife,' I yawn, exhausted beyond belief. 'What good if it's unsustainable and I pass out summoning it. Nogoth probably told me another lie to coerce me to remain in his service.'

'But why would he do that?' Lotane looks at me closely.

'He told lies constantly. Everything had an element of truth to make it believable, like delivering equality and bringing down the evil, greedy kings. It's how he manipulates people.'

'No. That's not what I meant, Malina.'

Lotane using my name like this sends a cold shiver down my spine, especially as his arm drops away when he turns to look earnestly at me.

'I can't understand why. I believe everything you've told us, from people being livestock to him being the antithesis of what we'd come to believe. But why did he let you live if not as a slave? Why were you allowed to wander his valley, and what did he hope to gain?'

Flashes of me naked in Nogoth's arms, night after night, the frenzy of our joining intruding on my thoughts. How could I ever explain them? I simply can't. I need to tell the truth, but not that truth. What can I possibly say that ...

'He believes I have the blood of the Saer Tel running through my veins.' Even this admission causes my head to drop in shame. 'From the last invasion a thousand years past, it would appear a child of fey and human came to be.'

'By the gods, that's hard to believe.' Kralgen doesn't sound too convinced by his own denial, and Lotane's arm going back around my shoulder is enough to send tears down my cheeks again.

'It might be true. You remember how I looked when I first arrived at the mountain. My mother, brother and I were always mocked for our deathly white skin and yellow eyes. Now, if I stood next to a Saer Tel, you'd see the similarity. Add to that my control of the four elements, and it's not so improbable.'

Lotane gives me a final squeeze, and let's go. I'm sure he knows I'm only telling half the story, but he laughs. I'm relieved and surprised because it actually holds genuine humour.

'So to summarise,' he says. 'We're soon to face an unbeatable, immortal Fey King alongside his monstrous legions. Our enemy outnumbers the armies of mankind combined, which weaken daily as they fight one another. Oh, and we have less than ten weeks to warn a world that will laugh in our faces in disbelief or kill us on sight for the heinous deeds we've committed. Have I missed anything?'

A faint smile creases Kralgen's lips, a glint of humour coming to the fore.

'You've only listed the negatives. You forgot to add that facing them is the King Slayer, part fey, part human, and her two magic-wielding accomplices; one incredibly handsome and the other incredibly strong!'

Lotane doesn't push the joke further. Like me, I know he's just grateful Kralgen still has a spark inside. Kralgen's the strongest of us all. I know he's hurting, but he's still a force to be reckoned with.

'So, Malina, what's the plan?' Lotane prompts.

'It's really rather simple. Warning everyone isn't enough; we need to unite all the armies of the warring kingdoms and present a combined show of force that makes Nogoth realise the cost won't equal the gain.'

'I was thinking along those lines,' Kral declares.

'Me too,' Lotane mutters.

'Then we can't all be wrong!' I say, relieved we're in full agreement. 'We must choose the perfect defensive battleground and ensure Nogoth faces us there. If we tie his army down and bleed them badly, they'll turn back from losses or lack of supplies while the civilian population hopefully remains unharmed.'

'High Delnor?' Kral asks.

'Yes, it's perfect.' Lotane nods. The city walls are strong enough, and that citadel is nigh on impregnable. With access to the sea, no siege will starve them into submission!'

'Agreed,' I say.

Lotane grimaces.

'But how the hell will we get armies that have warred for years and hate each other, to cease fighting, ally and come together there.'

'We'll tell them the truth or give them no choice!' I say.

'No one will believe us until it's too late,' Kralgen points out. 'Look at me. I might be large, but no one will take me seriously unless I've got a knife to their throat.'

'They'll believe you, Kral, don't worry.'

'Why? I still find it nigh on impossible to believe despite knowing Nogoth's invasion is true.'

'Where you're going, Kral, you'll give them no choice. Your mission is to return to Icelandia and reclaim that crown you gave up. Icelandia has remained stubbornly neutral in this war. Forewarn them, prepare them, and mobilise their fighting men and women.'

Kralgen nods, a genuine smile crossing his face.

'Alyssa always said I should go back there. She believed in me, and so do you. I swear on my everlasting love for her that I won't fail in this. When I succeed, I'll bring every axe and hammer-wielding giant of an Icelandian south to High Delnor as fast as possible.

'Which only leaves Astor, Rolantria, Suria, Hastia and Tars to convince. Ten weeks won't be sufficient to do this, whatever our approach,' Lotane sighs.

'It will have to be ... unless we can slow Nogoth's advance,' I muse. 'Convincing the Delnorians to send a delaying force west must be our first step, and then we'll have time to convince the other kingdoms to join our cause.'

'We need to carry provisions to last weeks ...' Kralgen's voice trails off as he starts counting on his fingers, concentrating as he makes a list of things to do.

'What about me? Do I get to be a king as well? I know deep inside I'd be a rather good one.' Lotane asks, eyes shining as a mission begins to take shape.

'Sorry, but no. I'll need you with me because where I'm going, I won't be able to succeed on my own. But after that, who knows!'

'We're heading back to High Delnor then, aren't we?' Lotane grumbles.

I nod.

'It's time we became reacquainted with Commander Farsil and Major Conrol.'

***

THE LAST HOPE

As Lotane and I trudge toward High Delnor, my shoulders sag. However hard I try to focus on what lies ahead, memories of our desperate escape from the Mountain of Souls and losing those I love, plague me. Had I done things differently, Lystra, Nestor, Alyssa, and Fianna might still be alive.

My dreams of Karson had always foretold nothing but death.

It appears they were uncannily prophetic.

I sigh, fatigued and burdened by the weight of responsibility. I haven't had nearly enough time to recover physically or emotionally. Talking late into the night and snatching only five hours of sleep hadn't helped.

But rising early, despite our tiredness, had. We'd carefully tended to one another's wounds while breaking fast, and those physical acts of compassion had helped the healing process begin.

When we'd parted from Kralgen a short while ago, we'd all cried unashamedly.

Kralgen had taken all three horses, the remaining food, my sword and all the sundry equipment. He had a long journey ahead of him, whereas Lotane and I could see High Delnor in the distance.

I don't doubt Kralgen will succeed, for he is a raw force of nature.

As for Lotane and me, I only wish I felt as confident.

Lotane, who'd been lost in his own thoughts, looks at me.

'Do you remember saying how you dreamed of a life where it was just you and I? Well, look at us now; dreams do come true.' He opens his arms wide, then picks me up in a bear hug. 'Even if it's for just one day, we're finally free. Free of the Mountain, free of the lies.'

'I just feel so guilty for the others who died, I ...'

'NO!'

Lotane puts me down and stands back, a rare seriousness about him.

'Don't go there. We both know our life span was always numbered in years doing what we did. Even if we hadn't died on a mission, we now know we'd probably have been culled and served up at some stage. Don't count the few who've died; count those you've saved, and I'm not just talking about me and Kralgen. It's those who might survive the coming apocalypse because you found the strength to do what you did!'

'I did nothing but try to keep myself alive, Lotane. This wasn't some heroic sacrifice but a desperate fight for survival!'

'Still, you don't see it, do you?' He groans. 'You're more like Kralgen than I care to admit. Look at where we are. We aren't running away with pouches full of gold to the furthest reaches of the known world to live that life of freedom you dreamt about. We're heading back to High Delnor, putting our lives at risk in the vain hope we might somehow save the people there. Whether that was your intention to start with doesn't matter. It's your intention now.'

Lotane's voice softens, as does his demeanour.

'You were always the best of The Chosen, Malina. That doesn't mean you have to be a shining paragon of virtue. It just means you must find a way to be what you once were; the King Slayer. But please, this time, you've just got to find a way to kill the right one!'

He always makes me feel better, and my back straightens.

I sigh wistfully as our footsteps take us along the trade road back toward Delnor. Would we be able to evade the coming storm if we hid away? Probably. But what kind of world would we return to when we came out of hiding?

I hold Lotane's hand as we pause, moving to one side as a line of wagons rumbles by. There's no point trying to talk above the noise. The oxen grunt and bellow loudly under the lash as the drivers encourage them to speed. Despite the beautiful morning, the burial mounds dotted everywhere serve as a reminder that death is never far away. So the wagonmasters push for the safety of High Delnor's walls. By contrast, the city holds nothing but danger for Lotane and me.

As the wagons leave us behind, a dust cloud their parting gift, we continue on our way.

'So, do you have any idea how we're going to approach Commander Farsil?' Lotane probes. 'I wouldn't suggest handing ourselves in. Even if they don't hang or gut us immediately, I doubt they'll bother listening to us either.'

Lotane speaks the truth, and I remember my earlier thoughts of having a captive audience.

'We need to take Commander Farsil or Major Conrol, prisoner. I don't think it matters which.'

Lotane's laugh is so infectious that I can't help but join in.

'By the gods, Malina. You've killed their king, and now you'll take one or both of them prisoner. The amount of gold for your head on a platter is already enough to sink a galley! Are you sure this is the best way?'

'How else are we going to get them to listen unless they're tied up? We lure them out, using me as bait, then kidnap them!'

'A simple and infallible plan,' Lotane chuckles. 'What could possibly go wrong?'

I roll my eyes in exasperation.

'Have you got any better ideas or perhaps something to add other than your gentle sprinkling of mockery?' I ask with a wry smile.

Lotane's cheeks dimple as he purses his lips in thought.

'Truly, I don't have a better idea, at least for now. So let's play yours through.'

'Right. We find ourselves a room or vacant property …'

'Close to the docks, so the lighting is poor?' Lotane offers.

'Good idea. Maybe in a whore house or tavern. We let someone overhear that we're on a mission. Once they recognise my eyes and skin, they'll run off to the palace for the reward and …'

'No.' Lotane interrupts. 'If Farsil or Conrol believe we're on a mission to kill someone, perhaps even them, there'll be no talking to them, captive or not. Also, whoever overhears us might try to be a hero.'

'What do you propose then?'

'We use someone trusted to deliver a message who won't do something heroic. Perhaps along the lines of we just want to talk, or even surrender,' Lotane shrugs. 'It's less threatening even if they don't believe it. Being overheard just screams clandestine operation.'

I kick a loose stone, watching it bounce along the trade road toward our destination. We'll be lucky to make it to High Delnor by nightfall, and passing through the gate at dusk won't be as easy as riding out pretending to be a noble first thing in the morning. Yet another problem to overcome.

Mulling over Lotane's comments, I believe he's right.

'I like the sound of it. I know just the right person to deliver the message.'

'Good. As long as it isn't me.' Lotane laughs. 'Then the biggest problem is getting them to believe our tale.'

Silence reigns for a while as we mull over this seemingly insurmountable obstacle. Even if we do convince them, will they have the power to act upon it?

A rumble of approaching carts interrupts my thoughts and has me looking over my shoulder.

'Shall we get a ride? Those merchants will probably just get waved through the gates if they're well known,' Lotane muses, no doubt also considering how we'll re-enter High Delnor.

'Good idea. You do the talking. I'll just pretend to be your shy obedient wife.'

I pull my hood close, ducking my head to give me a worn, stooped posture.

'Give me some money then, wife.' Lotane laughs, holding out his hand. 'Money always talks louder than words.'

Lotane's hand closes warmly around mine for a moment, and I smile. Him saying wife has sent a pleasant shiver down my spine. Then, the memory of Nogoth's quickening comes to mind, the unbridled passion, desire and thirst making that pleasant shiver insignificant.

Damn.

***

CHAPTER VII

It's late afternoon, but we're back in High Delnor, having been waved through the gates without incident.

'This place is disgusting,' Lotane says, wrinkling his nose at the smell.

I can't disagree. Our room is about as gross as can be. Plaster sloughs off the damp walls, rat droppings litter the floor, and the filthy mattress looks like it might get up and walk away; it's crawling with so many insects. I won't be surprised if the chamber pot hasn't been emptied and something is dead inside; the stench is so thick.

Our lodging is nestled in the roof space of the tavern and the cheapest they have, but it has one redeeming feature; a small balcony. Lotane had paid half a copper for the accommodation for two nights, and the tavern keep had leered, thinking me some noblewoman in an illicit relationship with a hired hand.

Certainly, my robes are new and of a fine cut compared to Lotane's, and he already looks like a ruffian. To conceal his identity, we'd fashioned a bandage from torn strips of cloth to cover one side of his face. His green and blue eyes would have given us away as swiftly as my skin.

'This is so romantic. I doubt there's a mattress in Delnor that has experienced more lovemaking than that one.' I grimace, pointing to the thick stains covering almost every inch.'

'I'm almost tempted to turn it over and see if it's the same or worse on the other side,' Lotane laughs, kicking it to the side of the room.

Walking toward the balcony, I wonder how the opened curtains have acquired more stains than the mattress, then decide I don't want to know. Opening the balcony doors, I breathe the salty air with gratitude as I crane my head to look up. The flat roof is but a small leap above.

Perfect.

'Right. You're in charge of getting us some weapons and finding us another basement room,' I say, conscious of the time. 'If you can also get some supplies, that'll be ideal. I'll be back before dark.'

Lotane nods. We'd had plenty of time to hone our plan. Now it's time to put it in motion.

We descend three flights of stairs, keeping our heads down as we pass the tavern keep at the front desk. I put my gloved hand playfully on Lotane's ass when we exit. I know the tavernkeep will be watching, and it'll reinforce his ideas of us being lovers rather than raise suspicions.

I turn east and Lotane west. I keep my head down and focus on where I'm going. My hood is pulled tight around my head, and I've also wrapped a scarf around my face, leaving only my eyes showing above the binding. I'm quietly confident no one will be able to identify me, despite the faded wanted posters plastered on almost every street corner.

Thankfully, the footfall on the streets is beginning to thin, and I make good time reaching my destination.

I feel trepidation and reluctance; two unfamiliar feelings that are returning now I've severed the rigid magical bonds that bound me. Yet my conditioning remains, as does the mission itself, and there's no physical danger awaiting me here, only emotional pain.

Keeping my head down and with heavy feet, I climb the steps to the city library.

The large entrance doors are open as I pad into the cool interior, staying close to the wall, thankful that the place is nearly empty at this hour. An assistant librarian is replacing books and tomes on shelves, looking bored.

'Where's Arcan?' I ask softly, watching in amusement as the young lad jumps in shock and frantically grabs at some books slipping from his grasp.

'In his office on the top floor.'

I walk swiftly away, ensuring he doesn't see me.

Memories flood back as I head up the spiral staircase; the kindness Arcan had shown me when he'd thought me a student of history. Then when I'd killed the men in his library, how that had changed. The gods know how he felt about me after I killed the High King. I just hope he agrees to help.

Assistants hurry about, casting annoyed glances my way as they turn down wicks on the scattered lanterns or blow out candles, encouraging the few persistent visitors to leave.

Then I'm standing before Arcan's office door.

I raise my hand to knock but think better of it and slowly twist the handle, letting myself in.

There he is, stooped over some ancient scrolls scattered about a large desk, a magnifying glass to his eye, a dozen candlesticks shedding a homely glow across his office.

'I'm busy. Go away,' he growls without looking up, shooing with his free hand.

I close the door softly behind me, then walk around the desk, ensuring my boots scrape on the floor so as not to startle him.

'Are you deaf or just dumb?' Annoyance rattles in his old voice as he pushes himself upright, turning to face me.

Reaching up, I push my hood back and pull the scarf from my face.

Arcan steps back. He already has a pale complexion from years inside these dusty halls, but whatever colour there might have been, drains away instantly, and he begins to shake.

I wait, standing still, hands at my sides, hands open, showing my empty palms to ensure he perceives no ill intent.

Arcan's mouth opens and closes a few times.

'You. It's You. IT'S YOU!' Arcan's voice begins to climb, a crooked finger rising to point at me.

He edges around the desk, banging a chair out the way, then opens a drawer scrabbling inside, and all the while, his rheumy eyes are fixed on me. He pulls out some kind of letter opener. The blade is thin and dull, and couldn't even cut a cake. He's shaking so hard I'm afraid he might drop it on his sandaled feet as he makes his way back around the table toward me.

'Arcan, please put the knife down,' I say quietly, keeping my voice low. 'I am unarmed and haven't come here to harm you.'

Despite my plea, he continues toward me, desperation and hatred shining in his eyes.

My heart aches. Is this how people will meet me for the rest of my days? Will I forever be an outcast, the assassin who killed the High King?

'You k-killed him.' Tears run down Arcan's face as he makes a clumsy lunge with the knife.

I palm the thrust to one side, backing away as Arcan continues his advance.

'You burned him alive!' Another clumsy thrust that I twist away from, but now I'm in a corner. Whilst I could leap onto the table or even kill Arcan in a heartbeat, this needs to be played out.

'What kind of m-monster are you?' Arcan wails, making a final desperate stab. This time I trap his frail wrist in a vice-like grip with one hand whilst grabbing his shoulder with the other, holding him firmly despite his attempts to pull free.

'Please let go of the knife. You're not in danger, but if anyone hears us and comes to investigate.' I pull an indifferent face and shrug as if I wouldn't care about the outcome.

Arcan's shoulders sag, and the knife clatters to the floor.

'A curse on you and your family!' Arcan hisses as I let him go.

I ponder his words briefly. If, as Nogoth insinuated, I have fey blood, then indeed, my family has been cursed.

'You're more right than you realise. They've been cursed for a thousand years.' I answer softly, brushing past to give Arcan some room.

The old librarian is intrigued by my response, but he bites his lip, refusing to be drawn.

'So why have you darkened my door this time. Are you back to research your Once and Future King?' Arcan scoffs maliciously. 'I was such a fool believing your lies. I was such a fool, and now the High King is dead.'

I ache to console Arcan as he sits on a stool and sobs piteously, his tears darkening the parchment before him. Yet I know my touch will only stir him to anger or, even worse, a rash action. The death of the High King has hurt so many people so deeply. He was truly loved, as much as I'm now hated, it would seem.

'I need you to deliver a message for me right away. It has to come from someone I can trust, and despite your hatred for me, I know if you say you'll do it, you will.'

'Hah. I wouldn't spit on you if you were dying of thirst!'

Arcan refuses to look at me, staring down at his parchments, finding strength in avoiding my gaze.

'I need to meet both Commander Farsil and Major Conrol tonight.'

'Why? Is it their turn to meet a grisly end?'

'No, Arcan.'

'Then why?'

My hopes lift. If Arcan is intrigued enough to engage in conversation, then that's progress over an outright refusal.

'I want to hand myself in.'

'More lies, girl. When will you learn? Are you so steeped in deceit, that's all you know?'

'You wouldn't believe the truth if I told you!'

Frustration adds an edge to my voice, but he's right. I can hardly tell him the truth. Lies come without conscious thought; it's second nature. Calming myself, I continue.

'Does it really matter what reason? I'm staying at the One-Eyed Gull in the poor quarter tonight, and then I'll be gone. Go to the castle, ask to see one of them, and tell them I'll be waiting there. My room is on the top floor. They must come alone, unarmed, at midnight.'

'I'd do it just to see you hang, even though that's better than you deserve,' Arcan snarls maliciously. 'However, whilst I might know of them, they certainly don't know me. Why would they see, let alone believe me? I'm a nobody, just a fool of a librarian.'

Arcan's right, but I'd already thought this through.

'Show them this. They'll believe every word you say!'

I drop the Heart of Delnor onto the table. It's caused me nothing but misery, yet now that it's leaving my possession, I suddenly don't want to let it go. It might remind me of killing the High King, but it was bestowed on me by a good man for a good reason. I just hope he remembers that reason when we talk.

Somehow I doubt it.

***

'Over there, the woman. See the way she walks,' Lotane whispers quietly. 'That makes forty so far.'

We hunker down, and even though Lotane's face is next to mine, I can only see the whites of his eyes. We've blackened our faces with chimney soot, and as this is a cloudy night, we're all but invisible.

As far as the tavernkeep knows, we're still in our room, whereas instead, we're watching wolves in sheep's clothing, position themselves at either end of the street. No doubt there are just as many in the alley behind the tavern, ensuring we have no avenue of escape.

So far, things are going as planned.

Earlier, after following Arcan out of the library, I'd returned swiftly to the tavern, ensuring my entrance was observed. Upon making my way upstairs, I'd found Lotane waiting. There'd been little need for words. Food, weapons and equipment were laid out on a cloth in our room, and we'd quietly eaten together before fashioning harnesses for our weapons. Once ready, with the sun having set, we'd lit a dozen candles, closed the curtains, climbed onto the tavern roof via the rickety balcony and light-footed our way to the rooftop at the end of our street.

'Do you think they'll wait till midnight when they're invited to join us?'

Lotane's breath tickles my ear as he brings his lips close. Suddenly his hand grips my shoulder hard, and his finger goes to his lips, then his ear, before pointing to the rear of the building we're hiding on.

Silently we creep to the back wall and press ourselves into the corner where the shadows are darkest, listening to the footsteps on a balcony below. Lotane's finger taps on my thigh five times. He's right; there are five people.

A grappling hook loops over the small parapet with a clang, and I know Lotane is waiting for my decision. We could cut the rope or kill the first soldier to come up. No one would follow, for it would mean their death.

Yet, this is our best and possibly only chance to get to Farsil or Conrol.

As the first hooded figure clambers over, feminine, supple, and lithe, wearing tight, black clothing, I conjure a sharp wind, blowing dust and debris toward her, so there's no chance she'll turn our way. A heavy crossbow looms over her shoulder as she leans over the wall, helping four more figures up. All are armed with crossbows, a terrifying weapon in the right hands.

THE LAST HOPE

'Mariem, you take this roof.'

'Yes, Sergeant.'

No other words are spoken, which means they've either been thoroughly briefed or are a tight unit, used to working together.

Lotane and I remain silent, unmoving, while Mariem uses a windlass to draw back the string on her weapon. It's a laborious task, but a hand-drawn crossbow isn't as powerful, whereas these could stop a horse.

The other four soldiers hasten away over the rooftops. These pathways above the streets were once our safe haven, our uncontested and unseen route, but no longer. Yet this is our vantage point, and with the other archers gone, it's time to reclaim it.

Silently, fluidly, I move to my feet, ensuring the wind gusts a little more, disguising my footsteps on the gravelly rooftop, Lotane a few paces to my right. As I approach, the woman stops cranking the crossbow. An almost imperceptible tilt of her head reveals that she's either heard or sensed something, and her hand drops toward a dagger hilt.

'Mariem!' I call. She turns toward me, recognising her name but perhaps not my voice, and I'm relieved when her hand doesn't grasp her weapon. In that instant, Lotane acts, rising from a crouch, his strong arm wrapping around her throat, lifting, then falling back onto the rooftop. His legs wrap around, inhibiting her struggles as he cuts off her breathing. It's a dangerous moment, but fortunately, her hands instinctively go to her throat, not the dagger at her side. Had she grabbed the weapon and stabbed it backwards, she could have injured Lotane before consciousness left her.

Staying low, I pick up her fallen crossbow and begin cranking it, taking her place on the roof, looking carefully around. My nearest rooftop neighbour is five buildings to my left and, like me, is busy preparing his weapon. I can just make out the other three together on the roof of what I believe is our tavern. They'll attack from above as others attack from below. Suddenly, a shadowy figure rises on the roof terrace of the building opposite, also armed with a crossbow, and my blood freezes. Yet whoever it is simply sketches a salute. Relieved, I return the gesture and watch as more figures climb over the distant rooftops.

Damn. I hadn't foreseen this!

Lotane slithers over, staying low, a quiver of bolts in his hand, which I gratefully take. I've no intention of killing anyone, but I'll fight to survive.

'She'll be unconscious for a while. Even when she awakes, she'll be no trouble,' he whispers.

I continue looking around, becoming the vigilant sentinel Mariem would have been were she not tied up like a hog.

'There are more troops on the rooftops on the other side of the road,' I murmur. 'You need to take care of the one directly opposite.'

This isn't good. We'd discussed numerous possible scenarios, but not one where we'd split up and be unable to communicate for a while.

'Do I take their place or come back?'

'Come back, if you can.'

I receive a grunt in reply, and whilst I want to wish Lotane luck, or give him a hug, now isn't the time. He slithers off toward the back of the building.

Damn, damn, damn.

There's no sign of our targets, just more and more soldiers dressed as civilians filling the street below. It might be two hours before midnight, but this trap is almost ready to be sprung.

I pull a bolt, inspecting it in the near darkness. It has a wide, killing head, and upon checking the rest, they're all the same. It appears our capture is not on the menu. Slotting the bolt into the groove, I hunch down, resting the heavy weapon on the stone parapet.

Sighting down its length, I study the street below, noting that there are twice as many disguised soldiers as genuine civilians. Suddenly, I see Lotane, weaving across the end of the street, hunched low to conceal his height and frame, barely keeping his balance as though drunk.

A few people glance his way but shake their heads in disgust before he disappears from view.

Then I notice a tidal shift in movement as the civilians are escorted from the street or told to go inside. There's no noise nor fuss I'd have expected from people being ordered about; I'm impressed.

It won't be long now. Any chance of collateral damage has been removed, and all the pieces of the trap are in place ... except for one. The one who will set it in motion. I swing my weapon slowly, noting a group of fifteen disguised soldiers on the opposite side of the road to the tavern, milling around a horse and cart. The armed men on the roof are the hammer, and these are the anvil.

Stealthy movement grabs my attention, and I catch sight of a dark shadow as Lotane eases his way onto the roof terrace opposite.

I cough loudly, knowing that this unprofessional breach will gain the attention of the crossbowman he's approaching. I raise my hand in apology and see the crouched figure shake his head in disgust just before Lotane's shadow covers him like a blanket. There's a loud twang as Lotane's victim squeezes the trigger of his weapon, and the bolt hisses overhead.

My heart thumps in my chest as I expect shouts to erupt at any moment, but for once, the gods of luck are smiling; no one seems to have noticed.

I continue to survey the streets and rooftops, yet my eyes always go back to where Lotane and his target have disappeared. Then, a crossbow appears, resting on the parapet, and a figure flops into sight to fall forward over the weapon as if sighting along its length.

It's a creative act. A missing sentry would draw immediate attention. To a casual observer, everything will appear fine.

A flare of light draws my attention to the end of the street below me. Three individuals are standing there, and my interest is piqued. One is a solidly built man wearing simple black trousers, boots, a white shirt and a dark, wide-brimmed hat. Frustratingly I can't see his face. Could it be either Conrol or Farsil?

Another man stands by his side, one hand tucked inside a robe, perhaps holding the hilt of a weapon. His head is constantly moving, alert for trouble.

The final one is a woman with long braided hair who has unshuttered the lantern that caught my eye. This street has several well-placed lamps, so it stands out as odd. She begins walking down the street, gently swinging it back and forth. As she moves, the disguised soldiers move with her like a wave, leaving just the two men who'd kept her company standing on their own.

She is like a tripwire.

Once she reaches the wagon, the trap will be sprung.

My eyes flick back to the two men. If the one under the hat is Farsil or Conrol, then now is the time, but if they aren't, then my mission is doomed.

Lotane staggers across the street behind them. He's procured a bottle from somewhere, and he sloshes liquid onto the cobbled streets. He bumps into a lamppost, then, to my horror, starts to relieve himself while singing something unrecognisable.

The two men flash him a look but return their attention to the lantern bearer, who is almost at the wagon.

Why the hell had Lotane done that?

I realise why. He must know who is under the hat and is playing for time, waiting for the trap to spring. Once the soldiers run shouting into the tavern, he'll make his move when everyone is distracted.

It won't be long now, but then further sudden movement meets my eye.

The crossbowman on the parapet opposite must have come around, for his weapon is wobbling, twisting back and forward as he tries to free himself. Then, the unthinkable happens. Almost as if in slow motion, it topples, balances for a split second on the parapet's edge, then tumbles end over end toward the street below.

NO!

I whip my weapon around, hold my breath, then exhale as I squeeze the trigger at precisely the same time as the dropped crossbow crashes loudly into the street below, alerting the two men.

The stock jolts against my shoulder, and then I fling it aside as I rise to my feet.

A whiny of terror and shouts of alarm shatter the stillness of the night as the lantern I'd shot on the back of the wagon sprays hot, burning oil everywhere. I don't pause to watch and charge across the rooftop, arms pumping.

Below, Lotane makes his move toward the two men. I see them all drawing weapons, and my heart sinks. We've no time for a fight. The distraction of the burning oil won't last much more than a minute, and I can only hope that the dozens of soldiers are storming the tavern and not running up the street.

I leap.

I'm three stories up, and Lotane and the others are twenty paces away, squaring off in the middle of a junction, weapons extended.

Even as I plummet toward them, I draw my sword and dagger. I'll have but one chance. My heart, which had been beating furiously, calms to a steady rhythm, conditioning kicks in, and everything slows.

Just before I hit the ground and break every bone in my body, my magic responds, slowing me dramatically. Unseen, from behind, I smack the sword pommel hard against the head of the man in the hat. As his legs are folding, I bring the dagger's edge up under the other man's chin.

He freezes, letting go of his sword, death but a gentle slice away.

I stand back quickly as Lotane fells him with a ferocious right hook, catching the man's body before his head smacks on the ground.

Then Lotane has the hatted man over his shoulder, and we're running for a dark alley as if the demons of hell are after us.

***

'Finished,' I say, exhausted.

We're in a cellar a couple of streets from where we'd kidnapped Major Conrol. Unquestionably, a search will shortly be underway for us if it hasn't started already, but we'd made it here unseen and without further incident.

I step back, casting a critical eye over the stone wall that has replaced the flimsy wooden entrance door we'd torn off of its hinges. If any searchers come across the steps leading down here, they'll encounter a rock wall at the bottom as if the cellar was never excavated.

Above us is an empty storeroom and I'm confident we won't be disturbed any time soon.

Major Conrol is blindfolded, gagged, tied hand and foot and secured to a chair that I've sunken slightly into the stone floor. It's more for the major's safety in case he struggles so it won't tip over. It's unlikely he'll be grateful even if he knew.

Two lanterns provide light, set upon a table with only three legs. Lotane could have used his magic, but as I know only too well from using mine, it would have drained him unnecessarily. A bag with some provisions also sits on the table. Lotane had been very thorough in his preparation.

Until now, we'd had a plan, several in fact, and despite a few hiccups along the way, we are exactly where we want to be. The problem is, from hereon, I've no idea how things will turn out. This will be all unplanned, uncharted territory.

I nod to Lotane, who steps forward and gently removes the blindfold and gag.

'Major Conrol,' I say.

There's no response. His head remains lolled forward, with no sign of consciousness.

'Major Conrol.'

Again there's no response.

'Cut off his left ear!'

Lotane draws a dagger and takes hold of Conrol's ear.

There's a subtle flinch, a tell-tale sign that the major is awake and knows what's coming. The pulse in his neck flutters, making my own quicken.

I shake my head, and Lotane steps back, sheathing his weapon. I'd have never let him carry through with my threat, but I'd have been prepared to see some blood flow if it would stop this charade.

'Right, let's stop with the act now, shall we?'

Conrol's eyes snap open, and there's nothing but hatred within.

'YOU BLOODY BITCH,' he screams, 'I've dreamt every day and night of what I'd do to you when I found you …'

Lotane's palm lashes across Conrol's face with such force that it twists the man's head around. Conrol opens his mouth to say something again, but it doesn't even leave his lips before Lotane lands another ringing slap. Blood flows from Conrol's lip, and he groans slightly.

Inside I do the same. Every act of violence will lead to more hatred, and take us ever further from where we need to be.

I wait for his eyes to focus a little, to meet my gaze before I speak. I want him to understand I don't want him hurt, that this doesn't need to be this way.

'Apart from the lump on the back of your head and now a split lip, you're unharmed. Please help us keep it that way. If you raise your voice again, Lotane will dissuade you the same way as before. We only want to talk. Do you understand?'

'BURN IN HELL!' Conrol shouts.

Lotane hits him twice.

'They'll find you, and when they do, they'll kill you.' Conrol spits blood, but he at least talks softly this time. 'I only wish to be alive to see it, but I'll go happily to my grave knowing it's coming even if I don't!'

Conrol continues for a while. He's had a year of festering anger and resentment, and there's no point talking until he's got it out of his system. Eventually, he runs out of insults and threats, which are replaced by a look that still says everything.

It hurts to be the target of such hatred, such vitriol, and it's not even directed at Lotane in the slightest, just entirely at me. I wait a while, letting the silence grow, unsure now how to start, how to clear the air.

'I'm sorry.'

The words leave my lips without thought. No truer words have I ever spoken, but the mocking laughter that follows makes me wish I'd never uttered them.

'Sorry. Why? Because a whole country wants you dead. Save me the pigshit and just kill me. Come on, set me on fire, damn you. That's what this is all about. DO IT!'

'No,' I say, both in response to Lotane, who has raised his hand, and the major.

'When I sent Arcan to the castle, I told him I wanted to talk with you and Farsil. Was that not the message that was delivered?'

'This is the message that's been delivered,' Conrol spits, wriggling his restrained hands and feet.

'Your people had orders to kill us on sight, yet here you sit, alive. That should tell you something,' I growl softly.

'Only that you've made a big mistake in keeping me alive. You're stupider than you look, which is saying something!' Conrol hisses back before laughing bitterly.

'We are just here to talk,' I reassure him. 'After this, we'll let you go unharmed, save the few bumps you already have. Then, depending on what we agree, we'll either stay or be on our way.'

'If you let me live, you'd better run, and never stop, because I'll hunt you till the end of days!' promises Conrol, eyes bulging, fists clenching.

'And that brings us neatly to why we're here.' Lotane smiles sadly, hunching down before Conrol.

When Conrol doesn't speak, Lotane looks at me, but I just nod for him to continue. Everything I say just infuriates Conrol, but perhaps if Lotane speaks, Conrol might just hear some of what he says.

'We're here because the end of days *is* coming,' Lotane says sincerely. 'For all the wrong we've done, we're here to try and do something right.'

'Let's cut the crap, shall we?' Conrol snaps. His shoulders sag resignedly. 'You're here to do the same job you did so perfectly before.

Why else would you ask to meet Farsil, other than you're aware he's going to be made regent. NO, don't even attempt to deny it. I hate you, but I also respect how good you are, so afford me the same respect. You've played your hand to get Commander Farsil out of the citadel, but you've failed, and your ploy won't work again.

'However, there's something I have to know. After the assassination, the ssythlan prince was cut to pieces by guards before I could question him. Since then, no ssythlan army has appeared to take advantage nor allied with our enemies. So what did they hope to gain? Just tell me, and let me have peace, before you kill me.'

'Then be silent and listen to all I have to say,' Lotane says, sitting cross-legged on the floor at Conrol's feet. 'I have a long story to tell, and you must hear it all before I get to the end, where you'll learn what you want to know.'

***

I sit and listen to Lotane, helping myself to some food and water as he tells the tale, or at least what he knows of it. He starts from the very beginning when we were first auctioned. It will take longer, but I agree it's vital for Conrol to know how we've been conditioned and trained, that this has been a plan of years beyond measure.

The longer Lotane talks, the more I'm sure Conrol is playing for time, sitting and listening without believing a word, hoping we'll be discovered and perhaps him rescued. He controls his temper, not shouting nor struggling, just studying our every movement and gesture.

As Lotane's story continues, I detect the sound of distant voices and footsteps.

'Time for a break. Gag him.'

'I'M DOWN HERE. I'M ...'

Lotane renders Conrol unconscious with a swift blow to the chin and reinserts the gag.

We extinguish the lanterns and sit in the dark.

Heavy boots stomp around above, and dust showers into our small room as soldiers search the premises above us.

'Lean back into me,' Lotane whispers.

I do as instructed, and what would have been a harrowing time changes into a comforting one with Lotane's warm breath on my neck and his arms around my waist.

'They're being very thorough.'

Lotane's breath tickles.

'That's good,' I whisper back. 'They won't return unless they find something.'

I sigh contentedly. A part of me doesn't want the soldiers to move on, so we can stay like this a while longer. But even as the thought crosses my mind, the footsteps recede, leaving us undisturbed and undiscovered.

Lotane lights the lanterns again.

Conrol's eyes snap open, and if looks could kill, I'd be dead.

'Lotane. Continue, but leave the major's gag in place.'

I make myself comfortable and listen as Lotane resumes his story while Conrol remains gagged. After several hours I remove Conrol's gag and offer him a waterskin. From his disparaging look, I can tell he suspects there's something wrong with the water, so I have a gulp before offering it again. This time he accepts.

'You're wasting your time, and it seems so am I,' growls Conrol after a few gulps. 'That you're trained assassins is beyond doubt, that the ssythlans gifted you with magic, likewise. I also believe your tales about killing the other monarchs and generals. But the rest; to destabilise and prepare the world for the return of this Nogoth and his army of monsters. By the gods, I'd rather die from a knife between my ribs than listen to more of that pigshit. Have the guts to admit that you're here on a mission to kill our next regent, and it's for the money, not because some fictitious blood magic left you no choice!'

This was always going to be the trickiest part of our plan. I can't blame Conrol for disbelieving us. Knowing that Farsil will soon rule until a High King can be anointed, along with our request to meet, certainly looks like another assassination attempt. But I can't give up. I mustn't let the deaths of everyone who've died to get this story told be in vain.

I kneel down before Conrol, my eyes level with his, clasping my hands.

'You have to believe us. If the current war isn't stopped and the armies of the warring kingdoms united to face the invasion, everything you've ever known will cease to be, Conrol. What can I do to make you believe I'm telling the truth?' I plead. 'I need your help!'

Conrol spits in my face.

The warm saliva runs down my chin, and I stand up, wiping it away with my sleeve.

I'm shocked. To hold someone in such high regard as I do this man, to see him so changed, full of hatred, and to be the target of that terrible emotion, is hard to bear.

'GET IT INTO YOUR STUPID SKULL. I DON'T BELIEVE YOU, AND I WON'T HELP YOU!' Conrol roars, then, as Lotane raises a hand, he lowers his voice. 'Controlled by blood magic; rubbish. A fey invasion; rubbish. You here to help save the world; rubbish.'

I sit on the filthy floor, my back against the cold stone wall. The major's eyes continue to blaze with anger and hatred, but at least he's now silent. I remember a time when he looked upon me with affection and respect after I saved his life.

My hands shake a little. This had been our best hope, and I can't see how anything else will work. I doubt Farsil will believe me either, but ultimately, if he's going to be Regent, then he's the only one who has the power to act on this. How many lives will end if I don't find a way to make myself heard and believed?

'I need you to take me to Farsil. I'll ...'

'Never.' Conrol snaps.

'I will go as your captive ...'

'No!' This time, it's Lotane who interrupts.

'It isn't your decision! Now, be silent!'

The shock of my command has the desired effect, and Lotane refrains from saying anything else.

Looking Conrol in the eye, I hold his gaze, trying to project my sincerity.

'I will surrender to you if you promise to take me to Commander Farsil.'

Conrol laughs.

'Oh, how I wish I could have you in my hands, but I tell you this. I've seen what you can do, but I know there's a lot I haven't seen either. I'd be stupid to take you anywhere near him lest you use your magic. But I'll do you a favour. Surrender to me, and I'll snap your neck, nice and

THE LAST HOPE

quick. You won't even have time to scream, not like the High King. No. He took a long time to die, his flesh peeling away from his bones.'

'Perhaps I should break ...' Lotane begins to say, when everything fades away, his voice and Conrol's becoming mere echoes.

Conrol has already given me the answer to my problem several times, and it lies in his disbelief over how we've had so little control over our actions. On the one hand, he doesn't doubt our magical abilities but, on the other, disbelieves the power of blood magic, the subtlest but most potent of them all.

Do I have the power to bind Conrol to me, to have him obey me against his obvious will? So far, I've only used it to break the chains with which the Chosen and I were bound. The biggest question I have is one of morality. Do I have the right to try and take away Conrol's free will, to bind and coerce him into doing things he has no wish to do? Then, what if Farsil doesn't cooperate? Do I take away his free will too? Would these be the first small steps toward becoming something like Nogoth?

'Lotane. We need to talk.'

Rising, I take his hand, and after pausing at the stone wall to listen carefully, I open an entrance and lead Lotane outside.

'I don't want Conrol to know what's coming and perhaps find a way to fight against what I'm thinking of doing.'

'Which is?'

I look to the stars for some divine sign that this is the right thing to do. Nothing.

'Use Blood Magic to bind him to me.' I cringe, waiting for Lotane to say something, but he remains silent. 'I've no idea if I can, but, if successful, I can pretend to be his captive and have him escort me inside the citadel.'

'Taking away his free will doesn't sit well with me after what we've been through, and there must be a better plan than having Conrol lead you in the front gate as a captive. Have him fetch Farsil for us.'

'I'd thought of that too, but it's too risky. We had years of conditioning and a belief in what we were doing to reinforce our orders, and I've never done this before. If Conrol is outside of my sphere of influence and meets Farsil, it probably won't end well. We can't afford to gamble.'

'At least let me come along with you. If anything goes wrong, the two of us will have a better chance to escape.'

I laugh softly, taking Lotane's hands in mine.

'There'll be no chance to escape, whether it is just me or the both of us. If I fail, then you must join Kralgen. If anyone is to survive what's to come, it will be the Icelandians in their homelands.'

'But how will I know whether you succeed or not?' Lotane rests his forehead against mine, his breath warm on my face.

'A good point,' I concede, my hands going to Lotane's chest. 'If all goes well and Farsil not only lets me live but allows me my freedom, I'll have him run up an Icelandian flag above the castle. If you see that within the week, you'll find me at the bottom of the approach road the morning after it flies. If in that time you see nothing, then it's time to forget me and move on.'

'Forget you? How can I ever forget you?' Lotane murmurs, turning his face to brush his lips softly against mine.

As I surrender to the moment, Nogoth flashes into my mind, his violet eyes half-closed in pleasure.

'Not now!' I whisper, gently pulling away, although whether I'm talking to Lotane or the memory of Nogoth, I don't really know. 'Come, we shouldn't be out here any longer than we need to.'

Leading Lotane back inside, I seal the wall behind us. I'm tired. Using my magic has drained me, and I wonder if I'll have the strength to do what must be done.

Sitting beside Conrol on the filthy floor, I shift around, to get comfortable, then reach out, laying my hand on his knee.

Conrol remains still and silent. I hope he stays that way.

I enter a meditative state, controlling my breathing, and find the blood magic pulsating and throbbing. Its enthusiasm to help is tangible, and I feel a surge of hope.

Using my ethereal sight, I focus on Conrol, hearing the powerful beating of his heart, perceiving the resulting swoosh of blood as it rushes around his body. There's something slightly sensual about the sound that fills me with ... hunger, but I force the thought aside.

Bind us.

In response, a red, serpent-like thread extends from my body. I focus on Conrol and watch uneasily as the thread probes around his body. Then, like a striking snake, it wraps around his heart, joining us both. Our hearts regulate, beating at the same speed, yet beyond this, I feel nothing.

Perhaps the bond isn't strong enough.

'Bind us closer,' I demand, and the thread thickens to the width of my wrist. Again, I feel nothing other than the synergy of our heartbeat.

What else needs to be done? I remember severing all the threads that had bound me and the mantras I'd heard when doing so.

Yes, the bond itself isn't enough. There needs to be reason and direction.

Love. Obedience. Loyalty. Trust. Protection. Devotion.

These and more I project, willing Conrol to be bound to me. I take my time, repeating them over and over, putting down layer after layer of commands.

Is it too much? I don't know. Will it overwhelm him? I've no idea about that either. But to do too little will have this plan collapse like a wall of sand.

Opening my eyes, I find myself the object of attention. Both Lotane and Conrol's eyes are looking down on me. There's only one way to discover whether I've been successful. If only I wasn't so exhausted, for this is a dangerous moment.

'Release him.'

***

CHAPTER VIII

You will do nothing to harm me and everything in your power to protect me.'

My voice is steady and clear as Lotane steps forward to untie the bindings on the major's feet. I stand away, giving him some room.

'You will obey my every command, and everything and anything you do will be to further my goal to meet Commander Farsil. We'll leave here with me as your prisoner, and you'll escort me to the castle without raising suspicion. You'll only share your plans or concerns when we cannot be overheard. You're loyal to me, devoted to me, and will love me as your own blood. Do you understand?'

'I understand.'

'You will do as I ask?'

'I will do as you ask!'

There's no conflict in Conrol's face, no hint of anger, far from it. He looks upon me with wide eyes. There's no way he could have known what I was doing, so this can't be some ploy to gain my trust. My attempt to bind him has succeeded.

Lotane looks over as he unties Conrol's hands, and I nod reassuringly.

I ease myself upright before the major. He won't have forgotten anything, far from it, but the desire to do as I've commanded will be overwhelming. Even now, I'm sure he's justifying to himself that my story makes sense and how he was wrong to judge me so harshly.

Lotane raises his hands, the leather bindings hanging loosely between his fingers, before bending to untie the final restraints holding Conrol to the chair.

As they loosen, Conrol grabs Lotane around the neck with one arm while pulling Lotane's dagger free from its sheath. It's such a sudden, unexpected movement after his docility that it catches me off guard. The next moment the razored blade is pressed hard against Lotane's neck.

I can't believe the blood magic failed. Conrol looked so subdued!

'Time to watch your boyfriend die!'

'No! Don't hurt him!' I yell, dragging my sword free, knowing I'm too late and that Lotane won't be able to stop him either.

But there's no bloody spray, no gurgling, just a moment where incomprehension binds us together. The blood magic is working, and then it dawns on me that I'd only bound Conrol to myself and not said anything about Lotane. Yet even though Conrol had been poised for an opportunity to kill Lotane, the moment I'd shouted, he'd had no choice but to obey.

'Put the weapon down, release Lotane, and sit!'

I'm shaking inside. A simple oversight had almost cost Lotane his life.

Somewhat ashamed, Lotane recovers his weapon from the floor and moves away from Conrol, who sits back down.

'You must never hurt Lotane or do anything that might lead to his being hurt, punished, captured, or anything else that might upset me.' I pause, wondering whether I've covered everything, but the danger is over for now.

Have I missed anything else?

'How would you propose we enter the castle and for me to meet Commander Farsil without being killed?' I ask Conrol.

'Through the front gate. You should be bound, gagged and hooded. I'll take you to the cells and have the commander summoned by telling him you're in custody.'

'What could go wrong and get Malina killed?' Lotane asks.

Conrol says nothing.

'Answer him as you would me,' I sigh. If I had the strength, I'd bind Conrol to Lotane the way I did with myself, but I'm exhausted.

'It's possible Commander Farsil will kill Malina at first sight before I can stop him or just order her execution without bothering to see her. It could be perceived I'm acting unusually, or that it's suspicious I've captured her after being kidnapped and going missing. Both scenarios might lead to us being held and, ultimately, Malina's execution.'

'Damn. There are so many things that might go wrong, Malina. Let's find another way.'

Lotane's pleading eyes melt my heart, but it has to be done, and it has to be now.

'No.'

Taking Lotane's hand, I lead him to the wall, parting it with a wave. I sway, almost entirely drained of strength.

'Stay safe, my love. Just know that I love you.' I kiss Lotane tenderly on the mouth, ignoring the images of Nogoth that come to mind, welcoming the rush of pleasure irrespective of its source.

'I will see you soon, Alina,' he whispers as our lips part. 'Don't forget the flag of Icelandia. I'll be watching.'

Then, with a swirl of his robes, he leaps lightly up the wooden steps and is swallowed by the night.

Conrol is waiting patiently as I turn around, no hint of threat apparent. He raises an eyebrow expectantly, awaiting my order.

'It's time for us to pay Commander Farsil a visit.'

***

The darkness has always been my friend, a comforting blanket I can hide under while awaiting my prey. But never before was I helpless, as I am now.

My hands are bound securely behind my back, not just at the wrists but also at the upper arms. Leather straps secured around my ankles hinder my movement, restricting me to a shuffling gait. A blindfold is drawn tight, holding cloth pads in place that allow me to see absolutely nothing. To complete my misery, a gag pulls my lips back, stretching them painfully, and I can't utter an intelligible sound.

I'm disorientated, and the noise of the awakening city adds to my anxiety.

Major Conrol shoves me from behind, sending me stumbling forward, and I frantically catch my balance before the next push.

His pace is merciless as he takes me through the streets of High Delnor toward the citadel. Have I misread the level of control I have over him? Has he somehow managed to overcome the blood magic and reassert his will?

Suddenly, shouts of alarm begin to echo from the buildings around me, followed by the pounding of feet.

'He's got her. The Major's got her,' a booming voice shouts the news.

'Get a rope. Get a rope. String the bitch up!'

Dozens of people take up the shout, which quickly becomes a chant.

Rough hands grab me, kicks and punches land, and I'm about to fall when suddenly I hear several cries of pain, and the crowd goes deathly silent.

'There'll be no lynching here today,' Major Conrol's voice is loud and commanding. 'The next person to lay a hand on her will lose that hand. Mark my words!'

A sob of relief fights for release as his hand pushes me roughly forward.

'But the other one's still out there, So, don't stand about looking all sorry for yourselves. Go find him!'

With a roar and a pounding of feet, the small crowd disperses, and we continue.

Shove follows shove, and occasionally Conrol warns soldiers away who want to vent their anger on me.

'We're almost at the approach road,' Conrol mutters quietly. 'So far so good.'

He punctuates the sentence with another push, and I sense the gradient beneath my feet steepen.

It isn't long before we stop, and I sway, trying to calm my thoughts and breathing. If only I could enter a meditative trance, use my spirit eye to look around, and reorientate myself a little, this wouldn't be so bad.

'Welcome back, Major.'

'We feared the worse, Major!'

'Why haven't you followed the commander's explicit kill-on-sight order, Major?'

The last comment has me listening intently.

'Those were general orders. I was given my own, Captain.' Conrol replies. 'Now, make way. That's an order!'

'Sorry, Major. I can't. Not until I clear this with the commander.'

I hear a heavy sigh.

'What's the penalty for disobeying a direct order from a superior officer in time of war?' Conrol growls.

'Death, sir!' The captain responds.

'So, let's both consider the situation. You *think* I'm disobeying a direct order by bringing this prisoner in. If so, then I *might* face the death penalty despite returning from an important mission, which, as you can see, has been successful.

'Yet, there you are, consciously disobeying my direct order as witnessed by your fellow guards. Do you think this course of action will end well for you?'

'Sorry, Major. Have a good day, Major,' the captain concedes, and then we begin the long walk up to the citadel gates.

Every hundred steps or so, guards welcome the Major's return. He's so well-liked and respected. In contrast, every word in my direction has been full of spite and hate.

The gentle warmth of the morning sun is replaced by the cold shadow of the citadel's curtain wall as I'm pushed forward a final time.

'Welcome to your new home, King-Slayer,' Major Conrol grumbles.

More guards' voices are followed by hands patting me down, checking there's nothing concealed. I'd already divested myself of weapons, but the search is thorough, even probing the bindings over my injured ribs, causing me to flinch with pain.

'Major. Welcome back!'

'Sergeant.'

'Yes, Major?'

'Please send word to Commander Farsil that I have the King-Slayer in custody and will await him in the holding cells.'

'Sorry, Major. The Commander left orders that you're to attend him immediately in the planning room should you return. We can take your prisoner from here, although I don't understand why she's still alive. Why haven't you killed her?'

A brief silence follows.

'Sergeant. As to why she's alive, I've already had the conversation with every soldier I've met from the poor quarter to here, so excuse me if I'm a little tired of answering that. Of course, I'll attend the Commander; however, your guard takes precedent. I'll grab someone with a less important role to escort this vermin.'

The major's palm rests on my back, and I'm pushed forward.

THE LAST HOPE

The crunch of gravel and the feeling of space helps me visualise where I am. The killing ground between the curtain wall and the keep. I remember seeing the defensive siege engines on the beautiful green grass and the long avenue to the castle gates.

Voices sound in greeting, others in disbelief as the major hurries me along.

The solid stone now underfoot indicates we must be at the keep gates. The major's hand presses on my head, encouraging me to duck, and he pushes me through a low door.

My footsteps echo softly, and I recognise our location. We're walking through the killing maze just inside the castle entrance. The hum of distant voices and thump of booted steps indicate the palace is alive and breathing with activity despite the early hour.

After so much aggressive shoving, the major guides me gently for a few minutes before we halt.

'There's no advantage in you remaining bound now,' Conrol says.

The next moment, my restraints are removed, followed by the gag and blindfold.

I look around, not recognising our location, massaging my limbs, waiting for my eyes to adjust to the light.

'The commander won't come to us, so we'll have to go to him,' Conrol says in a hushed voice. 'The main stairwell is beyond that door opposite. Four levels above us, at the top of the steps, will be a long corridor, at the end of which is the planning room. It will be barred from the inside. There will be guards at the entrance, and we'll have to kill them. Once they're dead, I can get the commander to open up.'

'No. There mustn't be any killing.' I place my hand on Conrol's forearm, looking him in the eye. 'I want you to know that I'm not here to harm anyone, including Commander Farsil. I wish you could believe me without being under my influence.'

Conrol looks confused, not understanding my meaning.

'They'll be veterans and too heavily armoured to subdue. What other choice is there?'

'A diversion. If you can get their attention and have them move away, even for a few moments, I can get through without the chamber door being opened.'

'But how can I protect you if I'm not next to you?'

'I'll be fine.'

The words ring hollow in my ears. I feel like I need a week's sleep.

Major Conrol pulls my hood up, then steps back, shaking his head.

'No one wears black robes, and you're instantly recognisable if someone sees your face. You'll be killed on sight from hereon. I'll do what I can, but ...'

I raise my hand, forestalling any more conversation.

'Then we must stay out of sight. But understand this. You won't kill to protect me. That's an order. Do you understand?'

A reluctant nod is all I receive in return.

'Lead the way, and let's hope we're lucky.'

Major Conrol opens the door without hesitation, and a buzz of conversation fills the air. Beyond is a wide passageway, a floor of polished stone tiles with ornamental columns lining the walls. Several people walk by deep in conversation without looking in our direction. Conrol steps forward and raises a hand as unseen people call out in greeting.

Smiling brightly, he strides across the corridor, then pauses briefly at the stairwell to adjust a bootstrap on the first step. Casting a glance left and right, he beckons me to follow, and I walk casually, keeping my head down.

There's no change in the flow of noise, no sudden fluctuation to indicate alarm, and with relief, I tread lightly up the winding stairs. My fingers trace the fashioned stone, finding subtle imperfections. In the Mountain of Souls, a haven of evil, the rock had felt alive, full of elemental power. Yet here, the stone, fashioned by human hands, is almost devoid of life.

Approaching voices and footsteps from above warn us of impending jeopardy. Major Conrol quickly pulls me into an alcove in the wall to allow them to pass.

'Put your arms around me,' he says quietly, enfolding me in an embrace, dropping his head down as if we're kissing. His heart thuds powerfully, and I'm fixated on the accompanying pulse in his neck.

I hear a woman chuckle at something a man says. Several more ribald comments are made, and Conrol laughs, looking over his shoulder.

'Rank hath its privileges,' he says before turning back as we wait for the group to pass.

Then, as they disappear down the steps, we're off again, passing two more landings before we pause just below the final one.

The major risks a glance around the corner and invites me to do the same.

It's like many of this castle's hallways; broad, with decorative columns that support the roof. Colourful stained glass windows with martial scenes paint a rainbow of light across the scene. Two guards in plate armour stand either side of the door facing each other. Thankfully they wear full-faced helms, so their view is restricted.

The major tousles his hair, making it look wild and unkempt. With his somewhat reddened and bruised face, he doesn't look at his best.

'I'll distract them,' he whispers. 'Use the columns along the left side to conceal your approach when I do.'

Moaning loudly, he puts a hand to his chest and then staggers up the last few steps, leaning briefly against the wall, gasping for breath before staggering to the far side of the hallway where he supports himself against a window ledge.

'I'm not feeling too good, lads. Lend me a hand, will you?' he grimaces in pain, then with a groan, sags to the floor.

The two guards come running into view. As they kneel over Conrol, I'm up the last couple of steps, moving swiftly and silently along the left side of the corridor. Major Conrol grasps their shoulders firmly in thanks, ensuring their focus remains on him.

The thick oak door is closed and supposedly locked from the inside, so I don't waste time trying to open it. Placing my hands against the cool stone, I sweep them aside and the stone parts, allowing me to step through into the chamber beyond. With a wave of my hands, it returns to its previous form, sealing me in.

I've made it.

Commander Farsil is on the far side, hunched over a huge map table. The problem is, alongside him, equally engaged, are three armed officers.

***

I hide behind a pillar, considering my next move.

The moment I announce my presence, two things are likely to happen. They'll try to kill me, or try to escape, perhaps both. Farsil escaping before I can make my case will be a disaster, which means sealing the room thus prompting a fight.

Looking at the door, I'm relieved to see a large key in the lock and wriggle it free. There are no exits other than through the windows, and being so high, that way won't end well for anyone except perhaps me.

The planning chamber is circular and fairly large, perhaps fifteen paces across. Wooden cases filled with scrolls intermittently line the walls, and detailed maps fill the spaces in between. Leaded windows make up the far side of the chamber, and the room reminds me a captain's quarters on a ship. There's even a large telescope on a tripod pointing northward over the city.

'Our forces are struggling against a Surian attack in the northeast,' a grizzled officer says, moving some carved pieces on the table. 'We've suffered five hundred casualties in the last few days, but reinforcements are already on the way.'

'The Rolantrians are pushing hard too,' says another. 'Our whole eastern flank is shaky. If we don't subdue the Hastians and Tarsians within the next month to free up some troops, we're in serious trouble.'

'The problem is, the Tarsians and Hastians know we're in trouble and won't capitulate,' growls Farsil,' slamming his fist down on the table. 'We are being bled dry on too long a front. However, to counter that, we've levied another five thousand civilians from the lands around Southnor. They're going through training and will be with us in about five weeks. When they arrive, we'll set up defensive works to the south, here, here and here,' he says, placing figures on the map. 'We'll pull our armies out of Tars and Hastia, then bring our full force to bear on Rolantria before heading north and dealing with Suria. There'll be no quarter, with those who stand against us put to the sword. May the gods forgive me, but diplomacy has failed without our High King, and this war will only end when rivers run red with blood.'

Murmurs of agreement meet Farsil's words from the officers.

I can't put the moment off any longer. The guards outside might announce Major Conrol, and the more bodies in this room, the more likely people will die.

'It's not the south or the east flank that should concern you,' I begin, watching the shock, fear, and hatred appear on the four faces that turn toward the sound of my voice. 'Nor is it me!' I raise my hands, palms showing. 'I'm unarmed, and I come here with no ill intent, or you'd be dead already!'

'Stay back,' I warn as the officers position themselves in front of Farsil.

One, a willow-lean woman, holds two short daggers in her hands, eyes shining with intensity. The two others, grey-haired men, are all wiry muscles covered in white scars with short swords held confidently in their right hands. The woman is the most dangerous of the three; I recognise that immediately, although there is of course, Farsil. No worry or concern is etched on his features, just a calm composure, his confidence built upon years of knowing only victory.

'Kill her!' Farsil commands, and the three sweep forward as he shouts for the guards outside.

The woman advances to my right around the pillar, daggers weaving, looking to quickly close the distance. Her footwork and balance are exemplary, and she's evidently a deadly opponent. The two men go left. Whoever I face leaves my back to the others.

Reaching left, I yank at a tall wooden map case against the wall. It topples, throwing scrolls to the floor, momentarily hindering the two men. As the woman runs at me, I thrust out with both palms. A blast of air plucks her up and throws her across the room to slam into a pillar. She hits with a thud and crumples to the floor, moaning.

'There's no need for this,' I say, spinning around to face the other two men, who leap over the toppled case and scrolls. They approach cautiously, swords extended. To my right, Farsil draws his sword and dagger, then circles, trying to get behind me.

'I'm here to warn you of a far bigger threat than you can ever imagine,' I yell, backing further away before running into the centre of the room so I can see my remaining three opponents.

There's hammering on the door, but the lock holds, and I have the only key.

'If I wanted you dead, you'd all be smoking ashes on the floor right now,' I growl, and my hands erupt in flames. I'm tired, and using my magic isn't helping. I can't afford to keep using it, but this fight has to stop. Unfortunately, my display has the opposite effect.

With a war cry, Farsil leaps forward, and the two men follow his lead. Vaulting onto the map table, I kick a heavy wooden figure of a swordsman into the face of the officer furthest to my left, who stumbles back, blood running into his eyes from a gash above his brow. Farsil and the other officer swing for my legs, and I leap back off the table to land near the window.

Despite his age, the officer gets around the table first, aiming a lightning-fast thrust at my chest. I twist left behind the telescope's tripod then right as he lunges around the other side, trying to get me again. Grabbing the telescope's eyepiece, I swing it viciously, and the heavy brass end catches him square in the temple, and he crumples to the ground.

I roll to the right, Farsil's blade whispering by as it slices through the space I was just standing in, and come to my feet holding the officer's short sword.

Backing away, I keep my sword extended as Farsil advances, murder in his eyes.

The hammering on the door gets louder, and it splinters under a rain of heavy blows.

Farsil's eyes flick to my right, and I spin, blocking a weak cut from the officer with the gashed forehead. Farsil launches his own attack simultaneously, and I'm not quite quick enough to entirely deflect his blow. His sword blade scrapes my hip, and I cry out.

I twist away, favouring my right leg, and as the officer swings again for my head, I duck under his blow and slam an uppercut into his jaw, sending him crashing to the ground. I sweep up his sword and spin to face Farsil.

'Can't you see I'm not here to kill you?' I gasp through gritted teeth as I deflect blow after blow from Farsil's blade. He's extraordinarily fast, and I realise it won't be long before one of his attacks land, even if I'm his better.

I stay on the defensive, not making any attacks of my own.

'The king I used to serve is launching an invasion in less than ten weeks. I'm here to warn you, share his plans, and give the world a chance!' I slam my second blade into the map. 'That's where the enemy will amass!'

'Like you gave the High King a chance,' snarls Farsil, a mighty swing punctuating his words. I skip back rather than parry it.

He glances at the map, a sure sign he's intrigued.

'Pine Hold, in case you're wondering.'

The door to the chamber finally gives way, and Major Conrol charges in, sword in hand. Of the guards, there's no sign. He stands warily, sword half raised, eyes sweeping back and forth between Farsil and me.

I step back further and toss my remaining sword onto the table, once again opening my arms wide, unarmed.

'Please just listen. I was blinded by lies and magic the last time we met, bound to an evil king who I believed was a champion of justice. By his order, I committed a terrible act on an undeserving victim, but if there's one positive of that heinous deed, it was that my guilt indirectly led me to discover the truth.

'You need to understand that my assassination of the High King, combined with dozens of others, was part of a bigger plan to keep the world at war, and so pave the way for an invasion of a type not seen for a thousand years.

'Unknowingly, I served Nogoth, the Fey King himself. His armies are going to pour out of Pine Hold in an unstoppable flood and end civilisation as we know it. Already a force of about six hundred ssythlans are there to welcome him. Please believe me!'

Farsil looks from me to the map. I can sense his confusion, but there's something else, although what, I'm not sure.

I kneel in fealty as Major Conrol approaches, pausing to check on the comatose victims. None should be dead, although the headaches they experience might have them wish otherwise.

'No sin-hawks have arrived from Pine Hold or Sea Hold in over a week. Is it coincidence?' Farsil mutters.

My hopes blossom. He believes!

'What now, Commander?' I ask.

'Major Conrol,' Farsil says, somewhat distracted as he bends over the map.

'Yes, Commander,' Conrol answers, just behind me.

'Kill this assassin.'

Damn!

***

Despite Conrol having obeyed my every order since binding him to me, I tense, anticipating the excruciating bite of a lethal sword thrust, yet thankfully it doesn't come.

'No, Commander.'

Pain and regret are evident in Major Conrol's voice, but one thing there definitely isn't, is uncertainty. The disbelief on Farsil's face might be funny were it not for the circumstances. I imagine he's wondering whether he's been misheard or somehow didn't utter the words he thought he spoke.

'Kill her, MAJOR!'

'No, Commander. I will not!'

Farsil raises his sword, stepping forward, and Major Conrol responds in kind, positioning himself before me.

'What are you doing, old friend?' Farsil asks, lowering the tip of his blade, confusion and hurt evident. 'Have you been injured? That's the King-Slayer. You limped for half a year and every day swore to kill her for what she's done. Please, stand aside, Dimitar.'

It's the only time I've heard the major's first name, which shows how close these two men are.

'She's surrendered. Would you be a murderer, like her?' Major Conrol pleads my case.

'You left here yesterday burning for revenge, but today you're protecting her. What kind of dark magic is this?'

'There's nothing here but right and wrong. What Malina did was wrong, but then what you're about to do is wrong too. You have to hear her out, for her crime pales in comparison to the good she's trying to do. You *will* hear her story, or else!'

Seeing such firm friends at the cusp of spilling one another's blood is awful and entirely my fault. If I don't intervene and Farsil attacks, the major will defend me, and at least one of them will die.

'STOP, the both of you!' My voice echoes around the chamber. 'Magic is responsible for the Major's change of heart. He's still your friend, still loyal to you and Delnor, but he's bound by magic to protect and obey me. Were I to order him to kill you, he'd do so. It would break his heart, but he'd have no choice. Knowing that, would you then hold him to blame?'

Major Conrol looks at me nonplussed while Commander Farsil's face whitens with rage.

'Of course not. Because if what you say is true, then it would be your fault and yours alone. No blame would attach to Dimitar.'

'Then answer me this. If I was bound by magic when I killed the High King, was the fault mine or that of the beast who controlled me?'

A long silence follows as Farsil considers my words. I cast my eye around the room, ensuring that no one is recovering enough to surprise me. I can only imagine the two guards outside must have been subdued by the major before he broke in.

My hopes begin to rise. Farsil's rage is being subdued by logic. He was always a fair man, and now his blood has cooled, a sense of that is returning.

'Don't seek to have me forgive you for your deed.' Farsil sighs, lowering his sword. 'That I'm not sure I could ever do.'

'I am not asking you to forgive or forget my deed, Commander. I'm asking you to listen and believe me.'

'But how do I know that your magic won't compel me to do your will as it has the major?'

'Do you still hate and want to kill me?'

'Yes!'

'Then evidently you're not bound to me.'

Commander Farsil nods slowly, then looks at the major.

'I will listen to you on one condition. You release Dimitar from whatever control you have over him. I want my friend back!'

My response is immediate.

'I agree. However, I have a condition of my own.'

'What is it?' growls Farsil. His knuckles white from gripping the hilt of his sword. The potential of death still hangs heavy in the air. Once I release Conrol, there's every chance they'll both seek to kill me ... unless I bind them, not with magic, but with something equally as strong.

Honour.

'It isn't that I don't trust you,' I say guardedly, 'but I've no wish to die here by design or accident. So I'll call on you to honour the King's Favour I'm owed. I want a pardon for Lotane and me.'

'You dare to call on the favour bestowed by the very king you killed!' Farsil splutters with rage.

But there's also a hint of panic in his eye. His strength of honour and duty is also his weakness.

I've got him.

***

CHAPTER IX

It all sounds so far-fetched. I'm sure torture would get the truth from her.' Major Conrol glares at me, back to his usual self. 'Even if she isn't here to kill you, she's still working for the enemy or personal gain.'

I sigh, looking at Farsil for support, but there isn't much empathy there. It would have been so much easier to abuse my power and take control over the minds of everyone, one by one. It's an alluring thought, and I can understand why Nogoth had taken this route. Undying loyalty, instant obedience, and unquestioning belief from everyone around you would make things so simple.

I push the tempting thought aside. I need to overcome the prejudices brought about by my actions, not whine about them.

'If that were the case, we'd be doing her every bidding, not arguing with her, and certainly not entertaining the thought of torturing her,' Farsil says, putting his hand on Conrol's shoulder. 'On a grander scale, our current war is because erstwhile allies became enemies. The High King always wanted them to become allies again. This is how we must view our situation with these two, however painful that may be.'

The major grunts, reluctantly acceding the point. Since I'd severed the magical bond between us, his rage, which had initially been incandescent, is just below boiling point. He bends to pick up a wooden troop marker off the floor, a leftover victim of yesterday's fight. His knuckles whiten as he squeezes it. I know he imagines it's me in his grasp.

THE LAST HOPE

The planning room has been tidied, but there are still a few visible scars of what occurred. It's been a whole day since Lotane and I were pardoned and he was brought in under escort after the Icelandian flag was run up on the citadel's flagpoles. The incredulous looks we continue to receive as we walk around unrestrained would be amusing if they weren't so swiftly followed by scowls of anger and hatred. Some people even make a sign to avert evil when they see us. We may have been pardoned, but that doesn't mean we're safe.

In addition to Lotane, Farsil and Conrol, three others are in the room. One is the woman who'd attacked me with the daggers. Syrila, the Head of Delnor's Military Intelligence, a spy recently promoted from operational work to manage Delnor's agents. She has a stern face, long wavy brown hair and a figure as toned as any Chosen. She reminds me of Lystra.

The next, Ardlan, a man I haven't seen before, looks like he'd slit someone's throat for a tankard of ale. He has a captain's insignia on the shoulders and chest of his battered but repaired cuirass. His weapons look as worn as he does, suggesting he's a man of action over words. Yet, there's also a twinkle in his eye, so he might not be as dour as it first seems.

Finally, there's Admiral Destern, a High Delnorian of noble birth in the worst sense of the word. He might be good at his job, but he sneers down his nose at everyone, and I've been tempted to smash his teeth in several times over his scoffing laughter. I've seen Lotane restrain himself more often than me.

I pick up a goblet of water and, out of habit, scent it for poison. I'm tempted to laugh, as now, more than ever, we might find ourselves the victim of such a ploy. I take a mouthful, then offer it to Lotane, who gratefully accepts.

I'm still thirsty and hungry to boot. The last two hours have felt like an interrogation despite not being chained or tortured. Often the questions are repeated in a different form. Perhaps Farsil, Conrol or the other three hope we'll trip up, revealing an inconsistency that proves we're lying, thus giving them a reason to go back on our deal.

Yet the time for lies is behind us. Or perhaps not entirely. Firstly, we haven't said a word about Kralgen's mission to Icelandia, and secondly, how can I reveal to anyone my relationship with Nogoth? It will damn me forever.

Farsil lets out a huge sigh and silently looks out over the city, pondering over everything we've said. After what seems an eternity, he turns back, fixing his three military advisors with his gaze.

'I might soon be Regent, and the decision is mine to make, but I want your thoughts solely on what Malina has told us.

'In summary, she believes a fey invasion is imminent and will come from Pine Hold, which according to her, is already under ssythlan control. Her advice is to not only recall all of Delnor's armies from the front lines but, having told our erstwhile enemies of the forthcoming fey invasion, invite them here as allies. This while we redirect some of our forces to the Elder Mountains leaving High Delnor undermanned.

'As we know, there's been no communication from Pine Hold or Sea Hold for two weeks, lending some legitimacy to the claim that something untoward has happened there. There's also no disputing that Malina and Lotane are magic users, as we've witnessed their escape using mirrors in times past. So if we know they can travel magically between kingdoms, then maybe an army can travel between worlds.

'Finally, they risked almost certain death to bring this story to us without, as far as I know, killing anyone. This could be considered a selfless act if, indeed, their motives are pure.

'Major Conrol, you first.'

The Major's face is twisted with suppressed anger as his dark stare sweeps around the room.

'To me, it's obvious. Sending a large force west to delay a fictitious army of mythical beasts whilst inviting our enemies onto Delnorian lands would be stupid beyond belief and will lead to our inevitable defeat. The tales of ssythlans are nothing but bait. In summary, these two assassins are trying to sabotage our war effort with their tales. We should judge them on what we actually know to be true. They killed the High King. They should be immediately executed, pardon be damned!' He glares at me as if to slay me with his words.

'Syrila.'

'I have dealt in lies and misdirection my whole life,' she begins. 'Never have I witnessed such a sublime and deadly deception as that played by Malina when she last walked these halls. I agree we can't send an army based on the spurious tales of these two. However, I can hear a lie in a person's voice or see it in their eyes, and I cannot detect one in theirs. So I think they believe they're telling the truth and are probably carrying out a further mission without realising it.' She drums her fingers on the map table. 'I side with the Major on this, especially the part about them being executed!'

Conrol looks at me triumphantly, and my hopes sink.

'Enough of the execution talk. They've been pardoned,' Farsil warns.

I only wish his voice held more conviction.

'Ardlan?'

'Gah. What do I know? I just get pointed in one direction and kill people. I don't do the pointing!'

Farsil's stare demands more of him.

'Alright. I agree with the others about the stupidity of following Malina's advice, nor do I believe all the foolery about fey monsters. However, we often wondered what the ssythlans were up to after the assassination, so perhaps this is it. Irrespective, wouldn't we still investigate Pine Hold and Sea Hold going silent even if Malina hadn't come forward?'

'Destern.'

Admiral Destern looks at Lotane and me down his nose. His customary sneer, which I'm sure he perfected in front of a mirror, is plain to see.

'What we have here are two uneducated peasants turned cutthroats responsible for our king's death. Despite her claiming the King's Favour, I'd still have them dancing at the end of a rope for their crimes. As for their children's stories of a fey army, I've heard more believable tales from a drunken sailor in a ship's mess.

'Regarding Pine Hold and Sea Hold, towns often go silent, mostly when falling behind with tithes or levies. They'll reach out when they're ready. We need to concentrate on the southern and eastern fronts and put the plan we'd recently agreed swiftly into action.'

With a snide look at Lotane and me, Destern switches to High Delnorian.

'I suggest if you don't want me competing for the Regency, commander, you ignore this simpleton and his little whore's tale!'

Barely has the final word left Destern's lips, than Lotane punches him full in the mouth. The admiral is catapulted off his feet to slide along the floor. My gods, if Lotane has killed him with that punch ...

Syrila's daggers are in her hand in the blink of an eye, and Ardlan is only a heartbeat slower in drawing a shortsword as they turn to face Lotane. Major Conrol looks gleeful as he advances, sword extended.

Lotane and I are unarmed, and as we back away, I'm ready to unleash my magic.

'SHEATHE YOUR WEAPONS,' Farsil booms.

He puts his fingers on Destern's neck before returning to the table to grab a water pitcher.

'I told you to sheathe them,' he growls, emptying the water onto Destern's face.

'That preening idiot,' he points, 'deserved what he got. He called Malina a little whore, thinking no one would understand what was said other than me.'

The admiral comes around spluttering, murder in his eyes and blood flowing freely from his mouth and nose. His hand goes to his sword as he clambers unsteadily to his feet.

'Think twice before you draw that,' Farsil looks at him with disapproval. 'Because if you demand blood to restore your honour, I'll have you duel Lotane, and I've a feeling that won't end well for you!'

'You dare take the side of an assassin!' The admiral shrieks in disbelief.

'I take the side of a man whose woman you disrespected right in front of him. It appears our guests understand High Delnorian quite well. Maybe they're not the uneducated peasants you deem them to be! You've made your opinion heard, now get out and clean yourself up!'

As the admiral leaves the room, Farsil turns furiously on Lotane.

'Hit an officer again, and you will be dancing at the end of a rope. Do you understand?'

'Yes, Commander!' Lotane barks, standing straight, eyes staring ahead.

Farsil snorts in frustration.

We wait silently as Farsil bends over the map, looking at the wooden pieces denoting Delnorian and enemy troops. Then he turns to gaze out of the leaded windows. He leans on one of the many beautiful statues adorning the room as if it were an old friend.

When he turns back, the look on his face isn't promising.

'I've come to a decision,' he announces, and everyone unconsciously leans forward. 'The story Malina and Lotane have weaved is beyond belief ...' He raises his hand, stopping the protest that's about to leave my lips. 'We're in the middle of a war that hangs in the balance, and we can't afford to be distracted ...'

'Yes!' Conrol agrees, slamming his fist onto the map table.

Farsil's disapproving gaze stops the Major from celebrating further.

'As I was saying,' Farsil continues. 'We can't afford to be distracted. Arcan, High Delnor's head librarian, has found no reference to any catastrophic invasion that almost destroyed civilisation, nor have our astronomers sighted a black moon. Without anything to validate Malina's tale, I can only conclude there's no immortal king impervious to weapons leading an army of monsters hellbent on our destruction.'

'Couldn't have put it better,' Syrila chuckles.

'Agreed,' Conrol murmurs.

Farsil pauses a moment.

'I also ask myself if this news were brought to me by a different messenger, would I have a different perspective, unsullied by historic events. The answer is still no.'

'Four of my friends died so we could bring you this news,' Lotane snaps, his fists clenched with restrained anger. 'You have to believe us!'

'And one of mine burned to death at the hands of the one who stands alive beside you,' Farsil shouts, eyes burning with rage. 'Just because she's claimed the King's Favour doesn't mean both your acts are forgotten or forgiven nor that you'll be automatically believed!'

Major Conrol's smug look slips as Farsil sighs and utters one word.

'However.'

Farsil fingers drum on the map table as he bites his lip, then shakes his head like a wolf tearing at its prey.

'The silence of Pine Hold and Sea Hold needs to be investigated. The western provinces are pivotal to our war effort, and their supplies must continue to arrive unchecked. We cannot afford to divert any of our regular troops away from the front line, but there are those whose presence can be spared ...'

Ardlan grimaces.

'I wondered why I was here. Well, my lot need something to do, or they'll be back to causing trouble before you know it.'

Upon seeing my look of confusion, Farsil smiles coldly.

'Ardlan's unit is the Last Hope. The day after tomorrow, they'll head east to investigate Pine Hold and your claims of a small ssythlan force. It's only fitting, Malina, that you accompany them because, just like you, they're murderers and thieves given a second chance instead of the gallows! However, if your tale turns out to be untrue, your chance will be lost. The pardon won't save you from the executioner's axe!'

Major Conrol looks happy again.

'How dare you threaten Malina!'

Lotane's muscles bunch, but Farsil isn't deterred, and before Lotane can say anything more, the Commander slams his fist on the table.

'I dare because, in this land, I'm the law. I dare because I could still have you and Malina locked up and throw away the key despite pardoning your deeds. However, this way, I can justly execute you both if it turns out you're deceiving me again, and that's definitely worth sending a few hundred men to Pine Hold to find out. So, Malina will head west, and you, Lotane, will remain here, never far from my justice!'

I can tell Lotane's anger is on the verge of boiling over. If that happens, dead bodies will be everywhere, which would be a disaster. So I put my hand on his arm, squeeze it hard, and lead him from the table.

Lotane leans in conspiratorially.

'If they don't believe us, we should get out of here and go to Hastia, Rolantria and every other kingdom to make them believe us instead,' he says intently.

I shake my head.

'We'll be met with disbelief and steel wherever we go, my love. It has to start here, because if Delnor leads, the other kingdoms just might follow. You know it in your heart; there's no other way. If these demands are what it takes for us to survive and for the truth to come out, then so be it. We've never turned away from adversity before. Let's not start now.'

'But you're not going with near enough troops. They'll be massacred and achieve nothing.'

'If it gets our story believed, it will have achieved everything. Even late is better than not at all.'

Our eyes meet, and the trust that exists between us guides Lotane's decision.

'As you wish,' Lotane responds, and the moment of danger is past.

We return to the others as Conrol grabs Farsil's shoulders.

'Don't you see! This is exactly what *they* want!' He points at Lotane and me. 'This is all part of their plan, causing us to divert resources and soldiers ...'

I feel sympathy for the Major. He was once such a jovial character, yet that must have all been burnt away when the king went up in flames beside him.

'Hush, Dimitar,' Farsil says softly, his arm wrapping around Conrol's shoulders. 'This is exactly what *I* want. Yet that's not all. I want you to go too, for I trust no one more than you. Be my eyes and ears, brother, but not only that ...'

Farsil turns Conrol away, speaking softly in his ear. I don't need to use magic to know how that exchange finishes. Major Conrol is to be my executioner should circumstances dictate.

The glare Conrol gives me as he glances back makes me wonder if I'll ever reach Pine Hold alive.

***

Lotane closes the door behind him, then leans back against it, sighing. I move about the room, lighting candles that smell faintly of honey. It's evening, and having just eaten dinner under guard in the mess hall, I'm mentally exhausted

'After all this time apart, and I'm supposed to just let you go again,' he says, moving forward to pull me into his arms. 'I don't like this. I don't trust them.'

'Nor do they trust us, with far better reason.' I sigh.

I rest my head against his chest, feeling the warmth of his powerful body through his shirt. We're no longer dressed in black clothes and robes but in something a little less assassin-like.

Lotane wears a cream woollen shirt with a wide collar that's stretched tight over his powerful chest while his belted dark green trousers are tucked into polished black calf-length boots. He strikes a handsome figure.

It was Farsil's idea to change our appearance, and it was a good one. We no longer receive as many instant scowls or murmured threats if we keep our heads down. I'm dressed similarly, but with a dark brown leather shirt.

'We are lucky to be alive and free,' I whisper. 'Now, keep your voice down. Everything we say that's overheard will find its way back to Farsil, be sure of that.'

'I could slip the guards and catch up with you on your journey,' Lotane murmurs, his lips gently brushing my forehead.

'We'd have to kill the Major if you did, probably Ardlan, and where would that leave our mission? No, we have to regain their trust to have any chance. Be on your best behaviour while you're here. Give them no reason to dislike you or have concerns about your behaviour. You got away with hitting the admiral, and you're my hero for doing so, but Farsil won't suffer insubordinate behaviour again and will gladly carry through on his threat to lock you up.'

'There's something about the threat of death that makes me want to enjoy life,' Lotane murmurs. His hands find their way to my shirt buttons, and he begins to undo them.

'I believe you said I'm your hero. Surely heroes get rewarded handsomely for their noble deeds!' Lotane whispers huskily in my ear as he pushes me towards the bed.

'We can't!' My willpower rapidly dissolves as, having finished with the buttons, he pulls my shirt off. 'There are guards outside; they'll hear.'

'Then try not to make a sound.'

I moan as his lips brush mine, his fingertips tracing my spine.

He stops, tutting in mock disapproval.

'Sssssh.'

Moving behind me, Lotane pulls me close, his hands gently running over my breasts as I grind back against him, enjoying the feel of his growing arousal.

'What are these?' Lotane pauses, brushing hair away from my shoulders, trying to turn me toward the light.

Has he spotted the bite marks Nogoth left there?

I turn swiftly in his arms.

'Surely there are other parts of my body you can give your attention to,' I tease, my heart beating wildly.

Lotane smiles, then pushes me back onto the bed, his hungry mouth moving down my neck. How hot can his mouth be? It traces fire across my skin, and as his lips close gently around a nipple, Nogoth's violet eyes flash into my mind before disappearing an instant later.

Lotane pauses, looking mischievous, then pulls the woollen shirt off over his head.

'If you can't be quiet, let's try the alternative and give the guards something to report, shall we?'

The next instant, we kick our boots to the corner of the room before yanking our trousers and underwear off. Laughing between hungry kisses, we pull the blankets over us, and the exquisite heat of skin on skin makes me squirm with pleasure.

'I haven't drunk my infertility potion in a while, so don't get too carried away,' I whisper as I manoeuvre Lotane onto his back.

Kneeling beside him, my lips move slowly down over his chest, past his stomach. My hands are busy too, gently stroking, softly pulling, until neither of us can take the anticipation anymore, and I take him in my mouth.

'Now, who is the noisy one?' I laugh several minutes later as I tap him on the nose with my finger.

'I was so close,' he groans, eyes half-closed, before sitting up and kissing me softly.

'Now, I think what's good enough for a king should be good enough for his queen, don't you?'

Lotane winks, and I can only sigh in agreement. He takes his time, lips and tongue moving down my body, teasing. He even gently kisses where my ribs are bandaged before continuing his descent. I raise my hips to encourage him, and then he slides my legs over his shoulders as I moan blissfully.

A flash. Nogoth's face, those intense violet eyes. I gasp, grabbing the back of Lotane's head.

Encouraged by my response, Lotane's hands caress my thighs and stomach while his tongue probes gently. Yet even though he takes his time, he doesn't finish me on purpose, leaving me no choice.

'Lie on your back, and don't you dare finish inside me!'

'Then you'd better go slowly,' he says, eyes closed.

Unable to wait any longer to join, I sit astride him, lowering myself down, inch by exquisite inch.

'That feels so good.' I bite my lip, mixing pleasure and pain.

His hands grasp my arse, urging me to go faster, but I know what I want and resist the temptation.

Leaning forward, I grab the headboard, using my arms and legs to control the rhythm, sliding up and down. Heat rises inside of me, a mixture of passion and magic, boiling up, and I feel perspiration break out over my body as the silken friction brings me closer to release.

Lotane sits up, his tongue and mouth working wonders in the curve of my neck. I wrap my legs around his waist, fingers digging into his back as we grind together.

'Give it to me,' I moan into Lotane's ear, and he increases his tempo.

Violet eyes, my magic burning, Nogoth crying out. Image after erotic image enters my mind.

'I'm getting close,' I cry out; the pleasure is so intense.

Dropping my head, I bite Lotane's shoulder in passion, my nails raking his back, the salty taste of sweat filling me with thirst. I succumb to the darkest depths of my fantasies, picture Nogoth underneath me, and ride Lotane in a frenzy, overtaken by my lust.

Faster and faster, hotter and hotter, then even as I reach release, crying out, I realise something isn't right.

Lotane is pushing me away, pain and confusion in his eyes.

He hasn't finished ... how cruel of me.

I grab his softening shaft, dipping my head, but he's saying something ... his hands pulling me off him, restraining me.

Finally, his words filter through the pounding in my ears.

'Enough, Malina. Please, no more. No more!'

I release him, unsure what I've done wrong, hurt at his sudden rebuttal.

'Lotane, what's wrong?'

I move toward him, but he turns quickly to sit at the edge of the bed, and I bite my knuckles to stop from crying out.

His back is a bloodied mess.

At first, I thought I'd dug too deep with my nails, but as I peer closer, they're just scratches. So, where is the blood coming from?

Then I see the puncture wounds on his shoulder.

I'd bitten him! The saltiness I'd tasted had been his blood, not sweat.

Lotane stands, moving across to a large mirror in the corner of the room. He turns his back, then, face twisting in concentration, summons a ball of fire to light the room with its incandescence.

I just sit on the edge of the bed in shock as he examines the wounds before going over to a chest of drawers. He rummages through before taking a small hand towel which he tears into strips.

'Let me do that,' I say, moving over to him, reaching for the linen.

His eyes are so full of hurt when he looks at me that I know he suspects, but he simply hands over the makeshift bandages and lets me get to work. I clean his back, dipping some of the cloth in a pitcher of water before applying the remainder to protect the wounds from infection.

'You've never been like that before. You were burning hot inside. It was painful ... and then ...' Lotane pauses, searching for what to say next, but then his resolve firms as he takes a deep breath. 'Those are bite marks on your shoulder too, aren't they?'

The last time I was this frightened and trapped, I hung from a strap in a ceiling above a bottomless pit.

'Answer me, damnit!' he roars, his face darkening. Turning his back on me, he wrenches the chamber door open and steps out naked into the hallway.

'If you're not at the end of the hallway by the time I count to five, I'm going to rip your bloody heads off,' he shouts at the guards.

Running feet can be heard as Lotane slams the door behind him.

His voice is quiet as he walks past me and begins pulling his clothes on.

'Nogoth?'

I could lie. It might save us both from a broken heart. Then again, neither do I want to deceive, lie, and be like Nogoth. I will be truthful, for only with the truth do we stand a chance.

'Yes.'

I feel like my heart will burst from my chest. I'm hurting so bad that I can barely breathe, and if I feel like this, then what about Lotane?

'I waited a year for you. Even when the others assured me you were dead, I never wanted to join with another. So, tell me, how long did you wait before ...?'

Oh, gods. Lying would have been better than this. Being stabbed with a dagger would be better than this!

'It doesn't matter. I regret it from the bottom of my heart!'

'Then why did you cry out his name?'

'I don't know. I really don't know!'

I cry, but Lotane's gaze is as hard as steel, unbelieving. It demands I continue to tell the truth.

'He used his power over me, over all his people. It was called The Quickening. It created lust amongst those around him. I had no idea what I was doing, nor choice in it!'

I consider telling Lotane it affected me because I have fey blood, but I don't know if I can ever share this with him or anyone.

Lotane finishes dressing and sits nervously on the edge of the bed.

'So is it all a lie? Him coming here to destroy the world? Did he spurn you, and you're just a jealous woman hellbent on revenge, having been cast aside for another lover?'

Lotane's voice breaks, tears beginning to replace the fire of anger.

'Am I your poor second choice and a convenient weapon with which to strike him down?'

'No, Lotane. Nogoth is coming to harvest the people of this world, and if anything, he's the one seeking revenge. I took the soul of his love, another Chosen, to pay for my passage back to the mountain. As for you being my second choice, that's not the case. Nogoth desperately wanted me at his side, but despite this, I wanted to return, not just to right the wrongs, but to be with you. I always intended to tell you about what happened, to find a way to explain it without breaking your heart ... but I never had the chance. This is certainly not the way I hoped it would come out.'

'It doesn't look good.' Lotane says, his voice solemn.

I want to hold Lotane to see if he'll allow me close again. However, after what he's just discovered, my nakedness isn't appropriate. I suddenly feel ashamed and turn away, picking up my discarded clothes.

'I know. But we can get through this. I know we can.' I reassure him, turning to look him in the eye as I pull my trousers on.

'Maybe we can, I don't know,' he says sadly. 'But that isn't what I'm talking about. I meant the bite marks on your shoulder. They don't look good, and he guides me to the mirror. His magic flares, and light banishes the shadows as I look over my shoulder, pulling my hair aside.

Damn.

Since the joining, my skin has been a multi-hued swirl of colours and whilst I carry scars that occasionally mar the artistic pattern, I've loved how it looks. Yet now I notice with concern that, whilst the bites have scabbed and seem to be healing, dark black veins like a broken spider web thread across the back of my shoulder.

'Does it hurt?' Lotane asks, bending closer, sniffing my shoulder for any scent of corruption.

'Not at all, nor is there any loss of strength.'

'Hmmm.'

Lotane opens a wardrobe, pulls out some spare blankets, and throws them on the floor before grabbing a pillow off the bed.

'We need to talk,' I implore as Lotane lies down on his side, his back toward me.

'In the morning. I'm tired.'

His response, the hardness of his voice, and knowing how I've wronged him keep me from getting angry.

'I'll be leaving tomorrow morning,' I reason, trying to keep my voice calm although I'm breaking up inside, ready to burst into tears.

'Then we'll talk when you get back.'

After pulling on my shirt, I extinguish the candles until only one is left.

I sit in bed, watching Lotane's back, willing him to turn, to come back to bed, to take me in his arms and tell me everything is alright.

Within my stomach, the blood magic twists and turns, vying for my attention, offering a solution.

Yes!

I could bind Lotane to me again. He'd never know, never suspect. He would simply worship me, eyes and heart full of love and loyalty.

The temptation is huge. How can I resist?

I blow out the last candle, and as darkness claims me, I begin a battle with my inner daemons.

***

CHAPTER X

Turning in my saddle, I look back at the faint bump of High Delnor on the horizon and, for the twentieth time, swear not to do so again.

Somewhere within its walls remains Lotane, and we hadn't said goodbye.

What was the point in winning a difficult battle with my inner daemons and resisting the temptation to bind Lotane when despite the victory, I'd lost the war? His disappearance while I slept obviously means he wants nothing more to do with me.

Not having a chance to repair the hurt I caused weighs heavily on my soul.

I swallow, hardening my heart, and call upon the years of conditioning to contain my emotions as I ride to my doom, followed by the scum of the empire.

The Last Hope. They're aptly named, for they avoided the hangman's noose by signing up for a battalion that offers them a final chance of a reprieve. From what I've learned, they need to survive two years, after which their sentence is lifted. Not that they take just anyone. Rapists never avoid the noose, but someone who killed a man in bed with his wife or cut a few purses too many might find a place here if they survive the brutal selection process.

No pay, no second chances, no glory.

Four hundred men unknowingly rushing east to meet a force the like of which this world hasn't seen for a thousand years. Four thousand might have slowed the advance in the narrow mountain passes, but four hundred!

Yes, they're the Last Hope in more ways than one.

However, apart from Ardlan, they don't even know my tale of Nogoth, and as I've been ordered to remain silent on the matter, they won't find out until it's too late. All they know is that they're being given a crap job, finding out why two towns have gone silent at the arse end of the empire.

The air is blue with coarse language and humour as we ride fast. Bizarrely, they seem to bemoan being given what they perceive as an easy job. They've a reputation for being savage fighters and want to be sent back to the front lines. If only they knew ...

However, having been given a job, they're pushing the pace. Following the column of mounted troops are wagon teams carrying enough water and supplies to see us to Midnor, where we'll replenish before continuing.

Ardlan and Major Conrol ride just ahead of me at the front of the column, deep in conversation. I'm tempted to join them, but being the focus of Major Conrol's unrelenting hatred is painful. Maybe a few more days, and he'll come to terms with my pardon, but then again, maybe not.

I slow my horse, edging the gelding to one side of the road, allowing the first rank of troops to come abreast.

They're a tough-looking bunch. It isn't because they scowl or anything like that. Rather it's because of where they're from. I'd warrant most, if not all, are low-born. Forced to live a life of crime where only the clever, fast or strong survive. Perhaps many are orphans like me who'd been sold into slavery and escaped to the criminal underbelly that infests every city, irrespective of the kingdom.

They all wear simple red shirts and trousers under brown, sweat-stained leather armour. I smile, for it's no different than the armour I trained in as a Chosen. They're armed with short swords and daggers and have large, rectangular, body-length shields slung from the saddle of their horses.

None are trained riders and most, from how they sit, have only rudimentary riding skills. In fact, several in the front rows are the butt of many jibes as they shift awkwardly astride the trained horses.

I'm the only woman here, unarmed and unarmoured. It appears my pardon hasn't extended to trusting me with any weapons. It seems that not all murderers are considered equal.

The man riding closest, who has three stripes on his shoulder, smiles at me.

'I'm Yeldom, one of the Hope's sergeants. Please excuse me if I don't introduce the rest,' he laughs.

Being a non-commissioned officer, Yeldom's not a convicted criminal and has the tough job of turning scum into obedient soldiers. Like Ardlan, he'll receive double pay and swift promotion at the end of his term.

'I'm Malina.'

'Yes, the King Slayer. We know who you are. Why are you riding with us and not dead with your head on a spike?'

There's no maliciousness in his question nor hatred in his eyes, and as I catch the gazes of those near enough to overhear our exchange, I'm relieved to find only interest in most of them.

'The short version is I claimed the King's Favour and got a pardon for my deeds.'

Yeldom's laugh is like a barking dog, and several others join in.

'Saved by the very king you killed,' he chuckles, scratching his stubble. 'There's something a little twisted about that. So, you're some kind of witch then? Is that how you set the king on fire and why you don't need weapons and such?'

'Not quite. I'm a magic-user, but prefer weapons.'

'Can you make potions to help Yeldom get it up? He's having problems with the women!' A man in the rank behind Yeldom calls.

'I'll have her cast a spell that makes yours drop off if you're not more respectful,' Yeldom growls.

Friendly jests fly back and forth for a while. There's no rancour amongst these men. I'd thought there'd be spitefulness, bitterness, or just plain nastiness, but there's a camaraderie that surprises me. Yeldom must be a hell of a sergeant.

I begin to relax in their company, yet something doesn't sit right. Until now, everyone I've come across hates me for what I've done. Yet if the men at the front of this battalion are anything to go by, hatred doesn't figure in how they look at me.

'I have to ask, Yeldom. You've said you all know who I am, so …'

'Why don't we all despise and want to kill you?' Yeldom interrupts, finishing my sentence for me. 'I would think that's obvious, but perhaps not. Well, as for my men, they're murderers and thieves themselves. You did what you did and had your own reasons for doing so. The same can be said of them. They're many things, mostly bad, but they ain't hypocrites.

'Now, many soldiers look down on them for what they've been found guilty of. Yet, soldiers kill half-trained farmers and such and don't consider it murder cause the other person has a sword. But they're no different to my lot, not really.

'Anyways, as for me, I'm the forgiving type and know anyone can find redemption, even a King Slayer. Now, I have an important question. Can you make a potion to help me get it up or not?'

'You'll have to buy that kind of magic from the next brothel we come across,' I laugh before realising the men behind Yeldom don't get paid and might not appreciate the joke. Yet nonetheless, everyone who hears, laughs and hoots while Yeldom slaps his thigh, tears running down his face.

'QUIET IN THE RANKS!' Major Conrol bellows, wheeling his horse around, his cheeks red with anger.

It appears my acceptance hasn't gone down well.

'I don't think he's getting any either,' Yeldom chuckles under his breath.

Laughter breaks out again, and the major spurs his horse back to me.

'Malina, you'll ride at the front. I won't have you impact the discipline of this battalion!' he snarls, beckoning me to follow, then yanks on his reins and heads back to Ardlan.

Yeldom leans over, talking softly.

'Give it time, King-Slayer. A man who's been made to look a fool will often go on making a fool of himself before coming to his senses.'

I smile in gratitude to some of the other men who nod or raise a hand in my direction as I heel my horse forward to join Ardlan and Major Conrol.

Mulling over Yeldom's words. I think he has it right. Major Conrol feels a fool having the High King die on his watch and then being caught a second time unawares. I just hope he comes to his senses sooner rather than later. Anger can blunt judgement, and I need him to be as sharp as he used to be where we're heading.

As we continue our journey, I don't antagonise Conrol by saying anything or looking in his direction. A fire can only burn if it has fuel, and this one needs to go out.

The gentle tugging of the blood magic lures me, offering its help. It can douse the flames.

It's so tempting. Blood magic is the answer to almost every problem I'm facing.

How did Nogoth resist the lure of controlling everyone around him?

The answer is simple. He didn't.

Of the many battles that lie ahead, perhaps this one will be my most challenging. If I don't want to become like Nogoth, it's one I'll have to fight daily and one I can never afford to lose.

***

Two weeks of hard travel, the last three days of which were on half rations, and we've finally made it to Midnor, the centrepiece of the Delnorian empire. Eight weeks until the end of days is upon us, while my warning remains unheeded.

Has Kralgen made it to Icelandia, or is it too soon? Will he overcome whatever obstacles lay before him and claim the throne? The task before him is almost as insurmountable as the frozen peaks rising up far to the northwest.

For a whole day before we came near Midnor, we'd passed sprawling farms teeming with workers overseeing field upon field of crops and livestock. When I think of how scarce food had been in Hastia when I was a child, it makes me wonder who all this food is for. Yet, they certainly don't keep it all for themselves. We'd often passed wagons bearing food and supplies to the capital and other Delnorian cities. The drivers' relief when they realised we were friendly troops was something to behold.

Midnor is a vast city, more extensive than High Delnor, but it isn't the capital despite its size and position and nor does it appear opulent.

Ardlan, the major, and I ride through a gatehouse where the guards sketch a salute. Ardlan speaks quietly to one for a few minutes, getting directions for the governor's residence, and then we heel the horses into a trot. Behind us, the battalion continues its journey around the city perimeter while we head inside to exchange pleasantries and information.

Supplies to enable the Last Hope to continue its journey should await the soldiers at the west gate. The empire's machinery is well-oiled. Sin-hawks had been dispatched from the capital before we left, ensuring everything we needed was ready for our arrival.

Something I find bizarre is the absence of a city wall despite the entrance fortification. As I look about, wondering why, I discover the answer. The buildings hereabouts are low and functional, with very few adornments save for signs that indicate a particular trade or service being offered. Yet it appears from their crumbling brickwork that the old city walls have been dismantled and used to provide materials as the population expanded.

Despite studying a lot of recent history to help provide cover on missions, I have no idea about Midnor's. Yet whatever their past, it's their future I'm worried about.

Occasional town guardsmen are visible, but it's easy to tell they aren't used to combat and are, in fact, mostly past their prime. Without a city wall, without anyone to protect them, this will be one of the first major cities to fall before Nogoth's army.

A pack of filthy but happy children, perhaps five or six years of age, run by with sticks, chasing a chicken along the dusty street, trying to catch their squawking prey. Their laughter should lift my spirits, but it will change to screams before long. They'll never escape capture and will be dragged away by monsters to another world unless, of course, they're slaughtered and eaten here.

Everyone we pass looks at us with curiosity. I wonder what reaction I'd receive if I lowered my hood. However, a few steps later, I see the answer. Fading wanted posters with my likeness and description are plastered on every street corner. I keep my hood raised.

Half an hour later, we dismount before a low, brown building with a solitary bored guard standing outside. A young lad runs over to take our mounts' reins and leads them away to an adjacent stable.

'The governor's expecting you. You were spotted this morning,' the guard offers when we approach, banging on the heavy door next to him.

It opens inward, and we're met and escorted by a nimble, grey-haired woman carrying a tray laden with food down several long corridors and out into a pleasant, sunlit courtyard.

'The governor will be with you shortly. Help yourself to refreshments,' she says before hurrying off.

Whilst Conrol eats, Ardlan and I decide to look around.

The courtyard walls appear ancient, yet they add to the charm. Set into the crumbling mortar are perches upon which several hooded sin-hawks sit quietly. As I step toward them, they whistle softly in greeting, aware of my presence. Darkest blue with yellow-tipped wings, hooked beaks and sharp talons, they're a deadly and beautiful predator, yet if raised from hatching, they bond to humans and are as docile with us as they're intelligent.

'I've often wondered why they're called sin-hawks. Do you know?' I ask Ardlan.

He scratches his chin as if he's trying to recollect the answer.

'It's the tear-dropped red plumage beneath their eyes that gives them their name. It's said they cry tears of blood as they witness the sins of humankind upon their travels. Now I think it will be a sin to let the Major eat all the food, so please excuse me!'

I take a few moments to gently fuss the birds' necks, rubbing my fingers together before I do so, ensuring they're aware of my impending touch.

Turning away, I take in the tranquillity of this private oasis.

A pond with a small, tinkling fountain creates a sense of peace, while a dozen small green trees bearing apples sit in red pots arranged around the perimeter. Rectangular tubs hold beautiful flowers, and someone obviously takes pride and joy in maintaining this place.

I love fruit and can't resist helping myself to a rosy apple. I bite into the skin, enjoying the sweet flesh and juice.

'A murderer and a thief!' Conrol mutters, yet his bitterness doesn't spoil the tranquillity.

Ignoring him as I crunch happily, I investigate the carved stone benches arranged around the fountain. It takes me a moment to realise that there's a partial mosaic on the floor around them. It's old and faded, barely visible, for the majority of the ground is covered in newly fashioned flagstones.

I walk around the courtyard, trying to work out what it's depicting. I kneel down, carefully brushing aside a little dust to see the faded image of an armoured woman, standing sword in hand before a huge mirror, then almost drop the apple core in shock. Could it be a World Gate she's standing in front of, and who is she?'

THE LAST HOPE

'I see you're admiring some of this old city's history,' says a warm voice.

A jovial rounded man ambles across the courtyard, arms spread wide in welcome.

'Not many people are interested in the old, only in the new. That applies to people too. As we age, we find ourselves ignored and, worse, forgotten!'

His self-deprecating remark is warming, but I can also detect a subtle fakeness to his charm.

'I'm Garbor, the governor here. Welcome to Midnor. You must be Major Conrol,' he says, bowing slightly, 'and you are Captain?'

'Ardlan, of The Last Hope.'

'Really? The Last Hope. I can only *hope* you aren't staying too long then.' The governor chuckles mirthlessly. 'There's virtually no crime in this city. It would be good to keep it that way! Wouldn't you agree?'

Ardlan's face darkens, but he says nothing, just staring hard at the governor. That kind of response must be the norm, but the governor outranks him, and he has to swallow the insult. Yes, Garbor's welcome is as fake as his smile, and I'm perhaps unreasonably angry for Ardlan and his men.

Somewhat uncomfortable, Garbor turns his attention back to me.

'So, who are you, and how can I address you, my lady? You've piqued my interest, hiding under your noble's robes and in the company of such nefarious types. Excepting the major, of course,' he hurriedly adds.

I pull back my hood.

'My name is Malina. Most people just call me The King Slayer. You choose.'

Garbor steps back in shock so quickly that he trips over a flower pot and squashes the beautiful blooms beneath him. Moaning in fear, he rolls off, then, as he recovers his feet, positions himself behind Major Conrol.

'Shouldn't she be dead?' Garbor squeaks.

Ardlan laughs at the governor's fearful reaction and smiles warmly at me.

'It appears news of your pardon has travelled slower than news of your crime.'

'As the captain says, she's been pardoned, however unjust that may seem,' Conrol says coldly.

Ignoring his dourness, I fix the governor with my stare.

'Who is the woman on the mosaic, governor?'

Having decided I won't harm him, he shuffles from behind Conrol and shrugs.

'How would I know? Midnor was built from the ruins of a crumbling ancient fortress about five hundred years ago. Whoever she was is long forgotten.'

'Take a look,' I say, beckoning Conrol and Ardlan over. 'Tell me what you see.'

'A queen of some kind standing in front of a mirror. What of it?' Conrol growls.

'It looks like a World Gate to me.'

Conrol's face turns red.

'I thought you'd given up on peddling that idiocy. You've tricked yourself a pardon, so why keep up the charade?' Conrol's hands clench and unclench. The anger burning inside never seems to diminish.

'If it's a mirror, then why isn't she reflected in it?' Ardlan observes, kneeling down and rubbing his chin.

'Oh, for the sake of the gods.' Conrol exclaims in exasperation, turning back to a confused-looking Garbor. 'Thank you for your hospitality, but we don't intend to stay. However, I want to know if you've heard anything from Pine Hold or Sea Hold since you received the news of our coming. It would save us a journey if you had.'

Garbor points at four empty perches.

'I've sent and lost four birds. Never in my days has that happened. I sent another to Iron Hold, and the governor there responded immediately. Said they hadn't had any timber or fish for a couple of weeks but weren't worried. It could be there's a sickness they don't want to spread, or they're late with their tithes. You know how it is.'

Major Conrol grunts but says nothing, scratching the new beard on his chin. After this long on the road, I'm the only one who hasn't got one.

'Send a sin-hawk to Commander Farsil at High Delnor.' Conrol commands. 'Let him know that as no news has been received from Pine Hold and Sea Hold, the Last Hope are heading off immediately. We should be at Iron Hold in six days, and our objective within three weeks.'

THE LAST HOPE

'Let's go,' Major Conrol orders, striding purposefully from the courtyard with Ardlan close behind.

I grab two apples from a tree before I leave and take a final look back.

As if in a dream, the courtyard is covered in rubble, a blackened smoking ruin, with half-eaten corpses scattered about, before it returns to normal.

'You look like you've just seen a ghost,' Garbor smiles nervously, relieved we're going so quickly.

'I'm looking at one right now if you don't do one, simple thing.'

'What's that?' Garbor gulps, sweat running down his face, thinking I'm making a personal threat.

'Get everyone out of this city and head north to Icelandia. If you're still here in a couple of months, you'll be dead. An army of fey will come from the west and wash this city away in a sea of blood.'

'Hah. You had me worried for a minute.'

Garbor's wobbly jowls shake with forced mirth, although he looks perturbed by my words.

'Don't say I didn't warn you,' I reply, then hurry after the others.

Will I forever be disbelieved until it's too late? The blood magic stirs within me. I could use it quickly, make him believe, and help save the city.

No. I admonish myself firmly, striding after the others. But the temptation is growing, and it's getting so hard to resist.

***

Sometimes banter around the fire continues long into the night, but tiredness is getting to everyone this evening. The pace since we left High Delnor has been fierce, and tonight we've stopped later than usual.

The horses had been cared for first. Despite initially being unfamiliar and indifferent about their mounts, the men of the Last Hope have now formed a special bond with these noble animals. To see them brushing down, feeding, watering, fussing or even talking to their horses has shown me these hard men also have a soft side.

There's definitely hope for the salvation of their souls ... if only they live long enough.

I take a wooden bowl of meat and vegetable stew from Yeldom and lean back against a twisted tree. The roaring fire, jovial company and tasty food should fill me with warmth, but despite them, I'm not feeling at my best. My stomach is unsettled and bloated, and I force myself to take a mouthful, chew and swallow.

There's a loud slap, and someone swears, causing a ripple of laughter. We're travelling through a marshy region fuelled by meltwater from large hills to the north, and the insects are annoying everyone. I've consciously chosen downwind of the fire, knowing the smoke will keep them away from me until it burns out.

We'd stopped at several small towns along the way to Iron Hold, but credit to Conrol and Ardlan, they don't take any privileges their rank might allow. No baths, shaving, or dining in a tavern. They sleep in bedrolls and eat around campfires with the men and, like me, have taken their turns preparing food.

Even above the stew's aroma, I can smell myself. We all stink because we've travelled light with just one set of clothes. Every river or lake we come across serves to replenish our water, but also a brief respite as we submerse ourselves, fully clothed, to try and rinse the filth away. We never truly succeed. None of us will step foot in this marsh though.

After three weeks of hard travel, I've gotten to know many of the Last Hope in Yeldom's company of a hundred men. I'm greeted with nods and grins, even the occasional slap on the back when I walk amongst them. It feels good to be accepted without judgement, even by murderers. I've heard some of their stories, and very few here are truly worthy of that badge, but there are those ... like the one staring at me now from a nearby fire, who are unwilling or simply unable to change their ways.

My unpleasant admirer has a full dark beard making his big head appear even bigger. He has tattoos all over his neck and the back of his hands, with small calculating eyes sunk into a swollen face. Whenever he opens his mouth to take a bite of his dinner, I see crooked, yellow teeth like half-fallen tombstones. With hands the size of shovels and shoulders barely able to fit inside his armour, he's a brute and revels in it. Yet he doesn't meet my gaze and makes a point of only glancing at me briefly, but I know he's watching.

Well, as long as he stays over there with his company, he can watch all he likes.

THE LAST HOPE

Tired laughter breaks out around my fire, and I smile, forcing myself to finish eating while listening to the distracting conversation.

If only Lotane could be here, sharing this camaraderie, humour, and my bedroll at night.

Does he think about me as often as I think of him? Has his anger faded or continues to grow like the Majors? For me to have called out Nogoth's name in the ecstasy of our joining would have cut very deep. This time apart might be what's required for him to forgive me.

I finally finish my food. The crackle of the flames is soothing, and there's the occasional hum of conversation coming from some nearby fires. Tiredness comes at me in waves, so I quickly finish my stew, clean the bowl with some stale bread, and wriggle into my bedroll. Around me, the rest do the same. No sentries are set, which irks me a little, but we're so deep inside friendly territory that even I have to admit it would be a waste. Speed is of the utmost importance, and tired men will only slow us down.

My eyelids are so heavy, and I feel my consciousness slipping away. The last thought on my mind is Lotane and the look of unbearable pain when he realised the truth about Nogoth and me.

.....

Has it been minutes or hours when suddenly, I open my eyes, unaware that I'd fallen asleep, to find myself surrounded by the corpses of the Last Hope.

I crawl out of my bedroll over to Yeldom. An arm and a leg are missing, yet despite no blood flowing, his eyes open as I lean over him.

'I wanted to see my mother again. Why didn't you say anything?'

I fall away in shock, crawling backwards on my hands and heels. My fingers push into something wet, and I turn with trepidation to find them in the entrails of a young corporal called Bandorn. His stomach has been torn open, but not by weapons, for I can see the talon and teeth marks all too well despite the gore.

'We didn't have a chance,' he cries, his remaining hand vainly trying to scoop his intestines back into the gaping wound. 'Why didn't you tell us?'

I stumble from body to body, and all the while, the cries around me build and build till they reach a crescendo of accusing howls and sobs.

... I wake up gasping.

My nightmare has lasted half the night. The fire has burned out, and everyone is sound asleep.

I use some breathing exercises to bring my pounding heart under control. Yet that doesn't stop my mind from racing.

The dream has shown me what I've known all along; the folly of silence. I'd allowed myself to be cowed, to follow the orders of Commander Farsil, to feel like I'd done all I could.

I need to do more, or these men of the Last Hope, however flawed they might be, will forever scream their accusations at me. I know I can't save them, nor myself, most likely, but I can prepare them for what's to come.

My stomach growls noisily, and my bowels protest, so I quietly extricate myself from my bedroll. As I carefully make my way into the marsh, I'm aware of being stalked by a looming figure, yet it doesn't bother me.

I'm a Chosen, and the night is mine.

***

I'm energised, and my thoughts are crystal clear as we continue our journey west. It's as if I've just had a long induced sleep like those I enjoyed within the Mountain of Souls. I've no aches or pains, nor do the recent injuries to my ribs and hip hurt.

Perhaps it was ridding this world of another dark soul that created this feeling.

Unlike most of the Last Hope, the brute from last night hadn't left his evil life behind and had hoped to find an easy victim as he followed me in the darkness. His corpse had been claimed by the marsh with a little magical help.

Strange that I can't remember how I killed him, but I'd certainly slept perfectly afterwards.

I smile as I recall the furore over the brute's disappearance. Fortunately, as his horse and gear remained, and he obviously hadn't deserted, it was decided he'd fallen victim to a misplaced step in the marsh. We'd all got underway shortly after.

A frown replaces my smile as a memory of my dream comes to mind. I have to say something.

Yet how do I approach the Major? Conrol rides ahead with Ardlan, but if I ride alongside and bring up Nogoth or my dream, he'll just order me back in line or ride away. The other problem is that he already knows the whole story, so what else can I tell him to make him believe.

It's a simple question, yet the answer is anything but.

We move off to the side of the road to let a convoy of wagons pass, heading toward Midnor. The oxen pulling them huff and puff, and I feel somewhat sorry for them. They have a long journey ahead.

'It's too fine a day to be wearing such a frown, King Slayer,' Yeldom says next to me. 'If you look any gloomier, I fear a storm might replace the sunshine.'

The men around chuckle at his gentle jibe. He means no harm, for his words are accompanied by a wide grin.

A smile threatens to replace my frown. Yeldom is well-positioned as a sergeant. The men under his command respect and genuinely like him, and despite the joking between the ranks, they obey his commands instantly. I like him too, for he understands the importance of morale and intuitively finds the right words for everyone.

Nor does his, or the men calling me King Slayer, annoy me.

As he'd explained the second day out from High Delnor, I was not officially part of the Last Hope or the Delnorian military, which posed a bit of a problem. I held no rank or office, yet the men held me in high regard despite my dark deeds and thus couldn't simply call me by name.

So, with something approaching pride, they'd decided to unofficially adopt me and call me King Slayer out of respect, not hatred. Once I understood, the title lost its sting.

The smile wins, and my frown recedes.

'Thank you, Yeldom. Now, if you could only solve my problem.'

Yeldom chuckles, leaning forward in his saddle to pat his horse on the neck.

'Well, that's simple enough, because the way you look at the major's back, you only have two options. You either need to plant a dagger there, which wouldn't go down too well, or you need to resolve your differences.'

'Want to borrow a dagger?' a man calls, and laughter accompanies his words.

'Don't listen to those reprobates,' Yeldom grimaces in mock disgust. 'They all like the major, and that life is hopefully behind you!'

'I know. I want to resolve our differences, but the major just isn't interested.'

'Therein lies the problem,' Yeldom explains. 'You want to be friends, and that's too difficult for him, so you need to approach it differently. Establish a working relationship, find things he can't disagree with even if he wants to, then build on that.'

I ponder the sergeant's words and can see the wisdom in them.

'You're quite something, Yeldom,' I say, reaching out to grasp his forearm briefly in thanks.

'Age gives you wisdom, and Yeldom's so *old*,' someone mutters loud enough to be heard.

Yeldom's mount chooses that moment to snort as if in laughter, and merriment ripples through the first couple of ranks.

Up ahead, Conrol looks back over his shoulder disapprovingly. He begrudges me for being liked or accepted by anyone.

However, I barely notice, for through the heat haze, rising behind him in the distance are the Elder Mountains. The geography of this land is imprinted in my head through years of training. With little effort, I recall how they reach from Icelandia's Frozen Sea in the north all the way to Tars and the Sea of Sand in the south, and what I can see is just the eastern boundary. Almost everything to the west is mountainous terrain, and yet nestled amongst it all is Iron Hold, South Hold, Lake Hold, Sea Hold, and of course, Pine Hold.

'It's good to be home again,' Yeldom sighs.

'I've missed how clean the air smells up there,' another voice adds.

'You're from here?' I ask, realising as the words leave my mouth they aren't the wisest I've ever spoken.

'Absolutely. Me and maybe another dozen or so of the boys are from this area. I'm from South Hold, as is Derwin just there,' and he nods at a youngish lad in his late teens. The other companies have a goodly number of mountain folk in them too.'

'How well do you know the whole region?' I ask, my mind whirring. How stupid of me to have assumed everyone came from the cities further east.

'As well as he knows his sister's body,' someone says to a host of guffaws.

'That's just disgusting. She was so ugly, I much preferred my brother's.' Yeldom fires back, rolling his eyes. 'Now, you lads be quiet and let us grown-ups speak.'

He turns back to me with a shrug of apology at the interruption.

'Not that well, to be honest. We were worked hard, and unless you rode the trade wagons, you didn't get to travel much. I spent most of my time down the coal mines. I visited Lake Hold a few times over the years but never got further west than that. I was always jealous of them, with their full bellies and days spent fishing. I'd often go weeks without ever seeing daylight.

'As for Pine Hold, I think they had a good life, too, farming those mighty trees. Of course, they have to live in the shadow of that ancient haunted fortress, so who knows …'

'Haunted fortress?' I interrupt.

'Honestly, that's what the traders said. It's supposedly halfway up a mountain, and the weirdest thing is that they say it's inside out.'

'What?'

'It never made sense to me either. You know how people like to embellish their stories. Mind you, I tend to believe 'em. After all, Iron Hold isn't exactly normal either.'

I'm about to ask what he means when Ardlan raises his hand to catch our attention.

'Double time,' he shouts, and then we're back on the road, with the pounding of hooves drowning out the possibility of further conversation. Ardlan obviously hopes to make it to Iron Hold by day's end, and I've got a lot to think about because tonight, I intend to talk with Major Conrol.

***

CHAPTER XI

Iron Hold. I don't know what I expected, but it certainly isn't this.

We've just finished making camp on the outskirts of the town that sits at the end of the biggest, crumbling wall I've ever laid eyes on. The majority of it is so tall that as you look toward the top and see the clouds drifting across the sky, it gives the impression that the wall is toppling onto the town. The length that had collapsed is at the far end of the pass, and I can only imagine the thunderous roar as it fell.

Unsurprisingly, everyone is starting to avert their gaze; it's rather unsettling.

The fires are set, and food is being prepared when Ardlan comes over.

'Let's go, King Slayer,' he smiles. Just like the other men, he now uses the title with warmth.

I follow him to the picket line where our horses are tethered, then mount up. Major Conrol scowls as though he's been kept waiting a long time. As we set off at a gentle canter along the trade road, we pass some supply wagons heading toward the Last Hope. The men driving the wagons wave as we pass, their clothes covered in black and red dust.

'Iron Hold is a mining town,' Ardlan shouts above the clatter of hooves. 'You won't be surprised to know that this is where most of Delnor's iron comes from.'

The mountains here have a reddish tint, and so do all the buildings. The streets are dust-covered, and our horses' hooves create an ominous-looking cloud behind us. Town dwellers pause, curiosity apparent on their faces as we ride by. I doubt they get many visitors this far west, and having a battalion of troops turn up on their doorstep must be quite the novelty.

We rein our horses back, slowing to a trot as the streets become busier, and Ardlan rides alongside, obviously keen to talk.

'Look at that wall. It's ridiculous,' he says, puzzlement in his voice. 'What was the point in building that here. This area is mostly uninhabited and, as far as I know, always has been. Only the gods know how old it must be. It predates the empire, of that, I'm sure. It reminds me of a dam I saw up in the mountains when on exercise near Astoria, just ten times larger.'

I'm not puzzled. First Midnor, built on the site of an ancient fortress in the middle of nowhere, and now this wall. Midnor lies directly between High Delnor and here, almost a straight line. This wall is definitely a dam of sorts, built to stop a fey flood. It must have been constructed after the last invasion, when the memory of what happened was still strong, yet with no knowledge of when the next one would come.

Major Conrol stops a few times, asking for directions, and soon after, we're dismounting outside a barracks. There's a small training yard, two open-sided sheds, one holding equipment and the other sin-hawks alongside some empty perches. A few town guardsmen mill about, looking at us apprehensively. They're well past middle-aged and, with bellies hanging over their belts, well past their prime too.

'Even towns as far west as this will have had most of their strongest conscripted into the army,' Ardlan says softly. 'Still, that's a sorry-looking lot.'

I'd already noticed that very few of the people in town were young men or women. With the war going on for so long, every nation has been bled dry of the very people who might have the strength to fight against Nogoth's invasion.

A grizzled old man comes limping from the barracks. He has sergeant's stripes on a uniform as old as he is. Perhaps they both should have retired a long time ago. Yet, as he draws closer, there's a spark in his eye.

'Major. Captain.' The man snaps a salute first to Conrol, then to Ardlan, before nodding at me. Then a puzzled look appears.

'Isn't she ...' he begins.

Major Conrol sighs.

'Yes, Sergeant. She is. However, let's not start that conversation, please.'

I'm grateful Conrol brought me along, but I wonder why. Perhaps the answer is obvious. He doesn't trust me out of his sight.

'We passed the supply wagons on the way here. Thank you for that,' Conrol continues as he dismounts.

Ardlan and I follow suit, and at the sergeant's nod, a guardsman waddles over and takes the horses' bridles, then leads them toward his friends. I'm pleased to see that they begin taking care of them immediately. It appears that whilst looking sloven, they work hard when required.

'Please tell me there's been news from Pine Hold or Sea Hold. It would be great to turn around and head home,' Ardlan says, stepping forward to shake the sergeant's hand.

'Hah. We only had two sin-hawks trained to go there, and neither has returned these last weeks. Such a shame, as they'd been with me since they hatched.' The sergeant sniffs, looking a little emotional. 'I also sent a couple of guards when we first heard from High Delnor, but they're a little overdue in coming back. I reckon they enjoyed the rest and hospitality a little too long.'

The major and Ardlan exchange a glance. Are they finally beginning to wonder if there's truth to my story?

'Damnit, but there's a war to fight,' growls the major.

'Don't I know it. My son died fighting it,' the sergeant snaps. 'Sorry, Major,' he apologises quickly, looking embarrassed.

'We've all lost someone we care for, Sergeant,' Conrol says, placing his hand on the man's shoulder in a show of empathy. Yet as he says the words, his eyes flash at me.

'Tell me. Has production been affected here?' Conrol asks, getting down to business.

'Not yet. We still get coal every couple of days from South Hold, and we're getting food from Lake Hold, but we'll run out of charcoal reserves soon, and that only comes from Pine Hold. We've had disruption in the past. They've probably got some sickness up there, which might explain my guards not coming back, in case they brought it with them.'

'But that doesn't explain your missing sin-hawks.' I point out.

THE LAST HOPE

'Nope, it doesn't.' The sergeant admits, scratching a sweat-stained armpit.

'It looks like the Last Hope might be chopping trees if there's sickness up at Pine Hold,' Conrol laughs, looking pointedly at Ardlan.

'Chopping trees or men, is there much difference other than trees stand still and don't chop back?' Ardlan grumbles.

I can barely believe my ears. Aren't they worried about the missing sin-hawks?

'You know. Evening's closing in, and there's not much point in you lot heading off before daybreak,' the sergeant notes. 'With all the smelting going on here and the meltwater off the mountain tops, we always have hot water. If you've a care, send your boys into town an hour after sunset, fifty at a time only, mind you. The baths are where that white smoke rises between those two buildings. See?'

We follow the sergeant's outstretched arm, taking our bearings.

Conrol turns toward the horses, intent on leaving.

'What can you tell us about the wall?' I ask swiftly.

The sergeant grins. 'For a moment there, I didn't think anyone was gonna ask. That would've been the first time a newcomer came here and hadn't. There's little I can tell you that you can't see with your own eyes. My kin have lived in these mountains for more generations than I can count, and no one knows who built it; it's been around that long.

'As you can see, the far end finally collapsed during some tremors around thirty years ago. However, what's standing is pretty solid. It might look a little beat up, but it was built to last, that much I can tell you. Saying that, there were supposedly lifts and such running up the back that rotted away way before I was born. Now the only way to the top of the wall is up lots of steps. There's a hundred and twenty if you care to climb them. It's still pretty safe, but I'm too old to show you. However, the view is certainly worth it, although not so much at night.'

'Where do I start?'

'The entrances are by the wall tunnel. If you ...'

'No. We're heading back now.' Conrol interrupts firmly, the tone of command evident.

I bristle, feeling my anger rise. Now isn't the time to let it loose, to say what needs to be heard, but it soon will be. Who knows, this wall might help my cause if there are further mosaics or paintings inside.

'I'll catch you up shortly then,' I say over my shoulder, setting off at a run.

I push myself fast as Conrol and Ardlan pound after me.

***

'Malina, STOP!'

The anger in Conrol's voice is tangible, but I can't help but laugh. I've been in a saddle for so long that I've forgotten how much I love to run. I turn around, running backwards, to see Conrol and Ardlan labouring after me. They've done well, burdened by their weapons and armour, but I'm unencumbered and fleeter of foot anyway.

'Almost there. You'll thank me when we get to the top,' I call.

I can see Ardlan smothering a smile, but Conrol is furious.

As we get closer to the wall, I feel dwarfed. The mountains on either side are incredibly tall with white caps, yet it's the sheer, near-vertical face of this construction that gives it such an overwhelming presence.

I dart through an arched entrance to one side of the gate tunnel, and sure enough, from within the small, gloomy, debris-filled chamber, a set of uneven steps is visible. I hurry upwards as Ardlan runs in, panting. After a few steps, it's hard to see, yet a glimmer of light beckons up ahead. As I get closer, I pass an arrow slit in the stonework that's been artfully concealed on the outside. Regularly spaced holes in the walls are barely visible and probably once held torch brackets.

'Malina,' calls Ardlan, his voice ragged. 'Enough. We've come this far, so let's continue together at a walk, shall we?'

'I'll wait,' I call happily, turning around to see them labouring up after me. I take a moment to wonder about the design. Unlike most castles with an anti-clockwise spiral staircase to aid with defense, these steps go diagonally up within the wall. Maybe this was a cost and time saving as no one knew when the next attack might come.

Major Conrol says nothing as they get closer, but I'm sure he's now just as intrigued to investigate as I am.

We're on the north end of the wall, and it's now getting so dark I can barely see a few steps ahead. I sense that Ardlan's going to suggest turning around because there's not much point in us going further without torches.

I hold my hand out in front of me, and with barely a thought, a glowing ball of flame appears in my palm. I pull up my sleeve just in case. Major Conrol hisses between his teeth, but I press on, ignoring him.

We tread carefully as many of the steps have fractured with age. Cobwebs are thick across the passage, but I increase the strength of the flame, and they peel back, burning, cremating anything entrapped within.

After twenty steps, we come to a long landing. Along both sides are heavy, perfectly rounded stone balls encased in more webs. Where the spiders are that made them, I've no idea.

'What are these for?' Ardlan murmurs, kneeling down to look at them.

They stand as tall as his thigh and are incredibly heavy. He sits on one.

'I think I've found the answer,' he laughs, stretching his legs out.

'I think not,' Conrol mutters, looking back down the steps. 'They're a brutal, simple defence to kill any unwanted guests coming up. If all of them were used, they'd block the entrance permanently.'

Conrol is right. The effect these stone balls would have on any attackers coming up the narrow stairwell would be devastating. Nothing would be able to stop their descent, and everything in their path would be pulverised.

We set off again, another twenty steps and more stones, but there's also a corridor with three interconnected chambers. We investigate and find them all identical, with a dozen wide stone benches spaced neatly apart in each.

'Sleeping quarters, perhaps infirmaries, or both,' Ardlan remarks. 'Yet there are only thirty-six beds. Unless there's more, that's a fraction of the number required to defend something this large.'

As we continue upwards, another landing appears; there are more stone balls and, this time, what might have been a storeroom. Mounds of rust, rat droppings and ancient debris are everywhere. This time the steps lead back in the opposite direction, heading toward the centre of the wall. Two more landings, each identical to the ones below, and the musty air turns fresh.

We come across a final chamber. Huge corroded steel wheels with a few rusted spokes remain. Gears and levers and pitted chain links as thick as my arm standing over a dozen large holes in the floor indicate this was some kind of gatehouse.

My legs gently ache, and the ascent reminds me of the Mountain of Souls. However, daylight shows through an arch to our right, and I sigh in relief.

We've finally reached the top, yet it's nothing like any of us expect.

There's no open wall; instead, we're in an enclosed tunnel with small openings every twenty paces. They're barely wide enough to lean through, but nonetheless, the tunnel is awash with light from the setting sun.

'By the gods, that's a view worth seeing,' Ardlan exclaims next to me, looking west, and I can only agree.

Below us, twisting like a serpent into the distance, is a steep-sided valley with the trade road nestled in its centre. The entire landscape is painted with red, orange, green, yellow, and black brushstrokes. Above, the sky vies for supremacy in this artistic competition. Clouds the colour of fire are streaked across the sky, set against a backdrop of deepest blue. It's breathtaking.

After a few minutes' silence, we begin to take stock of our surroundings. We're standing at the centre of the wall, where another exit probably leads down to the opposite side of the gate tunnel. Further stone balls are placed here.

'This is such a strange design, although I can see the advantage of a roof if it rains,' Ardlan jokes, looking up at the masonry above us. 'I hope it holds; look at some of those cracks!'

'More likely to keep off a rain of arrows,' Conrol muses. 'But why no towers, murder holes or proper arrow slits. This is just a wall, with no real defensive capability, beyond keeping those inside it safe.'

Major Conrol can't help himself. A military man, through and through, he starts examining everything closely.

'Ardlan. Take a look at the base of the wall. Tell me what you think,' he asks, having leant out through a narrow opening. He beckons the captain to take his place.

'I'd say it's to drain water away from the wall,' Ardlan muses. 'What's your opinion, Malina?'

Conrol snarls and moves away. I expect he's half tempted to grab my legs and tip me over. Sadly for him, with my magic, that won't kill me, and maybe that's what stays his hand.

I look around, and there, cut into the mountainside, curving down and along the base of this mighty wall stopping just short of the wall tunnel, is what looks like a wide sluice. A smooth, curved excavation as if a spoon has been dragged through butter. Another one mirrors it to the left, but it's now covered by fallen stone blocks and landslide debris.

'It could well be.'

Conrol snorts as if it were pointless asking me, but then my gaze falls upon the stone balls by the stairwell.

'However, I warrant, if we move to the end of the wall, we'll find a lot more of those ready to roll down. I think it's another defensive mechanism.'

Conrol shoots me a glance, then strides off rapidly, with Ardlan and I following. The tunnel floor everywhere is covered in the carcasses of dead birds, mounds of red dust and crumbled stone. Cobwebs covered in dust and ancient mummified remains of insects hang from the low ceiling, and I hate to think how many have ended up in my hair.

'You were right,' Ardlan says, clapping me on the back as we reach the end of the wall.

Sure enough, cut into the mountainside above the sluice is a covered platform. More stone balls rest in a channel waiting to be pushed through an opening just large enough for them to fit through.

There's also a narrow tunnel opening that descends into the mountainside.

I'm wondering whether we should investigate further when a rumble makes me look around.

'That's my stomach saying that dinner is well overdue,' Ardlan smiles apologetically. 'Time to head back, I think.'

Had it been Conrol, I might have ignored him, but I'm hungry too and using my magic after such a long day has only added to my tiredness. With a final look around, I lead the way back down the steps, deep in thought.

Even with the southern end of the wall nothing but a massive pile of rubble, this still might slow Nogoth's horde down. I say a silent prayer to whoever had the forethought to build this wall. What horrors they must have seen, and even after all these years, their labour won't have been entirely in vain.

***

I'm clean for the first time in weeks, and it feels good. My clothes are damp from being washed, and whilst I could have expended a little magic on drying them off, my body temperature will do that soon enough.

Everyone is in good spirits around the fires, for a bath is a luxury, especially a hot one, and for many of the Last Hope, this was the first they'd ever had. Laughter is loud on the night air as Yeldom tells a hilarious tale about a bath he'd had in his youth that involved a seductive woman, her angry husband, a chicken and a feather duster.

Yet I'm only half-listening, for there are more pressing matters on my mind. With only seven weeks to go until Nogoth's invasion, the whole world is walking blindly toward the apocalypse, and my dream has sharpened my focus.

It's time to convince Major Conrol and Captain Ardlan to take my claims seriously.

My determined footsteps take me toward their campfire, where they sit, taking a break from mingling with the men.

Ardlan raises his bowl in salute as he sees me approach. He and I get on, yet he isn't my problem. Major Conrol is. He's the ranking officer and in command.

'We all need to talk,' I say, sitting down on a log between them.

'No, we really don't. Not tonight or any night,' Major Conrol says, spitting into the fire for good measure. Picking up his bowl, he gets ready to leave.

For whatever reason, my anger gets the better of me. His pig-headedness will get so many killed.

'Sit down, or I'll make you sit down!' I hiss quietly, eyes blazing.

'Watch your mouth, girl, or I'll cut your bloody tongue out,' Major Conrol snarls back, his hand closing around his dagger hilt. 'Or maybe I'll just slit your throat and happily take my place within the Last Hope as punishment!'

'How will you do that if I make you cut your own throat instead?' I threaten.

'Enough!'

Ardlan might be the Major's inferior, but his commanding voice snaps loudly in the night air bringing the conversation around all the nearby campfires to a sudden halt.

'As you were, men,' Ardlan calls, then turns back to us both.

'Apologies, Major, and to you, Malina,' he says quietly but firmly. 'Now, what's all this about?'

'She's a bloody witch and should be burned alive, is what this is all about!' Conrol storms.

'Perhaps that should be my fate, Conrol. Yet if my killing the High King was bad, I'm now on the verge of doing something worse. I'm complicit in a crime that will make that pale into insignificance.'

'I bloody knew it,' Conrol chokes out angrily. 'What is it? Tell me, damn you!'

'So you can stop it from happening this time, unlike when you failed to stop me from killing the High King? When you stood by and watched him burn because you didn't act in time.'

'Yes, damnit. YES. I live with that failure every day, and I'll never let it happen again!'

Ardlan comes to stand between us.

'You need to calm down, both of you.'

'NO!' I hiss. 'He needs to hear this.'

'You were complicit in me killing the High King,' I say through gritted teeth, driving my verbal dagger home into Conrol's chest. 'Without YOU, I couldn't have done it. You brought me and my fellow assassins through the front gate. It was you who led me, murder in my eyes, to stand right in front of him. You were complicit then, and you're complicit now!'

'Damn you, girl. Damn you to hell. I tell you this, I will die before I let you commit this crime you allude to!'

'Then throw yourself on your sword now, because your anger and hatred are blinding you. The ssythlan's orchestrated this war and the death of your High King, amongst many others. They didn't do it for political gain but for their god. In seven weeks, that god, Nogoth, is arriving with an army the like this world hasn't seen for a thousand years.'

'When I uncover your lies and discover your real plan, you do realise the pardon you received won't keep your head on your shoulders.' Conrol growls.

I shake my head in disbelief.

'Are you so blind? Look behind you. What do you think that wall was built for? It wasn't to keep wild rabbits and mountain goats from ravaging the countryside all the way to High Delnor. The survivors from the last invasion built that, not knowing when the next would come, just knowing from where …'

'Gah,' snorts Conrol. 'One ancient wall doesn't add any credibility to your tale. Why wasn't a citadel built there, if what you say is true? Forty thousand troops in one would have been sufficient to hold the pass if this army of monsters came through. That wall resulted from a stupid decision and a stupid design, nothing more.'

'Maybe they didn't build a citadel because there weren't enough fighters left, or more likely because this area can't sustain such a population. As for a stupid design, perhaps there are no battlements because Nogoth's flying warriors would sweep them clear. I think the windows are small so that they can't get in. The stairwells, which are the only way to the wall top, can be blocked by those stones. It's designed to give those who defend it the greatest chance of survival.

'It wasn't built to defeat Nogoth's hordes but to slow them, giving time for kingdoms and armies to unite. Then there's Midnor. The governor said it was built on the remains of a fortress. It's in a straight line from here to High Delnor. Why would that have been built? Tell me that!'

Conrol's face reddens, and he talks to me as if I'm an idiot.

'Because it's near the border with Icelandia, and back then, they probably weren't pleasant neighbours!'

'Malina,' Ardlan intercedes. 'I have faith that you believe in what you're saying.'

For a moment, my hopes rise, but then they're dashed.

'Yet that doesn't make it true.' Ardlan finishes his sentence.

Yeldom's words come to mind about finding something they can't disagree with. I also remember the dream, the accusing eyes and the corpses asking why I hadn't warned them.

'So why are we here?' I probe.

'I've asked myself that question every day for three weeks!' Conrol laughs bitterly. 'I'd have slit your throat back at High Delnor instead of wasting time doing it here when your lies were uncovered!'

Ardlan looks shocked at Conrol's confession.

'It's in case the ssythlans actually are the reason behind Pine Hold and Sea Hold's silence. This area provides a lot of the raw materials we need for the war effort, and we can't afford it to be disrupted,' he offers.

'So why are we charging in like a bunch of amateurs with the men unprepared then!' I challenge. 'Both of you are veterans, experienced officers, and yet your leadership is a disgrace. The men under your command don't know a fight might await them.'

'Or so you say,' mutters Conrol, but I ignore him.

'My men can handle themselves in a fight,' Ardlan adds defensively.

'They've never seen a ssythlan, let alone fought one, so they'll have no idea of their strengths and weaknesses. Your blind hatred, Conrol, and your blind obedience, Ardlan, will get them slaughtered at their first encounter.'

I can sense a battle going on within both Conrol and Ardlan. Ardlan has to defer to Conrol's decision and doubts my word, but he makes his mind up first and speaks nonetheless.

'She has a point, Major. When would we ever go into a possible fight unprepared? I've no idea about ssythlans. What harm to learn something that might stand us in good stead?'

I can see Conrol wants to say no just out of spite, but as Yeldom had surmised, he can't disagree with sound military practice.

'It's your unit and your decision,' Conrol growls through gritted teeth. 'We leave at first light, and nothing slows us down. Nothing. Do you understand, Captain?'

The way Conrol speaks makes me think Ardlan has just made an enemy of Conrol too.

In the greater scheme of things, it's the least of Ardlan's worries.

***

We'd started off an hour earlier than usual, rising before sunrise, then getting underway as the first rays bathed the landscape in a sea of gold. Riding through the town before any residents were up sent a chill down my spine. It was all too easy to imagine them gone, some of the first to be shepherded back through the World Gate to a different life underground, with terrors far more horrific than a cave in.

It hadn't been pleasant riding through the wall tunnel. There were no open gates, and I don't believe there had ever been any. Instead, pairs of thick, fire-hardened tree trunks supported three rusting portcullises that looked as if they might come down at any moment. As we exited the tunnel, the final one lay flush against the front slope of the wall. It didn't have the traditional gaps between bars. Instead, it was a single massive panel of rusting steel. Slightly above it were two holes in the wall, streaked with rust where once-mighty chains had held the portcullis up before the trunks were put in place.

However, the wall is now a long way behind us, and we're making good time, passing through the centre of a sparsely wooded winding valley.

I look across at Ardlan, and he nods.

'AMBUSH. AMBUSH!'

My yell is echoed by Ardlan, and suddenly pandemonium breaks loose.

Shouts of worry and confusion tear along the ranks as men wheel horses about. Several mounts pick up on the panic and rear, tossing their riders. Some men jump down, drawing swords while trying to unsling shields. Yeldom does his best, and he starts screaming at his men to stay mounted, but, as I'd surmised, despite most being veterans, this was not something they'd ever prepared for. With conflicting orders and reactions all the way down the line, it's a disaster.

Ardlan looks ashamed, and even Major Conrol struggles to hide his shock.

'Your men aren't trained cavalry; they're infantry used to fighting in formation on foot, having been lined up in front of an enemy,' I shout above the noise, trying to lessen the disappointment.

'It's just a drill. JUST A DRILL.' Ardlan shouts over and over.

Slowly order is restored as the word finally filters back down the line, and men dust themselves off while suffering the verbal lash of the sergeants and corporals.

Major Conrol is looking at me, something different in his gaze.

'We'll be leaving the horses at Lake Hold,' he states before wheeling his horse around and setting off.

As the ride continues, Ardlan passes orders back through Yeldom on how to react.

A few hours later, when a third ambush is called during the late afternoon, the column of mounted men, four abreast, display signs of discipline. They split down the middle and turn outward, facing either side of the valley. Swords are drawn, but the shields stay slung as they're body length and not designed for fighting from horseback.

'Not perfect, but getting better,' Ardlan observes as we set underway again.

After the first ambush, we'd lost twenty minutes while discipline was re-established; this last one, only four. It's shocking how experienced soldiers are lost in a new environment. The set pieces of a battlefield or siege where everyone knows their place is what they're all used to, yet credit to them, I can sense their readiness creeping up a notch.

'Next, we need to have scouts ahead, behind and to the flanks,' I suggest.

Ardlan laughs.

'You put me to shame. Oh, to be part of a bigger army again. Someone else always makes the big decisions and sends the cavalry to scout ahead for us. Now, we *are* the cavalry.'

Shortly after, Yeldom and seven others canter past while the next few ranks peel off and make their way into the tree line. At the back of the column, other soldiers are doing the same.

Every hour the outriders are replaced, and as they return, I note they're holding themselves differently, seemingly more alert.

We make camp an hour early at an intersection in the trade road.

'How do you think we should handle giving the men the news?' Ardlan asks, looking to Conrol.

The Major shrugs and walks away, deep in thought.

'Have the sergeants and corporals report to us.'

Ardlan looks thoughtful, then shakes his head with a wry smile.

'You've already been adopted into the battalion, and this is your show. So, you give the order.'

'Yeldom!' I shout, catching sight of him brushing his horse down. 'I want all the company sergeants and corporals here within ten minutes.'

He pauses, looking to Ardlan, waiting for a signal, but Ardlan remains impassive.

'DIDN'T I MAKE MYSELF CLEAR?' I yell, and Yeldom hurries off to do my bidding.

'Don't make the mistake of thinking you'll get a rank, pay or pension now,' Ardlan laughs.

I can't help but smile. He's a good man, and having him on my side makes this so much easier. I just wished he and Conrol believed me.

Whether they'll see the light in time worries me, for surely death won't wait much longer to claim us all.

***

Ten men of the Last Hope face Ardlan and me. Five abreast, two deep, infantry shields locked. Their swords remain sheathed, but instead, they all hold heavy sticks, and for the first time since I laid eyes on them, they look like true warriors, confident in their ability.

This is what they've trained for; fighting in formation. The shields protect them from calf to neck, and as they hunker down, I can see only their eyes gazing firmly back at me through the slits of their leather helms.

Surrounding us are Yeldom and the eighty-nine other men of his company, and they're watching intently. This is why we'd started and now stopped early. I'd had word spread through the battalion by Yeldom and his corporals that this mission involved the prospect of death at the hands of a foe they'd only ever heard of. Everyone is now briefed on the ssythlans' speed, how they move and look, but now I'm going to show them how they might fight.

Yeldom's corporals are amongst those standing before me in formation.

'These are ten of your finest, put forward by you.' I speak loudly into the respectful silence. 'Just imagine I'm a ssythlan, which, considering how green I am, isn't too hard.'

A ripple of laughter runs through the watchers, and Ardlan smiles alongside me. Conrol's lips curl unpleasantly. Yet however much the Major dislikes me, he's come to watch and learn, as I hoped he would.

Unlike the swordsmen, I'm empty-handed, while Ardlan holds a long wooden stave I'd fashioned earlier.

'When I give the command, you have thirty seconds to overpower your captain and me. Lay a stick on us, shield-bash us, anything to lay us low whilst avoiding Ardlan's stave of death.'

I laugh, but behind the joviality, I'm deadly serious. From the narrowed eyes of those facing me, they are too, for pride is on the line.

Ardlan is less than sure.

'Are you crazy?' he whispers. 'They won't go easy on us.'

Turning to him, I grin.

'Have you ever dreamt of besting ten men at once, single-handed? Well, now is your time. Just trust me and attack when the chance presents itself.'

'I might have to wait until they're all asleep tonight then,' he mutters. 'Assuming I can still walk.'

'Attack!' I shout.

There's no hesitation, and I silently applaud our ten opponents for immediately breaking formation. It would have held them too immobile and unable to outflank the two of us. They're supremely confident, and they aren't stupid either.

Ardlan firms his grip on the stave. It will be useless against their shields, and he prepares himself for the coming punishment.

Yet it never arrives.

I don't need to put on a show, but I do. I raise my arms and then pull them down dramatically.

After the first few steps, the men pitch forward as the ground liquefies beneath them. Then, as they struggle frantically, elbow-deep in mud, I bring my hands together, and they're trapped as it solidifies.

Even the birdsong stops at that moment as everyone watching is stunned into silence. Only those struggling hopelessly moan and curse in frustration as Ardlan theatrically moves amongst them, tapping them unopposed with his stave.

I soften the ground a little with a simple thought, and the ten men gratefully pull themselves free and roll onto their backs.

The magical drain makes me dizzy momentarily, but I recover unnoticed as Ardlan returns to my side. A low murmur of conversation builds as I let those observing assimilate what happened.

'A ssythlan mage controls the four elements of earth, air, fire and water.'

As I speak, everyone stops talking and pays attention to my words.

'What you just witnessed is just one way earth magic can be used. Yet a ssythlan mage isn't all-powerful, for their use of magic is finite. Magic cannot be used at long distances, and sometimes it requires direct touch. Nor are their mages immune to weapons. If you see a ssythlan on the battlefield moving their hands as if they're about to cup your balls, target them first.'

Laughter runs through the watching men, and I'm glad. The show I'd just put on would have rattled them badly, but laughter can melt fear like butter under a hot sun.

'Throw spears, daggers, or even rocks to kill them or simply disturb their concentration, and then you'll just have their warriors to deal with. I'm sure you'll be pleased to know they relish single combat, not formation fighting.

'The ssythlan warriors use every weapon with the utmost skill, from short swords to javelins and double-bladed staffs. Even their engineers or civilians seem to have no fear and will attack with tooth and claw if they have no weapons to hand. Yet, irrespective of whom you might face, against your shield wall and stabbing swords, they will lose, but only if their mages are dead.'

I beckon Yeldom over.

'Yes, King Slayer.'

He stands to attention as if facing an officer, and I perceive Ardlan's nod of approval next to me.

'We have tents in the supply wagons in case of foul weather?'

'Yes.'

'Then the tent poles need to be turned into throwing spears. Fashion tips from daggers, knives, whatever you can. Then find those proficient in throwing, for they'll be our mage protection.'

Yeldom salutes, then hurries off, shouting orders which are echoed by the corporals. Soon they're heading toward the wagons.

'By the gods, I'd not have believed it,' Ardlan says, picking up the heavy sticks our defeated foes had left behind on our way to the next company. 'I don't know about the spears, but I'm glad we've got you to help us deal with any ssythlan mages. Assuming we encounter any ssythlans at all.'

'Well. If we don't, Major Conrol has orders to slit my throat,' I chuckle. 'So I guess we'll have to convince him otherwise. Anyway, I can't do as much as you'd think. They're more powerful than me. My reservoir of magic is smaller than theirs and replenishes slower. 'Don't get me wrong, I've killed one in combat, and another of the Chosen killed one before she died, but they are my betters.'

Yet suddenly, Nogoth's words come to mind about me being more powerful than I could possibly imagine. He is the king of deceit, yet, just like the ssythlans, I can control all four elements at will, and like the Saer Tel, with a simple thought, not forgetting the blood magic.

'Another Chosen?' Ardlan echoes, interrupting my thoughts.

'Her name was Lystra. The Chosen were what we were called. Chosen to serve the Once and Future King, Nogoth.'

Ardlan rolls his eyes at the last bit, and my hand itches to slap some sense into him.

Luckily for him, another hundred men of the next company are awaiting us. I've hardly spent time with them, although many faces are familiar. Most nod respectfully, and I hear many of them mutter King Slayer in greeting.

'I need ten of your finest to defeat Ardlan and me,' I shout as Ardlan throws the heavy sticks to the ground.

'Who thinks they've got what it takes?'

***

CHAPTER XII

It's been five days since my first display of magic. Weapons training is now undertaken before the evening meal, sharpening up the men and getting them into a combat mindset after three weeks of travel.

Conrol still barely tolerates me, but that matters little as long as he doesn't argue about keeping the troops combat-ready.

We're on foot, our packs bulging with supplies as we march two days west of Lake Hold. We'd passed through the town after a brief rest while Conrol talked with some of the inhabitants. It was a beautiful place, with small, well-built stone houses along cobbled streets positioned on a large lake's north bank. Small fishing boats drifted upon the still waters, nets hanging from their bows, while the looming mountains were reflected in all their snow-peaked majesty.

Despite Lake Hold's tranquillity, there had been concern amongst the townsfolk as we left them and our horses behind. A week earlier, they'd sent a dozen men and women with wagons and a week's worth of smoked fish to Pine Hold, and none had returned.

Yet they weren't fearful of ssythlans, not that any of the Last Hope mentioned them. Instead, they were worried about the plague. Several years before, many of them had fallen sick as disease had spread amongst the mountain folk like wildfire through a forest. Hundreds of others had died, and they were praying that this wasn't the case again.

If only they knew.

THE LAST HOPE

Guilt weighs heavily on my shoulders. The people of Lake Hold will be as good as dead, plague or not, for I'm cursed to be disbelieved, at least by those who matter.

One of *those* marches up ahead with Ardlan while I hang back with Yeldom and his company.

The crunch of booted feet is too loud, and I'm jittery. I'm used to stealth, concealment, and not marching around in the open. Although now they're on foot, shields in hand, the Last Hope appear more formidable than on horseback.

My eyes constantly scan either side of the trade road. The mighty trees that give Pine Hold its name are starting to appear, offering concealment for any number of enemies. We're but a day and a half from our destination, perhaps even our annihilation. Three ssythlan ships had been built and set sail from the Isles of Sin. Three ships with two hundred ssythlans apiece. Were all six hundred warriors, engineers, or both. How many, if any mages accompanied them?

But what if other ssythlan ships docked at Sea Hold, and we are marching to face thousands?

I stop briefly as that thought hits me like a hammer blow, then mutter an apology and hurry onwards as the marching men behind curse softly as I disrupt their step.

Then, my thoughts take me down a route that leaves me icy cold.

The one scenario I'd never contemplated is that there aren't any ssythlans or even a World Gate here. What if Aigul's slip of the tongue and the painting were just an elaborate ruse?

No. Whilst Nogoth is the king of misdirection and deceit, that would be beyond even him. Midnor, the wall at Iron Hold, the towns falling quiet ... this is where they'll come; I mustn't doubt it.

Movement in the sky catches my attention, and I squint into the sun. Birds circle on the air currents, wheeling then diving in an elaborate dance.

Malina, don't get distracted.

Pine Hold is less than two days' march, and with small copses of pine and wooded areas, I need to keep my eyes down, looking for danger.

A distant caw reaches me above the crunch of marching boots.

'What birds do you think they are?' I ask, pointing.

'Mountain Carks,' Yeldom answers. 'They're scavengers, a carrion bird.'

DAMN.

I raise my hands above my head, fingers extended. The corporals behind will now be copying my motion. Then, I close my hands into a fist and pull them down to the sides.

Behind me, the column comes to a halt, and the Last Hope takes cover behind their shields to either side of the road, weapons drawn. We have men in pairs out to the left and right flanks, and upon seeing what's going on, they take cover too.

A few steps ahead, Conrol and Ardlan turn at the sudden lack of noise, then hunker down and run back.

'Why did you order the column to take cover, Sergeant?' Ardlan asks, head swivelling left and right.

'It was me who gave the order, Captain.'

'You don't give orders!' Conrol hisses at me, eyes narrowing, but I note he still stays low.

Ignoring his comment, I point over his shoulder at the birds wheeling in the sky.

'Yeldom says those are Mountain Carks, a carrion bird. That's an awful lot of them for just a dead mountain goat. I suspect they're circling the site of an ambush.'

'Best we send some scouts ahead,' Ardlan says, rubbing at the rivulets of sweat running down his neck. He takes a water pouch, has a swig, offers it around then replaces it at his waist.

'No. I'll go.'

'You bloody won't!' Conrol shakes his head emphatically.

Yet I hold his gaze, fighting his will with my own.

'If I wanted to escape or kill you, I could have done it the first night we left High Delnor and not had to put up with your hatred these last three weeks. The men of the Last Hope aren't trained as scouts, hunters or woodsmen. If you send them, and they, in turn, get ambushed, those men will likely die, and our enemy will be forewarned.

'I'll go, because out of everyone here, I'm the only one trained in stealth. But, if that isn't enough reason, then this one really should be. The ssythlans will kill me if I'm discovered, and if I don't discover any ssythlans, well, you get to kill me instead by order of Commander Farsil.'

Conrol doesn't say anything. He just jerks his head back down the road.

Turning to Yeldom, I beckon him over.

'I need five daggers right now.'

He jogs off, and I can sense Conrol struggling with his anger. I've been kept unarmed and unarmoured over an enduring lack of trust, but there's no way I'll allow that to continue.

I shrug off my pack and water skin to ensure I'm as light-footed as possible.

A few minutes later, Yeldom is back. He's taken longer than I expected, but then I understand why. He's collected the daggers and attached them to a leather belt by tying the scabbards in place. He drapes it over my shoulder so that the weapons lay against my chest.

'Do you have everything you need?' Ardlan asks.

'Yes. It's time for me to get going. I'll be back within five hours. If I'm not, I'm dead.'

***

I set off at a ground-eating jog, parting with the road and heading toward the southern mountain slopes through the trees. It's midday, with not a cloud in sight, and anyone would be forgiven for not thinking of death this day.

Yet death is my trade, and it keeps me company like my shadow.

Despite enjoying the security of marching with the Last Hope, the relief at leaving them behind brings me close to euphoria.

I've only got five hours, although I'd have preferred far more. If an ambush awaits, as I'm sure it does, it won't be at the site of the previous one where the carks are, as nothing forewarns a target like dead bodies. The ssythlans won't be so clumsy, and they'll be far closer if they're here.

If I get past them and find the original ambush site unobserved, I'll ascertain the number of enemies that sprang the trap. Then, as I work my way back, I'll approach from a direction that the ssythlans think is safe. Their eyes will be on the road toward Lake Hold, so they won't see me coming.

I doubt there will be enough to put the column at risk, but if they warn their main force at Pine Hold, this mission will end in a bloody failure.

Despite putting speed over stealth, I'm confident I won't be spotted. Any eyes will be toward the road, and it's not as if I'm running in the open. I scurry low, from boulder to boulder, tree to tree, always choosing to move where there's cover, shadow, or ridges that I can hide behind.

I keep up a fast pace for an hour and am pleased with the ground I've covered. I'm now southwest of the carks, and it's time to find out what's excited them. This is a moment of great danger, coming down off the mountainside, not knowing if I'm spotted and walking right into the arms of the enemy.

I hunker behind a boulder twenty steps short of the forest and reach out with my magic, listening for something untoward.

Immediately I realise it's a worthless exercise. The forest is too alive, making it impossible to distinguish any threat amongst hundreds of noises. Instead, I rely on more traditional senses and take my time scanning the trees and undergrowth for any telltale shapes or signs of danger. Nothing is apparent, yet still, I'm not satisfied. Then, as a deer appears and begins to strip bark from a tree, I have an idea.

I summon a gentle wind and have it blow from every direction but mine. The deer pauses as the leaves rustle, raising its head, but then unperturbed by any foreign scent close enough to bother it, returns to grazing. I silently thank the magic within me, feeling it warm at my gratitude.

If the deer can't scent any ssythlans, it's safe to proceed, so I move into the forest's embrace.

The woodland is alive with birdsong. I'm grateful for their music as it disguises my soft footfalls, and they'll hopefully warn me of any predators. I spot occasional rabbits amongst the undergrowth and smile. The majesty of these mountains and being amongst nature calms my spirit.

Light filters through the canopy, and unconsciously I glide from shadow to shadow, weaving amongst the numerous shoulder-high pine saplings. My heart beats in time with the symphony of the forest, and if this were any other time, I'd simply lie down and let the positive energy of this ancient woodland wash over me like a soothing balm.

THE LAST HOPE

I move carefully, the road to my north just in sight, yet my focus ranges ahead as I scan the forest floor. Just like a muddy road will show footprints, so can the undergrowth. Studying nature's canvas, I detect and then discard the disruption left by rodents, rabbits, and even a goat as unimportant. Of human or ssythlan passing, there's no sign. No broken twigs, imprints, or scuff marks are evident. That doesn't mean no one is here; my own trail is nigh on non-existent, but ssythlan warriors aren't trained in stealth. Or are they?

I know so little of them, despite having been trained by some and fought others. So, I'd be foolish to underestimate them, a mistake that might get the Last Hope and me killed. I need to be cautious in the extreme.

Occasionally I discern the wheeling shapes of the Mountain Carks close by through the overhanging foliage, their cries harsh and brutal. Yet despite them hovering over my objective, I filter them out. I have to be in tune with the forest.

I take my time, reading the terrain before moving slowly.

It's counterintuitive, moving slowly. Your brain screams at you to find cover and shield your vulnerable body behind the next tree as fast as possible, but nothing draws an eye's attention like fast movement. So I take my time, taking no unnecessary risks.

Changing direction, I travel back east toward the Last Hope, knowing each step brings me closer to danger. The carks' cries get louder, and before long, my fears are proved correct. As I peer around a thick pine trunk, I spy three wagons facing west pulled amongst the trees at the side of the road.

A feeding frenzy is underway around them as hundreds of carks fight over whatever lies beneath the boiling mass of their black-feathered bodies and wings.

I'm confident the ambushers are gone from this place, but I still take my time, changing my position to get different perspectives. Crossing the road, I check the woodland north.

I'm glad I did, for here are the first signs of the ambushers. A trail leads from the road into the undergrowth. It's at least a week old, and nature has almost covered the trail, yet vague bootprints and flattened fauna show me where they went. Cautiously, I follow the trail, noting how it splits in all directions, showing where the ambushers took their places behind trees close to the road.

There had been eight of them, a solid-sized scouting group. It's a relief there isn't a more significant force abroad. Yet it had been more than enough against the unarmed fisherfolk from Lake Hold. The ssythlans believe there are no troops this far west, and if I can keep it that way, then the Last Hope will deliver them a nasty surprise.

I follow the bootprints from the trees down to the road. There are no signs of running, like scattered leaves or deep heel marks. It's almost as if they sauntered down, contemptuous and sure in their prowess to confront the wagons.

As I reach the road, the carks protest loudly. They're quite fearless and only begrudgingly give ground as I approach. I crouch, noting where the wagons had stopped and then been driven off into the undergrowth.

The birds have drawn back far enough for me to see a mass of rotting fish and the corpses of three oxen, but no human remains.

Had the drivers managed to escape?

No, that's very unlikely, which means they were taken prisoner and escorted to Pine Hold for questioning and execution.

I retreat, allowing the carks to resume their feast, and move stealthily east just inside the treeline. There are no further tracks, and I'm getting anxious about losing my prey. Is it possible the ssythlan scouts have returned to the main force?

I set off due north but don't bisect any trails rather than those left by animals. Returning to my starting point, I cross the road and repeat my search on the south side, but again encounter nothing. Is this the furthest east they've come?

No. They want to keep their presence a secret until Nogoth arrives. Those directly responsible for the ambush have either repositioned further east along the road or been replaced by a fresh party.

North or south of the road?

I choose the south and have no sooner stepped amongst the mighty pines than I hear running footsteps. Flattening myself against a trunk, I watch in disbelief as, down the road in my direction, four ssythlans race as if the very hounds of hell are at their heels.

***

My heartbeat rises, not in a panic, but rather in anticipation.

THE LAST HOPE

They must have spotted me, and undoubtedly their comrades are charging through the trees to cut me off at this very moment. Yet, I don't perceive any rapid movement amongst the forest, and as the hissing ssythlans draw closer, I realise I'm not their target after all.

They are indeed running from something, but what.

Of course!

They've just spotted the Last Hope and are running to Pine Hold to forewarn their brethren whilst their kin keep watch.

They each carry javelins and daggers, but other than green boots and loincloths, are unarmoured and unencumbered. Their hissing breath suggests they've been running a while, but I can't let them get any further.

As they pass, I step unseen from the trees onto the road behind them. I send my first two daggers spinning into the backs of the rearmost scouts, but as I'm about to release a third, the remaining ssythlans spin around. Two javelins flash through the air, forcing me to twist frantically, and the iron-tipped weapons swoosh by, one scoring my cheek as it passes.

It's two against one, and I'm only armed with three daggers. Yet one ssythlan turns and sprints off toward Pine Hold, its mission more important than risking its life. The bodies of the fallen scouts lie between the remaining ssythlan and me. We both react simultaneously, sprinting forward for the fallen javelins. I roll, grabbing one of the sleek weapons, then as my momentum carries me to my feet, I take three swift sidesteps, draw my arm back and cast it in one flowing movement at the back of the running scout. I don't take even follow its flight, trusting in my ability, instead immediately rolling again, avoiding the other javelin thrown at my back.

Then there's just the one remaining. It pulls a dagger as it lowers into a fighting stance.

'Traitor,' it hisses as it sidles toward me. 'Betraying your brethren to fight for the humans!'

I'm shocked, although I don't let it show. This ssythlan knows of my fey heritage. Had the ssythlans at the mountain known from the start, or, as Nogoth had intimated, it's because I'm changing? Yet, I don't feel any different.

'Do your friends have any idea of what you are? Do you even know what you are?' It hisses again, closing the distance, its hand weaving the glittering dagger in a small figure of eight.

Hissing, I bare my teeth, surprised at my reaction. Where did that come from?

I pull two daggers, throwing them in quick succession, and whilst my aim is true, the lightning-fast reflexes of my opponent see them dodged. Now I have but the one left.

Had I been Kralgen or Lotane, I'd have confidently duelled this creature. They'd likely win, whereas I know I'll lose.

I call upon my magic. The scout stumbles and sinks up to its thighs before the muddy road solidifies again, immobilising it. Hissing in defiance and with a sudden wrist snap, its dagger flies toward me, but the throw lacks power, and I snatch the weapon from the air.

Looking back over my shoulder, I'm relieved but not surprised to see my thrown javelin protruding from the back of the scout down the road. Satisfied, I walk around behind my entrapped foe, easily avoiding its grasping hands and cut its throat.

Time is of the essence. I've no idea if the scouts report back intermittently, even if just to restock supplies, so I can't dally. I swiftly gather up my thrown daggers, clean the blades on the dead, and replace them in their scabbards.

The sanctuary of the forest beckons, and I return to its embrace, at home in the shadows. My every footstep is unconsciously placed, soft as a falling leaf. Yet despite my silence, I travel smoothly, my peripheral vision finding the best route amongst the trees as I search for the other scouts.

They'll be watching the Last Hope from a good vantage point, which gives me confidence that I won't stumble upon them. If I can't see Conrol, Ardlan and the rest, I'm not near the ssythlans.

I pick up my pace and move up the wooded slope to the north, just inside the trees' perimeter. The valley winds slightly south where the battalion is hunkered down, so they'll be easier to spot from this side. The sun's position shows I've been gone about three hours. With plenty of time, I use it wisely, making my way stealthily toward the road.

Something untoward tugs at my senses … a trail!

Bent wildflowers, scuff marks and eight pairs of bootprints show this route has been travelled in both directions, and I'm confident this has been used by the scouts, the ones I killed, and the ones I intend to kill.

A thrill runs through my veins.

THE LAST HOPE

There's no greater test than hunting another sentient being. Whilst I might look back on many of my assassinations and soul gatherings with regret, there's no denying how alive I felt at times like this. I've missed the excitement, and the realisation surprises me.

Leaving the trail, I head back up the slope, keeping it just in sight. A foolish hunter might stay on the trail itself and stumble onto his prey or even traps. I doubt the ssythlans have set any, for they'll feel secure with the land behind them occupied, but why take a chance.

Slowly, I ghost from tree to tree, scrutinizing my surroundings and taking my time.

Finally, reflected light from a distant shield boss catches my eye. The scouts have to be close.

The trail splits, leading directly to four widely spread trees, no more than thirty steps ahead of me near the forest edge. There's some decent cover there, bushes and long grasses as well as the trunks, but nothing so dense that I shouldn't be able to spot my prey, knowing where they are.

A cold chill runs down my spine, and I turn, half expecting to find them standing behind me, blades thrusting for my body, but thankfully that's not the case.

I return my gaze to the trees and bushes. Confounded by my inability to see the scouts, I call upon my magic. The sounds of the forest are too loud even here, yet I'm sure I can make out the gentle hiss of ssythlan breathing. So, where are they? I could have the wind blow my scent in the direction of their hiding place; that would flush them out.

No, I mustn't get overconfident. I might have just killed four, but three were from behind, and only one had been face-to-face with magical assistance.

A yellow and brown bird flies down to one of the trees, then immediately flies away before returning and doing the same thing. It's odd behaviour, and I'm sure it can also sense or even see a danger I can't.

There's no ssythlan hiding in the branches, or the sparse undergrowth, of that I'm sure, so I fix my gaze upon the tree trunk. Am I wasting my time? It appears there's no ssythlan there. Yet as my attention flicks back and forth, I notice a strange uniform irregularity to the right side of each trunk, and once that becomes apparent, so finally do the ssythlans.

I knew my knowledge of them was limited, and now I understand why the scouts I'd slain earlier had been wearing so little. They can change the colour of their scaled skin to perfectly match their surroundings. Each ssythlan is motionless, hugging a separate tree trunk, heads turned toward the Last Hope. They've literally hidden in plain sight. I wonder how long they can stay perfectly still? There's no sign of their weapons that would have given them away, but no doubt they're within reach.

Summoning a long gust of wind that rustles the leaves, disguising my movement, I make my way to the far side of the tree of the northernmost ssythlan. Its arms are wrapped around a pine tree at shoulder height. The next ssythlan is obscured by another tree trunk, as are the others. This is the perfect observation place, but they broke a cardinal rule: to keep an eye on those who share their watch.

The impact of my dagger thrust under the ssythlan's armpit is disguised by yet another large gust of wind. The remaining ssythlans might think it strange that the wind appears out of nowhere on such a still day, but there's no reason for them to suspect a magic user is nearby.

The blow pierces the ssythlan's heart even as the wind carries away its dying hiss.

One down, three to go.

I smile. This is what I've trained for, and more than that. I enjoy it.

***

'Was this really necessary?' Conrol growls, inspecting the head of the final ssythlan I'd killed.

'You tell me. Would you have believed me if I'd returned without it?'

Conrol grunts as he tosses it into the undergrowth. It's the only answer I get, but at least the disbelief and scorn are gone. Only the anger remains, and hopefully, that will soon find another target.

Ardlan is more practical with his reaction.

'Report!'

'I came across an ambush site two hours' march down the road where the carks are feasting. There were signs of eight attackers ...'

'Eight?' Conrol interrupts. 'Where are the others hiding then, or did you let them get away to warn their brethren?'

Just when I thought Conrol's behaviour might be on the verge of improving, here's the suspicion that I'm still working for the enemy.

'I killed them all. The first four ...'

'You killed them all?' Conrol scoffs, not letting me finish the sentence.

'How long do we have?' Ardlan asks.

'I don't know their procedures, but I expect they'll rotate scouts or get resupplied every two days. We currently have the element of surprise as I stopped four heading toward Pine Hold. They were travelling at speed, implying they'd just got into position and spotted us for the first time.'

'Then we need to make the most of the opportunity you've given us.' Ardlan reaches out, gripping my hand. 'It seems you were right about ssythlan interference. Now we need to move fast, but we need eyes and ears out ahead to do that. You've proved yourself once. Care to do so again?'

I nod.

'Major?' Ardlan turns, seeking his superior's approval.

'As you say, Captain. We need to make the most of this opportunity.'

Conrol turns toward me, and I can perceive his turmoil. He sighs, his shoulders sagging.

'Malina, take Yeldom with you.'

Gah. Conrol still doesn't trust me and wants Yeldom to keep an eye on me.

'We'll march at double time,' he continues. 'If you spy anything untoward, you can send Yeldom back. I want us unobserved on the outskirts of Pine Hold tomorrow evening!'

It seems I've misjudged Conrol's reasoning. Yeldom accompanying me is tactical.

'Yeldom!' I call.

He's been loitering nearby and hurries over.

'Dump your pack, sword and armour. Just bring your dagger, a water skin and some dried meat,' I order as I retrieve some of my supplies. I drink thirstily and eat a little as Yeldom gets ready.

'The ssythlans can camouflage themselves,' I say between mouthfuls. 'They can adjust their scales to mimic the colour of their surroundings, and they're almost entirely invisible to the eye. If we take the trade road, we might run into another ambush as the woods provide too much cover.

'It will be tougher going, but I suggest we take to the mountain slopes above the tree line to the south. Any spying eyes will be on the road, and even if we're spotted, we can't be ambushed.'

'Good idea,' Ardlan agrees.

I'm relieved when Conrol nods. He pulls out a worn map and lays it on the ground as Yeldom returns, and we lean forward to get a better look.

'It's now apparent that the ssythlans either intend to disrupt our war effort by taking control of our iron mines or seek to acquire these lands for themselves at our weakest moment. It's a sound strategic move as we've never needed a military presence this far west in generations.'

'Major. That's not why they're here.'

'You'll respect my rank when I talk and remain quiet,' Conrol retorts.

At least there's no burning rage behind his comment. However, it's so frustrating that he still can't accept my story. I calm myself. If I push now, I might undo the little progress I've made. I just need to bite my tongue, whatever he says.

Satisfied with my silence, Conrol continues, a grubby finger running across the map.

'The ssythlans obviously landed with a small probing force at Sea Hold, unsure whether they'd meet armed opposition. Having met none, they've moved as far as they dared, occupying Pine Hold. Once reinforcements arrive, they could establish a bridgehead as far east as Iron Hold. To say that will put our war effort in jeopardy is an understatement. Also, the manpower required to retake this territory doesn't bear thinking about.

'We'll follow Malina's suggestion and move along this ridgeline from here to here,' Conrol says, stabbing his finger at the map. 'This will give us a good vantage point above the town, allowing us to see how best to engage the ssythlan forces within. With surprise on our side, we need to ensure our victory is swift and decisive, so we can free the citizens of Pine Hold and march swiftly to liberate Sea Hold.

'Thoughts?'

I want to say there will be no civilians left alive, and the ssythlans have no interest in Sea Hold, but instead, keep my mouth shut. Conrol will see the truth for himself soon enough. Then, once he's convinced, I hope we'll have enough time to evacuate this region and return to High Delnor.

No one else has anything to add. Yeldom leans forward, studying the map briefly, before nodding in satisfaction.

Ardlan stands up, groaning as he stretches.

'Malina. Yeldom,' he says. 'Time for you to go. Be our eyes and ears. We'll be right behind you.'

I nod, looking up at the mountains, remembering a time when I hunted a red wolf. Like then, I'll not fail, for failure means death, and not just mine this time, for the Last Hope of this world will die with me.

***

We've made it.

The gods had at first smiled, and we'd run into no further scouts or opposition.

The Last Hope has taken shelter in the pine forest behind whilst Conrol and Ardlan are beside me. The close-knit buildings of Pine Hold town are below us, and the sun still peeks over the peaks to the west.

Now the gods are laughing maniacally at our predicament.

We're crouching, hidden within a rocky outcrop at the forest's edge, halfway up the mountainside, whilst a ferocious wind smelling of the sea howls down the valley. I wonder if it's seasonal or batters this place all year round.

'You said there would only be around six hundred ssythlans,' Conrol growls accusingly. 'There has to be nearer two thousand, damn you!'

'Damn me? You didn't even believe there would be any,' I hiss back, equally unnerved, hardly able to believe my eyes.

'There's too many for us, and they've fortified the bloody place.' Ardlan mutters, frustration evident in his voice. 'There's no sign of any townsfolk either; I fear the worst has happened.'

He's right. At least eight hundred armed and armoured ssythlan warriors are standing guard over a host of engineers and workers on the mountainside. There are even more ssythlans in the town below, surrounded by a high, wooden palisade wall made of old pine trunks. There's no way the Last Hope can prevail with either a day or night attack.

'Looks like they're repairing that ruin to use it as a military base.' Conrol's eyes narrow as he looks up the slope.

The ruin is the old haunted castle, as Yeldom had once described it. Set against an enormous cliff face, a tall wall curves outward in a semicircle. The remnants of what might have been two towers rise like broken teeth at either end of its short length. It's apparent that superstition kept the resident lumberjacks well clear of the place as it's partially obscured by mature pines.

Punctuating his words, the sounds of picks and hammers are carried to us loud on the air as the ssythlans endeavour to fashion a smooth road from the ruin to link with the town. Occasionally the low sound of a hissing chant echoes out from the castle, as does a steady flow of ssythlans bearing rock debris that they deposit onto huge piles outside the walls.

I remember what Yeldom had said about it being inside out, and he was right. Rising along the outside, between decrepit buildings, broken steps lead to the top of the crumbling wall. The central entrance passage is the only part that appears solid from this distance. I warrant it's been widened, heightened and strengthened by magic. From our vantage point, I can't see inside, so it's impossible to know what's within.

Conrol's remark about the ssythlan's repairing the place would make sense if only the ssythlans were an occupying force, but I can't imagine Nogoth and his army dwelling here. Yet why repair it and build a road if not to use this castle as a base of operations?

A moment later, the answer crystalises in my mind.

The paintings I'd seen in the temple had shown humans being led through a gate, stepping directly from one world into another. I warrant this castle was built by the same historic survivors responsible for the wall at Iron Hold. The World Gate must be inside!

'We'll have to withdraw.'

Conrol's words shake me to my core. We can't leave, not without him understanding the truth.

'We don't have the numbers to overcome this force,' he growls. 'An attack during the day will see us beaten by both numbers and the terrain. I fear we'd suffer total losses. A night attack might have worked, but as they've fortified the town well, we'll fail there too.'

Ardlan smiles craftily.

'What about if we occupy the castle,' he suggests. 'Wait for the ssythlans to return to the town tonight and take it over. It might look old, but defending that will surely negate their numbers.'

Conrol sighs.

'It's an interesting idea, my friend. But without supplies or a relief force coming to save us, our supplies would run out in a few days. They could just ignore us, and we'd die of dehydration. As I said, we'll have to withdraw. Lake Hold is indefensible with our numbers, so we'll evacuate the civilians there, pull back and fortify Iron Hold.

'We'll have the men rest for now and head off before first light.'

No! We can't leave without everyone knowing the truth; we just can't.

Ardlan's suggestion gives rise to a desperate thought. If I can get Conrol and Ardlan to see the gate for themselves ...

YES!

If we creep up after dark, they'll see the World Gate hidden inside. Although will that even be enough to convince them of a fey invasion? I don't know, but there's only one way to find out.

As the sun disappears and darkness falls, the engineers and warriors begin their return to the safety of the fortified town below. However, twenty heavily swaddled warriors make their way into the castle gate.

My plan is disintegrating before my eyes.

Damn, damn, damn.

'Let's go,' Conrol orders.

With no other option, I follow him and Ardlan as we head toward the forest, back toward the waiting battalion.

What now?

Butterfly wings flutter in my stomach, and the temptation to use my blood magic on Conrol is huge. Yet what would I gain? There's an unbeatable force of ssythlans in town, and attacking the guards in the castle will bring them like bees to protect their honey.

Perhaps my best option is to go along with Conrol's plan and retreat to Iron Hold before taking a horse and riding like the wind to High Delnor. Then, Lotane, Kralgen and I can hide in the frozen wastelands of Icelandia for two years until the fey depart. Except Kralgen won't run, he'll want to fight, and Lotane might not even want to go with me.

The blood magic stirs again, reminding me it's the solution to all my problems.

No. I mustn't give in.

So what can I possibly do? Neither Conrol nor Ardlan believes my story of a fey invasion despite finally accepting I told the truth about the ssythlans. Until such time as they do, no word will be sent to forewarn High Delnor or the other kingdoms.

Not long ago, I remember saying to Lotane how we'd never turned away from adversity. I mustn't start now. I simply need to find a way to do the impossible; defeat these damned ssythlans and have Conrol see what they've been up to with open eyes.

Gods, help me.

The thick tree canopy allows a little light from the twin moons to light our path, but it's almost too dark to see our hands in front of our faces as we meet up with the Last Hope. To a man, they're hunkered miserably behind their shields, using them as a windbreak.

Conrol signals the sergeants to gather around and gives them the bad news to pass on to their men while I wrack my brains for a solution.

Yeldom comes to stand next to me. He's put his armour back on, yet he's shivering badly. I wonder briefly why I'm not, but a wiggling in my stomach tells me why. Even without asking, if the magic senses my needs, it helps subtly where it can.

The wind is so strong pine needles are being blown through the air like tiny daggers.

Yeldom leans against a pine, seeking shelter, but pulls away from the sticky trunk, a grimace barely discernible on his face.

'I think the lads would rather go now, as this will be a long, freezing night. I hear those lucky ssythlans are sheltered behind a palisade wall. I bet they've got fires going, the lucky bastards.'

'Lucky bastards, indeed!'

Then it's as if the sun has risen, for thanks to Yeldom, I can finally see the light. Reaching forward, I grab him and give him a swift kiss on his bristly cheek.

'What was that for?'

'You're the answer to my prayers,' I say playfully, leaving him standing there, mouth open, as I go to find Conrol and Ardlan.

***

CHAPTER XIII

The palisade gate rises above me as I creep forward. The stealth isn't entirely necessary, but my training is too ingrained to ignore, so as I cross the open ground, I take my time, testing every step.

I've approached from the west side of town along with twenty soldiers with the wind at our backs. It remains ferocious, and thankfully there's no way any ssythlan guard could discern our steps above its howl. Likewise, our scent is whisked away and masked by the sea's smell.

There's also little chance we'll be seen. The sturdy palisade, which stands about four times my height, is a simple, effective, but hastily constructed defence, and that's one of the ssythlans' mistakes. As I'd explained to Conrol earlier, with no guard step or walkway lining the inside, no lookouts are stationed on the walls.

I don't doubt a few guards are patrolling inside, ready to raise the alarm if an attack comes. Yet they're relying heavily on their now dead scouts and this impressive wall that protects them from any surprise attack.

Yet it's this very wall that will be their downfall.

On the east side of town, a safe distance from where the only other gate opens onto the trade road, Major Conrol waits with the rest of the Last Hope. Four hundred against nearly two thousand.

It will be a massacre.

The moons provide just enough light to operate by, and my twenty soldiers spread out and silently approach the walls on either side of the gate.

Two minutes later, they're back grasping wooden brands covered in sticky resin and pine needles. Yeldom's grimace as he'd leant against the tree, and his comments about the ssythlans having fires, was the beginning of the end.

In groups of five, the men gather around and push the ends of their brands together.

A silent wish, a simple touch, and my magic sets them ablaze.

The men run back to the walls where they'd pushed massive globs of sticky sap while I sprint to the gates.

Reaching out, I touch the pine trunks, projecting my thanks as my magic joyfully ignites the sticky wood. I step away, looking left and right to see if the soldiers need help. They don't.

The wind, the flammable resin, and the dried pine trunks the ssythlans had used to make the palisade wall were the ingredients of a firestorm waiting to happen.

The flames leap along the walls and onto the nearby buildings at breathtaking speed, whipped into a ravenous frenzy by the wind. As I look about, the faces of everyone are lit by the dancing flames, shining red and orange as they shout and laugh in glee, revelling in the destruction they've just unleashed.

There's no way any ssythlan can escape through this gate, so I shout to get the men's attention. Swirling my hand around my head to rally them, I head off at a run, heading for the south side of the wall.

We keep our distance, avoiding gobbets of fire as resin pockets explode and trunks split. The fire is already way ahead of us, having already reached the far end of the town, travelling as fast as the wind itself.

The light, the heat, and even the noise are incredible, and my stomach flutters as the elemental power within me responds to this incredible display.

Despite tiredness dogging my steps ... the toll of using magic, I feel alive.

A hand grabs my arms.

'Over there!' shouts a soldier, pointing, and I change direction, heading toward Major Conrol and the Last Hope.

THE LAST HOPE

They've changed position from what we agreed, but I quickly see why. Even though they'd been positioned a safe distance from the east gate, men are on hands and knees, coughing. Everyone is blackened by the smoke, and looks like they've stepped from the fire itself.

Ardlan is retching alongside Conrol as I approach, black spittle dripping from his mouth, but he stands up, wiping it away, and manages a smile.

'We blocked the gates, and only five ssythlans made it out. They must have been the mages, for the fire hadn't touched them. They're dead now too, and we haven't lost a single man, thanks to you.'

Conrol shakes his head, cold, dispassionate eyes surveying the scene.

'You slaughtered them all. You didn't even need us. How many more will burn at your hands?'

He doesn't wait for my reply, and I'm not sure I even have any words for him.

Ardlan turns back to his men.

'Move up the southern slope, out of the smoke!' he roars, trying to be heard above the conflagration.

'We'll head to Sea Hold at dawn. We need to secure our borders!' Conrol shouts at Ardlan. 'Have your sergeants pass the word.'

I can't allow that to happen, but I don't say anything.

I'll save the good news for the morning when the fire and Conrol have cooled down.

***

It had been a long and sleepless night.

Initially, it was because of the noisy coughing from those who'd inhaled too much smoke. Then, when the wind shifted and the northern slopes caught fire, fear spread as quickly as the flames. I think everyone prayed then, imagining what would have happened to us had the wind swung the other way.

Despite being tired, I'm up stretching and exercising before the sun rises. Rest is important, but keeping my body supple and strong is as much a habit as caring for my weapons.

As the makeshift camp begins to stir, I lose count of how many men come over, greeting me or simply grasping my shoulder.

'They're all a little in awe of you,' Yeldom says, coming to stand beside me. 'In fact, I'm a little in awe of you too.' He laughs softly, a little embarrassed.

'It was thanks to you that I came up with the plan.'

'Hah. I don't suppose if I come up with more bright ideas, I'd get another kiss?'

'I've got an idea!' Someone calls.

'So have I.'

I laugh as several nearby soldiers shout out, overhearing Yeldom's remark.

'Damn,' he mutters, scowling over his shoulder, then breaks into a smile and laughs heartily along with them.

'Don't get the wrong idea, Yeldom. I like you, but my heart belongs to another!'

'What's his name, this lucky man?'

'Nog… I mean Lotane. His name is Lotane!'

Yeldom shakes his head, merriment in his eyes.

'Well. It seems you're a little confused. Maybe you can add my name to the growing list one of these days.'

He tramps off, calling to his men to get out of their bedrolls.

Damn. Why did I say Nogoth first? I certainly don't love him. Lust for him, yes. His skill in the bedroom was beyond sublime. But love? I can only imagine the further hurt Lotane would have suffered were he aware of the slip.

As I finish my routine, I stare up the mountainside to the distant castle. I have to get Conrol and Ardlan up there, but how.

Then I perceive movement, and smile.

The ssythlans have again provided the answer.

'Major. Captain!' I call, jogging over to where they're deep in discussion over Conrol's worn map.

'Not now, Malina,' Ardlan answers. 'Get ready to move out, then we'll talk as we march. We have to make Sea Hold by day's end.'

'We can't leave yet!'

Major Conrol stands, eyebrows drawn close. Like everyone else, his face is blackened with soot, yet his eyes are bright, and they're shining with anger once again.

'The men might want to follow you, but don't ever forget, you follow me. The captain has given you an order, so I suggest you obey it.'

His finger shakes as he points for me to go away.

I've had it. Day after day, week after week. It doesn't matter what I do; it's never enough.

'Perhaps they want to follow me because I'm not blinded by stupidity or anger,' I rage. 'What competent leader would leave an enemy at our rear to wreak havoc and revenge upon the innocents of Lake Hold or Iron Hold? Stop acting like an ass. Your anger is clouding your judgement!'

Conrol's hand goes to the hilt of his sword, a bleak grin creasing his face.

'Draw that sword, and it will be the last thing you do!' I hiss.

'Why, because I'm going to be the next one you burn alive?' he growls, eyes narrowing. 'Maybe I'm fast enough to cut your damned head off before you can!'

Ardlan steps between us and, to my surprise, turns to Conrol.

'She's right, Major. Your judgement is clouded, and it needs to stop. The man I knew would have come up with Malina's plan himself last night. To make matters worse, I'm guilty of following your lead because of your rank, not because you're right. But enough is enough.'

'How dare you side with her?' Conrol's voice shakes as he spits out the words.

'We all have blood on our hands, Major. Every last stinking one of my Last Hope are murderers and thieves, yet they'd lay their lives down for you, and I know you'd do the same for them. She killed our king, but you and I have also killed brothers and fathers, sons, and the gods know who else.'

Ardlan turns to me.

'Malina. What are you talking about? Sea Hold is the key to securing our western borders, but ... Oh, by the gods, it's the ssythlans in the castle. How did we overlook them?'

Conrol twists around to look up the hill, and his hands go to his face, rubbing furiously as if to wash away the soot.

'YELDOM!' Ardlan shouts. 'Your company, fully geared with me two minutes. I want those with spearmen from the other companies too.

'Malina, come.'

I swiftly grab a drink from my waterskin and then toss it onto my pack.

Yeldom's company are forming up, ten abreast by ten deep, heavy shields at the ready. The last rank are carrying their makeshift spears. A further thirty spearmen from the other companies are getting ready behind.

I join Ardlan at the front of the column, and he passes me a heavy shield and sword.

'The owner will want it all back. Don't get attached to them,' he laughs.

'You might need this as well.'

To my surprise, Major Conrol holds out a stained and blackened leather helm. He looks embarrassed as I take it with a nod of thanks.

'The soldier it belongs to is puking his guts up thanks to your bloody ...' He stops, shrugs apologetically, and then tries again. 'Thanks to your well-thought strategy.'

I refrain from saying anything, afraid to break the spell, so I just nod gratefully.

'Men!' Ardlan shouts, catching their attention. 'Our object is to retake the castle from the remaining ssythlans.' He raises his hand and chops it downward.

I've never marched into battle before, always enjoying the freedom of solo or small group combat, and it feels restrictive and unnecessary. I want to run ahead and be the scout but hold back for fear of upsetting Ardlan or Conrol now there's a fragile truce.

We'd seen twenty ssythlans enter the castle the night before, and who knows where they'll defend. Their best option would be a narrow corridor or a room with a small entrance that will funnel our numbers and prove costly.

My magic wriggles, reminding me not every fight needs to be won by force of arms. With the smoking ruins of Pine Hold behind us, I should hardly need reminding. Yes, magic will be the better option. I could seal them in to die in the darkness. I smile grimly; they deserve no better.

As we get closer, the sun fully crests the peaks to the east, and yellow light bathes the valley.

'FORM AND HOLD!' yells Ardlan as the ssythlans suddenly fly out of the castle like angry wasps to protect their hive.

THE LAST HOPE

Ardlan closes in on my left, as Conrol does the same on my right, locking their heavy shields with mine. Moments later, the front rank presents a solid barrier as the ssythlans leap at us.

The spearmen haven't the time to throw, and with the ssythlans so close, this will be decided by steel on steel.

I'm not used to fighting this way and feel completely hindered by the formation. Yet I force myself to trust in those around me. As the ssythlans smash against the shield wall, weapons bouncing off the hardened surfaces, Ardlan raises his voice again.

'PUSH!'

As we step forward, bashing with our shields, several ssythlans go down, and our short swords do their work. The remainder gives ground slowly, hissing in anger, hindering our advance by darting forward to land heavy blows with sword or spear. Despite several men falling injured, the Last Hope aren't drawn into breaking ranks, and we're soon at the massive entrance.

Daylight only illuminates the first dozen steps as the ssythlans retreat into the gloom ahead of us. Yet, it isn't pitch black, for behind them, I can see a faint light shaped like …

I was right. The World Gate is here.

The ssythlan warriors back away as we advance down a huge tunnel. There are no passages or archways leading off, just massive rocks lining the walls, some of which have been smoothed or strengthened by magic. The rest are scarred by pickaxe or hammer, and it occurs to me this isn't an existing gate tunnel that's been expanded.

The massive piles of debris outside the walls are a clue to this jigsaw. This had never been a castle but was instead a giant stone barricade to prevent the fey from coming through the gate. Over the last few weeks, the ssythlan mages and engineers must have made this tunnel themselves through rock that was laid here a millennia ago.

'Just a moment longer, brothers.'

It takes me a moment to realise that it's one of the ssythlans exhorting its kin. A little longer till what … them meeting their gods in the afterlife?

But then the answer is made clear to me.

As I stab a ssythlan in the chest, it stumbles back, retreating away with its kin just as light floods the tunnel. For the sun rises, not only in our world but the land of the fey, revealing a landscape of dreams and an army of nightmares.

Belief dawns on Conrol's face while Ardlan's mouth opens and closes like a fish out of water, and the Last Hope's footsteps falter.

The remaining ssythlans take the opportunity to turn and run. The one I'd struck staggers after them, clawed fingers fruitlessly trying to stem the spurt of ichor. As we watch, dumbstruck, the ssythlans pass through the gate as an evil-smelling wind blows through the other way.

The enormity of what I'd just witnessed hits me like a physical blow; the gate has just opened.

Nogoth and his ssythlans had lied. I thought we had another five weeks.

The end of the world has come early.

***

Despite the ssythlans racing down the ramp on the other side of the gate, the fey army is only just beginning to rouse. In response to their appearance, around three dozen sinewy creatures, grey leathery skin, all knees, elbows and bulbous eyes, sidle up the ramp, long tongues hanging from their lips. They appear female, with long knotted black hair falling to their knees and cloth wrapped around their breasts and waists. Despite being unarmoured, they pull long black daggers from their belts and lick the blades in anticipation.

Twin temples rise up either side of the ramp, a horrific reminder of what lies beneath.

'By the gods, you were telling the truth.' Conrol's hushed voice sounds loud in the silence as the Last Hope stares wide-eyed upon another world. 'You were telling the truth.'

'What do we do now?' Ardlan asks, but more of himself than anyone else.

'What are those things?' Someone cries, and others echo the words.

Fearful murmurs begin to rise, and the front rank shuffles backwards. Without leadership, a rout will soon occur. This situation is already dire, but it could quickly worsen. Something needs to be done. There are two good antidotes for fear ...

'I'll tell you what they are.' I shout as I step forward from the ranks and turn my back to the gate. 'Those hags are Yeldom's sisters. They might be as ugly as he is, but there's enough to go around.'

Nervous laughter meets my poor joke. It's a start.

'Seriously though, you asked what they are.' I pause briefly, considering how to deliver the news. I shrug nonchalantly as if I were telling them nothing more worrying than the time. 'What you see behind me is no different from the armies you're used to facing. Like the others, they're about to invade your homelands. If they prevail, they'll slaughter or enslave your fathers and mothers, brothers and sisters. They might look like the creatures of nightmares, but that doesn't matter.'

'Why the hell doesn't it matter?' A man asks, having pushed to the front.

Everyone looks at me expectantly.

'What's your name?' I shout, pointing at him.

'Derenas.'

'Give me your spear, Derenas!' I order, holding out my hand.

The soldier tosses me his weapon, and I catch it midway up the shaft, hefting it and testing the balance.

Looking briefly over my shoulder, I see one of the creatures ahead of the rest, turning back to its kin, undecided on whether to advance further.

I spin, take three swift steps and throw, turning my hips and shoulders for extra power. The spear passes through the gate, arcs, and plummets to take the creature square between the shoulder blades, pitching it forward at the feet of its brethren.

'It doesn't matter because we can kill them!' I yell.

I've almost got them back from the brink. Seeing me kill one of those weird harridans has straightened the mens' spines, but they need something more.

I laugh out loud as something outrageous comes to mind.

'Captain. Would you mind if I took command briefly?' I say, stepping over to Ardlan and grabbing his shoulders as I look him in the eye.

'N-no. N-not at all,' he stammers.

'Derenas. Get your arse moving down the mountain and get the rest of the Last Hope back up here. On the double man. MOVE!'

Derenas turns and bolts along the tunnel.

'Wedge formation!' I yell, positioning myself between Ardlan and Conrol.

'Didn't you whoresons hear me? WEDGE FORMATION!'

'WEDGE FORMATION!' Ardlan echoes, snapping out of his stupor, and then Conrol shouts it out.

'ADVANCE AT THE DOUBLE!' My voice cracks as I shout, but it doesn't matter, as one hundred men of the Last Hope jog through the gate.

'You're crazy,' Conrol shouts as we surge forward, but then the time for conversation is lost as roars erupt from hundreds of thousands of throats as we do the unthinkable ... invade the land of the fey.

We slam into the shocked creatures on the ramp, our armoured wedge splitting them apart, tossing them aside. As they fall, they're trampled, stabbed, and kicked to death in a panicked frenzy that cleanses the men's fear. Only a victory can do that, and however short-lived, this is ours.

The ramp where we stand is at least twice my height, and creatures of every shape and size are leaping and scrabbling to get to us. Several hundred tusked creatures wielding wicked-looking swords and body shields are forming up at the far end, discipline apparent despite the hunger that's no doubt consuming them. I look about, wondering if I'll see Nogoth, but he isn't in sight. Our job here is done, and it's time to withdraw.

Yet just as I'm about to shout the order, a beast leaps onto the ramp twenty steps ahead of us. It's thrice my height, and a bull-like bellow erupts from its jaws as it spreads its legs and arms wide. It holds a giant sword in one hand, twice as long as I am tall, and in the other, a standard adorned with feathers and human skulls.

'I claim the blood rights on these pathetic humans!' it roars, the common tongue sounding twisted and brutal coming from its cavernous maw. It shakes the tribal standard above its head before tossing it into the sea of watching fey.

'We're undone,' Ardlan murmurs next to me.

He's right. This one beast alone could swat the men behind me aside as if they were flies. Yet the taller they are, the more vulnerable to low attacks they become, or so I found when practising against Kralgen. Yet I'd never ever once managed to beat Kralgen, and this beast would make him look like a dwarf.

'Give me your sword,' I command Ardlan, taking it from his shaking hand.

Now isn't the time to hesitate. I'll either be dead or victorious in the next twenty seconds.

THE LAST HOPE

Tossing my shield aside, I spring forward, feet pounding, a wind pushing me from behind as my magic senses the urgent need.

Corded muscles bunch, eyes flare, and that ghastly sword swings. Without question, it will cut me in half. Yet at the last possible moment, I roll, the swoosh of the blade so close that the wind of its passing almost unbalances me. As the sword tip gouges into the ramp behind me, stone fragments thud against my back, but then I'm on my feet, running between those mighty legs. I spin, adding power to my blows, feeling my swords cut deep, glancing off bone as I cut left and right. Then as I pass through, I slow to a jog as the army around falls quiet in stunned disbelief.

Behind me, I hear painful grunting, followed by a huge thud and the moans of the mortally wounded behemoth. It's likely my adversary had been a general or champion, and its swift defeat momentarily shocks the fey army into silence.

Every eye is on me as I stand there, arms hanging loosely at my sides, the two swords dripping black blood. I look around at the fey horde, challenging them with my stare.

I need to use this victory for all its worth. I will use the weapons of The Once and Future King himself; deceit and misdirection.

Calling upon my magic, a wind blows through my hair, but the reason isn't for dramatic effect; I want my words to be carried on the breeze and heard by everyone here.

'I will give you this one day to prepare for death!' My voice carries like thunder as I raise my swords, sweeping them around to encompass them all. 'For tomorrow, I will return with the vengeful human armies at my back to burn you and your world to ashes!'

Turning, I walk slowly, careful not to slip in the river of black ichor that still pours from the gaping wounds to the insides of the beast's thighs. I climb onto its corpse, remove my helm, throw my arms wide and let forth a war cry.

'Tell Nogoth when he arrives,' I yell, 'that Malina, the King Slayer, is coming for his head at noon tomorrow!'

***

'Withdraw the men in formation,' I say firmly as I approach the ashen-faced Conrol.

He moistens his lips and nods.

'Form up, lively now! Shields high. Company, about turn!'

With the precision borne of automatic obedience, the men pivot around.

'At a slow march, forward!' Conrol orders, and they stamp back through the gate in perfect unison.

I've never felt so vulnerable as I stand there, letting them leave while I turn around a final time, taking careful note of the forces around me. The names of monsters used to scare me as a child come to mind.

The one I'd slain must have been a troll, while in the distance, giants tower over everything.

Formations of the winged creatures I'd encountered on my last visit circle above. Gargoyles.

Closer, furred wolf-like creatures with intelligence shining in their yellow eyes snap and howl. They can only be wolfen. However, the majority of this horde are brutish, tusked monsters. Ogres?

My gods, every creature I ever believed was made up can be found here, and I realise that a warning of this day has been told for a thousand years.

Every instinct screams to run and never stop, but I can't let this army know my fear.

I look upon them, the silence building, then shake my head as if disgusted. Reaching down, I pick up my discarded shield and saunter back through the gate into the transient safety of the tunnel beyond without looking back.

If I'd been surprised by my victory, nothing could have prepared me for Conrol coming over to throw his arms around me. After a moment, he steps back, looking embarrassed, nervously looking over my shoulder through the gate.

'Forgive me, Malina. I was wrong.'

I know he wants to say more, but now certainly isn't the time.

'Why did you say the armies of man would be invading tomorrow?' Ardlan asks, confused.

'To buy us a day,' Conrol answers for me, his awe at my ruse evident. 'They believe a vast army will invade on the morrow and will prepare to slaughter us as we march through.'

'But what do we do with a day?' Yeldom asks, joining us. 'We can't seal up this tunnel, and from the size of some of those beasts out there, they'll make short work of any barricades we erect.'

All eyes turn to me.

As if understanding my unspoken question, Major Conrol clears his throat.

'From hereon, Malina, you lead. I'll advise if there's a better way, as will Ardlan here, but you're in charge for now.'

The weight of responsibility on my shoulders is almost unbearable, but indecision will never be something I succumb to.

'We need fifty men in a shield wall across the tunnel to be rotated every hour. They must be visible and ready to dissuade any fey that becomes too inquisitive. If we keep up the appearance of preparing to attack, there's nothing for them to gain by forcing the gate. Have spearmen ready, just in case. I don't want anything passing through.'

'Every other man needs to be tasked with building a barrier. We'll use rock debris and the trees from outside the tunnel. The higher we can make it, the better, as they have Gargoyles that fly.' I struggle to voice the word out loud, but neither Conrol nor Ardlan blink.

'It won't be enough, but every hour it gives us will be more precious than gold. But first, every man needs to see what we're facing. Then, those who survive will have the belief to persuade everyone they come across of the danger the world faces.

Conrol nods at Yeldom, who moves away, shouting orders at the waiting men.

'What about your magic?' Ardlan asks. 'Can you use it to seal this tunnel again?'

'If I had a month, maybe. I'll do what little I can, but using it drains me terribly and won't leave me fit to fight.'

'Damn,' Conrol mutters. 'But perhaps it's better that way. To have too much power would make you a god in a world of mortals.' Then he chuckles. 'I never thought I'd say this after what I've been feeling recently. But, when I look at those creatures, I'd happily worship you if you could save the world.'

We laugh together, and even in this dark moment, it feels good to have our wounded relationship begin to heal. It's been open and raw for far too long.

'Now comes the hardest part,' I sigh. 'We need to decide who'll be given the slim chance of escape.'

I pause, gathering my thoughts, picking and then discarding countless ideas.

'Major. You have to be one!'

'No. That I can't do!'

'You have to, Major,' Ardlan says before I can voice my reasons. 'Commander Farsil will never believe Malina if she returns alone. He'll have her executed, as you well know. He trusts you over and above anyone. Your duty is to notify Farsil, not stay here and die. That's for me and the Last Hope. The first in and last out, that's our way. It always has been.'

'I'm staying too, and don't even think of trying to dissuade me!' I stare at them both, resolute.

Ardlan and Conrol exchange a swift glance, and then they both shrug.

'Having seen you slay that giant creature when I thought our end had come early, I'm not going to argue,' says Ardlan. 'It will give the boys who fight with us all the courage they need. How many need to stay?'

'To give Conrol as much time as possible to get back to Lake Hold, grab some mounts, and return to High Delnor as fast as he can ... I'd say three hundred. The hundred he takes can protect him from the gargoyles when they get past us and verify his story to Farsil if they make it.'

Ardlan pulls his ear lobe.

'They'll all want to stay, believe it or not. I know they took fright to start, we all did, but they're sworn to protect one another. The Last Hope is a family, and you don't leave a brother behind.'

Conrol puts his hand on Ardlan's shoulder, gripping it tightly.

'Be that as it may, Malina is right. Take three hundred, my friend, and make those creatures pay dearly. Put fear and doubt into them like Malina did.'

We move back down the tunnel as fifty men of the Last Hope form a shield wall ten steps inside the gate. The rest of the Last Hope are making their way, wide-eyed, to see for themselves the new world and monsters they've just heard about.

THE LAST HOPE

As we emerge into the open, Conrol and Ardlan step away, so I take a quiet moment to myself.

I pause, staring at the charred, smoking ruin of Pine Hold in the valley below and sigh. How many cities and towns will soon look like that? I'm glad I'll die here, so I don't have to witness the world in flames.

If only I'd had a chance to make amends with Lotane, to know his love again before I died. Even as I try and recall his caress and the love in his green-blue eyes, Nogoth flashes into my mind. I want to cry in frustration. Why am I so fixated on that beast? Maybe it is blood calling blood. Yet, my blood is red, not black, and I'm more human than fey. Yet as I look at my hands, I wonder if that's entirely true.

Conrol giving out orders efficiently and with authority catches my attention. It's something to behold as the soldiers, most of whom will die here, now respond to the command in his voice without hesitation. Finally, I have some hope, for if he's back to his former self, I have confidence he'll make it to High Delnor. The fey invasion will still come about, but Nogoth's army won't find the easy pickings they're hoping for.

Ardlan is equally effective, although his style is somewhat different. He has an easy familiarity with his troops, cajoling and insulting as he directs his men, and I can see their love for him shine in their eyes.

I wait for a pause in the shouted orders.

'Major. I need a brief word.'

Conrol turns to me.

'What is it, Malina?'

'I have a confession, but not a bad one. At least not now.'

Thankfully he laughs, and a white smile splits his filthy face. It's all the invitation I need.

'There are allies on the way to High Delnor.'

'More Chosen by any chance?' Ardlan butts in, overhearing our conversation.

'Well, yes, but just one. However, he won't be alone. You see, he'll be bringing an Icelandian army with him.'

Conrol's astonishment turns from disbelief to acceptance in a matter of heartbeats.

'I can understand why you didn't disclose that earlier. It would have led to your immediate execution. Assuming we could carry it out,' he adds with a wry smile. 'To lead an Icelandian army, I assume your fellow Chosen will have a position of high authority.

'The king. His name is Kralgen.'

'Oh, just the king.'

'The problem is he only left for Icelandia the day before we captured you and has no idea Nogoth is coming through the World Gate five weeks early.'

Conrol purses his lips thoughtfully.

'You're worried they'll arrive too late.'

'Exactly,' I sigh. 'Which brings me to Lotane. Lotane and Kralgen are close. If the Icelandians arrive in good time, I'd suggest having Lotane around, so things go smoothly. Kralgen can be a little hotheaded, but he looks up to Lotane … and there's one final thing.'

It's all I can do to choke out the words that need to be said.

'Just tell him I'm sorry and that I'll love him forever.'

Tears flow unchecked, irrespective of my self-control.

Ardlan comforts me, his arm going around my shoulders, pulling me against him.

'Tell him yourself,' Ardlan says, and as the words register, a cloth is clamped over my mouth and nose. I don't even have time to react before pungent nightloom fumes overcome me, and everything goes black.

***

CHAPTER XIV

'Hold my hand, my love.'

Lotane's voice is soothing as I fight the waves of pain that rip through my body. The contractions are coming closer and closer together, shaking me to my very core.

He looks as tired as I feel, for this has been an abnormally long labour. Yet the midwives seem happy, no concern evident in their eyes. Nor does Lotane look worried. I simply perceive the deepest love and affection in his gaze. He's forgiven me as I knew he would, and soon our world will be complete.

'Push, my love. Push.'

I strain with all my might. The magic writhes within me, and I know my baby will be imbued and gifted with power just as I am. I feel strong despite the tiredness.

I scream, and even though it's full of pain, that's outweighed by joy. I'm bringing a baby into this world. A new life, a new hope. Yes, that will be my baby's name if I have a girl. Hope. She'll be my first Hope, but as I love Lotane so much, she won't be my last.

From my bed, I can see out the window. We live in a beautiful valley, with tall, snow-capped mountains on either side. We're so lucky.

'I can see the baby's head,' a woman cries with excitement. 'Push harder, now. Push.'

So I push again, my head swimming.

The bed shakes with my agony, but Lotane steadies me, his words of encouragement and love reaching through the haze.

Then, it's done.

From one moment to the next, the baby is part of me, and then, there's a brief moment of emptiness.

My heart stops, but as a baby screams, it starts again, and then a swaddled bundle of happiness is pushed into my shaking, grateful hands.

'She's a beauty, just like her mother,' Lotane says, kissing the baby's forehead.

I blink away the tears, looking at this tiny life in my arms, with multi-hued skin and already with black hair, she's just like me.

'Just look at those eyes, exactly like her father's,' I laugh as Hope opens them for the first time.

It's true, they're the most beautiful violet I've ever seen.

Violet!

'What have you done?' Lotane cries in horror, grabbing my shoulders and shaking me hard. 'What have you done?'

I begin to cry. This is all wrong … and the shaking. I wish Lotane would stop shaking me so I could think properly. Nothing makes any sense!

…

'I think she's coming around, Major.'

The voice is unfamiliar, loud and unwelcome to my ears.

That shaking continues, the baby screeching.

'Push harder now. Push.'

But I've already given birth. Why push harder?

I open my eyes to see trees swooshing past above me. It takes me a moment to distinguish a drug-induced dream from reality, yet the sense of loss is so real.

I'm in a low cart, and the wheels squeal as it bumps along the trade road at speed, pushed by four soldiers. I'm foggy, the after-effects of the nightloom. Yet my anger, and no doubt magic, clear it away, leaving me sharp as a needle.

'Stop!'

The Major's voice echoes mine. The shaking cart comes to a halt, and I leap out like a cat. The soldiers retrieve their shields and move away with swift salutes, leaving me standing opposite Conrol.

'I have to go back,' I growl, reaching into the cart to retrieve my own equipment.

'It's too late, Malina. I'm sorry.'

'It won't take me long, I can assure you!'

Conrol doesn't answer; he just points upwards.

Looking through the canopy, I discern the circling shapes of hundreds of birds ... but there's something wrong. They're too big and ungainly, hovering around like butterflies.

Gargoyles.

'You've been out a full day. It's past noon, and they began appearing a short while ago. It seems your ruse worked, but it also means Ardlan and his men are dead.'

Conrol rubs his temples, wincing, smearing dirt on dirt. Everyone looks and smells of fire and death. I'm no different.

'I'm sorry about the Nightloom, Malina. We can't afford to lose you; you're too important. You've already mobilised a nation to fight at Delnor's side, and you're the only one who knows our enemy. Not forgetting your magic and martial skills. You don't get to die yet, Malina. Too many lives are in your hands!'

My anger is overshadowed by sadness at the loss of so many men. Ardlan and ...

'Is Yeldom here?' I look around, searching the sea of faces.

'He stayed. All the sergeants and corporals stayed. They led by example.'

Conrol's voice catches a little, and I know he suffers the same guilt that all of us do. Yet, at the same time, his eyes shine with some hope.

'Lake Hold is just ahead. We've made it, Malina. Thanks to you, we've made it!'

The men around me are panting and sweatstained. They've discarded their armour to give them more speed, and apart from sword and shield, they carry only their packs.

'DOUBLE TIME!' Conrol bellows and sets off.

I jog alongside, thankful my head has cleared so quickly. Unfortunately, my legs feel a little heavy, but I know that will wear off.

Every fifty steps, I turn and briefly run backwards, noting the gargoyles getting closer. They're Nogoth's scouts and are carefully combing the trail behind us. I've seen what they're capable of, and it's a good thing the trees provide cover. I reckon we're an hour ahead of them, maybe less.

As we reach the western outskirts of town, Conrol turns to me, an expectant look on his face.

It seems I'm in charge again.

'My first order is, don't you dare use that Nightloom or anything else on me again. Understood?'

Conrol looks sheepish but nods.

'Take eighty soldiers. You have thirty minutes to round up and saddle all the horses you can. Wait with them on the trade road just east of town. I'll meet you there with the other men. Every second counts, Major. Don't let anything slow you down.'

Conrol turns away, shouting, and within a minute, eighty men are sprinting off, their footsteps rumbling like thunder on the cobbled streets.

The remaining twenty soldiers stand silently, their eyes bright, expectant. By comparison, their red shirts and trousers are filthy, sweatstained, and covered in soot. They look like the murderers, thieves and vagabonds they used to be. Hopefully, that will help.

I take a deep breath.

'We owe it to the townsfolk here to try and give them a chance, however small it is. Major Conrol will be on the trade road east of town with our horses in thirty minutes. If you're not there, we'll leave without you. In the interim, do what you can, spread the word, and get people to join us ... there will be spare horses after all.

'Be brutal, rough, and frightening, for, in an hour, the gargoyles will be here, and when that happens, anyone left will have no chance at all. Let's go!'

I run toward the first house, kicking the door down, bursting in on the terrified inhabitants.

What should I tell them? That a fey army has invaded, that gargoyles are coming here to feast on them? They'll think I'm a madwoman and disbelieve every word I say until it's too late.

I draw my sword.

'You have to the count of ten to start running east to Iron Hold. If you stop, and I catch you, I'll cut your throats. NOW MOVE!'

***

'From now on, we'll have to burn everything down,' I shout above the steady beat of the cantering horse beneath me.

'What?'

Major Conrol raises his hand high, two fingers extended, and reins his horse back to a trot. The column behind us follows suit.

'What are you talking about? Burn what down?'

'Everything. Nogoth's army is huge, and while he'll no doubt have a supply train following behind, his army needs to eat and drink. If we have time, we need to torch everything that burns, kill any livestock and poison every well or water source we come across.'

'What is it with you and burning things?' Conrol growls, then shakes his head. 'I'm sorry, Malina, that wasn't fair. I hadn't contemplated a scorched earth policy, but you're right. At least those gargoyles have disappeared, so that's a bit of good news.'

I look over my shoulder, and sure enough, there's no sign of them. Then I shake my head sadly as the realisation sinks in.

'It's not good news for the people of Lake Hold. I can only imagine the carnage there,' I choke with emotion.

I might have succeeded in driving people from their homes, but so few had heeded my or the other soldiers' warnings. Only two dozen townsfolk ride at the rear of our column, barely hanging on.

'We should make camp and rest the horses. We'll rise an hour before sunrise and get an early start before those gargoyles take to the skies. I want us in Iron Hold by midday,' I say.

Conrol nods, and a few minutes later, he's picked a spot for us to camp.

As we rein in and dismount, some of the men start to unsaddle their horses.

'Leave the horses saddled,' I call. 'Make sure they're well-watered and fed. We'll replenish our supplies tomorrow. No fires, and from now on, keep the noise down.'

I hear my orders repeated amongst the men and smile in satisfaction.

'You, soldier,' I point to a swarthy, scarred individual. 'Look after the major's horse and mine once you're done with your own.'

I receive a salute in return and walk through the camp with Conrol beside me and pick eight men.

'The first watch is your responsibility. Each of you choose another to stand alongside you. Position yourself so you always keep the next pair of sentries in sight. Major, please pick their relief to take over in two hours.'

As Conrol stomps off, I walk amongst the men, pausing briefly here and there. I speak softly to them, keeping the conversation casual. I make a few jokes, ask their names and where they're from before moving on to the next bunch. I'm well versed in Delnor's geography, but there are dozens of places mentioned I've never heard of.

Darkness has fallen as I return to where I'd thrown my pack. Conrol has already laid my bedroll next to his and has put dried meat, cheese and bread on my shield.

'It isn't poisoned,' he laughs sadly as I automatically scent the food. 'A short while ago, maybe, but not now. Not ever again, I hope.'

'Thank you, Conrol.'

'You can call me Dimitar when you care to do so.'

I smile my thanks, and for a moment, tears threaten to well up. I hadn't realised how much this man's friendship meant to me until now, and he's trying his best to make amends.

We eat in companionable silence, and my heart mends a little. I can only hope Lotane and I can reconcile, for only that will truly make it whole again.

'I've been talking to the men, and it's given me pause for thought,' I say softly, aware of my command to keep the noise down. 'Us returning to High Delnor is paramount, but that's just one city, and there are a hundred towns and villages north and south of our route between here and there. We should have the men spread the word as far and wide as possible. We'll travel just as fast without them and draw less attention split up.'

Conrol finishes chewing on some meat before washing it down with a gulp of water.

'You saw what happened at Lake Hold. They witnessed four hundred men pass through and one hundred return looking like we'd been through the fires of hell. How many came with us?'

'Twenty-three,' I say sadly.

'Twenty-three out of nearly a thousand souls took heed of our warning. It took me to step into another world and see those monsters to believe. If the men save a couple of hundred, it will be a miracle.'

THE LAST HOPE

'Perhaps those couple of hundred will be the future of the human race. Every soul we save gives us a chance at a better future and will be one less to feed his horde. Don't forget, they're here for us, not gold or land. They're rounding up livestock!'

'As long as your scorched earth policy doesn't involve slaughtering civilians, so they don't fall into enemy hands!' Conrol's accusing glower is back.

For a moment, I consider the implications but then shake my head.

'No. I'd prefer everyone to come with us, but those who don't will live to play their part. Either they'll slow Nogoth's army down as they're eaten or drain his army as they're escorted back to the fey world. Either way, they'll buy us time with their lives.'

'Damn, Malina. That's brutal,' Conrol mutters.

Thankfully it's a statement, not an accusation, this time.

'You're right. I've got to start thinking differently. This is not the type of army I've ever had to face. Even in the current war of independence, villagers and townsfolk are left alone as much as possible. I'm just not used to thinking this way.'

The light from the twin moons shows the pain on Conrol's face, but I keep my distance. He isn't the type of man who requires consolation. He's the type of man who takes that pain and fashions it into a weapon. The Major Conrol I once knew is back, and it couldn't have come at a more critical time.

Old mantras come to mind, and I smile.

In the days to come, only the strong will survive.

From here on, we'll live to kill and kill to live.

***

I awake with a start, unease making the hairs on my neck rise.

A blood rush causes my heart to beat faster as my senses strain to understand what caused this fight or flight feeling.

Reaching over, I shake Conrol's shoulder.

He's awake instantly, aware of my tension. The glimmer of an approaching sunrise brightens the horizon, the sky is clear, full of stars, and the moons cast their cool light upon the ground. It's beautiful. But something is wrong.

I rise and draw my sword slowly, unwilling to make any noise, afraid that if I do, I'll invite something terrible to happen.

'What is it?' Conrol whispers, standing beside me, his own sword shining silver.

'I'm not sure,' I respond, just as quietly.

The two nearest pairs of sentries are standing quietly, with no sign of concern evident. Maybe I'm just too tightly sprung.

A mournful howl of a wolf lingers on the night air. A solitary call, so lonely that it tugs at my heart. I know how it feels, bereft of my mate, Lotane.

As it dies away, all hell breaks loose.

The ferocious beasts I'd spied from the ramp explode from the shadows and undergrowth. Reminiscent of wolves but standing tall on their hind legs, fanged and clawed, they tear into the camp in a snarling frenzy.

Horses whinny and rear in terror, and maybe a dozen break loose from their tethers. They gallop through the camp, knocking men aside but also half a dozen wolfen in their path. Thankfully, being war-trained, the rest stay where they are, shivering in fear.

As if in slow motion, I watch in dismay as one of the nearest sentries receives a clawed swipe that tears his face away, leaving him screaming without eyes, nose or lips in the moonlight.

Yet I don't have time to dwell on his misfortune.

A wolfen charges on all fours at me, its speed terrifying. It leaps, jaws open wide, and I drop to one knee, raising my sword to slit it open from head to tail. A flash, and I roll, claws hissing through the air as I bring my shield up, only to be borne to the ground under the weight of another beast as it tears at the stout wood between us. I'm on my back, and I stab frantically around the side of the shield, feeling the sword bite deep, and the weight lifts away as the wolf runs off howling.

'SHIELD CIRCLE!' Conrol bellows as I come to my feet, breathing heavily, and the call is taken up, interspersed with the screams and howls of the dying.

Conrol has his back to a tree while three huge wolfen lunge and swipe, trying to get past his swinging sword. His left cheek is lacerated, and blood runs from a deep gash to his thigh.

Two more beasts attack me, but this time I'm ready, ducking and twisting under their claws, my sword biting deep, leaving them dead on

THE LAST HOPE

the ground. As I recover, a soldier stumbles past, eyes wide with shock, holding his severed arm. Blood pumps furiously from his shoulder, and I'm about to grab him when he's eviscerated with a swipe from one of the three beasts facing Conrol.

I leap forward, hacking my sword through the neck of one of Conrol's assailants, before swinging low, taking a leg from another. As it goes down, I slam my blade through its back while deflecting an attack from the remaining one with my shield.

It howls as a sword erupts from its chest and Conrol nods his thanks as he rips it free and kicks the body to the side.

'SHIELD CIRCLE,' he bellows again and runs into the fray, pulling men into a semblance of the formation while fielding off fresh attacks.

As shields begin to lock, the wolves' attacks lose effectiveness, and they withdraw, snapping and howling. Unfortunately, our success will be short-lived. If they don't leave, nor can we, and any moment now, they might turn their attention to the remaining horses. There's no way the injured will make it out on foot, and I'm sure more of these beasts will come and overwhelm us if we can't break away now.

I push through the middle of the circle, finding Conrol.

'We're well and truly buggered,' he shouts while tying off a bandage around a soldier's hand that's missing three fingers. 'We need to get our horses and ride out of here, but if we lose formation, they'll tear what's left of us to shreds!'

It's good to know we're on the same page about what needs to be done.

I nod, catching my breath, trying to devise a solution. These are intelligent creatures, but they're also beasts, and what do beasts fear the most.

Fire.

It seems all my troubles started with the High King and fire, and yet it now offers the solution.

'I'm going to try and drive them back and give you a chance at getting on the horses. This time, you leave without me. I'll catch you up. Do you hear me, Dimitar?'

I grab his shoulder, keeping eye contact, making sure he sees my determination.

'Whatever you're thinking, find another way,' he shouts back.

'There is no other way. I should have died alongside Ardlan and his men. Don't worry, I'll try not to die now; I just can't promise it!'

I push through the shield wall, leaving its safety.

Before I became the King Slayer, I was the Wolf Slayer.

That time I returned victoriously, yet there are far too many this time. Yet before I die, there's time to collect some more heads!

***

Fire magic.

So destructive and, because of that, so draining.

Over time my reservoir of power has increased a little, but I don't know how many of these creatures I can set aflame before I succumb firstly to exhaustion and immediately thereafter to their claws and fangs. Yet, however many I manage to kill doesn't really matter as long as the Last Hope escape.

As I lift my sword, the blade is enveloped in incandescent white fire from hilt to tip, lighting the forest brighter than day. I don't hesitate and run at the massed creatures, watching them scatter before me, keeping out of reach of my flaming sword.

Damn. This isn't going to plan. I'd expected to be attacked from all sides, my sword setting furred bodies ablaze, sending them howling to their deaths. Instead, there's no panic to their withdrawal, and the Wolfen ranks close behind me, keeping a safe distance.

I know without turning around that the Last Hope are still in a shield circle, unable to break away from a foe still ready and intent on ripping them to shreds. If the pack doesn't attack me, I'm too slow to chase them. Should I return to the shield circle or continue?

Mind made up, the pack continues to separate before my steady advance. Ahead, I see a wolfen, larger than the others, watching me intently, rippling muscles clearly defined despite its glossy pelt. This must be the alpha male of this particular pack. Beside him are two smaller wolves, still fearsome and deadly, yet definitely subservient to this mighty creature.

Will this pack run away or seek revenge if I kill their leader?

I'll soon find out.

There's caution in the alpha male's yellow eyes and no immediate threat to its posture. Nonetheless, I don't let my guard down as I approach, my shield protecting my left side while I hold my sword loosely but at the ready.

With a wave of those deadly paws, the writhing mass of black wolves pulls back, except for the two smaller wolves. One has teats and is probably the alpha's mate, and the smaller male possibly his cub.

I stop just outside the reach of the leader's claws, unflinching as I meet his callous gaze. Its yellow eyes are full of dark intelligence, and it leans forward, sniffing, acquiring my scent. Thick lips pull back in a half-snarl, half-smile.

'You are the one called Malina, who slew Galgarath, our general?'

Do all the fey speak the common tongue, I wonder.

I nod, subtly turning my head, ensuring the pack keeps its distance.

'Why would a Saer Tel kill another fey over pathetic humans?'

I remember the words this Galgarath had used.

'Because I have blood rights over these humans. They were not his to claim.'

The beast snorts in laughter, confusion or disbelief, which I don't know.

I'm not fooled by the civil start to this conversation. The way the creature drools gives its hunger away. It will attack in time, and I'll be ready. But I'm interested in what it has to say, and with the sun beginning to climb, the Last Hope will shortly be able to fight in the daylight.

'What if I claim blood rights over them?' it growls.

'Then you'll die, like Galgarath.'

'I'm no more afraid of dying than are you, traitor ... but killing you will bring me great honour in Nogoth's eyes.'

It growls, a long loop of saliva dripping to the forest floor.

'Killing you will bring me none!' I reply, sensing the moment of attack drawing closer. 'Even killing Galgararth was too easy.'

'Galgarath wasn't cunning like I am.'

The alpha leers, its gums drawing back to reveal enormous, yellowed fangs.

I think it's talking to bolster its own courage. How encouraging to know these creatures are fearful. Yet fearful or not, they're also evil and deadly; the evidence of this lies bloodied in the forest behind me.

'Gah. You can have your small band of humans. We already ate our fill of your friends at the tunnel. It appears there's no army of humans to fight us, only you running away. You're no King Slayer, Saer Tel, just a cowardly traitor.'

I lower my sword and shield as if they're too heavy, knowing the invite won't go unanswered.

The alpha turns away but spins in the same motion, claws gleaming as it lashes out with a lightning-fast swipe intent on taking my head from my shoulders.

Fortunately, I'm already ducking, twisting under the blow, but even if I have the opportunity to gut the creature, I forgo the pleasure.

As the alpha recovers its balance, my sword has already claimed another victim, as it cleaves through the neck of the female wolf just before my kick sends the cub sprawling. I leap onto its back as the alpha, having recovered, howls in torment at its fallen mate.

Those eyes burn yellow with hatred as it turns toward me, but I yank the cub's head back, my fingers knotted into its fur, and I place the tip of my burning blade against its neck, eliciting a howl of pain.

'I believe you when you say you're not afraid to die. But no father should witness the death of both mate and son on the same day!'

'I'll eat you alive while you scream for mercy!'

'No, you won't. You'll order your pack back to the town along the road. Once they leave, I'll let your cub go. You have my word!'

The alpha prowls back and forth whilst the pack snarls and growls with hunger and hatred. With a simple thought, the sword flame increases, and the cub's fur begins to burn. The resulting piteous whimpers are enough to force the decision I'd hoped for.

'Back. Back to the town. Go. GO NOW!' the alpha growls, rounding on the pack angrily as if it's their fault. He sends them on their way with a long howl, and I watch until they disappear from view amongst the trees.

I yank the cub to its feet. If I was unarmed, it could probably rip me to shreds like its father, but for now, it's as subdued as a pet dog.

'You kept to your side of our bargain,' I say, shoving the cub stumbling forward.

As the alpha leaps forward to catch its falling son, I leap too. My sword sings as it cleaves through the father's skull, and before the cub even realises what's going on, it dies in its father's arms.

I pause briefly, looking at their bodies, locked together in death, and for a moment, I begin to regret my action. Then I visualise the children

THE LAST HOPE

that will be ripped screaming for their parents' arms before being devoured alive, and I turn away, with a grim smile of satisfaction.

For I am Malina. Both King Slayer and Wolf Slayer.

***

'All the civilians died in the attack, and we only have eighty-six soldiers left, sixteen of whom are badly injured,' Major Conrol shouts as we ride hell for leather toward Iron Hold.

As I glance behind me, the empty stares of the Last Hope look back.

Gargoyles begin to fill the sky in the distance. Intuitively, I know that they need the sun to warm their cold blood and the thermals to keep their ungainly bodies aloft for so long.

Returning my attention to the road ahead, I squint into the sunlight at the once-mighty wall. If only one end hadn't collapsed, this could have held up Nogoth's army for quite some time.

Yet it doesn't mean it won't still slow them down. The wall blocks three-quarters of the pass, and the mounds of rubble are still half the height of the wall. Nogoth's army will be funnelled up and over the precarious rockfall unless they use the gate tunnel.

As we enter the wall's shadow, I lean toward Conrol.

'I'll meet you at the barracks shortly. I have something to take care of.'

Guiding my horse to one side, I watch as the Last Hope thunder past, then single out a rider.

'You there.' I bellow above the thunder of hooves, pointing at the man. 'Hold my horse.'

The soldier pulls on his reins reluctantly, casting a fearful glance back along the road, then comes over to take mine.

'Don't worry, soldier. We'll be joining the others shortly. Wait for me at the end of the tunnel.'

He doesn't need further encouragement and canters off, leading my horse.

Looking up, I study that huge portcullis of iron propped on those old, fire-hardened tree trunks.

It's time they burned some more.

I lay my hands on first one, then the other trunk. Setting them ablaze with elemental fire, giving it a purpose, to consume until nothing is left, then walk down the tunnel to the next pair. Once again, I leave them burning behind me as I head to the last portcullis. I'm exhausted but call upon my dwindling power a final time, and as they ignite, smoke billowing skyward, the first trunks collapse.

Walking backwards, I fear the last barrier will remain welded to the wall after so long. But then, with a crash that hurts the ears, the portcullis slams into the ground sending stone shards bouncing everywhere.

My horse rears, frightened by the noise, and I go over, taking the reins from the struggling soldier. Talking softly, I blow into the horse's nostrils and pat its neck, ensuring it's calm before I leap into the saddle.

'Come on, let's go!' I say.

Heeling my horse into a canter, we clatter through the streets, heading for the barracks. Another boom comes from behind, and people stop and stare in concern at our appearance and the smoke coming from the wall.

I want to tell them to run, to get out of Iron Hold, but these people will never escape in time. Nogoth's gargoyles will fall upon them like a rain of death, and they'll die in agony, eaten alive.

A final boom reaches my ears, and I smile in satisfaction. The trolls and giants might rip away the first portcullis, but the tunnel is too small for them to get inside and do anything about the other two. Nogoth's forces will be slowed, and every day counts.

Conrol is waiting impatiently, as are the men, as I ride up to them. Standing beside him is the worried-looking barracks sergeant.

The major steps forward and holds my horse's bridle as I dismount.

'I've got bad news. The sin-hawk we sent to High Delnor when we first passed through has yet to return. We can't get the news out!'

'Damn! Have you told him?' I ask Conrol.

'Told me what?' asks the sergeant, eyes flickering back and forth nervously, giving me my answer before the major can respond.

I ignore his question, instead asking one of my own.

'Where's the nearest food store?'

'Erm, down there, the second street on the left,' he points with a filthy finger.

'Major. Get everyone's packs, saddlebags and water skins full. I'll meet you there shortly.'

Conrol sketches me a salute, surprising the sergeant and then begins shouting orders. A few moments later, silence falls over the barracks courtyard with just the sergeant and me left.

'What's going on?' the sergeant demands. 'What's with all the smoke and noise; did you bring the portcullises down?'

I nod grimly.

'You need to listen carefully and act on what I say without hesitation. You've seen the state of us and how few are left out of the four hundred who passed here but a few days ago. There's an army of creatures heading this way a couple of days west. However, you don't have that long. Their scouts are but an hour behind us.

'Do whatever it takes to gather as many people and supplies as you can before that time's up. Then, seal yourself inside the wall. You'll remember the round stones at the top of each stairwell. Roll them down to block the entrance, and you'll be safe. Stay inside whilst your supplies last, but when they run out, take the passage leading into the mountain from the north end of the wall. There'll be a hidden exit at the other end.'

The sergeant scoffs in disbelief, a response I've come to know so well.

'What are you talking about? An army of creatures and sealing ourselves in the wall ... you're crazy! Whatever army is coming this way, they'll want our expertise. This is a town of over six hundred skilled people. We'll just surrender and work under another taskmaster, High Delnor be damned!'

With defiance and determination, he turns away, fists clenched, stamping back toward the barracks. Who else can I turn to? This man, the head of the town guard, is the only one who might be able to save someone. What can I do?

'WAIT!'

He pauses, and I run over to stand in front of him.

'I'm sorry,' I say, resting my hand on his shoulder. I close my eyes and lower my head.

'Don't worry, girl. We'll be just fine. Don't worry about us!'

I'd made a promise to myself, but what does that matter. I can claim to be honourable, honest and all kinds of things, but that's hardly true anymore, and only when it suits me.

I open them again, looking the sergeant square in the eye.

'You will do everything I told you to do as if your life depends on it … because it does. Seal the wall the moment you see the enemy scouts in the skies. Whoever is outside at that time stays outside. Do you understand?'

The sergeant snaps to attention, reverence and obedience now shining forth.

'Go now, and the gods be with you!'

The sergeant runs off, screaming for his men, who come tumbling outside.

My magic squirms happily, yet I don't feel the same. Breaking my promise to never bind someone to me again had been all too easy.

Malina, you've done it to save people. You had no other choice. Just don't do it again.

Who am I kidding?

***

'They're turning back,' Conrol shouts as we thunder along, the horses creating a dust cloud behind us.

Thankfully it appears he's right, and I feel like whooping with joy and relief. But how can I when we'd just lost over twenty men? We'd become lax through tiredness and believing we were safe, having travelled for nearly two weeks without further incident from Iron Hold.

Then, two hours ago, as the evening had drawn close, the gargoyles had attacked, their approach concealed by the blazing sunlight. The first we'd known of their presence was the javelins raining from the sky, followed by the screams of injured men and horses.

Conrol's gelding had fallen with a javelin through its neck, throwing the major. Still, he'd rolled with practised agility, and I'd ridden past, grabbing his outstretched wrist, and almost had my shoulder pulled from its socket as he swung onto the saddle behind me.

Others hadn't been so fortunate and had run pleading and screaming after us, only to fall to the shining rain one by one. Hopefully, they're dead because if not, I'm sure their deaths will be hideous, for the gargoyles aren't giving up; they're just returning to feed.

With darkness approaching, I feel confident we're now safe. Raising my hand to signal those following, I slow my horse to a walk, feeling its mighty heart beating furiously beneath me. Looking around, I'm relieved to see some empty-saddled horses. They're trained to stay with their fallen riders, yet the panic had been infectious, and several had followed our rout as we fled east.

'We need to rest the horses a little,' I say to Conrol over my shoulder as I bring my mount to a halt.

Conrol dismounts groaning in discomfort.

'Keep walking,' I shout, and the command is passed back.

While the major fills two nose bags with grain, I lead our horses. Without wagons, this was the only food we could pack in the saddlebags in sufficient quantity, but now it's running low, as are all our supplies.

We'll all be hungry before we reach Midnor, assuming we make it. Yet I'm hopeful, as we're only two days out. I pull my last biscuit from a pouch and push it into my mouth all at once, not willing to risk it crumbling.

'There are three vacant mounts, Dimitar. See if there's any food in the saddlebags, will you?'

My stomach grumbles, not remotely satisfied by the morsel it had received.

I walk in silence, thinking of what needs to be done once we arrive at Midnor. The sheer scale of what lies ahead is nigh on overwhelming. We have to convince tens of thousands to leave their family homes in a city of prosperity during the middle of summer. Even with the Major and the remnants of the Last Hope behind me, I just can't see us making any kind of impression. It's an impossible task.

But what if I use blood magic, the end justifying the means ... how many people could I reach and convince to leave?

If we stay half a day and I have a willing audience, maybe a couple of hundred, but that's assuming that using the blood magic prolifically doesn't drain me.

What if there's a limit to the number of people I can be bound to?

No, I can't think like that!

I feel like sobbing in frustration because two hundred is a drop in the ocean.

Yet I still pursue the thought because there needs to be a plan and an obvious solution comes to mind. If I just stay longer, I'll reach more people. Whilst I'm doing this, Conrol can carry the word to High Delnor.

I'll start with the governor because he can order the city's evacuation! Realistically though, most people will disobey that order.

Only those I've reached are guaranteed to take heed and leave. As for the rest, they'll only take the fey threat seriously as they're having their throats ripped out.

My maudlin thoughts are interrupted as Conrol joins me.

'Look what I have.' He smiles and tosses me an apple. 'I have one, too, so don't worry about sharing.'

After my dark thoughts, I feel like clapping with joy. It's something so simple, but on this terrible journey, devoid of anything but hardship and death, this one little offering of pleasure has me giddy with excitement.

Taking a bite, I revel in the sweetness, then guilt washes over me as I realise it's a dead man's food ... something a soldier had saved for when he really needed it the most.

'Thank you,' I mutter softly, offering a silent prayer to whatever god might be listening that the dead soldier's soul finds peace.

My horse snickers softly, and I give it a sidelong glance. Without question, I wouldn't be alive without this incredible beast.

'Alright, alright,' I sigh. 'You deserve this as much as me, if not more.'

I slip the fruit into the nose bag and receive a snort of appreciation for my kindness. I pat the horse's neck. It feels good to be appreciated.

Conrol's new mount swings its head and nudges the major.

'Now look what you've gone and done,' Conrol grumbles, rolling his eyes and offering up the remnants of his apple to his new charge

I laugh. It's been so long since I've done that, and it feels strange.

We walk in silence, our throats parched, deep in thought.

When the sun had set, I can't remember, but nightfall's cool hand has laid its claim firmly across the land. We've definitely put a lot of ground between us and the gargoyles, and it will soon be time to make camp. Not that there'll be any fires, food, or laughter.

Instead, everyone will take turns to stand watch or snatch some restless sleep.

I'm just about to signal our column to stop when a distant howl causes my horse to whinny.

I can't be sure whether it's Nogoth's fey or a wolf calling to one of the moons. Whichever, there's no way I'm taking the risk.

'Get ready to mount up!' I shout. 'We ride throughout the night!'

***

CHAPTER XV

Midnor.

The relief I'd felt as the city hove into sight begins to evaporate as I ride toward the western entrance with Conrol by my side and the Last Hope following behind. The fields that should be buzzing with workers are half-empty, and the men, women and children who see us run into houses, slamming doors behind them.

'I wonder what's happened,' says Conrol loudly, above the clattering hooves on the cobble trade road. 'These people appear worried about something. Unless, of course, it's just seeing us!'

Whilst we look decidedly battered, filthy and generally disgusting, I'm a little surprised if that's the case. I wonder if some gargoyles or wolfen have reached Midnor ahead of us, yet there's no sign of bloodshed or battle anywhere, nor are these people exactly panicking.

'There are no guards about, so it can't be that bad, whatever it is,' I point out as we pass through the unmanned gate tower into the city proper.

Yet, several shops and commercial premises we pass are closed. Some have boards over their windows; others are secured with heavy shutters.

With so few people on the streets, we make steady progress along the main thoroughfare. The slow clip-clop of our horses' hooves reflects how tired our mounts are. As I gaze upon the riders, that same tiredness is etched upon every face. The Last Hope now appears more like the Lost Hope. It's a sobering thought.

Finally, the governor's residence hoves into sight, and it's now apparent where the town guards are. Around fifty of them are gathered around the entrance, and from my vantage point astride my gelding, I can see Garbor waving his arms, addressing them.

'Let's wait until he's finished,' mutters Conrol as we rein in our horses and dismount.

'Sure. Whatever he's doing, we can wait a little longer,' I reply, nodding at the soldiers behind us as they almost fall from their saddles. 'The men and horses need a break. I suggest we leave the day after the morrow and get them fed and watered in the interim. Everyone needs some good sleep.'

The major sighs.

'Good sleep. What's that? Every time I close my eyes, I see that army of creatures stretching to the horizon, and I wonder how Ardlan died. I hope it was quick and he didn't suffer.'

'Dimitar. Ardlan would have died surrounded by a pile of corpses, with a war cry on his lips right up until the last beat of his heart. He'll have put fear and doubt into our enemies, and his loss won't be in vain.'

The lie hurts. The truth, and perhaps the major knows, is that Ardlan, Yeldom and the others died screaming in rage, panic and bowel-wrenching fear, knowing that however many they killed, they only delayed death by a few more heartbeats. Then, unless they died outright, they'd have suffered the unbelievable pain of tooth and claw as they were overwhelmed and eaten alive.

The stables are next to the governor's residence and barracks, and we leave our horses in the care of the stablemaster, whose shouts have stable boys scurrying around like frightened rats. Conrol has temporarily promoted three of the remaining Last Hope to corporals, and he calls them over.

Together we enter the barracks and find the quartermaster in a messy office full of crates. He's so round that I can only wonder how much of the guards' food he appropriates for himself. In fact, crumbs and grease cover the chest of his dirty uniform as he rises from behind a desk in surprise at our unexpected intrusion.

'Do you know who I am?' Major Conrol asks, his eyes sweeping over the poor excuse for a guard with disdain.

The man shakes his head slowly, looking puzzled. His eyes constantly flicker to me, and I know what's going through his mind. *What's the King Slayer doing in my office?*

'I am Major Conrol, aide to Commander Farsil of High Delnor.'

Sweat beads on the quartermaster's greasy brow, and he stands to a semblance of attention, although his legs are so fat he can't even bring them together. I wonder how many fey he'd feed and for how long.

'My men will stay here for two nights. Tomorrow, when I inspect them, they need to be washed, in clean uniforms, with full bellies and enough supplies in their packs to last two weeks of hard travel. If you fail to provide what I'm asking for, you'll be seconded to a unit on the front line against the Tarsians. Do I make myself clear?'

'Yes, Major,' the man squeaks, his jowls shaking.

'Corporals. Have the men ready for first light tomorrow. Ensure they eat, sleep and do nothing else in the interim. The only talk is to be amongst yourselves. Do you understand?'

'Major!' they all acknowledge in unison.

With a swift salute to his men, Conrol turns to me.

'Let's go see the governor.'

As we leave the barracks, Conrol places his hand on my arm and pulls me aside.

'We haven't talked much about what needs to be done here. I guess I've been avoiding the subject until I could come to terms with what I'm about to ask.'

I say nothing, letting him continue in his own time.

'We can't afford to stay here any longer than necessary to rest the men and horses. Getting the message of the fey invasion to High Delnor and the other cities is of the utmost importance.

'There are over thirty thousand souls here, and we must try to get at least some of them to leave. The fate that awaits those who stay doesn't bear thinking about. We failed so miserably at Lake Hold, and this is a vast city where we cannot hope to reach more than a fraction of the people.

'You talked about a scorched earth policy before, and I'd considered getting the men to set fire to the city and have you use your magic like at Pine Hold. But this city is made of stone, not wood, and I doubt it would take, let alone spread.'

I nod but keep my lips sealed, wondering where this conversation is heading.

'Yet what if you didn't use your magic to destroy but rather to control?' The Major's voice lowers to barely a whisper, and his eyes look at the floor. 'I don't know how many you can get to do as you want, but it doesn't matter how many it is … every single one is a victory, however small. I'm sure you've been thinking of this too.'

There's no point in me denying it.

'I agree. It's the only way I can see us getting even Garbor to leave, let alone some of his subjects. No one will obey an order to abandon their homes without seeing proof. By then, it will be too late; whether it's here or back in the fey world, all these people will die horribly.'

'Right, let's get started then, shall we,' Conrol says with a sigh.

It's taken a lot for him to ask this, and it makes me feel better about my own decision. The end does justify the means.

The guards are muttering as we push through their ranks, and when Garbor sees us, I'm not sure who is more surprised, Conrol or me, when he runs over, rolls of fat wobbling, to greet Conrol with a hug.

'Major, Major. It's so good to see you. I've been praying for guidance, and it's as if you've been delivered by the gods themselves!'

I exchange an amused glance with Conrol.

'What are you talking about, Governor?' Conrol demands, extricating himself from the embrace.

Garbor turns toward me and opens his arms but decides better when he sees my face and remembers who I am. Recovering his composure, he continues.

'One of our trappers claims to have spotted a terrible army of monsters about two days north of the city heading this way. He's been telling everyone who'll listen, and the rumour has spread, making people nervous. Now, he's known to enjoy his grain spirit way too much, so he's either seeing things or aiming for free drinks. My guards are trying to reassure people, but with your appearance, I'm sure everyone will calm down, and the workers will return to work instead of using it as an excuse to slack!'

I'm sure the shock on Conrol's face matches mine as we exchange a quick glance.

A force of Nogoth's has travelled parallel to us, and this city is already doomed!

***

'Just two days away,' Conrol murmurs. 'They've moved far faster than I'd have thought possible. It must be Nogoth's light troops come to cut the city off!'

'This trapper might be the saviour of this city. If people are already frightened ...' I look meaningfully at Conrol.

I'm surprised when he shakes his head.

'Not necessarily.'

'What are you talking about, and who is this Nogoth? Garbor asks. 'It's all just a story. Take my word for it.'

'Let's talk in private,' Conrol suggests.

'Of course, how remiss of me.' Garbor looks flustered. 'Let's go inside, and I'll have refreshments brought.'

As we walk through the cool, tiled corridors of Garbor's residence, he enthuses over the crop yield and how much wheat and flower he'll be sending to High Delnor over Midnor's quota. He's already discounted the trapper's tale and is returning to his exuberant self.

'I won't be a moment. I'll just organise the food,' Garbor says, gesturing to the sunlight at the end of the passage.

The courtyard is the tranquil oasis I fondly remember as Conrol and I sit on a stone bench awaiting the governor's return.

'What did you mean?' I prompt. 'If the citizens are fearful, surely more might heed our orders to evacuate the city and head for High Delnor.'

Conrol sighs.

'On the face of it, that's true. But this force has matched our pace. If they're Nogoth's wolfen or gargoyles, anyone escaping without a horse will be overtaken, caught in the open and slaughtered!'

A groan escapes my lips.

'I hadn't thought of that! In which case, they'd be better staying here, fighting for their lives, having barricaded the streets and their homes.'

'Exactly,' mutters Conrol. 'Without knowing our enemy, how can we know what to do?' He rubs his eyes, frustration evident as he scowls.

'Then I'll have to scout them; there's no other way.' I state firmly, brooking no dissent. 'While I'm gone, we'll have Garbor ready as many supply wagons as this city holds. We can't afford to spread panic now, but we'll have a clear course of action once I return.'

'And I'll send word to High Delnor by sin-hawk,' Conrol says, gesturing to the hooded birds. 'If nothing else, by reaching here, we'll succeed in forewarning them.'

'That alone won't be enough; you must get to Farsil in person. You mustn't die here because, however you word that message, he'll only believe it when he sees you and your injuries.'

'You're right. Now, do what you have to do with Garbor. His town guard will obey him without you controlling them all, then head north on the fastest horse you can lay hands on.'

Garbor chooses that moment to return.

I'm exhausted. My eyelids feel like lead; it's been so long since I've slept, but I can't afford to rest, not at this pivotal time. However, at least I can eat the platter of food placed before me. Bread and honey with a goblet of milk, a feast fit for a queen.

I surprise Garbor by reaching out to hold his arm as if in gratitude, smiling into his started eyes. I don't even use my spirit eye. I just call silently to my magic and feel it respond instantly.

'You need to obey the Major and me without hesitation or question, believing it's the right thing to do. Do you agree that's the best course of action?'

Garbor smiles nervously, looking back and forth.

'B-but, of course,' he stammers.

'Then you must prepare as many supplies as possible for an immediate wagon journey to High Delnor. Whether it's from the city reserve or private stores, every kernel, grain, loaf or ham, in fact, anything that can fit onto a wagon, must be ready to leave as soon as possible.'

'As many wagons with water barrels as food.' Conrol adds.

I nod my thanks. How could I forget water?

'Of course,' Garbor gushes, smiling broadly.

'Then make haste and set this in motion immediately,' Conrol orders.

Garbor waddles off faster than I've ever seen him move.

Conrol shakes his head in wonder.

'What I've just witnessed is powerful beyond measure. It would have been beyond most mortals to have resisted using it all this time. To take away someone's freedom of choice is a dark deed, but in this instance, a necessary one.'

THE LAST HOPE

Would Conrol judge me harshly if I told him about the sergeant at Iron Hold? I'll never know.

'Here, you finish the food; you need it more than me.' Conrol says, offering me his plate.

My stomach has been so poor recently, the lack of sustenance giving me a ravenous hunger, and I dive right in. I finish every morsel on the platter, yet I don't feel any better. Nor when I quaff the milk does it quench my thirst. My stomach growls in protest, and I swallow down bile. To distract myself, I walk over to the mosaic I'd noticed on our first visit. Kneeling, I study the depiction of the queen in front of the gate, wondering again who she might have been.

A moment later, Conrol joins me.

'It's amazing,' he whispers. 'This has happened before, and people actually forgot. Why weren't better records kept so we knew what was coming?'

'I often wonder that,' I reply. 'Why build walls and fortresses and not bother writing records. However, it probably was done, but I suspect the ssythlans were responsible for those records disappearing over the centuries.'

'By the gods, it beggars belief, but I don't doubt it anymore.' Conrol looks around in a rare show of embarrassment and wrings his hands together. 'I'm sorry, you know. Sorry that the ssythlans made you do their bidding. I'm sorry that I hated you for it when I now realise you had no choice. You're a good woman, Malina, and I hope I can call you a friend.'

Tears well in our eyes as we embrace, and the moment is only broken as we hear the huffing of Garbor's return.

It's time for me to leave, as only I have the skills to approach the fey army unseen.

'May the gods of luck shine on you, Malina.'

I smile in thanks. If only I believed in a god other than Nogoth.

***

It's approaching dusk as I stand atop the flat roof of a house on Midnor's north-western fringe. From this vantage point, I can see a mighty army spreading across the land like a dried, bloody stain.

Flickering torchlight highlights fangs, tusks, and blood liberally splashed across armour, skin or fur. Drums boom like thunder or the beat of a mighty heart, and the roof under my feet vibrates to the rhythmic tramp of thousands of boots and clawed paws.

Beside me, Garbor stands shaking, his face white with fear, along with a dozen other people in a similar state. On every rooftop, at every door and window, the population of Midnor stares upon this mighty horde, unable to believe their wide eyes.

Stay and fight, or flee? It's the thought on everyone's minds, and the next few minutes will see the whole city do one or the other.

After two nights away, I'd returned earlier in the afternoon, sweat-stained and sore, my horse lathered, to find Conrol awaiting. Worry, anxiety, impatience and frustration all manifested as we hurried off to make desperate, last-minute plans.

And it was the culmination of those plans, a final desperate roll of the dice that the whole city has come to watch.

'The bravery of that man is without peer,' Garbor whispers, almost to himself.

'And those with him,' adds another, equally hushed.

My eyes follow the object of Garbor's adulation as Conrol and twenty men of the Last Hope march out. Fresh white cloaks billow around them as they go to barter for our lives or find a diplomatic solution.

Murmurs of hope replace those of fear. Admiration for Conrol and the twenty men of the Last Hope strengthens spines and resolve. Surely the gods can only applaud and reward such an act.

The drums stop, and the enemy horde comes to a ragged halt.

It's as if the whole world holds its breath.

The sun rests on the horizon, hesitant to set, casting long shadows, the gentle breeze seems to die away, and even the bird song disappears.

Conrol and his men continue, closing the distance until they stand before the enemy leader, who sits astride a gigantic beast.

It's hard to see. The setting sun has everyone squinting. Conrol is too far away to hear what's being said, but it's evident from his broad gestures and the sweep of his arms that he's doing everything he can.

The enemy leader dismounts. Even from this distance, the enormous tusks curving over his face look frightening. He looms above

Conrol like the shadow of death, and what can only be his bodyguard move forward too.

Then, in the dying light, the leader raises a gigantic axe. The blade glitters as he momentarily holds it aloft, then, in a blink of an eye, it sweeps down, and Conrol collapses to the ground. Distant screams follow as the bodyguard butcher the twenty men who'd accompanied Conrol, and suddenly those screams are echoed by those around me as panic sets in.

'Run! Run for your lives!' The town guard and the remaining men of the Last Hope start yelling, chivvying those who freeze in terror, pushing, shoving, and doing whatever it takes to get the crowd moving.

Thankfully, the cry is taken up instantly by a thousand panicked voices.

I turn and grab Garbor's shoulders, watching the terror settle upon him like a heavy mantle.

'What are you waiting for? Save yourself!' I yell. 'The supply wagons are on the south trade road. Get them and head to High Delnor as fast as you can!'

'Escape to High Delnor,' I shout, my voice magnified and carried by the magical wind. 'They're coming to kill us all!'

People take up the chant as they run, screaming for their lives.

Blood-curdling howls come from the enemy horde, and their drums resume their furious beat. A tidal wave of people surges through the city streets as if a floodgate has opened. Like the firestorm in Pine Hold, the panic spreads as fast as the wind. Even those who hadn't witnessed the massacre run from their houses, clutching their meagre belongings or their loved ones close.

Looking around, I realise I've been left alone on the rooftop. The streets below are almost empty, but for some barking dogs and blowing papers.

I won't run with the fleeing crowd; that isn't my way. I turn around to see the distant bodies littering the ground. It's time for me to join Conrol.

Leaping from the roof, my magic cushioning my descent, I run toward the horde as the sun slips below the horizon. I run steadily, conserving my strength, lightfooted across the plain.

The enemy leader stands, arms crossed, holding that horrendous axe. As I approach, he spreads his arms, and I throw myself at him.

Those gigantic arms close around me, squeezing the breath from my lungs.

Yet I don't struggle.

'How did I do?' Kralgen asks, his smile bright under the Nastalian skull, a sea creature's remains he's taken from a standard and worn as a helmet.

'Kral. You did amazing. Nigh on the whole population is now heading to High Delnor. Alyssa would have been proud of you!'

'Can I get up yet?' Conrol asks, his face muffled by the grass.

Kralgen's giant mount, a blue bear, ambles over, sniffs Conrol, then sneezes, covering him in goo.

'I would if I were you. That's the beginning of a blue bear's mating ritual!' Kralgen laughs.

As Conrol and his men climb to their feet, genuine smiles are everywhere.

It's the first time in weeks I've genuinely felt positive. With Kralgen's army advancing, the town population won't stop running until they reach safety. The supply wagons will keep them fed, and if anyone falls behind, they'll be looked after.

Other towns along the way will also run before this mighty horde, which unbeknownst to them, is anything but their enemy. The lives Kralgen will save with his timely arrival will be beyond count.

Despite only just reuniting with Kralgen, Conrol and I need to leave him behind. Speed remains of the essence, and we've lost two whole days executing this plan.

But just as I'm about to suggest we need to get going, I change my mind. I might never have another night like this where I feel totally safe. Of course, I also need to hear all about how he reclaimed the throne and got the Icelandians marching so quickly after such a long absence. Somehow, I think his missing right ear and little finger have something to do with it.

I can't wait to hear how.

***

'I can't believe we've made it,' Conrol shouts, his face lit by a rare smile.

The nine soldiers we have with us whoop gleefully as the walls of High Delnor rise proudly in the distance. We'd left Midnor two weeks ago with ten men after saying farewell to Kralgen as his Icelandians chased Midnor's fleeing population. Conrol had been furious for days over the one deserter, and it's a relief to see his good mood returning.

In direct contrast, I feel better than I have in weeks, albeit filthy, needing a wash and fresh clothes. I smile, recognising the reason; Lotane ... he'll be waiting within those walls. My excitement has me full of vigour despite the poor rations we'd survived on as we crossed the countryside.

Several times we'd swapped horses as we pushed them to the limits of their endurance on our race here. How far we're ahead of Kralgen and his Icelandians or Nogoth's fey is anyone's guess. The last time I'd seen a gargoyle was before we'd reached Midnor. Since then, there's been no indication that this world is about to be torn apart by something other than the current War of Independence.

'It seems a lifetime ago we set out from here,' Conrol says tiredly, bringing his horse alongside. 'Four hundred men and a good friend I left with, now with the Last Hope all but destroyed, I'm returning with just nine. I've failed so miserably.'

Then he leans over and grasps my forearm.

'But at least I ended up doing something right. I found a friend who I thought was lost!'

I smile, warming under his genuine warmth.

'Don't be so hard on yourself, Dimitar. No blame can attach to you. This plan's been in the making for nigh on a thousand years. Even though I was once a part of it, I was still deceived countless times, perhaps more than most. It's what we do from hereon that the gods will judge us by. The game is now afoot, and even if we have the weaker side, we're more prepared than our forebears ever were.'

Conrol scratches his thick beard, eyes serious beneath his bushy brows.

'The problem is, even with Kralgen's Icelandians by our side, it's not near enough to give Nogoth's army more than a brief pause. Mind you, those bears were scarier than half those creatures on the other side of the gate.'

'Scary? I thought the one you encountered was about to get a little too friendly.' I laugh to lighten the mood. 'So how many soldiers can Delnor call upon?'

Before answering, Conrol looks upwards as if the answer is written on the few clouds that dare to break the perfect blue, then returns his attention back to me.

'As you know, not enough. Around ten thousand fighting Tars and Hastia in the south, and roughly twenty thousand split between Astor, Suria and Rolantria in the east. Southnor has raised a levy of about five thousand, and there's always around that amount passing in and out of High Delnor. So, perhaps forty thousand in all. With Kralgen's army, we have a combined force of sixty thousand. I didn't have time to count how many fey were waiting to come through the World Gate, but your estimate of two hundred thousand seems frugal.'

'It's too beautiful a day to worry about such things. We'll let Farsil sort out the insignificant details,' I reply with a smile.

Conrol's horse tosses its head, whinnying, and we laugh.

'There, that's decided,' Conrol agrees. 'We've a straight road ahead, blue sky above, and the horses have their wind back. What say we race to the north gate?'

'How's it going to be a race if I win so easily?' I wink smugly, then with a flick of the reins and a kick of my heels, I'm off.

The thunder of hooves and the shouts of Conrol and the men tell me the race is on, and I lean low, my hair whipping behind me. Everything is exhilarating, the speed, High Delnor getting closer, Lotane awaiting. I know everything will be alright. Lotane and I had something even the gods would be envious of. He'll have forgiven me, and together, we'll find a way to beat Nogoth.

For the first time in a long time, the Fey King's face doesn't enter my thoughts, and I shout joyfully, urging my mount to even greater efforts.

Wagons and people move to the side of the road as we approach, and I wave my thanks as I fly past. Seeing them shake their heads in exasperation makes me laugh. The gate is getting closer, and I rein my horse in slowly, allowing the others to catch up. All of us, despite our filthy state, are grinning broadly.

The gate guards greet the major like a long-lost brother as he dismounts to embrace them, and then we all laugh as they complain about how much he smells.

Passing through the wall tunnel is like passing through the World Gate. It had been quiet on the roads, with only the sound of nature, our conversation and the horses' hooves to disturb it. Yet suddenly, my ears are being assaulted. Vendors shout, selling their wares, along with

THE LAST HOPE

hundreds of civilians bartering or talking loudly to be heard. Gulls add to the cacophony, wheeling above in their hundreds.

We leave our horses at a stable just beyond the gate tunnel. There's no point trying to ride through the crowds at this time of day, and we make our way slowly toward the citadel sitting high on its hill to the south.

People give way before us quite quickly when they see us coming. We are all sweat-stained, with tangled hair and smell like vagrants. Even the salty sea air struggles to compete with our aroma.

However, I soon realise it isn't the group's appearance that has the crowd muttering and starting to point. With nothing but the clothes on my back and no robe to disguise me, it's plain for all to see that the King Slayer is amongst them again. I'd forgotten for a while how hated I am, but it doesn't take long to remind me. Someone throws a handful of horse dung, and then an egg just misses me, but thankfully, other than that, only names and insults are called.

Conrol and the soldiers close around me, shielding me with their presence. Nonetheless, my good mood begins to evaporate.

'Enough of this.'

Conrol moves to a clothing stall, grabs a hooded green cloak off a hook and tosses it to me.

'Ask for Major Conrol at the palace, and I'll ensure you get double what it's worth!' he growls at the indignant vendor.

Once my identity is disguised, the catcalls and insults fade, my mood improves, and excitement returns. Every step I take brings me closer to Lotane.

Conrol is talking to the others about how we'll be debriefed and how important it is to tell the truth, but I can only think of Lotane. He consumes my thoughts; those beautiful eyes, strong arms, and gentle touch. I think of everything I love, all the moments we've shared, the list of which goes on and on until suddenly, I'm amazed to find myself at the citadel's outer gates, and I can't remember a single step of the way.

'Welcome back, Major!' the guards snap to attention.

As Conrol had said earlier. We've finally made it.

***

CHAPTER XVI

The major takes time to shake the guards' hands and ask their names. Small gestures like this endear him to the troops, and whilst I can't wait to find Lotane, I curb my impatience.

One of the guards hurries off, bow-legged, to advise Farsil we've returned, and we're about to follow when the guard sergeant raises his hand.

'All of you, weapons, please,' he demands. 'That includes you, Major.'

'Why, Sergeant?' Conrol asks.

'I apologise, Major. They're new standing orders that apply to absolutely everyone. No one is allowed to carry weapons inside the palace unless on guard duty.'

A dozen guards step forward to help take our weapons and shields. I feel strangely vulnerable being unarmed again, and I can sense the others aren't too happy either.

The guards smile apologetically, revealing gapped yellow teeth as we're all respectfully patted down. A few of the Last Hope joke that it's the first time they've felt the touch of a woman's hands in a long time. It's meant in jest, but the scowls they receive show it's not appreciated.

'It's good to see security is as tight as when you ran things here, Dimitar.'

'Hah,' he says, grimacing. 'If only I deserved that compliment, but I let you in having checked for weapons, not knowing you *were* the weapon. You're right, though. Farsil is taking things seriously, which bodes well.'

'Major!' a familiar voice peels out.

THE LAST HOPE

We turn together, and there's Syrila, Head of Delnor's intelligence, striding toward us. She cuts a striking figure, wearing tight dark green leathers that show off her toned body and calf-length boots. Her hair is pulled back from her face and pinned in a tight bun, which only serves to accentuate her high cheekbones and hazel eyes.

Leaning close to Conrol, I whisper in his ear.

'There's no way she's carrying concealed weapons; those clothes are so tight.'

Snorting in amusement, he steps forward to grip Syrila's hand as she looks quizzically at me.

'You're alive,' she observes. 'I'm not sure whether to be happy about that. If you're still breathing, either you're controlling the major or what you previously claimed is true. Neither is good news!' She smiles to ensure I don't take offence at her words.

I understand what she means. My return is a double-edged sword.

Conrol shakes his head sadly.

'I can assure you, I'm in full control of myself, Syrila. You'll have no doubt been privy to the message I sent by sin-hawk.'

'The Once and Future King has returned,' she says quietly.

Then, she's all business again, the cold tone of command in her voice.

'Sergeant. Take these brave soldiers to the barracks and ensure they're well looked after.' Syrila indicates the remaining men of the Last Hope. 'However, keep them from wandering, as I'll need to debrief them.'

I'm touched when the men turn to embrace Conrol and me. We've shared so much that, at this moment, the difference in rank doesn't matter at all.

'King Slayer,' they whisper respectfully in my ear before they head off, escorted by the guard sergeant.

Syrila steps forward, commanding our attention.

'As for you two, you'll have to wait a while for some rest and respite. The Commander will want to see you immediately. Let's go!'

She spins away, turning into the side entrance, guiding us unerringly through the killing maze and into the grand hallway beyond. The palace is bustling with minor nobles and staff, just like the last time I was here. However, it appears Farsil has put the whole place on alert, for more guards are visible, and there's a sense of disquiet in the air.

Syrila and Conrol are just ahead of me, deep in conversation, heads bowed, their voices lowered. I drop back, letting them have their privacy.

I wonder if there's anything romantic between them, then laugh to myself. Since Conrol has gotten over his hatred, the bright, humorous and quick-witted man I'd liked so much is returning, whereas Syrila is always so serious. It would take magic to bind those two together.

Syrila looks over her shoulder.

'Amongst other things, I'm just telling the major we've caught a spy and are questioning him. Commander Farsil is in the dungeon, so we'll join him there.'

Syrila sets an easy pace, and I take the opportunity to look around. I've seen so little of the citadel's interior, and it's truly striking. Vaulted ceilings, statues, tapestries and small stained windows abound. Carpets, rugs, and beautiful mosaics cover the floor, and whilst most of the light comes through the windows or from large candelabras, here and there, moon globes adorn walls and ceilings.

We approach another two guards who salute sharply, tattooed hands snapping to their foreheads. The guards pull open a panelled wooden door and allow us to pass before it bangs closed as we descend a flight of wide circular steps.

Discipline is certainly tight, and I should be relieved, yet something is niggling me. No, not just one thing, several things.

I watch Lystra walk down the steps beside Conrol.

Lystra, hah. She reminds me so much of Lystra, and then my footsteps slow as cold creeps down my spine.

When she'd greeted us, she'd mentioned The Once and Future King, and I'm sure I'd only referred to him as Nogoth since entering these walls. Then the guards. Conrol hadn't recognised the sergeant, and he always knew the names of his men. One had run bow-legged, like a sailor, to bring news of our return, and then there were the tattoos.

Marines don't guard the palace unless ...

We've reached a landing, so I stop, lean against the wall and groan loudly as I close my eyes.

Yet I can still see, for I open my spirit eye, and there is the affirmation of my fears. Thin, red lines, barely distinguishable, fan out from Syrila's body. From the moment I'd first seen her, her toned physique, the way she moved, and even the role she held had made me compare her to a Chosen.

Now, here she is, leading us like sheep to our doom.

Even Syrila's lie about seeing Commander Farsil in the dungeon holds an element of truth to make it sound smooth and of no consequence. But we'll find him incarcerated along with anyone who supported him.

Admiral Destern now rules in High Delnor, of that, I'm sure.

I don't believe Destern is a Chosen, but he's either been bribed or just took the opportunity of power when it was offered to him.

'Are you alright, Malina?' Conrol asks as he retraces his steps, Syrila beside him.

I push myself away from the wall, swaying slightly.

'Not enough food or sleep,' I mutter. 'I'm just tired. Do you mind if I lean on you a little?' I ask Syrila.

Her lip curls. No Chosen can stand weakness, another obvious tell, but she nods anyway.

Smiling my thanks, I rest my arm around her shoulders, a prelude to putting her in a chokehold. At precisely that moment, Syrila grabs my hand, twists, and throws me hard over her hip to crash into the corridor wall.

I curse from the pain and my stupid mistake; a Chosen would never show such weakness unless as a lure.

With a flash, her hand goes to her bun, pulls forth the long needle which had held it in place, and slashes at Conrol, who leaps back, a red score mark on the palm of his hand.

My head is swimming. I've hit the wall so hard, and I struggle to regain my feet.

Through blurred eyes, I see Conrol drop to the floor, clasping his hand. He's in agony, his face twisted, a silent scream unable to leave his lips. The tip of Syrila's needle must be poisoned. She'd been armed all along with something far deadlier than a dagger.

How long ago she infiltrated the citadel, I don't know, but it must be recently, or she'd have been the one to kill the High King. Where did she come from? I certainly don't recognise her from the Mountain, but then again, she's in her forties …

Syrila lunges for me. I barely dodge the blow, rolling out of the way, then get to my feet, keeping the distance between us.

I'm concussed and weak. My magical power and physical strength are intrinsically linked. Without one, I can't call upon the other, yet every passing second brings it closer.

My magic wriggles sluggishly, but I can't focus enough to direct its help.

Syrila leaps, and I grasp her wrists as she pins me back against the wall.

The needle tip hovers just before my left eye, and Syrila laughs.

'Whatever happened to the stone-cold killer, the vaunted King Slayer? Only the strong survive!'

My arm trembles as she pushes her weight forward. Behind her, on the floor, Conrol displays a rictus of unbelievable pain. I focus on his face, my anger rising like an inferno, burning away the pain and melting my weakness. Then Lotane comes to mind, and I wonder if his body lies dead and cold somewhere or is imprisoned below.

My strength returns in a rush.

Conrol's plight, frozen in agony, strikes a chord, and I smile maliciously.

'It's a little cold in here, don't you think?' I say, my breath clouding before me.

Syrila's scream dies in her throat, and I watch in fascination as a frosty crust skims across her eyes in a heartbeat. I'd have liked to make it slow, to have her experience the agony Conrol feels, but I can't afford her demise to alert anyone, and I need to help the Major.

As I push Syrila's rigid body away, I almost topple after it. With a crash, she shatters on the flagstone floor, parts of her spinning this way and that.

I touch the back of my head, feeling a sticky mess, and as I look at my fingers, they're glistening with blood.

Barely able to focus, I kneel beside Conrol.

Taking his hand, I'm horrified to see it's completely black. I quickly pull up his sleeve and grimace at the darkness that's advanced halfway up his forearm. He's been poisoned with black rot, a fast-moving and deadly necrotic toxin derived from the deathwatch bee.

The only thing to do is to cut off the limb above the spreading black tide, but I've no weapon and certainly no time for that.

'Dimitar. Listen to me,' I say, tearing off his sleeve, sickened by what I must do. 'I have to take your arm below the elbow. I don't have any other choice if you're to live.'

I'm not expecting a reply as he's paralysed with pain. I'm surprised he's still conscious, or his heart hasn't already given out, yet I want him to know, to be prepared.

Do I burn his flesh away? No, the trauma might kill him. Nor can I freeze it, as once thawed, it'll rot ... but what other way is there. With each passing moment, the blackness creeps up the major's arm. Then some of Syrila's last words come to mind. Maybe if ...

I have no idea whether it will work or how, but that's only for my imagination to project, and if my magic can deliver, it will.

Holding the major's hand still against the cold floor, I close my eyes and entreat my magic to save this good man, whatever the cost. As I visualise what's needed, magic pours from my body.

Then the pull on my strength fades, and Conrol gasps, sucking in a deep, shuddering breath.

'Thank you, Malina,' he chokes, residual terror and pain still apparent in his voice.

I cry with relief as his arms wrap around me, one soft and the other hard and cold, made of stone.

***

'What's going on? Why did Syrila attack us?' Conrol asks shakily as we slowly let go of one another.

We don't have time for explanations, but neither is Conrol ready to continue, and I could do with a moment's respite. However, every moment that passes brings us closer to discovery and death. I draw a deep breath, trying to clear my head of the fog encroaching on my vision.

'Destern rules here now, and Farsil is either dead or incarcerated below. Syrila was a Chosen, an agent for Nogoth, and she was leading us into a trap when I realised her true nature.'

Conrol lifts his stone arm, eyes wide, and tears form in the corner of his eyes. He's teetering on a knife edge.

'Look at this, look at this,' he moans.

'Ssssh, Dimitar. We need to focus. Farsil needs us. There's a trap below, and without you, we're all dead.'

'But, look at this,' he moans again, lifting his left arm.

I can't help but look. Conrol's hand is perfectly closed in a stone fist, every vein, knuckle, and nail as hard and polished as the flagstone we're sitting on. The stone continues halfway up his forearm before changing seamlessly into living flesh.

'There's no sign of the black rot.' I sigh, relieved.

'But just ...' the major beings to moan again, and fast as a striking snake, I slap him hard across the cheek. He'll wear my handprint for at least a day, but as he shakes his head to clear it, the vagueness has gone from his eyes. Instead, they clear, his old self returning.

'How do you feel?'

Conrol smiles, his eyes creasing.

'On the one hand, I feel great, but on the other ...'

I groan, but I'm immensely relieved. If he'd have gone into shock ...

'Good to have you back, Dimitar. We have to find the trap and turn it on those who've set it before they come looking for us. We're in no shape to fight, but we can't shy away from this one either.'

Conrol levers himself to his feet.

'Damn, this hand is heavy,' he mutters.

Leaning down, he picks up Syrila's needle and smiles grimly, looking at its tip.

'Let's go find my friend,' he states firmly. 'The dungeons are another two levels down.'

We head toward the next set of steps, and before long, I'm leaning on Conrol's shoulder for support.

Conrol stops and gently turns me around to look at my head.

'Oh, Malina,' he whispers softly. 'Syrila got you badly too.'

'It doesn't matter,' I say, pulling away. 'This will be over and done soon. Now, be quiet; I need to listen.'

Despite fatigue and injury making it difficult, my magic quests down the stairs, seeking out any hidden presence. Before long, I hear the sound of shallow breaths and stealthy movement. I put my finger to my lips and then lead the way. As we arrive at the next landing, it's lined by three closed doors on either side.

Leaving Conrol at the entrance to the landing, I move as silently as a cat along the right side to the final door. Nausea washes over me, and I lean against the wall, waiting for the moment to pass.

It takes three attempts for my magic to answer. When I'm strong, a mere thought is enough, but instead, I use my hands to roughly mould the stone frame, closing it around the edge of the door so it can't open.

The hammer of the trap has now been secured. It's time to find the anvil.

Motioning for Conrol to join me, I begin the final descent.

Deeper we go until we come to a short hallway. A large wooden desk and chair stand unoccupied close to a thick, iron-studded door that's slightly ajar. A quick search by lantern light reveals nothing of use in the drawers. Only papers and two large bottles of grain spirit with a goblet tucked away to keep a guard from getting too bored or cold.

As I peer carefully through the grille in the door, lanterns cast an unholy glow across a tragic scene. Row upon row of barred cells, crammed full of men and women wearing tattered finery or filthy uniforms.

By contrast, the cell almost opposite the door I'm behind only holds a dozen vicious-looking men and women. They're dressed in rags and appear as bedraggled as the other inmates, but they're part of the trap. Their tattoos give them away, and the blankets piled on a bed no doubt conceal weapons. The door to their cell is closed, but I'm sure it's unlocked.

They are the anvil.

It seems the trap would have been sprung when we passed through the door as those above came from behind.

At the far end of the chamber, Admiral Destern talks to a marine officer in a pristine uniform. Farsil isn't in sight, but I'm sure he's amongst the prisoners if he remains alive, and hopefully Lotane too.

Fourteen against two, and I can barely stand.

Conrol takes my arm and leads me to the desk. I lean gratefully against it, the whole room spinning. I try to picture Lotane needing my help, tortured and bleeding, anything to get my anger to rise and give me strength, but there's nothing left.

'Any ideas?' Conrol whispers in my ear. 'That bunch in the cell aren't prisoners!'

He looks hopefully at me as I desperately try to focus, and I can only shake my head slightly. Even that makes me want to lie down, close my eyes, and never wake up.

Conrol moves out of sight, I hear the soft glug of liquid being poured, and then a cold goblet is pressed to my lips.

'Just a little, or you'll cough so hard, you'll alert the guards.'

I take a sip, liquid fire burning my mouth, and clarity returns briefly as the neat alcohol pushes back the encroaching darkness.

Fire.

It always comes back to fire.

Lurching around the table, I grab the two bottles of alcohol, then point at the lantern at the end of the desk.

A grim smile creeps across Conrol's face as he picks it up. He's still holding the needle, and I hope he doesn't stick himself.

'I can't help with Destern. That's down to you,' I mumble.

'Ready?' he mouths in reply.

'I live to kill,' I whisper back, pushing through the door, throwing the bottles of grain spirit toward the *anvil's* cell. One shatters against the bars, the other against the floor. Glass shards fly, and the liquid splashes liberally across the cell and the people inside as they look up, open-mouthed in shock.

Conrol's flaming lantern follows a heartbeat later, and the screams begin.

As Conrol charges down the cell, roaring a battle cry, I grab another lantern from the wall and toss it after the first. The smell of burning flesh is as thick as the smoke that carries it.

I'm unsure how I ended up on the floor, but it's remarkably cool against my cheek.

From where I lie, I watch as Conrol jams that damned needle into the marine officer's arm, even as the man's dagger finds Conrol's right shoulder.

Conrol staggers back, trying desperately to pull the dagger free.

Destern raises his sword high. It's all over, Conrol's going to be cut in two, yet he still raises his hand high in a last desperate bid to grab the blade.

The blade sweeps down, and I laugh maniacally as it shatters against Conrol's stone arm. As Destern gapes in disbelief, Conrol pulls the dagger free and guts him.

'Only the strong survive, Dimitar,' I whisper as I close my eyes.

***

'Malina.'

THE LAST HOPE

I hear my name called once, or is it a hundred times. One part of me wants to escape the endless dreams of death and destruction, but in between those dreams, there's sometimes an empty blackness, and during those times, I know peace.

'Malina.'

What awaits if I make the effort to return to the living? Surely nothing that anyone would wish to face. I recall my dreams when Karson appeared and how my future, whichever way I turned, was surrounded by the dead.

Yet there are those I call friends who need me, and there are those I need now more than ever, especially the one with green and blue eyes. Lotane.

'Malina.'

It hurts to open my eyes, the piercing light and a pounding in my head make the darkness all too appealing, but I know Lotane will be waiting. For him, I'll overcome any pain, any adversary.

I force them open, blinking in an attempt to focus, and am rewarded as the pain recedes to a dull ache while my vision sharpens. I'm in a small chamber with an open window. The walls are lined with wooden shelves that groan under the weight of different herbs and potions. Under the window, on a table strewn with glass tubes, open tomes, and a pestle and mortar, something burns in a small pot that releases a fragrant smoke.

'Malina.'

Conrol sits on a stool beside the bed I'm propped up in. His eyes are wet, red and puffy. Behind him, at the back of the chamber, a kind-looking woman with smile lines looks on disapprovingly as he leans forward to kiss me gently on the forehead.

'We didn't think you'd make it, but it appears you refuse to die!'

I'm happy to see Conrol, but I'm disappointed that Lotane isn't waiting there. No doubt they've been taking turns to watch over me, or Lotane is busy with some tasks.

'How many hours have I been asleep?' I murmur. 'Is Farsil alright; did you save him?'

'So many questions.' Conrol smiles and uses a damp cloth to wipe around my eyes.

'It's not been hours, Malina. You've been unconscious for nearly two weeks. As for the commander, he was officially declared acting Regent five days ago. After we saved him, it was a dark time, and too many good people died to right the wrongs Destern committed.'

I smile, remembering the admiral's end.

'How's your arm?' I ask. 'The last thing I remember is Destern's sword shattering on it. Who'd have thought it would save your life, eh?'

Conrol's smile gets even broader.

'It's even more amazing than that. Take a look at this.'

He lifts his left arm onto the bed, and that smooth grey stone is only marred by the slightest scratch where the sword had hit.

'Almost as good as new,' I say, running my fingers over the imperfection.

'No, Malina. That's not what I'm talking about. Look again.'

As I focus on his clenched fist, the stone veins shift, and the fingers tremble.

Conrol laughs at my expression.

'For days, there was a chunk out of my arm where Destern's blade had hit, yet each morning when I awoke, I swore it was smaller, and sure enough, it's now almost gone. Then maybe three days ago, I bumped my hand against a table and actually felt it. Now, I can move my fingers a little.'

'That's unbelievable,' I breathe, touching his arm. 'The stone is quite warm yet still hard.'

My magic wriggles happily in my stomach as if proud about what it's achieved, and I take a moment to silently express my joy, to thank it with all my heart.

The woman at the back of the room clears her throat, and Conrol rolls his eyes at me.

'Marianna here didn't want you to have visitors for a while after you awoke, but wild horses couldn't have kept me away. However, I don't want her upset because we'd have lost you if it wasn't for her. Anyway, you still have more visitors. I'll see you on the morrow.'

He leans forward to plant a final kiss on my forehead.

I have so much more to ask, but I'm tired, and there's only one person I really want to see.

Conrol smiles over his shoulder as he passes through the doorway, and then the frame is filled as Kralgen ducks down to fit through.

THE LAST HOPE

He certainly looks the part of an Icelandian king. The new tattoos on his arms and face are striking, and the white furs he's wearing are daubed in red war paint and serve to make his already sizeable frame enormous.

'Only the strong survive, King Slayer. You prove yourself yet again,' he booms.

'Good to see you too, Kral. Perhaps you can keep your voice down; my head is still pounding like a drum! Now, tell me, did you get everyone here from Midnor?'

'Yes, and more besides. In every town and village we approached, the populace fled before us. Now we've been here a week, and there are a lot of angry civilians in High Delnor baying for an explanation and recompense. Most want to return home now they know we won't kill them. Farsil hasn't told them yet, and there's been no sign of Nogoth or his army.'

'You're amazing, Kral,' I say sincerely.

'Of course I am,' he laughs, glowing under my praise. 'Yet, however amazing I might be, my warriors are getting impatient. I promised them a fight against impossible odds, and they're now hundreds of leagues from home. Our bears aren't too happy in this heat either, the poor things. If Nogoth doesn't show up soon, I'll be fielding off challenges for my kingship!'

He rubs the side of his head where his ear is missing, then looks down at his hand.

'I don't suppose you could regrow me a stone ear and finger? Conrol's stone arm is amazing. He can wriggle his fingers now!'

With a smile to soften my response, I shake my head.

'Sorry, Kral. What's lost is lost. You're as hard as a rock anyway. Turning you to stone would only soften those muscles of yours.'

Kralgen beams with delight, flexing his biceps happily.

Marianna comes over and lays her hand on Kralgen's shoulder.

'Get better quickly, King Slayer, or you'll miss all the fun.'

'See you soon, Kral.'

My heart beats with excitement, for I know Lotane will be coming through the door next, and my eyes are brimming with restrained emotion as into the room walks ... Farsil.

'Malina,' he greets me with a gentle smile. 'Until a short while ago, I'd have happily seen you dead, but now I'm glad to see you're still with us. I'll never forget what you've done, not just in saving Conrol or me, but so many others besides. I've spoken to the surviving men from the Last Hope, and they all talk about you with reverence. I only wish the populace knew your exploits and could understand the good you've done. All they've been told is that enemy forces are afoot, and they're here for their own protection. They bemoan being crammed into this city now their fear has faded. Now even I'm beginning to ask. ... where is Nogoth's army?'

He looks at me, hoping for insight, but I don't have that answer.

'Knowing I've been unconscious for two weeks, I'd have expected him at the gates already, or at least on the horizon. Yet, surely every day we're given to prepare is a gift?'

Farsil nods.

'That much is true. Our engineers are busy building defensive war engines, and we're cramming the tunnels beneath here with supplies to last months. Our armies are returning at the double, and they'll start arriving in the next two days.'

'What about the other kingdoms. Are they uniting with Delnor?'

'Not quite, but they're coming too, except for the Astorians.'

'That's amazing news. How did you convince them to join us?'

Farsil snorts.

'They aren't exactly coming to join us. There's no way the Rolantrians or the others would believe a messenger about a fey invasion, so I didn't try. I just followed your idea and ordered all our forces to immediately withdraw. Now all of our enemies are pursuing intent on High Delnor's destruction and will gather here. When they see the fey horde with their own eyes, circumstance will make allies of us all once again.'

I smile. Farsil's approach was devious and perfect; no one had so far believed what was happening without seeing it for themselves.

'What happened with Destern?'

Farsil grimaces.

'He considered me a traitor for pardoning you and gained support by implying it was because I was complicit in the High King's assassination. I woke up one morning to a sword at my throat.

'Dimitar tells me that Syrila was a Chosen, and now it makes sense. She's been bedding Destern for a while, and even if the admiral knew where her allegiances lay, I doubt it would have made a difference. Love can be blind, and he was an ambitious bastard.'

Love can be blind ... Such true words, but I can see clearly who my true love is, and my heart aches for Lotane.

'Commander. I'm exhausted, and I can barely keep my eyes open.'

'I'm so sorry, Malina. Of course, I'll let you rest,' Farsil says, getting up to leave.

'I'm sorry. It's just that I want to speak with Lotane before I fall asleep.'

Farsil's face drops, and he sits down again. A cold hand grips my heart, and tears come unbidden to my eyes.

'What's wrong. Is he alright? Tell me!' I cry, my hand going to my head as pain shoots behind my eyes.

Marianna comes over.

'You need to leave,' she commands Farsil. Then looks at me. 'You need to calm down and get some more sleep,' and she moves to the desk and puts some herbs into a goblet.

'Don't you dare go without telling me,' I demand, gripping Farsil's wrist.

'In truth, I don't know, Malina. He was in a black mood after you left to go to Pine Hold. I had him confined to the palace under constant guard. But then, two days later, he just vanished. I thought then that everything you told was a lie, and he'd escaped to rejoin you ... but now, I've no idea. I'm sorry.'

Farsil continues talking for a moment, but I just hear a buzz as my mind replays that terrible moment when I broke Lotane's heart. He couldn't forgive me for my sins, and now he's gone. I wonder if I'll ever see him again. Marianna presses a goblet to my lips, and I drink automatically, just wanting the blackness to reclaim me.

I don't want to give in to despair, but what will I fight for if not for love?

As my eyes start to close, violet eyes come to mind, and there is my answer.

I'll fight for revenge.

***

CHAPTER XVII

Another barrel full of thrashing fish, mouths gasping in panic, desperate. A touch of my hand and the water they're in freezes instantly, the fish entombed, dying terrible deaths ... as if there's a good way for them to die.

How many barrels I've frozen, who knows, and it amazes me that this act costs so little strength. As the fish wagons leave for the tunnels beneath the citadel, I remember the bodies frozen beneath the Mountain of Souls. Am I any different from the ssythlan mages? They also ensured their food didn't spoil ... and just preferred the taste of human flesh over fish. At least their victims were dead before being encased in ice.

My stomach cramps and sweat breaks out on my brow. Since discharging myself from Marianne's care, I often suffer from sickness. I know it's not unusual for head injuries to have such an effect, so I'll have to get used to it.

I wave goodbye at the galley captain I've been helping. It's almost dusk, and enough is enough.

He salutes, his expression worn and grim.

As I walk along the wooden quay toward the city proper, I'm close to puking. Nonetheless, I force a smile and nod back to dozens of dock workers who wish me a good evening. Whilst they recognise me as the King Slayer, stories are now told of how I helped save the Commander and successfully led battles against Delnor's new enemy. I've been forgiven by some and am at least tolerated wherever I go.

Some navy marines salute as they march by. Despite them reeling from the news of Admiral Destern's failed coup and death, they've mostly put their resentment behind them. All the war galleys now fish the waters whilst on patrol, supplementing the fishing fleet that it used to once look down upon.

Frenzied activity and construction are everywhere, yet so are lethargy, fear and resentment. The city of High Delnor is full to bursting with people, with every homeowner forced to share their property with refugees. Skilled labourers are being put to good use, but many others stand idle, shrouded by an aura of defeat. Then there's the criminal underbelly, seeking to profit from this situation, circling like sharks around a sinking ship.

As I look back across the harbour's calm waters, I pause to admire the ingenuity of the new complex pulley system that raises or lowers a thick metal chain to ensure no uninvited vessels enter. A dozen defensive bolt throwers and catapults also guard the approach. I know others are being constructed and positioned along the city walls, with additional ones installed at the citadel.

To the right of the harbour entrance, there's another chain, but this time of despondent people. Rationing is already in place, and these poor souls are coming to collect the fish offal soup that's cooked throughout the day and distributed for free. It smells awful, yet nothing is being wasted, and these people are willing to eat anything to help keep their stomachs full.

I pull the hood up on my robe. I prefer being inconspicuous and don't enjoy any attention.

The main streets are too crowded for my liking, so I take a detour. Almost immediately, I come across a dead man and woman lying in the street. Once, murder would have been uncommon in the daytime, but not any longer. They've been dead a while, but even if the rats haven't found them, another scavenger already has, because they're completely naked apart from bloodied shirts.

Two dozen town guards march by, ignoring the corpses as if they're just garbage. Half of the guards exude nervousness and wear new uniforms that don't fit. They're some of the hundreds of inexperienced young men and women who've been conscripted into the guard to help police the city's swollen population as public disorder grows. Yet despite the enlarged military presence, muggings, assaults, and murders are rising, and people are beginning to speak out against Farsil's rule.

Deep voices singing a maudlin dirge have me step to one side as six drunk Icelandians stagger down the road arm in arm. There's never a time of day in the Icelandian culture that doesn't allow for drinking because, in the frozen wastes, it helps keeps them warm ... although it's anything but cold in High Delnor. Their furs are filthy, no doubt from creating the defensive earthworks alongside the returned soldiers of the southern and eastern armies.

'Keep the noise down,' a woman shouts out of a window.

'Drunken Icelandians,' an unseen heckler calls.

Further insults rain down as people vent their frustration.

Everyone's tempers are short. Fear is tightening its grip on this city, and the initial unity brought about by common peril has frayed under constant stress. Once it snaps, this city will be on the brink of devouring itself before any of our enemies arrive.

In response, the Icelandians raise their voices, bellowing at the top of their lungs, challenging bystanders with their stares.

I sigh. These men have come to fight, to lose their lives on foreign soil, and they're just letting off steam after a long day. They're doing little harm when everyone is still awake, but this situation could easily get out of hand.

I move to stand in their path.

'Brothers. Your voices are as strong as your sword arms, yet they also carry as far as a thrown axe,' I say in Icelandian, a smile on my lips. 'Would you care to lower them a little, as the ancestors you honour can hear your tribute whether you sing loud or soft?'

The group comes to a ragged halt, and one steps forward, looming over me. He leans down, peering into the darkness of my hood, then breaks into a foolish grin.

'Hush, everyone, it's the King Slayer. Join us for a drink?' His exaggerated whisper echoes off the walls like thunder.

'Not tonight, but it will be a yes next time, as long as you promise to keep up!' I challenge.

Their booming laughter is even louder than their singing, and I wince as a barrage of angry curses and shouts erupt from nearby houses.

As the Icelandians pass by like an avalanche, *hushing* each other loudly, they slap me on the shoulder, and I fight to stop my knees from buckling under the onslaught. I can't help but chuckle; they're such friendly giants.

I yawn. It's been a long, busy day, and I'm exhausted. I'm up daily before dawn, throwing myself back into training for three solid hours, honing my weapon skills either on my own or with a growing number of soldiers who now embrace me. Then I keep myself busy as much as possible, doing what I can, where I can, helping on the walls, the docks, or barracks, sometimes with magic, yet most of the time with muscle.

I'm not some master strategist, and whilst I attend most meetings, I've already shared all I know with Conrol and Farsil. Well, almost all I know. Nogoth comes to mind. The guilty secret I keep. His image frustratingly still invokes desire but also, thankfully, anger.

Street lanterns are lit as I wander aimlessly for a solid hour along roads as familiar to me as the swirls on my body. Sometimes, despite my tiredness, returning to the citadel doesn't appeal.

My stomach lurches, but not from hunger, and I curse silently. It doesn't matter what herbal remedies I take; nothing good settles it, although there's one thing that helps a little, not just with my stomach but with my chaotic thoughts.

Alcohol.

I toy with the idea of tracking down those Icelandians instead of returning to my empty chamber in the citadel, and I find myself ambling back toward the docks. In the daytime, it's owned by the military, but during the night, by the city's flotsam. The taverns, whorehouses and bars surrounding the harbour thrive at night, and the streets hereabouts begin to fill again now the sun has set.

Scantily clad women, young men, and their pimps appear, loitering in doorways or alleys, fake smiles plastered on their faces alongside nasty makeup. Rowdy sailors and off-duty marines mingle amongst them, but as their uniform is off, so being the rules they usually abide by.

Loud shouts shatter the night, and it won't be long before they mingle with screams of pain as fights break out, blood is drawn, and lives are brought to an untimely end.

There are so many good people in High Delnor, but at night it floats on a cesspit of insatiable greed, and evil boldly shows its ugly face. If only Nogoth was simply coming to collect the unworthy of this world as he was supposed to.

I remember collecting souls when I hunted these streets, and they were safer for it.

Gah.

What am I thinking?

The truth. But what a dark, twisted truth ... is that I collected the souls of evil to feed a greater evil, and afterwards, I partook in the feast too. So what does that make me?

I wander by establishment after establishment, the bright lights, music and laughter tempting, but at the same time, repulsing me. Lotane is the only company I want tonight. So I turn my back on the noise and head toward the industrial district, hoping to find peace and solitude in this overcrowded city.

The number of people gradually thins, and I relax, happy with my decision.

Another growl from my stomach.

Enough, damnit!

It twists again, but not like before. My magic is disturbed, and my senses heighten in response.

Yes, there it is. A single pair of footsteps subtly echoing my own.

In a heartbeat, my loneliness, lethargy and, in fact, any negative emotions are swept away by euphoria. How can I pretend I am anything other than what I am; a predator of the night.

I'm in a shadowy street lined by old warehouses, locked tight and secure with only the moonlight to show my way. I slow down, and the footsteps behind match mine immediately. It's enough to inform me that my stalker is experienced and up to no good. Perhaps I should draw my dagger and give him a chance to reconsider. But no. Where's the fun in that?

Instead, I turn a corner and, within moments, effortlessly clamber up an iron drainpipe onto a flat roof. I feel like laughing with exhilaration as I turn the tables, becoming the hunter. As I peer over the edge, a thin-set man in loose-fitting clothes enters the narrow passage I'd just vacated, a length of cord in one hand and a dagger in his other.

He stops, flummoxed as to where I've gone. After a brief pause, he treads cautiously down the alley, quietly checking the warehouse doors on either side to see if they're secure. All the while, I shadow him from above, my footsteps matching his.

THE LAST HOPE

My stomach rumbles loudly, and I bite back laughter as the man spins around in a panic, his dagger extended, only to find himself alone. Rattled, he picks up his pace, and I know he's given up on the hunt, his instincts warning him that all isn't as it should be.

Do I let him go? I could. But will he find another victim who will die bound and helpless if I did?

Somehow I doubt he'll mend his ways ... unless.

I move swiftly, leaping across rooftops as my quarry twists and turns in the alleys below to put off a pursuer his fear tells him is just behind.

Then, I step off the tall building, cloak flapping as magic slows my descent to the ground half a dozen steps ahead of my prey. The thin man comes skidding to a halt as I raise my hands, flames glowing, Illuminating the rubbish-strewn and rat-infested passage he was trying to escape down.

I twist, his thrown dagger sailing past my shoulder to clatter along the ground.

Next, I catch the whip-like cord in my hand as he snaps it at my eyes, and it turns to ash instantly. Credit to him, He's rather skilled.

I advance, and instead of running, he falls to his knees, shaking uncontrollably.

'You don't have to kill me!' he cries, sobbing in fear, hands pressed together beseechingly.

'You're right. I don't have to,' I reply

His screams die away quickly.

It's good to be back.

***

The pillar I'm leaning against vibrates with the music of elemental energy as I run my fingertips over its rough surface. A small hoverfly darts around the room, and I'm sure I can hear the thrum of every wing beat. Then there's the cadence of everyone's hearts as they listen to the guard captain's daily report.

My every sense is so finely tuned, unlike anything I've ever experienced, and I'm bursting with energy despite a morning training session that had left all my sparring partners gasping. Even my stomach is settled, no doubt the consequence of a good night's sleep.

'Fifty-four murders yesterday, a new high,' the guard captain drones.

I wonder if they're counting my victims, although I'm not sure I actually killed them. Hmmm. I must have let them go.

'Sewers are beginning to overflow ... civil unrest ... a riot in the market. More guards ... night patrols ... stores at full capacity.'

On and on, I find it hard to listen. I look through my spirit eye to distract me, watching the colourful flow of elements cavorting around the packed chamber.

Full of love, I mentally embrace my magic as if a child. It will never let me down, not like Lotane.

Kralgen's meaty hand on my shoulder shakes me back to the present.

'He's looking tired,' Kralgen rumbles in a whisper that can probably be heard at the back of the room.

Major Conrol glances in our direction and then stares across the gathered officers as everyone awaits Commander Farsil. We don't have to wait long.

I study Farsil as he enters, his confident stride, the look of resolve on his face and in his eyes. Despite being armoured and armed for war, he somehow projects calm and belief, and as I look around the room, I note the effect on those attending the briefing.

'You've heard the rumours for weeks,' Farsil begins. 'You've listened to the testimony of the remaining soldiers from the Last Hope, Major Conrol, and more recently, our returning scouts.

'Soon, my friends, the enemy of whom they speak, will be at our gates. The army of Nogoth, King of the Fey, will be upon us in less than five days. Nogoth's goal is simple ... to defeat our armies and subjugate those remaining, leading them into slavery on another world as food for his legions.

'You've read the reports. The creatures we face are those spoken of in stories told to us as children. Giants and trolls, wolfen and gargoyles, ogres and more. Those stories were handed down to warn and prepare us, but over the centuries, we just came to believe they were bedtime tales, their true meaning lost.

'Yet the gods have smiled on us in the strangest of ways. Amongst us stands Malina, once our most wanted foe, now a valued ally without whom we'd be walking blindfolded toward the abyss. You've all been made privy to her incredible story, and because of her, we're forewarned and forearmed.

'I tell you this, my friends. Humankind has lost the battle we're about to face countless times in the mists of the past ... but this time, it will be different, for this time, WE WILL WIN!'

Farsil's voice is a clarion call, and his belief is infectious. Shouts of approval echo around the room, along with the pounding of mailed fists on armour, and I can't help but get caught up in the excitement, my doubts diminishing.

Kralgen roars so loud in approval about five seconds after everyone else that the room falls silent in shock, which is shortly replaced by good-natured laughter.

'Now, I'll stand aside for Major Conrol to give you some specifics of our preparations and plans.'

Farsil bows to his friend and stands back, letting Conrol take centre stage.

The major's smile is broad as he looks around the room, gauging his audience and ensuring everyone is focussed. Like most, he's armoured, all except his left forearm. No gauntlet graces that side, for his stone hand doesn't require it. He winks slightly in my direction before taking a deep breath.

'We've now got forty thousand men digging oversized trenches all around the city, here, here and here,' Conrol says to the assembled officers in the planning room. Every eye follows the red-painted stick he grasps in his stone hand as he points it at a large-scale model of High Delnor and its surrounding areas. 'Each trench will be lined with oil-soaked hay and wood, while the earthen ramparts will be topped with fire-hardened sharpened stakes. They'll be finished in two days, hopefully sooner.

'I doubt these will entirely stop the giants or the trolls.' He shakes his head in disbelief. 'To even say these words sounds so strange to my ears. Anyway, what matters is that it will slow them down, making them vulnerable to our defensive siege weapons whilst funnelling Nogoth's smaller ground troops toward two potential killing grounds, the approaches to the west or northern gates, here and here.'

Like Farsil, the major is a man who inspires, and in truth, the summary of the preparations underway are impressive, to say the least.

'The best news is that we now have fifty bolt-throwers and fifty catapults taken from our galleys positioned on the city walls, whereas before, we had none. More are under construction as we speak to strengthen the citadel's defences.'

Smiles and nods of approval meet his words as heads crane forward to see the model engines atop miniature walls. Thin red cord marks each unit's range and overlapping arcs of fire.

'As you can see,' Conrol continues. 'They cover not just the killing grounds, but beyond the fortified approaches in case the giants and trolls take that path. The siege weapons will operate in units of four pieces under the control of marine engineers who are expertly trained and supremely proficient in their use. They have guiding orders to target the larger fey first but have independent fire control once any battle commences.

'We have five thousand archers to defend the walls, who'll also be pivotal in protecting our troops and city from aerial assault. We already have enough stores of spare arrows to last a solid month of fighting, and each day we have fletchers, carpenters and volunteers crafting ten thousand more.'

I can see Kralgen counting on his fingers next to me, his face screwed in concentration. Before he arrives at the result of whatever sum he's doing, a captain raises his hand.

'What is it, Denault?' Conrol asks.

'If we have five thousand archers, that's only two arrows each per day. If our stores last a month, each archer will only have about sixty arrows in their quivers after that time, assuming they're all still alive.'

Conrol shoots a glance at Farsil, who nods with a wry smile.

'Well observed, Captain,' Conrol says, slamming his hand down on the table to emphasise his praise. 'That is nowhere near enough. We need someone with an eye for such detail. You're now in charge of reviewing logistics, which means you'll get a promotion. Congratulations!'

Denault looks pleased with himself, and well he might be. Ten thousand arrows a day seemed incredible, but now we can see it's laughable.

Kralgen turns to me, holding up six fingers.

'Well done, Kral,' I whisper. 'Don't worry, Denault just beat you to it!'

Farsil steps forward again, taking over from Conrol.

THE LAST HOPE

'When it comes to fighting steel on steel, we have nigh on twenty thousand Delnorian swordsmen, fourteen thousand spearmen and a thousand light cavalry. Most of these are hardened veterans. We also have twenty thousand of our northern Icelandian friends under the leadership of the giant king in our midst, Kralgen.'

I can't help but smile as Kralgen puffs out his chest, beaming. He's death incarnate with a weapon in hand, but also a simple, gentle soul after Alyssa tamed him. She would have been so proud of him. The thought brings tears to the corners of my eyes, and I drop my head, allowing my hair to fall and hide my emotions.

'Don't forget our bears,' growls Kralgen, hooking his fingers like claws.

Everyone nods. Five hundred of those terrifying beats are positioned northward along the banks of the River Del. They'll be a devastating force under the direction of their riders.

Farsil spreads his arms as if to embrace us all like a family.

'In total, we already have sixty thousand of the finest troops the world has known, ready and waiting to defend our city. Yet, my friends, that won't be all. The independent alliance armies are coming to besiege us, unaware of our Icelandian allies or Nogoth's invasion.

'In doing so, they'll place themselves between Nogoth's horde and our walls. Once they recognise the situation and that their only chance of survival is with us, we'll welcome them unconditionally into our city as the brothers they used to be. With a combined force of nearly one hundred thousand soldiers, well supplied in a highly defensible position, I don't think Nogoth and his horde will have a chance to win.'

Rapturous applause meets his declaration, and mine joins the rest.

It's incredible and undeniably true. An attacking force needs approximately five times the number of heavily fortified defenders to overcome them. A siege to starve the city also won't work because of the fishing fleets. Farsil's plan is sound.

Major Conrol raises his hands, and the room eventually quietens. His face is serious once again, grabbing everyone's attention.

'Now, despite planning for success, we have also planned for setbacks, as no battle ever goes entirely as planned. I want everyone to speak and question freely. Challenge what you see and what you've heard, just like Captain Denault earlier.'

Thoughtful silence descends as everyone mulls over the unthinkable.

'I've heard it said they have mages. Can they summon lightning to destroy us?' a voice calls from the back.

Snorts of laughter greet the question.

Conrol looks at me and nods.

I step forward, the centre of attention.

'It's true,' I say clearly. 'There are ssythlans that can summon magic, and maybe they'll accompany Nogoth's army, although they normally never venture this far north. As to lightning or fireballs, I can't see it happening. Every mage has a finite amount of power, and using it tires them immensely depending on how much they expend, just like physical exertion. It can't easily be projected either. A mage would have to touch you to set you on fire, and ...'

'Thank you, Malina,' Conrol interjects quickly, motioning for me to return to my place. 'Given the choice between fighting a mage or a troll, I'll take the mage every day. They can die with a sword in their guts or an arrow to the chest, just like any other ugly beast. Next question!'

I curse myself for my choice of words. How stupid can I be?

'What if the city walls are breached?' a highly decorated lieutenant asks. His armour is covered in ribbons, whilst every bit of exposed skin is a patchwork of scars.

A few officers scoff, but Farsil's stern gaze quietens everyone.

'It's a damned good question,' he scolds the group.

'If we can't immediately contain the breach, we concede the walls, and our forces will affect a fighting retreat back to the citadel,' Farsil answers. 'Archers will traverse and fight from the rooftops, whilst our infantry fight in the streets, erecting barricades to slow our enemy's advance. Our heavy spearmen and swordsmen will excel in those circumstances. The navy will leave the harbour and take up station off-shore under the control of Admiral Skylin. They'll continue to assist us by fishing the surrounding waters, and their catch will be hauled up the cliffs.'

'But what about the civilians?' asks a heavyset, tanned officer.

'At the first sign of our defence being in trouble, we have town criers who'll direct them to the citadel.' Conrol answers. 'As you all know, leagues of tunnels beneath us have been fully stocked in anticipation of a long siege. The citadel has never fallen in living memory and has never been so heavily defended as now. Those who shelter behind its walls or within its tunnels will be safe!'

THE LAST HOPE

'What about our other towns and cities? I have family in Highnor!' a voice calls out.

This time Conrol and Farsil exchange glances. I note the subtlest drop in Farsil's shoulders, resignation replacing his confidence. I know what Farsil is going to say before he does.

'I've been sending out sin-hawks to our cities and large towns, ordering the populace to flee to the mountains or countryside with whatever supplies they can. I've even tried warning the other kingdoms. Regretfully, the responses have been of disbelief and refusal. May the gods be with them, for otherwise, they are on their own.'

'Some of us could go save our families if you let us leave!' cries another.

Shouts of confusion and condemnation ring out. This could get messy. Love can push aside duty as if it never existed.

'ENOUGH!' Kralgen booms, and those closest step back in consternation. 'The greatest chance of survival of everyone we love is on our shoulders. Nogoth is coming here to crush us. The more losses we inflict on his army, the more chance your families have!'

It's the truth, and Kralgen has summarised everything with his few words.

Murmurs of agreement fill the chamber.

'Are there any further questions?' Farsil asks.

Silence.

'Then we still have lots to do, so let's get on with it. We have a war to win!'

***

'It feels weird being astride a horse again,' Kralgen shouts. 'I far prefer my bear!'

'Looking at your poor mount, I think he'd prefer you ride your bear too,' Conrol laughs. 'I swear you've got bigger in the last few days. How that's possible, I don't know.'

It's true. Kralgen is putting on even more muscle. Added to his height, he truly is becoming a giant amongst men. The furs he wears, irrespective of the heat, only add to the image.

Kralgen laughs happily.

'Well, it's because I'm not staying in your city, and our bears are experts at fishing. They spend all day in the River Del staying cool and catching our supper ... plus we have our own supply stash!'

'Sounds like I should have dinner around your campfire then,' Conrol grumbles good-naturedly.

'I'm sure Kralfax, my bear, would be happy to see you again,' Kralgen winks.

The laughter feels good. In fact, I feel good, better than in days. When did that start ... the morning after I killed those men? Perhaps being close to Kralgen and his never-ending good humour is a balm for my soul. I remember the banter between him and Lotane would always make me smile.

Damn. My good mood evaporates in a heartbeat, replaced by the emptiness of loss. I know Kralgen misses Lotane too. He can't understand why he's disappeared, and I don't have the strength to explain.

'You, sergeant,' I call to an engineer covered in dirt overseeing a group of men. 'That trench needs to be deeper and wider by half again.'

'I don't understand,' he says, affronted, hands on hips. 'It's wide and deep enough to stop a horse, let alone an infantry charge. Any deeper or wider is a waste of effort. It's alright for you on your high horse, but we're exhausted.'

The disrespect doesn't sit well with me nor Conrol, who is about to tear a strip off the sergeant when Kralgen's booming laughter splits the air.

'On your high horse. Do you get what he means? He means ...' Kralgen gasps.

'I get exactly what he means,' I say, eyes flashing as I leap from the saddle.

The sergeant gulps, realising he's gone too far, but Kralgen laughing behind me is so infectious, I can't help but shake my head and smile.

'Listen, sergeant,' I say, my anger fading. 'You received your directives, and it isn't for you to question them, however tired you or your fellows are. However, now I'm down off my high horse, perhaps I can help a little.'

I step to the edge of the trench. It's been dug with precision, a long rectangular excavation, with the dirt piled high on the side closest to the city. Sharpened stakes, large and small, are piled nearby and once pounded into the newly compacted earthen rampart, they'll present a bristling hedge of points to an attacking enemy. He's overseen a good job, but unlike the surrounding trenches that this will soon join up with, it isn't large enough considering the foe we'll face.

'Stand back,' I order, sweeping my arms for emphasis to encompass the sergeant and his large group of soldiers.

Grumbling, they pick up their picks, spades and sundry other equipment and move to where Conrol and Kralgen sit astride their horses.

Leaping down into the trench, I land lightly and move to the end. It's about thirty paces long and as deep as Kralgen is tall. We've inspected hundreds of these defensive fortifications so far this morning; for the most part, they've been perfect.

This one must be no different.

Kneeling, I channel my thoughts, thrusting my hands down as if to bury them in the soil, then push my palms away, feeling the earth shift below my feet.

From the base and sides of the trench, the earth pares away like the skin of a fruit. I follow, exhorting my magic, feeling my strength diminish but nonetheless feeling equal to the task. As I near the end of the trench, the earth churning like an avalanche before me, I lift my hands. As I do, like a wave breaking on the shore, the earth rolls over the trench top and settles.

I expend a little more magic climbing the trench wall and come to my feet before a wide-eyed audience.

'Now we're all exhausted, sergeant. Please continue with the good work.'

I don't allow weakness to show as I return to my friends. Projecting strength and confidence is pivotal in maintaining our forces' morale which is currently riding high.

'Show off,' Kralgen chuckles as I mount my horse, the shouts of the sergeant rising behind us.

'Hah. You, of all people, should know how much that's tired me, Kral.'

We flick the reins and head off toward the next trench. The air is filled with noise. The thrum of bows as archers hone their skills, the sounds of picks, axes and shovels. The grunts of labouring men and women.

Conrol looks back and forth between us as we ride, an unspoken question in his eyes.

'Kral's a magic user,' I explain. 'Fire magic.'

'Fire. Why is it always fire?' Conrol rolls his eyes.

'I barely use it,' Kralgen shrugs. 'It's useful to light a candle, torch or campfire, but I don't have anything like Malina's power, and I can't use it in combat like she can. Then again, I prefer the power of my sword arm anyway!'

'How come Malina can use it in combat, and you can't? Conrol asks, intrigued.

'It's probably because she's part fey,' Kralgen laughs, then a look of horror replaces the laughter as he realises what he's just said.

I turn toward Conrol, a rare feeling of panic gripping me. I've only recently regained his trust and friendship, and Kralgen has revealed one of my darkest secrets with one clumsy comment.

The major looks at me, and I swear my heart pauses as I await the accusations and condemnation that will spew from his lips.

Instead, he just shrugs and sighs.

'Don't worry, Malina. Farsil and I had already come to that conclusion ourselves. As your head is still upon your shoulders, you can safely assume that we're judging you by your actions and friendship, not your lineage.'

'How did you know?' I gasp in shock.

'Your head injury. It bled so much, and Marianne initially thought you had a terrible infection because your blood was almost black. The wolfen had black blood; the troll you slew, the same. What else could it signify?'

My head is spinning as the magnitude of what Conrol tells me sinks in, yet I still can't believe it. Drawing my dagger, I prick my little finger with the point and watch in horror as a bead of blood wells up.

Black as night.

'It used to be red … I should know; I've seen enough of it. It should be red, not black. I'm not a monster … I'm not a monster!'

Suddenly the landscape is spinning.

'Malina. Malina!'

The voices seem to come from far away, and the spinning recedes.

I'm in Kralgen's arms on the ground, Conrol kneeling beside me, love and concern etched on their faces, the sky blue above them.

THE LAST HOPE

'I'm sorry. The blood ... it came as such a shock!' I cry.

But perhaps it wasn't. Nogoth had told me I was changing, and Lotane had shown me the black veins running from the bite wounds to my shoulder.

I'm becoming more fey than human.

***

CHAPTER XVIII

We're ready. It's hard to believe, but against the odds, we're ready.

A stiff breeze causes signal flags to snap angrily above us on their poles as I wait with Farsil, Conrol, Kralgen, and a dozen other officers on the gatehouse guarding the western entrance to High Delnor.

From this vantage point, I can see the completed earthworks spread out on the plains, like waves frozen on an earthen sea crested with giant spikes. Along the walls to my left and right, archers stand ready with giant bolt throwers and catapults looming over them. Ranks of spearmen and swordsmen stand to attention behind their large shields, presenting a barrier every bit as formidable as the walls they stand upon. Kralgen's twenty thousand Icelandians stand quietly visible outside the base of the walls, their massed presence saying more than shouts or war cries.

Yet despite this display of martial strength, the mood isn't ugly or charged with restrained violence, for no one will die this day, or at least we hope not.

In the distance, just beyond our defensive siege weapons range, the armies of Rolantria, Suria, Tars and Hastia have finally come together. Forty thousand enemy soldiers from four nations united to break the backbone of the old Delnorian empire once and for all. They make a formidable appearance. The midday sun shines from countless spear points and polished shields. Small units of cavalry continually circle the main forces, acting as scouts. Large wagon trains full of supplies and equipment further swell their number. If we walked down to the harbour, we'd also see their galleys prowling the waves.

'Perhaps it's a good thing the Astorians didn't join them,' an officer mutters behind us. 'There's certainly a lot of them.'

Conrol looks over his shoulder. 'You need to stop seeing them as the enemy, Captain. Shortly they'll be our allies, and the more, the merrier.'

'I wonder if they're thinking about going home now they've seen the defences and Kralgen's Icelandians,' I muse.

Farsil shoots me a look.

'Damn. You could be right. It would be a disaster if they do, and we can't take the risk by waiting.'

'Corporal! Horses for Malina and myself. At the double!'

Conrol raises his hand, forestalling the woman's departure.

'Three horses, surely?'

Farsil laughs.

'I always want you by my side or watching my back, old friend. But, it would be the height of folly to have us both fall into enemy hands, don't you think. Let's not put temptation their way any more than we need to!'

Farsil nods to the corporal, and she hurries off, shouting orders of her own, while we wait, watching for any sign of movement in the distance.

'How many would the Astorians have brought to the fray had they joined?' I ask.

Farsil scratches his temple.

'They field about fifteen thousand troops, mostly cavalry. They excel at skirmishing and utilise mounted archers as the backbone of their force. Historically, there's a lot of bad blood between our kingdoms, so it was a surprise when they didn't try and join the war.

'Honestly, I wish they were here, but perhaps against the odds, they heeded my warning of Nogoth's invasion and intend to defend their lands. May the gods smile favourably upon them.

'Now, Malina, it's your responsibility to ensure that whoever leads the alliance armies heeds the warning too and joins our cause. Are you still alright with this?'

I nod, albeit reluctantly.

Initially, we'd planned on the appearance of Nogoth's army forcing the alliance's sieging armies into desperately asking for sanctuary.

However, we agreed the risk of things going wrong was too high. Whilst I've no wish to use blood magic to take away anyone else's free will, I'll now bind whoever is necessary to ensure our plan's swift success.

'Commander!'

The corporal's voice interrupts my thoughts as she calls from below, and we enter the coolness of the gatehouse in response to her summons. Bundles of arrows are carefully stacked, along with spare weapons, bandages, barrels of water and a hundred other items.

Walking down the stairwell, we exit onto the main street behind the gate. Once, this thoroughfare would have been crowded with pedestrians, traders, market stalls, and goods. Now, every building adjacent to the wall has been taken over by the military, and these streets are kept clear for the movement of soldiers or equipment.

The corporal is waiting with our horses and a white banner.

'Good thinking,' Farsil shouts as we mount up.

Almost immediately, the gate creaks open, and we heel the horses through the tunnel, hoofbeats echoing loudly around us.

'Kralgen?' I shout as we exit into the sunlight.

Several warriors point to the north, and as I look across the massed ranks of Northmen, leaning on their heavy weapons, there sits my friend astride his bear.

'Thank you,' I shout in Icelandian as we urge the horses into a canter along the road, out past the mass of warriors, then head toward Kral.

'A fine day,' he shouts, lifting a double-handed war mallet in salute as we approach. The fact that he wields it in one hand like a toothpick isn't lost on any of us.

'Fancy coming for a ride?' Farsil asks.

'Is there a chance of a fight?'

'Quite possibly!'

'Then count me in!'

Kralgen looks positively jubilant. He shouts some orders to his bodyguard and urges his bear forward.

Our horses snicker, unhappy at the approaching beast, but they're well-trained, and Farsil and I both spend a moment soothing them, our voices calm.

Shortly after, we're heading west along the trade road that in happier days saw wagons flow freely between High Delnor, Hastia and

Tars, but now take us through the killing ground and toward the massed enemy ranks.

Farsil holds the white banner of truce high, and it streams in the wind signalling our peaceful intent. As we reach the end of the earthworks, we rein our mounts to a halt and sit, waiting. Farsil jams the banner pole into the ground.

There's no doubt we've been seen; the enemy cavalry screen is but a javelin throw away, but to press any further uninvited could be deadly.

We sit patiently for an hour, then impatiently for two.

'The bastards,' Farsil growls. 'They're just letting us bake in the sun here. How much longer will they keep us waiting? Every hour is pivotal, damn them!'

Kralgen chuckles, catching my attention.

'Care to join me?' he asks.

'I've got nothing better to do!'

Farsil looks back and forth between us.

'You can't. Don't be foolish!' but even as he says the words, Kralgen is plucking the banner from the ground and urging his bear forward with me alongside.

'This is insanity!' Farsil shouts as he catches up, grinning broadly.

'Dimitar put us up to it,' I shout. 'If we die, he gets to be Commander Conrol. It has a ring to it, don't you think?'

Kralgen bursts out laughing, and then Farsil joins in, wiping tears from his eyes.

The alliance cavalry forms a line ahead of us, lance tips gleaming.

As we get closer, consternation grows on the faces of those before us. We're approaching under a banner of truce, laughing as we do so, and they obviously don't have orders to engage us, or they'd have attacked long ago.

'I'm not stopping,' howls Kralgen gleefully. 'This is too much fun.'

Kralgen's bear roars, and the line of cavalry breaks apart, horses wheeling and rearing in terror as the riders frantically seek to control their mounts.

'Good morning!' Kralgen shouts joyfully as we ride through their lines.

Frantic movement ahead draws our attention. Spearmen are being cajoled into formation by a screaming officer before a colourful tent the size of a small house.

'Maybe it's time to approach a little more carefully,' Farsil shouts.

For a moment, I think Kralgen will ignore the advice, but the hundreds of glistening spearpoints help him see sense.

'It was fun while it lasted!' Kralgen smiles and leaps from Kralfax's saddle as the bear slows to a walk.

Farsil and I follow suit, leading our horses. Kralgen's bear doesn't even have reins but just follows at his shoulder.

Three men and a woman exit the tent. All wear armour decorated with symbols of rank. There's no doubt these are the generals of the four alliance armies.

Farsil doesn't hesitate.

'Welcome to High Delnor!' he shouts, opening his arms wide.

From the look in the generals' eyes, they aren't happy to see us.

***

'Hand over your weapons!'

The demand comes from a black-skinned general who could have been Alyssa's sister, the resemblance is so striking. A flicker of sadness mars Kralgen's otherwise happy face as he also registers the likeness. She must be the leader of the Tarsian contingent, but as she gives the order, I wonder if the others defer to her in other matters.

It doesn't matter; I'll get to all four of them.

Farsil nods briefly, so I unhook the scabbards of my sword and dagger.

A thin, pock-marked captain steps forward, a look of distrust upon his face. He holds a ceremonial cloth draped across both arms. Farsil carefully lays his sheathed sword and dagger across the richly embroidered purple material. Next, the captain approaches me, and I reluctantly repeat the action. Finally, he moves to Kralgen.

'Are you sure?' Kralgen asks softly.

The captain's lip curls slightly.

'Hand over your weapon, Northman!'

With a smile, Kralgen lifts his war mallet as if it weighs no more than a dagger, holds it at arm's length, a handspan above the captain's arms, and then drops it.

Kralgen steps to one side as the captain pitches forward to the floor, dropping all our weapons as he cries out in surprise and pain.

THE LAST HOPE

Farsil and I assist the embarrassed captain in regaining his feet as Kralgen turns to Kralfax.

'Guard,' he whispers into the bear's ear, pointing. The next moment, the enormous creature just lies down on our weapons.

The captain shakes himself free of Farsil and me, his face red with anger, then spies Kralfax baring its daggered teeth and backs away toward the waiting ranks of spearmen.

'I'm Commander Farsil of High Delnor. We come under the banner of truce in good faith and peaceful intent. Is it too much to ask that we be met with civility?'

'Stand aside!' The Tarsian general orders and the ranks of spearmen separate, allowing her to approach.

She's about as tall as Farsil but broader of shoulder, and her skin is crisscrossed with dozens of white scars. This woman has fought her way to the top and is no stranger to the sword.

The other three generals follow. The missing fingers, ears and scars show they were warriors once, but that was some time ago. These men have gone soft of body and obviously enjoy their food and wine too much. However, if their minds are as sharp now as their reflexes once were, then they are still to be respected.

'I'm General Tyral, overall commander of the independent alliance forces. These are Generals Gast, Avarez and Usutul, and she points to each in turn.'

Farsil salutes Tyral, and I mentally get ready. My magic squirms as it senses my need. We'd planned for this moment.

'May I present, Kralgen, King of Icelandia.'

Kralgen steps forward, reaching out, and Tyral automatically accepts the gesture, grasping Kralgen's forearm in a warrior's greeting.

'Well met, King Kralgen.' Tyral smiles briefly, bowing her head slightly in respect, and the other generals follow suit.

'May I also present ...' Farsil begins.

General Tyral steps back quickly, distrust replacing the smile, her eyes narrowing.

'You claim to come in good faith and peaceful intent, yet bring the very assassin who killed your High King, who is wanted across the five kingdoms for similar crimes! Do you take me for a fool? Am I supposed to shake her hand and die with my flesh on fire?'

Damn! I stand impassively, although inside, I'm reeling. Tyral or the other generals will never allow me to shake their hands or otherwise get close to bind them to me now.

I know Farsil will be fuming too, but he doesn't let it show and answers smoothly.

'No, General, no. My apologies. This is indeed Malina the King Slayer, but whereas she was once our most wanted foe, now she is my most trusted advisor. She's not here to harm you or anyone else. You have my word and life as a guarantee. But it's her words and wisdom that had me recall Delnor's armies and finds us here today.'

'You recalled your armies because they were getting beaten!' General Usutul snarls. 'Now you want to talk your way out of a siege. I don't think so! We've all been waiting for this moment for years. My warriors are thirsty for your blood, Delnorian!'

'They've got nothing to say that we'd want to hear unless it's begging for mercy. Even then, I wouldn't give it to them.' Avarez adds. 'Send them on their way!'

General Gast says nothing but doesn't need to, for he nods along vehemently, his face full of hatred.

The moment hangs in the balance, we need this opportunity to plead and win our case, or the consequences will be horrifying. Yet this hatred, bitterness and distrust brought about by years of fighting is suddenly an insurmountable obstacle in our way.

'What happened to the laws of hospitality?' Kralgen booms, rising to the occasion. 'I understand you not liking these two, but what do you have against me? Aren't you interested in finding out why I'm here? By the gods, I'm thirsty. You should offer me a drink ... I swear I'd consider being your ally if it's a good one!'

Tryal snorts and shakes her head.

'Is there any time of day you Icelandians don't drink? Gah. Allow yourself to be searched, and you can join us for a drink over lunch and say what you have to. I wouldn't want a High Delnorian looking down on us as uncivil heathens.'

'Captain. Do a better job this time,' she says, raising an eyebrow as she stares at the unfortunate man.

Then, followed by the other generals, she turns back and heads toward the tent.

Farsil smiles at Kralgen and I.

THE LAST HOPE

We're in.

***

'I've never heard such rubbish in my life, and it's been a long and colourful one, I can tell you,' General Usutul shouts. 'They're buying time, for what I don't know. Let's send them on their way and start digging in our troops. The time for talking is over; it's now the time for killing!'

'You haven't got enough men to win this siege, let alone the brains. You've seen our defences, and it's obvious they aren't for you. Why would we make our earthworks so high and the trenches so deep? Ask yourself that!'

'Maybe because I don't underestimate a Delnorian's capacity for stupidity,' Usutul sneers.

I watch as Kralgen shovels more meat into his mouth, finishing the platter meant for us all. He holds it out to a serving boy.

'Another one and some more wine; there's a good lad. This is pretty good!'

Kralgen is enjoying the arguments immensely.

We're sitting in the middle of a large campaign tent. Farsil and I are on small camp stools, whereas Kralgen has decided to lie on the floor and watches through slightly glazed eyes.

I sip on a goblet of water, whereas Farsil hasn't touched his. Then again, I'd done most of the talking till now, telling a heavily redacted version of my role in preparing for Nogoth's invasion, his duplicity, and his arrival at Pine Hold with an army to enslave the world. Surprisingly they'd let me finish without interruption.

I sniff the water. I know it's not tainted, but something is bothering me. There's a familiar smell that I can't quite place, and I don't know where it's coming from.

'We have forty catapults and forty bolt throwers on the walls. You'll have seen them through your spyglasses if you care to look.' Farsil offers. 'Why can't you see the futility of attacking? You'd be slaughtered!'

Tryal nods to an aide who disappears out of the tent to verify Farsil's claim.

'I'd even allow you to enter the city and see our preparations. They're not for you, but you wouldn't have a chance if they were. We have the weapons and the numbers. Were we so inclined, we'd march out with the Icelandians, and then you'd find yourself fighting sixty thousand men and a load of savage bears! You'd be butchered!'

'My Icelandians aren't going to fight this lot. This wine is too good!' Kralgen laughs uproariously.

Farsil's face goes red with rage as he looks down at Kralgen drinking straight out of a bottle.

'You wouldn't fight us?' General Tryal leans forward. 'Seriously, you wouldn't fight us?'

Kralgen sits up and puts the bottle to one side, and thankfully he recognises the seriousness of the situation, or perhaps he's been playing up all along.

'My Icelandians won't attack your alliance; that much is true. My Northmen aren't here for you.'

'Your allies are deserting you already!' crows Avarez delightedly.

'In fact, my warriors' will fight and die at your side.' Kralgen adds emphatically, slapping his thigh.

Avarez's smile slowly disappears.

'When we face this Nogoth and his armies, I suppose?' he says, finally understanding Kralgen's game.

'Indeed. There can be only one alliance now. The humans against the fey!' Kralgen nods sagely. 'But if you attack or siege High Delnor, then, however good the wine, my Icelandians will stand with Delnor!'

'Enough!' says Tryal loudly, her face angry. 'I've listened to your stories and lies out of courtesy and tradition. Now listen to what I have to say. My orders are to lay siege to your city and starve, burn, or put to the sword every Delnorian in High Delnor. Those are not just my orders, but my personal desire ... and I intend to carry them through!

'The only thing that will prevent this is your surrender. The civilians will then be spared, and your soldiers sold into slavery ... except for you, Commander. Your position and reputation will ensure you and a few others will be tried for war crimes leading to a death sentence!

'As for you, Kralgen, King of Icelandia, I say this. Despite our nations not being at war, it will be so if you obstruct us in our mission! So march away now in peace and friendship!'

THE LAST HOPE

Farsil looks desperate, not for himself, but for our plan and the survival of everyone. We feared this would happen unless I could use blood magic to have them believe me and follow my orders. Even if I leapt upon Tryal now, I wouldn't have time to bind her before I was killed.

Yet something else is wrong.

The way my story hadn't had an effect was my first clue something was up.

I know General Tryal recognises High Delnor is too well prepared and could survive a siege or march out to defeat the alliance forces at any time. Likewise, the others are too experienced to not recognise this. They're not even overly worried by the presence of Kralgen's Icelandians.

Usutul had earlier accused us of buying time with our meeting, but I'm beginning to believe it's the other way around. Why would they stay if they knew their armies couldn't prevail?

It's because they believe they can win!

But how? Surely, they can only win if they have a far larger army ... or another is on the way.

By the gods ... have they allied with Nogoth?

No. Nogoth wouldn't have had time to meet, let alone persuade them, and one look at his army would show anyone the folly of such an act.

'It's time for you to leave!' Tryal commands loudly.

'Please, just a minute. I'm not feeling well,' I say, lifting my hand, buying some time.

But if not Nogoth and his fey, who else do they believe could come to their aid?

Ssythlans.

Yes, that is the scent I can discern. Now I've identified it, there's no doubt.

Tell a lie but give it enough of the truth to make it believable. The alliance generals must have already heard another version of my story from ssythlan lips. They've been led to believe that Delnor's forces have retreated due to the threat of a conquering ssythlan army marching from Pine Hold, not an army of fey.

'They've lied to you!' I state loudly, looking Tryal in the eye. 'It's what they do. Lies entwined with a pinch of truth, sprinkled with what you desire to hear, to make you believe!'

Tryal looks hard at Farsil, who in turn looks back. Even Kralgen is focused.

'Not the commander.' My voice is loud, bringing Tryal's attention back to me. 'It's the ssythlan travelling with you who has lied. It's got you believing there's a ssythlan army coming to siege and capture High Delnor, which explains why you're not worried about our defences or the Icelandians.

'What's the price for a ssythlan alliance? Probably that you lay siege and attack before they arrive to ensure we're sealed tight. You'll suffer grave losses, but that will be an acceptable butcher's bill if High Delnor is subsequently humbled. Share the glory, share the spoils and return home as conquering heroes.'

From the shocked silence and looks, I'm right on the mark. It's time to take advantage before the opportunity is gone forever.

'Only you'll never see your homes again!'

I pause briefly, letting those words sink in.

'I swear, there's no ssythlan army coming to your assistance, only a fey horde. When they arrive to find our armies locked and bleeding in combat, they'll destroy you first. You won't have a chance as they smash into your rear, and everyone and I mean everyone, will perish, trapped between our fortifications and their merciless claws.

'General Tryal. I know you want to disbelieve everything. Why should you trust an assassin and the enemy leader you hate and wish to kill ... over a ssythlan? A race you've traded peacefully with for generations? But what if a ssythlan told you the truth of the matter. Would you believe it if it told the same story as us?'

'How do you know all this?' hisses Tryal.

'Does it really matter?' Farsil speaks up. 'Have the ssythlan brought here. If it refuses to speak, its silence indicates guilt; otherwise, we'll get it to admit the truth!'

'She wasn't speaking to you, Delnorian dog,' Usutul growls. 'She was asking the assassin!'

I nod to Farsil, and he subsides.

'I know all this because my life has been shaped by the ssythlans and recently by Nogoth, their god. Yet now is the time for truth, not deceit, so I'll speak honestly. You were right not to shake my hand, for I would indeed have worked magic upon you.'

Tryal scowls, her eyes narrowing, yet I press on.

'The magic I'd have wielded can only be done through touch. It wouldn't have been to kill you but to have you believe our story so that we could be allies, not enemies. To face death by each other's side, not at each other's throats.

'Have the ssythlan brought here. I'll charm it with a simple touch. Afterwards, ask anything ... and know the truth.'

'Don't trust her,' Gast says to Tryal.

He rarely speaks, and I wish he'd kept it that way.

'It would be foolhardy to risk the ssythlan's safety and help by bringing it to her!' Avarez mutters darkly.

'If I harm it, then we'll no longer be protected by the banner of truce. Surely our deaths are a reward worthy of the risk?'

'Don't include me in that,' rumbles Kralgen.

'Guard sergeant,' Tryal turns to one of her bodyguards. 'Have our ssythlan friend join us immediately!'

He leaves through a flap in the back of the tent. It's a possibility the ssythlan might know me or attempt to resist, so I need it distracted.

'Commander, Kral, greet it.'

My friends stand facing the flap as I position myself to one side. I miss Tryal's gesture, but guards move closer, their weapons poised, ready to strike us down if we attempt anything untoward.

It's not long before the flap is pulled back, and the ssythlan walks in.

'I'm Kralgen, King of the Icelandians!'

Kral extends his hand as Farsil does the same.

As Kralgen and Farsil distract the ssythlan, I slip behind and gently lay my hand on its shoulder

This might not have been our original plan, but perhaps it's better.

I nod confidently to the assembled generals.

'My friend,' I say, noting the flare of the ssythlan's nostrils and the scenting of its tongue as it recognises a Saer Tel behind it. 'Please sit before General Tryal and answer her every question as truthfully as if I'd asked you myself!'

The ssythlan is bound to obey. This is going to be interesting.

***

Kralgen's laughter booms from the other side of the gigantic campfire, and I can't help but smile across at my friend. It amazes me how far he has come.

Blood has called upon blood, and he's found his way back home amongst his Icelandian brothers and sisters where he belongs.

So, what about me?

Black blood flows within my veins, and the change leaves me sick as my humanity is pushed aside by what Nogoth has done. Where's home for me now, and who are my brothers and sisters?

Pushing such thoughts aside, I bite into some skewered rabbit, trying to enjoy the food, crackling fire and company. Farsil sighs, catching my attention.

'The sooner we lock those gates behind us, the happier I'll be,' he says, looking toward High Delnor.

I follow Farsil's longing gaze, in tune with his sentiment. The city walls are lit with the homely glow of a thousand torches, while the gates are wide open, beckoning, offering sanctuary for everyone.

'You and me both, but let's relax and enjoy ourselves in the interim.'

'Kralgen's crazy idea definitely seems to have paid off.' Farsil laughs, looking around. 'He might not seem that smart, but I think that's all show!'

'Too much drink can create enemies of friends and friends of enemies,' I say in a deep voice, mimicking Kralgen.

I think back to earlier and Kralgen's genius.

Under questioning, the ssythlan had ratified everything I'd said in such grotesque detail that it had left little doubt about the fey invasion or the horrors that would soon be visited upon the human race.

Unfortunately, despite the imminent threat, the enmity felt by the alliance generals was too longstanding to overcome so quickly, and some disbelief still remained. So, despite Farsil's initial entreaties and subsequent insistence, Tryal had pointedly refused to march the alliance warriors into the city. The following arguments had become dangerously heated until Kralgen's intervention had cooled things down.

I look around, smiling, as recent enemies now mingle, toasting one another with wine, overseen by the gigantic Icelandians who have spread out as peacekeepers. Even drunk, no one would want to be on the wrong side of one of them, and their laughter is infectious anyway, soothing ruffled feathers whenever required.

Tryal comes over to squat before us, her back to the fire.

'Gast and Usutul have left with a hundred lancers as an escort. They're still not entirely convinced, so they'll scout west for signs of this Nogoth's army. I've also got our cavalry screening north and west of our positions.'

'We should get everyone inside the city tonight,' Farsil presses again. 'I've led my men into the lion's den, bringing them out here … and you've shown yourself to be true. We may never be friends, but we're no longer enemies. Look around; the men and women of both our armies are relieved and happy to have avoided this bloodshed.'

'I'm sorry, Commander, but neither my soldiers nor those of the other kingdoms will enter High Delnor tonight or any other day,' Tryal says firmly.

'What do you mean?' I exclaim. 'You heard the truth, and your scouts will confirm this on the morrow. If you stay out here to fight, you'll be overwhelmed. It's utter folly!'

Tryal sighs softly, ignoring my outburst.

'Now your High King is dead, Commander. Who is your duty to?'

'My people.' Farsil answers without hesitation.

'Exactly. My duty is also to my people and my queen. Honour and duty require me to return and protect Tars with my army if this fey invasion is true. The other generals will do the same. So, tonight we drink together, but tomorrow, we shall return home!'

'And leave us to buy you the time with our deaths!' growls Farsil.

Tryal laughs bitterly, shaking her head as if in despair.

'I see the truth of the matter, Commander. Your armies retreating was a ploy to bring us here to defend High Delnor, leaving our homelands undefended. If anyone should be aggrieved, it's me. Yet despite your deceit, I admit it was a masterful plan!'

'That's not fair,' I say firmly. 'If together we deplete Nogoth's forces here, Tars and the other nations might escape unscathed!'

Tryal shakes her head. 'I wish I could believe that. Now, enjoy the night, for I fear none of us will enjoy many more.'

She nods to us, then moves away to mix with her soldiers.

I reach out, putting my hand on Farsil's shoulder, feeling it tremble with retrained anger.

'What we have is enough, Farsil,' I say reassuringly.

My words sound hollow, but then, as I look at the earthworks and high walls, I realise that perhaps I do have faith.

'I believe in you,' I say, just loud enough for him to hear. 'From the moment I met you, I realised you were someone special. No, more than that ... someone extraordinary. Since then, the faith I have in you has only grown. If there's anyone who can lead us to withstand the fey, it's you!'

'With an additional forty thousand alliance warriors, I felt confident. Now I have doubts,' Farsil sighs.

'Then let's wash away those doubts,' I say, passing him a wineskin.

'Spoken like an Icelandian!' Farsil laughs wryly.

'Spoken as a friend,' I smile warmly, then reach out to embrace him, pulling him close.

'Dimitar will be so jealous if he hears about this,' Farsil smiles as we separate.

'What?'

'You don't know?' Farsil looks at me closely as if to detect that I'm joking. 'From the moment you saved his life, he was smitten. Of course, he'll never admit to it, and he's too honourable to pursue you, knowing Lotane is in your life. Dimitar was always one to fall for someone quickly, but I've never seen him fall quicker and deeper than for you. When you killed the High King, he felt betrayed and heartbroken, which turned his adoration into hate, but the hate is all gone now. It's one of the reasons he was upset with you for so long.'

I'm lost for words, and Farsil laughs at my astonishment.

'You might be the deadliest assassin I've ever known, Malina, but you're also as blind as a bat. So, now you've enchanted my friend again, it's your responsibility to ensure you don't hurt him!'

I grab the wineskin back from Farsil and drink until I feel my head spin.

***

The pounding of hooves penetrates the thumping in my head, and I open my eyes to see a dishevelled lancer leap from her lathered horse and rush straight into Tryal's command tent. There's barely a hint of light on the horizon, and her early appearance doesn't bode well.

Farsil is already awake, stumbling toward a signaller who'd stayed nearby throughout the night.

'Sound to arms!' he orders, shaking the woman's shoulders to wake her.

I'm on my feet quickly and jog alongside as Farsil heads toward Tryal's tent.

The bugle rings out into the still morning air to be met by a barrage of curses and threats, but the signaller continues to rouse the Delnorian troops.

Without waiting to be announced, we push past the guards to find Tryal putting on her armour while listening to the lancer's report. As we enter, General Avarez enters through the rear flap, cursing.

'Someone shut that damned signaller up,' he growls, holding his head.

'No,' Tryal interjects. 'We need everyone roused and standing ready!

'Guards. I want all officers convened outside my tent in thirty minutes, including the Delnorian ones!'

She looks at Farsil, who just nods in thanks.

'Tell them,' she orders the lancer.

The woman turns to us, a haunted look in her eyes.

'We spied the army of creatures before sunset last night. Even though I'd been told what we might find, they were like nothing I could ever imagine. We left our horses in a dried stream bed and took position behind the rim of a small hill to observe when wolves started howling.

'I was sent to protect our mounts, but as I waited, the sounds of fighting and screaming came from the ridge. The fighting didn't last long, but the screams continued for hours. I crept back when it all went quiet, and ...'

The woman suddenly bends over, throwing up. I grab a goblet from a table, and even though it has wine inside, press it into her shaking hands.

'Drink this before you carry on!' I say.

She drains the goblet, and some colour returns to her face. There's silence in the tent, whether from horror or respect, I don't know, but she continues to the captivated audience.

'Everyone was dead, and there was hardly anything left of them, just bloody bones, discarded weapons and armour. Whatever attacked them, ate them, even if they were still alive!'

'By the gods!' Avarez exclaims.

I put my arm around the lancer's shoulders and guide her to a camp stool.

'Get her more wine,' I order a guard, tossing the now-empty goblet at him. He rushes off without even looking at Tryal.

Farsil crouches down before the shaking lancer.

'I'm sorry, but I need to ask you some questions. Please answer as best you can.'

The woman nods.

'If they marched at first light, how long before they're within sight of High Delnor.'

'We didn't see any mounts, so maybe by noon if they move swiftly.'

'Damn!' Tryal exclaims.

I know she's calculating whether she can get her army away and out of sight before Nogoth gets here.

'Describe the creatures you saw.'

'They were much the same. Large hulking beasts around the size of an Icelandian and hundreds of what we thought were war dogs.'

'What about giants and trolls or flying gargoyles?'

'No, sir. Just the … what was it you said they were called, general?' she asks, looking over at Tryal.

'Ogres.'

'Yes. Just ogres and those wolves.'

'Was there any sign of Nogoth, their king?' I ask.

'We were too far away to see. I don't even know what he looks like.' She shrugs apologetically, but then her face lights up a little. 'However, there was a command tent.'

'If there were only ogres and wolves … how many were there?' Farsil asks.

'Around eighty thousand, Sir.'

Farsil stands up, his gaze distant as he absorbs this information, but Tryal speaks first.

'The bastard has split his forces; who knows how many times! He's probably sent sixty thousand north to conquer Icelandia and another sixty thousand south to Tars. I'm too late, too late,' she cries, slumping into her chair, distraught.

THE LAST HOPE

My heart goes out to her because I'm sure she's right. Nogoth has launched a three-pronged attack. I walk over to a campaign map on a large stand.

'Assuming Tryal is right, and I fear she is. Once Nogoth's southern army defeats any remaining local forces in Tars and Hastia, some of his creatures will round up the population for escort through the World Gate. If he uses ten thousand for the job, he'll still have fifty thousand marching north to rendezvous with his main force here to join the siege. Once his northern army finishes with Icelandia, they'll be more than enough to deal with the eastern kingdoms.

'I'm sorry, Tryal,' Farsil says sincerely. 'I didn't anticipate Nogoth splitting his forces. I assumed he'd bring them all here.'

'Typical bloody Delnorian. You think the world revolves around you and your failing empire, but it doesn't!'

Tryal paces back and forth, her visage foreboding, her fists clenched.

Kralgen ambles into the tent, a broad smile on his face.

'Why is everyone so serious? I thought we were all friends now?'

'Not now, Kral,' I say softly. 'Nogoth is only half a day away with an army of eighty thousand ogres and wolfen. He split his forces, and we believe the rest are heading directly to Icelandia and Tars.'

Kralgen's smile slips, and he becomes serious.

'I sent my remaining people to the frozen sea. They'll survive on the ice flows.'

'Well, good for you!' Tryal growls.

Kralgen starts counting on his fingers, and his face brightens considerably.

'No, it's good for us all,' Kralgen laughs. 'I can count, can't you!'

Silence follows Kralgen's statement before Farsil slaps him on the shoulder, his eyes gleaming.

'We have a hundred thousand soldiers to Nogoth's eighty! He hasn't anticipated the Icelandians or the alliance armies being here. We have the superior force, and if we meet this bastard in the field, we can crush him.' Farsil declares.

'Kill the leader, and this war could be over,' Tryal murmurs in disbelief.

Farsil pulls the campaign map off the stand and sweeps goblets, empty bottles and platters off a large table with a sweep of his arm.

'Malina. Return immediately to High Delnor, find Major Conrol and tell him what's happening. Have him order every soldier to rally here immediately. Only the town guard must remain to maintain order. We'll also need a field hospital set up beneath the walls.'

The sun is shining as I run from the tent.

Nogoth has made the biggest mistake of his long life … and this will be the first battle toward winning the war.

***

CHAPTER XIX

The sheer size of the armies spread across the plain is hard to comprehend.

Shining in the noon sun are the forces of good. I know some of our soldiers are killers, murderers, thieves and general neer-do-wells. But on this day, they're the hope of mankind, and they stand in a battle line from north to south, whether full of courage or fear; it doesn't matter.

In the centre are fifty thousand heavy infantry, the solid backbone of any army. Equipped with full-length shields, wearing a mix of plate and scale mail armour while wielding long spears make them a formidable defensive or offensive unit. Their effectiveness lies in cohesion, presenting an unbroken wall of locked shields behind an impenetrable thicket of bristling speartips. Their drawbacks are mobility and versatility. There's no individual glory to be found in the shield wall because if a formation breaks ... but no, today, it won't.

At either end of their line are ten thousand light infantry. A mix of body-length, kite and round shields can be seen there. Most wear leather armour reinforced with metal strips and wield short swords. They're fast due to their light equipment and excel in attack and manoeuvrability.

On each flank are the Icelandians, a force of nature who fight as individuals, their long, heavy weapons requiring space to wield.

Behind the crescent line await two thousand light cavalry armed with lances and sabres alongside three thousand archers. There's also a reserve of eight hundred cavalry acting as both Farsil's bodyguard and a quick reaction force. The only missing piece of the alliance army, currently marching at the double from the city, are the five thousand Delnorian archers.

Their arrival will herald the start of the battle.

I can't help but smile as I gauge humanity's last hope.

Six independent nations with different religions, skin colours and languages, and yet together, we're stronger.

My smile slips as I look two hundred paces further west, for there awaits the army of evil itself.

There's little cohesion, no uniformity, just a mass of obscenity.

The scout had been right. There are no giants, trolls, or gargoyles. Luck has smiled upon us, and fortune will today favour the brave.

Before us is a force of mostly ogres, perhaps seventy-five thousand in rough ranks with large spiked shields and jagged swords. Their full heavy plate armour and weaponry are dull, soaking up the light rather than reflecting it, made of the ceramics I'd seen in Nogoth's mansion. On their flanks are perhaps five thousand wolfen, a boiling mass of fangs and claws.

Then there's HIM.

He's wearing plate armour dyed the deepest purple, sitting astride a gigantic, armoured, pitch-black horse. I squint and can just make out a monstrous spiked ball and chain hanging from his saddle pommel.

It seems pointless for him to wear such heavy armour when no weapon can hurt him ... unless that's another lie. I know mine hadn't harmed him, but maybe he's vulnerable if his magical power is drained.

I unconsciously check my own equipment for the dozenth time. I have a long sword and dagger at my waist while a horn bow rests in a sheath on one side of my saddle and a quiver of arrows on the left. I'm also wearing worn leather armour that feels like a second skin. A lance awaits point down in the earth beside my horse.

'How can he side with all those monsters?' Farsil asks, drawing my attention.

'Don't make the mistake of thinking him human because of his looks,' I reply. 'He drinks the souls of the dead and is every bit as evil as those he lords it over!'

'He seems hesitant now he's outnumbered.'

I can only agree. The light infantry and Icelandians had stayed hidden behind the ranks of the spear wall until Nogoth's army had

THE LAST HOPE

closed the distance, then swept out to position themselves like a bull's horns. The light cavalry rides in two units, back and forth behind the north and south of our main line, ready to flank once the main forces engage.

'Have the Icelandians at the north draw back a little,' Conrol orders a messenger, and the man gallops off at speed.

'Good call,' Farsil says, peering north. 'That'll bring the enemy closer to Kralgen and his bear riders hidden by the river.'

Conrol touches a finger to his forehead in a casual salute and acknowledgement. His eyes are everywhere, but now they're lingering on the slow-moving archers coming from the city.

'Tell those fools to run. I don't care how out of breath they are when they get here!'

The rider he's shouted at gallops off. Time is of the essence. The sooner we attack, the less chance of reinforcements coming to Nogoth's aid or him retreating.

'I think he's coming to parlay!' Tryal exclaims.

Sure enough, as all eyes turn toward Nogoth, I see him spur his horse forward, with half a dozen ogre bodyguards running alongside.

'We should just ignore him.' Conrol advises. 'The archers will be in position shortly. Let Nogoth sit there and have a front-row seat while his dreams end.'

'It's tempting. But it's never bad to know one's enemy and see his face,' Farsil declares.

'I'm with Conrol on this, if my voice matters,' I warn. 'Nogoth has nothing to say that we want to hear, and anything he does will be twisted! He might not even honour a parlay and seek to kill us.'

'Your opinion always matters,' Farsil says, leaning over to grip my shoulder. 'That's why you're coming with me, Farsil, Avarez and Tryal. We need the King Slayer with us in case he tries anything.'

'Please tell me we're taking some others too!'

'Let's go,' says Farsil, heeling his horse forward.

We canter toward the rear of the battle line, and I find myself strangely reticent. I've wanted revenge on Nogoth, and it's been a driving force to keep me strong, but now the moment has come to face him; I wish I could forgo the dubious honour.

'Sergeant. You and a dozen of your finest with us!' Conrol shouts, and the next moment we have a strong escort as the spearmen part before us, allowing us through.

We slow to a trot as we enter the space between the two opposing armies, and it's strangely quiet. A sense of unease ripples through me. Have I missed something?

I look for any archers in the enemy's front ranks, but there's no sign. If the breaking of the parlay happens, it will be Nogoth and his ogres who make an attempt on our lives. I only wish Kralgen were with us.

'He's a handsome devil,' Tryal laughs next to me.

How apt her choice of words, for if anyone has come from the pits of hell, it's him.

Up ahead, Nogoth flicks his hands, and his brutish escort stops while he moves forward alone.

'Wait here.' Farsil instructs the sergeant of lancers. 'But don't wait to be called if trouble starts!'

My horse snorts as we continue, sensitive to the charged atmosphere. We pause maybe half a dozen steps short of Nogoth, and I hold my head high, forcing aside any misgivings.

Nogoth leans forward in his saddle, a wide smile showing his white teeth.

'I'm Nogoth, King of the Fey, The Once and Future King. Who are you?'

'Commander Farsil, acting Regent of High Delnor, General Tryal of Tars, Major Conrol of High Delnor, General Avarez of Rolantria, and …'

'Malina,' Nogoth interrupts, opening his arms wide. 'I can't tell you how good it is to see you. Come join me! No Chosen has ever served me better in all these years. To bring the human armies together to fall at one time … you've done everything that was asked of you!'

My stomach flips at his words, and the others stare at me in shock.

'What's he talking about?' Farsil gasps.

'I warned you he'd twist things!'

Nogoth howls with laughter.

'My apologies. I'm just having some fun at Malina's expense. Did you really start to doubt her on my word? How marvellous. However, let me tell you some truths about Malina.

'Firstly, she looks just as good with her clothes off as she does with them on. I bet she hasn't told you were we lovers!'

THE LAST HOPE

My cheeks burn with shame, and I hiss impotently as the others exchange glances. Nogoth's laughter rings loud, and if I believed my weapons could harm him, I'd cleave him in half, parlay be damned.

'I've saved the best to last,' Nogoth says slyly. 'Malina really isn't human at all anymore. She's almost a fey. Can you ever really trust one of the enemy?'

This time there's no response from the others. Farsil and Conrol already knew, and whilst I'm sure Tryal and Avarez are reeling at the news, they're keeping it well hidden.

'From your own mouth, you've damned yourself,' Conrol says, gripping my hand in support. 'You can never be trusted, so if you're trying to make us doubt Malina, it firms my belief in her instead!'

Nogoth appears disappointed that his revelations haven't had the desired effect, but then his eyes widen as he catches sight of Conrol's stone hand holding mine.

However, he composes himself, looks squarely at me and extends his hand.

'Come join me. We are as one!'

'Enough!' Farsil roars. 'You're outnumbered and soon to face a reckoning. So, unless you have something more to say ...'

'I'll make you an offer!'

The calculating smile on Nogoth's face makes my skin crawl.

'No offer will interest us other than your unconditional surrender,' Farsil snaps back.

'Don't be too hasty!' Nogoth drums his fingers on the pommel of his saddle. 'Hand over Malina to me. She'll live, as will you all.' He gestures to encompass the army behind us. 'This world needs to be repopulated for my next visit. One life to save over two hundred thousand. I'll march away immediately if you agree!'

A shocked silence follows his offer, and for every second it lasts, a part of me dies. Nogoth is the ultimate strategist; he always has another move to play.

'Make the trade!' Avarez and Usutul voice their opinions strongly without hesitation or shame. Are they cowards trying to avoid a battle or simply believe it's better to not have a fey around?

Nogoth smiles warmly at me, and I glare back.

Conrol leans and whispers something to Farsil, who in turn speaks softly to Tryal.

I'm surprised when Tryal answers on behalf of the alliance.

'King Nogoth,' she hisses. 'You're just playing for time and in no position to make demands or offers. Our forces are superior, and you're facing defeat. This offer is nothing but a desperate ruse to escape that. For your sins against humanity, when you beg for mercy when this battle is over, there will be none. You'll die slowly, I promise!'

Nogoth nods, his eyes narrowing.

'You're right about just one thing ... I am playing for time, and you've given it to me. As for your promise, I'll return the favour. You're a marked woman, Tarsian. We'll meet again before the day is out, be sure of that!'

Nogoth yanks on his horse's reins and gallops past his waiting bodyguard, who lumber after him.

As we return through our lines, Nogoth's words play on my mind. He was playing for time, and we'd given it to him. The question is, was this just another deceit? Only time will tell.

***

Avarez has taken control of the archers, and the whistle of their arrows as they whip like angry clouds across the sky is chilling. Farsil and I stand in our stirrups, watching as the falling volleys find their mark, but surprisingly few enemy fall.

The ogres' heavy armour and the large shields held above their heads allow them to mostly ignore the withering rain as they stomp unperturbed toward our lines.

'Tell Avarez to focus on the ogres' rear and the wolfen,' Farsil shouts to a messenger, who gallops away.

Major Conrol is commanding the right flank, and General Tryal the left, and they're looking our way, awaiting Farsil's signal. We should wait for the ogres, but it weakens a warrior's spirit to simply stand, watching an opponent approach.

'Sounds the advance!' Farsil shouts.

The waiting horn bearer behind us blows a long soulful note that's picked up by a dozen more signallers.

With a battle cry, the massive line begins to move forward. The heavy and light infantry keep their shields locked, presenting a solid, unbroken line. The Icelandians, even from this distance, look like they're out for a walk.

'There's no sign of enemy reinforcements,' Farsil calls loudly, raising his voice over the thousands of stamping feet.

'Nogoth's parting words still worry me,' I shout back. 'Those ogres of his are fearsome, and despite being outnumbered, perhaps he believes he'll win the day. I just can't believe he'd take the risk if he wasn't certain!'

'Hubris!' Farsil replies. 'He's won so often, he can't fathom ever losing. But, if reinforcements appear or the battle turns in his favour, we'll withdraw back to the killing ground, don't worry!'

I nod. Deep down, I know what we've done is exactly how victory will be achieved, and a sense of well-being settles over me.

A mighty roar fills the air, and the ogres suddenly break into a charge. It's a fearsome sight. They're wearing full plate armour and wielding heavy weapons, yet they sprint as if unencumbered. Their tusked jaws are open as they bellow and roar in a blood frenzy. There's no tight formation, just a solid rolling wave of brute force, bunched muscles, armour, and wicked swords barrelling toward the tightly packed shield wall.

To their flanks, the wolfen dart north and south, using speed in an attempt to get around the ends of our line.

It's impossible to hear the shouted orders, but the first five ranks of heavy infantry lower their spears in unison. A moment later, the light cavalry on both flanks gallop to meet the wolfens' manoeuvre.

Farsil nods in satisfaction. Conrol and Tryal are his equals and have seen the threat and responded accordingly. With an army this large, command and control can't be held by just one person. Even the corporals and sergeants will have a degree of autonomy on the battlefield.

'Hold. Hold. Hold.'

Farsil says the words like a prayer, and I repeat them silently as the ogres hit the alliance lines like an avalanche.

'By the gods!' Farsil exclaims.

I can only agree.

The first three ranks of infantry go down like wheat before a scythe. Normally spear wall casualties are minimal to start as their long weapons and heavy armour turns a fight into a battle of slow attrition, but thousands are down in the first few seconds. Individual ogres are thrown from the shields of their brethren, leaping and landing deep in the spear formations, causing chaos before they're cut down as swords replace dropped spears.

For a moment, the spear wall wavers, and then it solidifies. The next five ranks angle their spears down, and the leaping ogres are killed before landing.

'Damn. We almost lost that in the first few minutes!' Farsil exclaims shakily.

'The light infantry are doing better,' I shout, watching the ebb and flow of the battle closely.

'Individually, they're better fighters,' Farsil shouts back.

Despite their first few lines being broken here and there, they're giving as good as they get.

The screams and roars are deafening, mixed in with war cries, shouts of pain, and the clash of weapons. Arrows still hiss and darken the sky, but they aren't proving to be decisive in the battle. This will be decided by sinew and steel.

Farsil points excitedly.

'Just look at the Icelandians to the north!'

Standing tall in my saddle, I can determine they're pushing the ogres back. Even above the noise of battle, their deep voices rise in song, a haunting complement to the slaughter. Then, Kralgen and his five hundred bears smash into the ogres' flank like an avalanche, adding to the carnage.

A sharp-eyed messenger grabs my arm.

'They're in trouble to the south!' I cry in dismay.

It takes me a moment to realise why. The cavalry there have been routed by the wolfen and have left the Icelandian flanks and rear undefended. The wolfen are darting in and out, rending and biting, disrupting the Icelandian's ability to effectively fight the ogres before them.

I lock eyes with Farsil, and he nods, tilting his head toward his bodyguard.

'Take them. Go help those Icelandians. We'll win this battle, Malina. If you can keep the south from folding, it's just a matter of time until it's ours!'

THE LAST HOPE

He's right. After the initial shock of the ogre charge, the centre is faring well. The north is winning decisively, and whilst the battle will continue for hours, it's swaying in our favour. The south just needs to hold.

'Captain,' I shout as I grab my lance and spur my horse toward the bodyguards. 'We need to support the south flank.'

The captain is a scarred veteran, and I know he's already seen the danger and was just awaiting his orders.

'It'll be an honour if you ride by my side, King Slayer,' he replies as I approach.

I wheel my horse next to his as we canter south. The sense of urgency is overwhelming, and the desire to gallop is hard to resist, but blown horses won't help anyone.

Despite the lancers laughing and whooping, full of bravado and camaraderie, their discipline is apparent. They maintain perfect order as we advance, two hundred lancers across with a perfect five-horse distance between the following three lines.

'We'll skirt the Icelandians by a hairsbreadth and take down those bloody wolves,' the captain shouts. 'Then, how about we continue past the ogres' south flank? That way, we might be able to charge from the rear or at least have them turn their attention to us!'

'You're the expert, Captain. I'll follow your lead,' I yell back.

We go past Tryal and her aides. She's too busy to notice our passing as she sends riders along the flank wherever she sees the need.

The captain lifts his lance above his head, the bright blue pennant of Delnor snapping like a snake behind it. Three times he pumps his weapon high in the air, and seamlessly the line on either side of us drops back to create a wedge formation.

These men must have fought together for years. They respond to their captain's lance and understand his intentions without the need for shouted communication or anything else.

We're closing in, the howling mass of wolfen drawing closer, and the horses' nostrils flare.

This time when the captain lifts his lance, he lowers it to point right, and we turn slightly in that direction.

'Stay in formation!' he yells, kicking his horse into a full gallop.

We lean low, and I firm my grasp on the lance shaft, picking out several wolfen who'll likely be my first targets. A few more seconds, and we'll be upon them.

'This is what I live for,' the captain shouts, his face ecstatic.

As the blood rushes through my veins, I can only agree. This is exhilarating beyond belief.

The wolfen notice us. Some begin to turn and face us, while others run, recognising their doom approaching, but it's too late.

My lance punches a wolfen from its feet, and I automatically loosen my grip, allowing the point to drop with the creature's falling body, then slide free as I ride past without straining my wrist. It doesn't matter whether it's a clean kill because those behind me will finish the job, or the pounding hooves will do it for them.

I don't even try to pierce the next one with my weapon, I simply nudge my horse to the right, and the howling beast is thrown from its feet, shattered by the horse's charge.

Another looks to dodge the point of my lance, but however quick, the point takes it in the shoulder, spinning it around in a bloody spray as the weapon tears its arm off.

Two more wolfen fall to my lance, one to the chest as it turns to fight, the other from behind. I don't care; this is war, not a duel, and then the remaining few flee, howling as they scatter in all directions.

A few bloodied Icelandians raise their weapons in salute before returning to their grisly task of holding back the ogre horde. Then we're past, nothing but an empty plain ahead with the massed ranks of ogres to our right.

Ecstatic laughter surprises me, and as the lancers' wheel to the left, putting distance between us and the battle, I realise I'm laughing along with everyone else.

'Seven!' shouts the captain, shaking his bloodied lance. 'Anyone else close?'

A few voices respond with fives or sixes.

'You did well, King Slayer. I saw you take down five. That's an impressive feat when you don't live in the saddle like we do!'

Several lancers ride close to slap me on the back in congratulation. Why is it that taking lives brings such highs? Then again, maybe it's the joy of remaining alive, having just faced death.

THE LAST HOPE

We walk the horses, a calm moment, yet I feel awful. While we're allowing the horses to recover their wind, thousands are dying every second without the luxury of a final gasped breath.

The captain looks around, his smile fading.

'We lost a good two hundred lancers,' he notes grimly. 'Still, it was worth it. If only we could win this war by ourselves with a final charge!' He points his lance at the distant figure of Nogoth, sitting calmly astride his horse as rank after rank of ogres push by toward the fight.

A chill runs down my spine, for even though Nogoth is a long way away, I swear he's smiling.

***

'We'll cut a shallow swathe out of the ogre flank and give the Icelandians some more respite,' Captain Lanachi, as I now know him to be called, indicates with a sweep of his arm. 'Then we'll return to the Commander.'

'Sounds good, Captain,' several lancers loudly voice their approval.

With a minimum of fuss, everyone begins to form on my right. Only Lanachi is to my left in the front rank.

He turns to me with a grim smile.

'Rank hath its privileges and risk! We'll bite deepest into the enemy ranks, but have the chance to kill far more than those at the other end of the line. We'll charge in with a flank attack, wheel to the right, and then out again before the charge gets bogged down. Our lances won't last long against that armour, so get ready to use your sword!'

As we trot back east, parallel to the ogres waiting to enter the fray, several turn to roar and bellow in our direction. A few daggers and hand axes arc through the air toward us but thankfully fall short.

'Ready?' Lanachi winks at me.

A lift of his lance, then he's pointing it at the wall of flesh and armour jostling to our left, and the line wheels in perfect unison as I heel my mount into a gallop.

There's no laughter or whoops of glee to forewarn our enemy, and as I glance across at Lanachi, his eyes are narrowed in concentration. The clamour of battle covers our approach, although some ogres to our left begin to shout and bellow to catch their brethren's attention in front as we charge in from behind.

I pick my target, a musclebound beast that bulges from the armour encasing it. I focus on the gap between his helm and shoulder armour, where the back of its thick neck offers an enticing target. Just as we're about to strike, the ogre spins around and crouches, causing my lance tip to glance from its helm.

Nonetheless, the blow snaps the creature's head back, sending it reeling. I'm already targeting my next ogre, the lance tip punching through an eye socket and out the back of the creature's helm.

The beast falls slowly, and I feel the lance snap rendering it useless.

The momentum of our charge is flinging ogres left and right as I drag my sword free to hack down at armoured heads and shoulders. More often than not, my sword bounces off without finding flesh, but the weight of the blows aided by my momentum still cracks skulls and breaks bones.

My horse is also reaping a terrible toll, but I can feel it slowing as it forges through the packed ranks.

'Wheel right,' Lanachi screams.

I pull on my reins, and my horse responds, heading toward the edge of the ogre line and safety. Several lancers and horses to my right fall, and I glance over my shoulder and see massive holes in the cavalry lines behind.

The next moment I'm flying through the air as my horse collapses beneath me, then smash into the back of an ogre warrior, sending us both sprawling.

Half-dazed, I stagger to my feet, blinking some dirt from my eyes just in time to see a jagged sword swinging for my head. I sidestep, bringing my own blade down to sever the hand holding the blade. The ogre roars in anguish, yet despite the horrific wound, it throws itself at me, only to be knocked aside as a horse thunders by. Another line of lancers passes, and I sprint after them into the gaps they make, knowing that to hesitate is to die.

Even trampled and half-dead, broken ogres still try and grab me or thrust swords in my direction from the churned, bloody ground.

I'm gasping, barely able to catch my breath as the final line of lancers gallops by. The last rider turns, wheeling her horse, lashing out with her blade as she rides back toward me, leaning down, stretching out her hand.

I frantically grasp at her wrist, and my arm is almost dislocated as I'm yanked up onto the horse's rump as she rides past. I half sob in relief

THE LAST HOPE

as we turn and race back after the others, ogres closing in from all sides, the gaps ahead disappearing quickly.

'Yah. Yah!' The woman shouts frantically, urging her mount forward. Its mighty heart pounds, and muscles swell as it gives everything, but it won't be enough; the edge of the ogre flank is sealing.

'NO!' I cry, flinging my hand out, calling upon my magic, and the half dozen ogres who've positioned themselves in our way are flung aside by a mighty gust.

'YAH!' the woman yells as we lean forward, a hastily thrown dagger spinning past.

Then we're free, riding after just sixty-odd lancers, the paltry few who'd made it.

'You saved my life!' I shout gratefully as we race toward the others, ensuring we're safely away from the horde behind us.

As we catch up to the waiting riders, my saviour slowly reins in the horse, looks over her shoulder and smiles at me. Her eyes are full of tears, her skin is pale, but a smile tugs at the corner of her mouth.

Suddenly she coughs, and a bloody spray erupts as she begins to fall.

I grab her, slide off the horse, and pull her into my arms. It's only then that I see the injury. A gaping hole in her chest armour draws my attention to a wound the size of my fist.

Her breath rattles as I lower her to the ground.

'You saved my life,' I whisper like a prayer, knowing there's nothing more I can do.

She reaches up to gently caress my face, her fingertips like a butterfly's wings. Then her eyes close, her hand falls away, and with a final sigh, she exhales her last breath.

A horse walks to stand above me.

'You're a hard woman to kill, King Slayer,' says Lanachi, but his voice holds no humour, just sorrow. 'Let's return to the Commander, although we're not much of a bodyguard anymore.'

He grimaces, and I note he's also covered in wounds.

As I look tiredly at the other riders, everyone is injured to a lesser or greater degree, with some hanging onto their mounts through sheer force of will.

'She falls off her horse and is the only one without a scratch. How bloody fair is that?' Lanachi grumbles, smiling wanly.

It's not fair at all. Tens of thousands are dead, and more are dying every second, all because of Nogoth. Yet as I look across the battlefield, I allow myself a small smile.

The Once and Future King's army is definitely losing.

***

CHAPTER XX

'We've really got the bastard!' Farsil declares to no one in particular.
I'm exhausted and don't have the strength to answer, but there's no denying it.

The heavy infantry advance smoothly, driving the ogres back, and the butcher's toll is starting to be revealed. Broken and rent bodies, some locked in a deathly embrace, but all trampled into the ground, appear behind the advancing ranks.

Here and there, movement is visible amongst the fallen.

'Tell Avarez to have his archers cease shooting,' Farsil orders a messenger. 'They're to kill any wounded fey and take our injured back to the walls. You, and you, advise Major Conrol and General Tryal to pursue the moment the ogres' rout. It won't be long now!'

The riders gallop off, excitement evident on their faces.

I sigh with heartfelt relief ... all my worries were for nought. On this day, victory will be ours. What happens in the following weeks or months with most of Nogoth's forces still at large remains to be seen, but that's a worry for another day.

Farsil has read the sway of battle perfectly.

Enemy horns sound, a deep noise as if from a giant beast, and the ogres begin to fall back in a hurry. They move swiftly despite their bulky appearance and heavy armour.

'YES!' Farsil shouts.

With a roar, our front lines pursue the routing ogres, newfound strength giving them speed.

My stomach squirms like a nest of snakes. Something feels wrong, but I can't identify what.

'Captain Lanachi!' Farsil shouts. 'Would you care to accompany us?'

'It would be an honour!' Lanachi calls back.

Farsil kicks his horse into a canter, and soon we're riding through the morass of churned dirt and bloody mud after the charging troops. I try and guide my horse around the corpses, but I realise it's impossible and give up unless I see obvious movement.

Archers are everywhere. None carry bows anymore, and most of their quivers are empty anyway. They're running around like ants, pulling the wounded free, administering what aid they can before fashioning stretchers from fallen spears, broken armour and cloaks for the long haul back to the city.

It's impossible to tell how many from both sides have fallen, but the toll is horrendous.

Groups of wounded ogres who were too slow to keep up with their brethren are being surrounded. When the infantry sees us coming, they stand back, and we charge down the snarling beasts.

Farsil always leads with Lanachi on his right, and me on his left. My sword arm is exhausted, and my horse is laboured.

Lanachi's unit is down to thirty lancers, yet we still push toward the front of the pursuit, where I can see the slowest ogres turn and fight, giving their brethren a chance to escape.

Not far to the north, I spy Major Conrol astride his horse and an arrow's flight beyond him, Kralgen astride his bear with a half dozen bear-riding bodyguards.

The blood rush that had given everyone strength for the pursuit is ebbing away, and soldiers begin to stumble with fatigue. Just as I note how ragged and dispersed our ranks are becoming, that mournful enemy horn sounds again and again.

In that instant, the fleeing ogres about-face, roar and bellow a challenge, then bash swords against their shields.

'It's their last stand. The beginning of the end!' Farsil shouts. 'Form a line of battle. Form a line of battle!' He looks around for messengers, but none are left.

THE LAST HOPE

'You and you,' Lanachi shouts at two of his lancers. 'You heard the commander. Go deliver his order!'

'Yah!'

The riders gallop away to reinforce discipline.

I nod in admiration. Farsil is the consummate leader leaving nothing to chance.

The ogres continue to make a deafening racket as they await their end, roaring and bellowing their defiance. The surviving wolfen have also returned to join them, but it won't make a difference.

It's hard to take my eyes off this boiling mass of evil awaiting its destruction.

From behind their lines, signal horns blare a desperate rallying call echoing across the plains and back again.

Except there should be no echo back.

Twisting in my saddle, looking over my shoulder toward High Delnor, I see the beginning of the end, as Nogoth's strategy and greatest deception become clear.

The Once and Future King hasn't split his forces to attack Icelandia or Tars, they were here all along, and High Delnor has already fallen. Nogoth simply used this smaller force to bait our attack, then lured our army further from High Delnor's walls with his faked retreat.

No long siege nor war of attrition for which we were prepared. No retreating back to the citadel atop its cliff if the city walls fell. Those would have cost him far more than he's just lost.

Smoke boils into the sky above High Delnor while swarms of gargoyles swoop back and forth, their deadly javelins raining down.

Nogoth's slow journey from Pine Hold and even his parlay before the battle were precisely orchestrated to give his forces the time to move into position and attack simultaneously.

Giants and trolls by the dozen climb over High Delnor's walls from the *inside*, knocking the defensive engines and their marine crews to their destruction as they do so. I watch horrorstruck as they rush across the plain toward our rear. An unstoppable force.

We'd overlooked the obvious; these behemoths could attack from the sea, wading through the depths and into the city with almost no opposition. The Delnorian galleys were in the harbour, their weapons and crew atop the walls, facing the wrong way, unable to do anything.

The alliance navy would have been beached nearby, similarly vulnerable.

To make matters worse, waves of ogres and wolfen pour from the western gate. I've no idea how they entered the city, but it doesn't matter anymore.

'Malina,' Farsil shouts without turning around.

He's focused entirely on the battle before us, unaware it's already lost, that it was always lost because we were just pawns in a game we never had a chance of winning.

'We'll join up with Conrol and then Kralgen,' he points excitedly. 'We've got to start thinking about how we'll bring down Nogoth at the end!'

I'm tempted to not say anything, to allow Farsil's joy to continue a while longer, for his heart to feel relief that he's protected his beloved city and brought about the end of a tyrant. Why take all that away when a giant's club will do that for me without Farsil even seeing it coming.

Instead, I nudge my horse to his side and pull him close, wrapping my arms around his shoulders.

'Thank you for forgiving me. My soul might be darkened forever, but you helped me bask in the light again for a while.'

Farsil's face creases in a smile, but he shakes free of my embrace.

'Save your hugs for later,' he laughs, but his happiness fades as he registers the sadness in my eyes.

I don't say anything, just lift my arm and point back toward the city.

The life and hope drain from Farsil at that moment, but to his credit, the realisation of our impending doom doesn't break him.

He grabs my wrist.

'Let's die with our friends beside us, and our enemies around us,' he says, his gaze steady.

Then he's shouting orders as we ride hell for leather toward Conrol and Kralgen.

He's right.

I want to die with my friends beside me.

***

'Malina. Watch your left!' Tryal shouts from behind me.

THE LAST HOPE

I spin, barely deflecting a sword thrust, feeling it glance from my leather armour. Had it landed squarely, it would have passed clean through, but even so, I'm winded, gasping for breath.

Lanachi lances his sabre through my attacker's eye with an expert thrust, and the creature crashes to the ground as I recover my balance.

'Thanks!' I gasp.

He smiles, then staggers as a spear slams into his chest. He collapses a moment later, the smile frozen in place while the life fades from his eyes as blood pours from his mouth.

Farsil pushes me behind him and locks shields with Conrol as they take the lead, forging north. I gather my senses, taking brief stock of our numbers. There are about four hundred warriors around me, a rag-tag mix of infantry and dismounted cavalry, and they're dragging more into our midst as we go, swelling our ranks. They're the best of whatever units they once belonged to who've survived against these terrible odds.

'King Slayer?' Tryal shouts, grabbing my shoulder.

'I'm fine!' I yell back, shaking off her hand, annoyed at my momentary lapse.

Tryal wrenches the spear unceremoniously for Lanachi's chest and launches it. I watch it punch a howling wolfen lifeless to the ground.

Around us, tens of thousands of fey and humans, hack, claw, and scream, in fear or anger. Overall there's no longer a chain of command, and cohesion is diminishing. Each group fights to last as long as it can. Some fight in one place, small islands in the sea of fey that batter against them in waves, the pile of bodies around them aiding their defence. Others try to find strength in numbers, seeking to join with other groups.

As I catch my breath, I look east to see the giants and trolls tearing through the spear wall Avarez had formed in a vain attempt to slow them. One wields a giant chain, and I recognise it as the one that had blocked the harbour entrance. With one enormous swing, at least twenty warriors are flung into the air, broken like dolls.

'Almost there,' shouts Farsil, and I turn to see Kralgen, five Icelandians and a mix of other warriors numbering about a hundred pushing south toward us.

Warm blood splatters my face as an archer next to me crashes to the ground, a thrown hand axe deep in her skull. I sweep up her bow and pull two full quivers of arrows from her shoulder. At a glance, I can tell they've all been scavenged from the battlefield. Bloodstained shafts and twisted feathers mar their simple perfection, but I couldn't care less.

As my group pushes north, one moment, I'm standing at the crest of a pile of bodies, shooting down into the massed enemy ranks, then running down the macabre slippery slope to find the next vantage point. Waves of ogres batter us, joined by howling wolfen who leap over the shield wall only to find death awaiting them.

I've always loved the bow, and I remember the time Lotane and I had ridden along the beach, shooting targets rising and falling on the surf. I smile at the memory, finding joy as I recall his laughter, his twinkling eyes, and the kiss that had followed as we ran back through the forest. Of course, there are little differences between then and now, especially his absence.

I exhale, release, and am already drawing another arrow before the first strikes a wolfen, punching through its muscular neck. The next shaft has a missing feather, but I compensate, aiming high and to the left, and grunt in satisfaction as the arrow crunches between a bulky ogre's shoulder armour and cuirass. I'd aimed for its face, but the gods of luck had smiled this time.

Lystra's voice sounds in my head, reminding me that every time I miss is a chance for a foe to kill the king I'm trying to protect. Once that king had been Nogoth.

Now, that king is Farsil.

Our group finally breaks the line of fey between us and Kralgen.

He whoops like a child when he sees me. His white furs, which had once been daubed red with war paint, are now black with fey blood. I've seen less blood flowing from a corpse, but Kralgen doesn't appear to notice.

He sweeps me into his arms as if I weigh no more than a feather and gives me a bristly kiss on each cheek before setting me down again. I don't think I've ever seen his eyes so bright or full of life than now.

'Do you have to look so happy?' Conrol shouts as he blocks a sword cut and punches the attacking ogre in the face with his stone fist. Tusks snap, and the ogre goes down, blood flowing from its flaring nostrils. Farsil finishes it off with a sword thrust to its neck.

Kralgen laughs.

'My Icelandian brothers and I have taken a fearful toll today. The gods will want us to tell our tales at their table before the day ends!'

'I bloody hope there's room for all of us, Icelandian!' Tryal shouts.

THE LAST HOPE

The five Icelandian bodyguards begin their throaty maudlin song as Farsil calls for a pause. Ogres continue to throw themselves at the shield wall; men fall screaming, guts spilling, arterial blood spurting. I take the opportunity to practice my archery, Tryal pointing out targets beside me. There are so many, but she picks those with less armour or who pose a threat with throwing weapons.

I reach for another arrow to find my quiver empty. I've loosed nearly fifty arrows, and my fingers are raw from releasing the string. I scavenge amongst the corpses at our feet but can't find anything useable. With a sigh, I cast the bow aside, grab a fallen shield and draw my battered sword again.

Roars of victory draw my attention, and I turn to see the last of the rearguard swept aside by the giants and trolls. Maybe half a dozen of the gigantic beasts lie dead on the ground, but it's hard to take any pleasure when their demise was bought by thousands of lives.

'We've not got much time,' I shout, coming to stand behind Farsil and Conrol. Avarez is dead, and the trolls and giants are coming!'

Farsil and Conrol step back as they defeat their respective opponents, and two scarred veterans take their place.

'I don't know how, but we've got to kill that bastard, Nogoth,' Farsil yells to make himself heard, pointing at the king who sits impassively astride his horse a hundred paces to our west. 'We kill him, and that's a victory right there whether we live or die!'

'Spread the word! We kill the king!' Conrol orders.

Like wildfire, the order spreads across our group in a matter of heartbeats.

I look around quickly, doing a quick count. We'd had four hundred before Kralgen and his group joined us, but with the ogres constantly attacking, we're down to less than three.

'My bodyguard will clear the path,' Kralgen states emphatically. 'Just give them some room and get ready to follow!'

He embraces the three men and two women, resting his forehead briefly against theirs, whispering to each. Bizarrely, they toss their gigantic weapons to the ground and stoop to pick up two discarded ogre shields each. They're heavy and body length, with a wickedly pointed centre boss.

'NOW!' Kralgen roars, and his bodyguard charges out into the mass of ogres.

They hold the shields before them, their muscular legs driving them forward like rampaging bulls, flinging ogres aside, creating an empty space in their path.

'Charge!' Farsil and Conrol yell, and with me and Tryal on either side, we become the point of an attacking wedge. We sprint, hacking down at the fallen ogres who've been bashed aside, not caring if the wounds we inflict are deep or shallow. I slip on some bloody entrails, but a hand grabs my leather weapon belt, pushing me forward while I retain my balance.

I subconsciously count the distance, every step I take matched by the swing of my sword.

Ninety steps, eighty. Every step, something or someone dies.

Screams come from around me as men and women fall at the front of the wedge, only to be replaced by others, their faces twisted in rage and desperation until they also disappear in a bloody spray. Several more fall to my right, and then Kralgen is next to me. He holds his mighty war mallet in one hand to block incoming blows while dealing death with a scavenged ogre sword in the other.

Seventy steps.

A fallen ogre slashes my right thigh as I run across his body, but it doesn't live more than a heartbeat longer to celebrate the blow. Conrol is bleeding from a forehead wound, the blood running into his eyes, but he presses on regardless. Farsil appears unscathed, although, with the amount of blood and gore on him, it could be he's bleeding from a hundred wounds.

Sixty steps.

Something tears the leather helm from my head, but I'm relieved; the heat is stifling, and my vision is no longer hindered. Kralgen throws his sword high into the air, snatches a thrown spear before it can skewer the woman to his right, and then launches it back. The next moment he catches his sword, laughing maniacally. It's as if we were back in the training circle again, and he's showing off simply because he can.

Fifty steps, and suddenly two of the Icelandians go down under a half dozen wolfen who leap seemingly from nowhere. As we run past, we hack at the beasts, and my blade bites deep into a furred, muscular neck. Even as I do, my right leg buckles, and a swordsman runs past to take my place at the front.

THE LAST HOPE

I don't have time to bandage my thigh, so I call upon what little magic I can and scream in agony as the fire in my hand sears the wound, stemming the blood flow.

We're only twenty steps away from Nogoth, but no more than forty of us remain. For a moment, I stand protected by those around me, and I turn, seeing how few of the alliance forces are left standing. Small pockets of resistance remain here and there, but towards them comes swift and certain death in the form of giants or trolls.

Making matters worse, gargoyles are now entering the fray, throwing their javelins down into the ever-decreasing circles of humanity.

The remaining Icelandian bodyguards fall, and suddenly, we're making no further headway.

Shields that once blocked blows with ease are now in tatters; weapons are notched and dull.

It's the end. Our numbers are insufficient, and we've fallen short of our goal.

Nogoth is out of our reach, and we'll never know what might have happened had we tried to kill him. Then I hear Kralgen's voice lift above the cacophony of combat.

'NOGOTH!' I hear Kralgen bellow. 'FIGHT ME, NOGOTH!'

I turn to see Kralgen wading out from the protection of our small band, scattering ogres aside with sweeps of his mighty hammer.

Now he's on his own; ogres dash in behind, but Kralgen seems to lead a charmed life, for he spins, twists and turns, dodging every cut and thrust as if he's seen them coming his whole life.

Then those violet eyes turn to fix on Kralgen, watching, measuring, and assessing.

'HOLD!'

It's not over yet!

***

Nogoth's command is enhanced by magic, crashing like thunder upon us.

'CEASE FIGHTING!'

Without hesitating, the ogres stop their attack and step back, snarling and gnashing their teeth and tusks. For a minute, isolated sounds of combat continue until even they stop.

The wounded and dying continue to moan, to call for help, or their mothers, even a quick death, but if it weren't for them, I swear even the end of the world would have brought no deeper silence.

'It's been years beyond count since I've been challenged by someone worthy,' Nogoth calls as he dismounts from his horse.

'It's years beyond count since I've fought someone so ugly!' Kralgen laughs as the ogres move back, creating a corridor for him to approach Nogoth.

Even Nogoth roars with laughter, no sign of enmity or anger on his face.

I want to run after Kralgen, to tell him how much I love him, but the opportunity for that is past. This is now his time, and if anyone can kill Nogoth, it's Kral.

Hobbling over to Conrol, I put my arm around his shoulder. He turns to me and smiles, looking strangely contented.

'I always thought if the world were to end, I'd like to watch it by your side,' he smiles, then pulls me into a gentle hug.

'Before my world ends, I want to see Kralgen rip that bastard's head off,' growls Farsil next to us.

While Kralgen ambles toward Nogoth as if he has no care in the world, the few bloodied alliance soldiers that remain take the opportunity to feel the warmth of another's embrace.

'I AM KRALGEN!' Kral shouts, lifting his arms wide, still holding the war mallet and sword. 'MAY THE GODS WITNESS MY VICTORY OR DEATH!'

The ogres have cleared some ground, tossing the dead and dying aside to create a circle for the two kings to fight in.

Nogoth steps forward with that nasty spiked ball and chain held loosely in his right hand. In his left, he holds a long sword with practised ease, gently whirling it around. They circle one another, first one way, then another, studying the other's footwork and balance, gauging their opponent.

I'm surprised, for Kralgen usually attacks immediately, but Kralgen, despite playing the fool, never was one. He is, in fact, the mightiest and best.

THE LAST HOPE

Nogoth attacks first, pivoting and twirling, a graceful move worthy of the god of dance. His sword whips out, missing Kralgen's forehead by a hairsbreadth, and then as he closes the distance, the spiked ball whistles.

Kralgen moves smoothly back, but not fast enough, and one of the spikes tears open his furred jerkin even if it doesn't score his skin beneath. Kral smiles in respect, and they're back to circling again.

Weapons clash, not overly committing, just testing reflexes and responses. I've always marvelled at Kral, yet, despite my hatred for Nogoth, I can see he's a superlative warrior. With lifetimes of practice behind him, he would be.

Then, the time for testing is over. The sweep of Kral's war mallet swooshing through the air, the whistle of the ball and chain, and the harmonic ring of sword upon sword accompanying the exhalation of breath and the scuff of booted feet.

Nogoth's sword lashes out, then, before the move is finished, he spins, the spiked ball smashing Kral's blade to shards as it lunges for Nogoth's exposed neck. It was a daring move, yet, being invulnerable to weapons and encased in plate, was it really?'

'Come on, Kral,' I mutter and find myself squeezing Conrol's shoulder as the duel unfolds.

Kral knows Nogoth can't be stabbed or cut, so I'm sure this is why he's chosen a war mallet. I smile, for, without question, that's Kral's gamble. Another hope is that, like with any other magic, invoking it depletes the user's strength. If Kral lands enough blows, maybe he can not only injure but kill Nogoth if the Fey King can no longer summon it to protect himself.

However, now Kral's a weapon down, will he even be able to lay his remaining heavy weapon on his fleet-footed and fresh opponent?

Nogoth begins to attack fluidly, and Kral is forced to evade, his footwork perfect, his speed for someone so large incredible. However, he can't dodge everything, and he has to use two hands on his heavy weapon to deflect his opponent's swift blows. I cringe every time he does so, for it's incredibly dangerous. Nogoth's blade and spiked ball barely miss Kral's hand time and again, leaving the shaft notched and splintered.

Kral counters a ringing sword thrust, then ducks the hissing ball, sweeping the heavy head at Nogoth's legs. Nogoth leaps up, but in a show of ridiculous strength, Kral yanks the mallet upwards, changing its hideous momentum through brute force, catching Nogoth's foot to send The Once and Future King tumbling. Yet the tumble turns into a fluid roll, and the heavy mallet sends dirt and earth flying from the follow-up swing instead of landing a crushing blow.

Nogoth raises his blade in salute, and the dance begins again.

For a moment, I drag my eyes away from the spectacle and realise that even this show of martial arts is part of Nogoth's plan. The blood lust and fury that had driven every man and woman to fight with desperate strength, killing as if possessed by hell's daemons, has disappeared like mist before the sun. Wounds continue to bleed, draining survivors' strength; limbs recently full of vitality now tremble with exhaustion, and hands that moments ago wielded swords with precision now shake uncontrollably.

The fight has been taken out of almost everyone ... even Kral.

He's already fought for hours, swung his heavy mallet a hundred times, parried a thousand blows, and he's now fighting Nogoth, who for the whole battle simply sat astride his horse.

Kral backs away from a flurry of lightning-fast cuts, then stumbles. Nogoth, in a flash, lunges with his sword, a picture-perfect strike, the sword an extension of his arm. My cry of despair is echoed by every human throat, and yet it goes unheard as the watching fey horde roars at their master's triumph.

For a moment, the two combatants stand there, the sword protruding out past Kralgen's back, but then, Kralgen laughs and spins, and at that moment, I realise he's trapped the blade between his arm and side. With a sound like breaking glass, Nogoth's ceramic blade shatters, and this time, human cheers lift skyward.

Kral roars, lifting his mallet to shake it toward the heavens.

By contrast, Nogoth looks at the useless hilt in his hand and then throws it aside in disgust.

'I've never seen his like,' Farsil says to my left. 'To witness such skill before I die is a gift. Kralgen is a giant amongst men.'

But no further words are said as the battle resumes.

Kral has the longer reach, and his weapon increases it further still, yet however fast he moves or strikes, Nogoth is as slippery as an eel and evades every sweep, lunge or blow with apparent ease.

His ball and chain is a constant blur, and every miss by Kralgen is met with a stinging counterblow, and as the battle progresses, my hope begins to fade.

THE LAST HOPE

Kral's stamina is beyond anything humanly possible, yet even he has his limits.

As tiredness creeps in, Kral's attacks slow, while Nogoth's only seem to get faster. One after another, bloody gashes appear on Kral's arms.

'No!' hisses Conrol next to me as Kral stumbles. His mallet head drops, forcing him to block the next attack with his bare hand leaving it mangled and useless.

Kral leaps back, blood flowing freely badly injured.

More exchanges, more blood, and Kral breathes like an ox, sucking air in great gasps. He can barely stand and struggles to hold his heavy weapon. His eyes widen as he stares death in the face, swaying like a tree in a storm.

'Oh, Kral,' I sob, and Conrol's arm go around my shoulders.

It isn't just that when this battle is over, so are we. It's more that Kral simply can't understand what's happening. The look on his face is one of childlike incomprehension. He's not lost in countless years, and now the moment of his death is upon him; he seems dazed and confused.

I want to hug him and whisper that everything will be all right. That he did his best, and Alyssa would be so proud and is already waiting for him on the other side.

Nogoth nods as if in understanding, then spins like a whirlwind.

The awful spiked ball flashes out, and despite wanting to turn away and close my eyes, I determine to watch the death of my friend. To give him the honour of witnessing his bravery right to the very end.

The ball goes to hit the side of Kral's head, but at the last possible instant, Kral brings the wooden mallet head up and the spikes jam into it. Using the momentum of the blow, Kral twists, yanking Nogoth off balance and the weapon from the Fey King's grasp.

Then, in a blur, Kral continues the turn, pivoting, the war mallet extending outward as Nogoth tries to recover.

But The Once and Future King is too slow.

With a sound like a ship's bell, the mallet hammers into Nogoth's chest plate, shattering it. In disbelief, I watch as the Fey King is thrown upward by the impact and flies through the air to land ten paces from where he was standing. He slides along the ground on his back as silence falls.

It's the most devastating blow I've ever seen land. The level of deception, skill and audacity used to carry it out is beyond comprehension, and everyone, fey or human, is astounded.

'I don't bloody believe it!' gasps Conrol next to me.

Nor do I. But the sad thing is it's not Kral's defeat of Nogoth that has us cursing in disbelief.

Nogoth picks himself up and brushes himself off as if nothing untoward has happened.

Kralgen's shoulders slump, and I know it's not feigned as he sinks to his knees.

He's done everything, even taken horrific wounds to lure the Fey King into a position that left no chance of escape. The blow he'd landed would have killed a giant, and even Nogoth puts his hands together and applauds Kralgen.

'THOSE WHO WISH TO SURRENDER MAY DO SO. THOSE WHO WISH TO DIE WILL DIE!' Nogoth orders. He flicks his hand toward Kralgen, and a dozen ogres leap forward, and he's lost from sight beneath them.

'Bastard,' yells Farsil, charging forward.

Conrol and I sprint after him as Farsil hacks left and right with his sword, trying to reach Nogoth. Screams, yells and roars rise up as the battle is rejoined in a final frenzy of bloodletting. Black ichor spurts over my face as I open a wolfen's throat, and I lick my lips, surprised by its sweet taste. I duck an axe, then sever an ogre's leg cleanly at the knee.

An unseen blow to my left shoulder has me stumble, and I drop my shield, my arm completely numb. I've no idea what hit me. Farsil is suddenly thrown backwards by a shield bash, and he lands at my feet dazed, so Tryal, Conrol and I stand around him as he gathers his senses.

Maybe ten remaining soldiers protect us, but they fall one by one to the pressing horde of fey.

Tryal screams. A javelin has hit her from above, passing through her right shoulder and out through her chest. She collapses to her knees, the weapon propping her up.

An ogre charges at me. I lunge, horrified that my weak thrust glances from its breastplate. The creature stabs me in the shoulder with a dagger, barrels me over, and lands on top, knocking the air from my lungs. I can't bring my sword to bear, so releasing the weapon, I grab the dagger embedded in my flesh, yanking it free and wrap my arm around the creature's neck, pulling it close. Again and again, I ram the point into the struggling ogre's armpit in a final desperate attempt to take one more to the grave.

Conrol suddenly falls to the ground beside me, eyes glazed, unseeing, a dent in his helmet evidencing the blow that had brought him low.

As I struggle, something tears through my armour and out through my back, pinning me to the ground. The pain is excruciating, and my scream joins a thousand others. With the last of my rapidly fading strength, I stab the ogre on top of me in the throat, feeling it finally give up the fight as its black blood spurts across my face.

Through a hazy mist, I see Farsil stagger to his feet, barely able to stand, sword held weakly before him. An ogre walks up behind him and raises a double-bladed axe. I'm glad Farsil won't see it coming. It flashes down, and Farsil is almost cleaved in two and drops like a stone.

Then, HE is standing next to me, but I'm not the focus of his attention; Tryal is.

'Feast on her, my brothers,' he orders.

The next moment her pitiful screams split the air as she's literally eaten alive.

'ENOUGH,' Nogoth's voice echoes across the battlefield. 'THE INJURED ARE TO BE KEPT ALIVE. THE DEAD ARE FOR YOU TO EAT.'

He says something else, but I can't understand what. My vision is going dark, there's a roaring in my ears, and my heart beats erratically. The dead ogre's weight on me makes breathing nearly impossible, and I feel something approaching relief.

I'm dying.

***

THE END

Dear Reader and fellow fantasy lover.
PLEASE REVIEW THIS BOOK
If you enjoyed this tale, then please take a moment to rate or review it on Amazon. It would mean SO much to me.
Thank you
Marcus Lee

MARCUS LEE

THE CHOSEN TRILOGY

If you're ready to find out what happens to Malina and her friends next, then don't wait, and continue the adventure.

Book 3 - THE RIVER OF TEARS

***

Are you looking for a new magical adventure?

THE GIFTED AND THE CURSED TRILOGY

A dark fantasy trilogy set in a dystopian land, with heroes that are at times more demonic than the evil they face. The bloody battles, quests for revenge and fights for survival are artfully balanced with light romance, tales of redemption, and breath-taking magical gifts.

Book 1 - KINGS AND DAEMONS

Book 2 - TRISTAN'S FOLLY

Book 3 - THE END OF DREAMS

Printed in Great Britain
by Amazon

THE LAST HOPE

THE CHOSEN - BOOK II

Against incredible odds, Malina has not only become a Chosen but has found friendship, love, and a home in the Mountain of Souls.

Yet, despite the rewards, this journey has taken a heavy toll. Plagued by remorse and with her conscience stained by the many lives she's taken, Malina's growing doubts give rise to difficult questions.

Only the Once and Future King has the answers, but seeking the truth can uncover lies capable of destroying the foundations of the even strongest belief.

And hell hath no fury like a Chosen deceived.

ISBN 9798371329653